Anne Baker trained as a nurse at Birkenhead General Hospital, but after her marriage went to live first in Libya and then in Nigeria. She eventually returned to her native Birkenhead where she worked as a Health Visitor for over ten years before taking up writing. She now lives with her husband in Merseyside. Anne Baker's other Merseyside sagas are all available from Headline and have been highly praised:

'A stirring tale of romance and passion, poverty and ambition' *Liverpool Echo*

'Anne Baker has blended the perfect ingredients to create a top class saga' *Historical Novels Review*

'Highly observant writing style . . . a compelling book that you just don't want to put down' *Southport Visiter*

'Anne Baker imbues her heartwarming Merseyside novels with rich local characters' *Nuneaton Evening Telegraph*

'A gentle tale with all the right ingredients for a heartwarming novel' *Huddersfield Daily Examiner*

A Pocketful Of Silver

Anne Baker

headline

First published in 2003
by HEADLINE BOOK PUBLISHING

First published in paperback in 2004
by HEADLINE BOOK PUBLISHING

10

ISBN 978 0 7553 0872 9

Typeset in Times New Roman by Avon DataSet Ltd,
Bidford-on-Avon, Warwickshire

Printed and bound in Great Britain by
CPI Antony Rowe, Chippenham and Eastbourne

HEADLINE BOOK PUBLISHING
A division of Hodder Headline
338 Euston Road
London NW1 3BH

www.headline.co.uk
www.hodderheadline.com

A POCKETFUL OF SILVER

Chapter One

As soon as her teacher had made sure she'd done up the buttons on her red coat, five-year-old Eleanor Jane Valentino ran to the school gates looking for Franco. She weaved through the group of waiting mothers with prams and toddlers, and realised with a flutter of anxiety that Franco wasn't here.

Gran had said she must wait if this happened, but it hadn't before. Franco was twelve, the youngest of the Baldini brothers. He went to the school for big boys which was right next door and had collected her and taken her home once before.

Quaking, Ellie stood against the railings, trying to take strength from the solid bars against her back. Usually Gran came to meet her, but she was having new teeth and had gone to the dentist this afternoon.

'You'll collect little Ellie from school, won't you?' she'd said to Franco. 'Don't forget now.'

'Course I won't.' He'd smiled at Ellie. She liked Franco, though he teased her.

She chewed on a few strands of her wispy amber-coloured hair. Gran said it was a bad habit she must break because only nervous babies sucked their hair. Big girls never would. Ellie watched boys and girls from the big school coming past her in

1

droves, but there was no sign of Franco. Even the mothers were fewer now as they set off home with their children.

As usual, the big pink ribbon her mother used to tie back her hair had slid off. She checked to make sure the bow was still in her pocket. Mam would be cross if she'd lost it again, but it was there.

She mustn't be scared, she'd been coming to school for two weeks now. Walking the streets between here and her home four times each day. She was almost sure she could find her way. Franco lived next door but one, she'd go there and look for him. Even if he wasn't there, she could get into her back yard and sit on the doorstep until Gran came home.

The crowd was thinning and still Franco hadn't come. She was afraid he'd forgotten and wouldn't now. No point in waiting any longer. Ellie broke into a run along this street of soot-blackened terraced houses, she recognised the corner shop on the end, this was definitely the way. Ellie looked longingly at the lollipops and sticks of liquorice in the window as she undid her coat. She felt hot.

On again, here was the church. The bike shop where her mother was working was just a little way down that street. She could find it, though Gran said it was better if she didn't go while Mam was supposed to be working.

Flooding with relief that she'd got it right, she ran up the back entry behind Harcourt Street. She was reaching up to the latch on the Baldinis' back gate when it was dragged open from the inside. Franco's dark brown eyes were laughing down at her. With his wavy hair he looked typically Italian. Behind him stood his brother Carlo, who looked very like him but was bigger.

'Ellie! I'm sorry, I forgot about meeting you!' Franco jerked her up in the air and gave her a hug.

2

Carlo said, 'Forgot? I never forgot to collect you from school, and she's just a baby.'

'I'm five.' She struggled to be set down.

'You look more like three.'

Franco said, 'Don't tell your gran, will you? She'll flatten me if she knows I forgot. Anyway, you're a big girl now, you can find your way home by yourself.' Ellie enjoyed a moment of triumph, she could.

Carlo said, 'Franco hasn't been to school today, that's why he forgot.'

'Shut up, can't you?' Ellie saw knowing glances pass between the brothers.

Franco said, 'You'd better come with us now. We're going down to your bike shop to see the car.'

Ellie knew all about the car. Everybody was talking about it. 'Gran took me to see it last night.'

'Did you have a ride in it?'

'No, and she said I'm not to go there any more.'

'Why not? Anyway, she needn't know. We won't go in.'

The bike shop was round the corner, only a few hundred yards from where they lived.

'Not that way.' Carlo caught at Ellie's arm and pulled her in the opposite direction. 'We'd have to pass our caff and I don't want Pa to see us.'

'I've just come this way,' Ellie told them. They both towered over her and they both seemed grown up. Carlo really was, he'd been working in his father's business for two years.

'Carlo's been sick for a few days,' Franco confided, 'so Ma has to work in his place. He's feeling better now, but she mightn't like him going out.'

It was further through the back streets and Ellie had trouble keeping up with them. She could see the bike shop now, as familiar as her home. She'd learned to spell out the gold letters on the scarlet board above the shop front before she'd started school. It read, Mario Valentino and Sons Ltd.

Gran had told her the story many times of how her grandpa had started this bicycle business before the turn of the century. It had prospered; cycling had been a popular pastime for many years. It occupied a big corner site, but now her Uncle Mick thought push bikes were less profitable and wanted to turn it into a garage.

'Look at those motor bikes,' Carlo breathed. 'I'm saving up for one.'

'I'd rather have the car.' Franco's handsome face glowed. The model T Ford was standing on the forecourt, all shiny black paint and chrome. It had been brought here only yesterday. A car was still a rarity in this district and this one was attracting a lot of attention. 'Isn't it lovely?'

Ellie longed to have a ride in it. 'Mam and Gran are against cars.'

Grandpa's shop had both sold bicycles and hired them out, and he'd added a workshop behind where he did repairs. The doors to the shop and the workshop stood wide open on this sunny afternoon. As they crept towards the car, Ellie could hear Uncle Mick shouting something. He sounded angry.

'Get in.' Franco opened the car door and pushed her on to the back seat. He and Carlo climbed in the front. Carlo was gripping the steering wheel and putting his feet on the pedals.

'Can you drive it?' Ellie asked.

'I wish I could.'

Uncle Mick was roaring at her mother. She could hear her mother's voice too, so angry she could hardly get her words out.

Ellie said, 'Wouldn't it be lovely if we could go for a ride in this?'

'Why don't you ask your Uncle Mick to take us,' Carlo giggled.

Ellie shivered. 'No fear. He wouldn't anyway.'

'Be quiet, he'll come out and chase us if he hears us.' Franco laughed. 'Move over, Carlo, I want to sit in the driving seat.'

Ellie slid back on the big leather seat. Her feet didn't reach the floor. It was the first car she'd ever sat in, but she had seen one like this driving along the main road.

'Get down,' Carlo was hissing urgently. The two boys suddenly ducked to seat level so they wouldn't be seen.

'You're all right, Ellie.' Franco was peering between the seats at her. 'You're so tiny nobody would see you there anyway.'

Ellie got up on her knees to peep through the window. A man was wheeling his bike across the forecourt to the workshop. She saw her mother come forward to talk to him, her face stiff and white. She took his bike inside.

'She's cross, in a paddy,' Ellie said. 'I'll get into trouble if she sees me playing here.'

'We all will.'

When the man went, the angry shouting started again. Uncle Mick was swearing, her mother's voice shrill.

'They're kicking up a real shindy,' Carlo sniggered. 'Just listen to them.'

Ellie thought her mother was coughing and spluttering. There was a shriek followed by a screech of pain, then a clatter as something fell.

They looked at each other. 'What was that?'

The silence that followed seemed somehow threatening. Carlo's mouth was open. Ellie watched his tongue moisten his lips. She was scared, she grabbed at Franco's shoulder, but he brushed her off.

'Get out,' he whispered. 'Be quiet.'

He and Carlo did so, just closing the doors to. Ellie tugged at the rear door catch, she couldn't get it open, tears were prickling her eyes. Franco did it from the outside and pulled her out beside him.

'You stay here,' he whispered. 'I'm going to see what's happened.' All was silent now.

'No,' Carlo protested. 'Let's get out of here.'

'Come on, don't be such a yellow belly.'

Ellie kept the car between her and the workshop but climbed on the running board and looked through the windows as the brothers crept towards the workshop. She was shaking. Within moments they came sprinting back.

Behind them she saw Auntie Wilma's stringy figure come out on the forecourt. 'Carlo Baldini,' she yelled, 'what are you up to?'

'What did you see?' Ellie gasped, as each boy snatched one of her hands and started to tow her along. She dug her heels in. 'No, I want my mam.'

'Come on, Ellie, don't be a pest. Let's get out of here.'

They gave her no choice. Her feet were hardly touching the ground, she felt she was flying between them. They took the long way home. 'What happened?' she puffed.

'Nothing.'

'What about my mam?'

'She's all right.'

'What was that clatter?'

'Just a bike falling over,' Franco panted.

When they reached the Baldinis' kitchen, it seemed a place of safety. They all collapsed round the table, out of breath.

After a few moments, Carlo straightened up on his chair. His voice shook. 'We haven't been there, Ellie. You didn't sit in that car, we just talked about it.'

Ellie's heart was going pitapat at twice its usual speed. She could see the brothers were frightened, and terror was stabbing at her.

'Don't forget.' Franco's face was close to hers. 'I picked you up from school and brought you here. I gave you a drink of milk.' He leapt to his feet, half filled a cup and pushed it in front of her. 'And you had a jam tart.'

'But I haven't.'

She stared at him. That sounded ordinary and normal. His mother made lovely jam tarts.

'No, we ate them all before you came. D'you want a biscuit?'

She shook her head and her wispy hair lifted round her face.

'Ellie, this is just pretend, a game you and me and Carlo are going to play. If anybody asks, you must tell them I brought you straight here, and we've all been here ever since. Promise me that's what you'll say.'

It seemed a very different afternoon to Ellie, and it was becoming even more strange. Franco's mother had just come home when Gran came round.

'A cup of tea, Bridie?' She was reaching for the kettle.

'No thanks, no time today.' Gran liked nothing better than a chat.

'How's the new teeth?'

'All right.' And Ellie was rushed straight home. Nobody asked if Franco had met her. Mam was already there. She was wearing a scarf twisted round her neck although it was a warm evening.

'You've hurt your cheek,' Ellie said.

'It's nothing, love. A bit of a graze.'

They didn't mention school though usually they wanted to know exactly what she'd done there. Their minds were

7

elsewhere, absorbed in something else. Gran started to put their evening meal on the table, it was what she always did at this time. Mam tried to help her but broke a plate.

'Slipped through my fingers, I'm sorry.'

'Doesn't matter.' Gran was straight lipped and usually that sort of thing mattered a lot. Ellie thought Mam and Gran were scared, they were whispering together about something they didn't want her to know about.

Mam was trying to smile. 'Eat up your boiled bacon, Ellie. Gran said you chose this for our tea tonight.'

She had, Ellie was fond of it, but that had been this morning, and now they were all pushing the food round their plates.

'I've got some aspirins somewhere.' Gran got up to burrow noisily in the sideboard drawer. 'Take two, Orla, and lie down on the couch until you feel better.'

To Ellie, it felt as though the whole room was filled with fear. 'What's the matter, Mam?' she asked. 'Did you hurt your face at the bike shop? Did Uncle Mick . . . ?'

She stopped. She hadn't meant to say anything like that. She'd promised Franco she wouldn't.

'Just a scratch, love,' Mam said, but she looked really shaken up.

When the table had been cleared, Ellie got out the playing cards. 'A game of snap?' she suggested. They often played cards together in the evenings.

'I'll play with you, love,' Gran said. 'We'll let Mam rest.' But Gran's mind wasn't on it, she wasn't shouting snap when she should. The game wasn't much fun.

It was always Mam who took Ellie upstairs and saw her into bed, but tonight, Mam was dozing when Gran said it was bedtime. Gran took her upstairs and tugged so hard on her jersey to get it over her head that it felt as though her ears were being pulled off.

'I can do this,' she complained. 'I can dress and undress myself, I'm not a baby.'

Ellie was sure she'd been put to bed early. Gran said she'd read her the usual story, but she raced through *The Three Bears*, missing bits out.

'Your mam will be up to tuck you in and say goodnight,' she said before going. It seemed to Ellie that she waited ages, and when Mam came, she was sniffing as though she'd been crying.

'What happened at the bike shop, Mam?' Ellie was afraid it must have been something dreadful.

'Just a little accident, love. I slipped and fell, I've hurt my side. Off you go to sleep now, see you in the morning.'

Ellie almost told her she'd been there and about what she'd heard, but Mam's kiss came down on her cheek and she whirled out, taking the candle.

Ellie woke first in the grey morning light to find Mam stirring beside her. They shared a double bed in Gran's back bedroom. Ellie rolled closer for her usual morning cuddle. Mam's sharp intake of breath shocked her.

She asked, 'Did I hurt you?' She knew she had.

It was only when the alarm clock went off and Mam pulled herself out of bed to draw back the curtains, that Ellie saw the bruises on her neck.

'Mam! What's happened to you? There's blood on your nightie too, here round the back.'

'I told you, a bit of an accident at the shop. Up you get, love, and get yourself ready for school.'

Mam was moving stiffly and trying to pretend she didn't hurt. She stumbled out to Gran's room. With her heart pounding, Ellie crept after her. Mam had taken her shoulder out of her nightie and Gran was strapping a fresh piece of lint over the cut there. A used dressing, soaked with blood, was on the floor.

'It's still oozing a bit,' Gran said. 'Real nasty.'

Ellie asked fiercely, 'Did Uncle Mick do that to you, Mam?'

'It was an accident, love. Nothing for you to worry about.'

Ellie saw Gran's lips harden into a straight line. A few moments later, Mam's hand was on her shoulder urging her back to their own room.

'Let's race and see who can be dressed first,' she said, sounding quite different. This was more like Mam.

Ellie threw herself into her clothes, so she could chortle, 'I've won.' This morning, Mam was so slow she hadn't even got her stockings on or her blouse buttoned by the time Ellie was dressed.

But she snatched up the comb from the dressing table and pulled it through Ellie's fine straight hair so it crackled and flew up in bright clouds round her face. Then she tied it back with a big blue bow of ribbon.

There was pain in Mam's brown eyes as they met hers in the mirror. 'You're such a totty for five.' She sounded sad. 'Tiny for your age, too thin.'

'I'm like you, Mam.'

Gran told her often enough that she'd look like her mother when she grew up, though her own eyes were the colour of amber. When she'd been a baby her hair had been yellow and now that was sort of amber too. Mam's colouring was much darker. They both had soft pink cheeks but this morning Mam's face was grey. Gran looked bad too and said she had a headache, but it didn't stop her talking about the bike shop again.

'Mam, did Uncle Mick hurt you yesterday?' Ellie asked.

'No, love. I fell, I told you.'

Gran started spelling words out after that. Ellie knew it meant something was being kept from her. She thought it very strange, because both Mam and Gran had explained that their problems had started years before when Grandpa had died. Nobody had thought to spell things out then. They'd talked and argued and fought openly about the bike shop.

It was just round the corner from where they lived – if you went past the shops and Baldinis' cafe. Gran had brought up her family in this terrace house in Harcourt Street, between the docks on the River Mersey and Birkenhead Park. She'd had five sons, two of whom had died in childhood and two who had been killed in the Great War. Ellie's mother Orla was the youngest and her only daughter.

Grandpa had retired before the war and handed the shop over to his children to run. The trouble was that conscription came and they were called up. One went straight away, the others as they became old enough. Grandpa had to come out of retirement to run the business again and Orla had helped him.

But he'd been ill and had died in January 1918. Orla had hired another girl to help, and had managed it for another year before her brother Mick had come home. They'd fallen out within days. He had very different ideas about how the bike shop should be run and wanted things changed. As the man of the family, he expected to run the business. Orla felt he was trying to push her out and maintained there was no point in changing things that were working well.

In this will, Grandpa had left his business to be divided in equal shares between his surviving children, but it stipulated that the first call on the profits was to pay a pension to his wife for her lifetime. Ellie used to love going to the shop. She was told she was welcome as long as she didn't get in the way. Her mother took her turn of looking after the shop, selling and hiring out bikes; and she also kept the accounts.

The place always seemed busy. There was usually a bike upended on its saddle and handlebars in the workshop as Uncle Mick repaired it. The place smelled of bike oil and the glue they used to stick patches over punctures.

In the main part of the shop, there were shiny new bikes of every sort. Ellie loved to study the latest fairy cycles for children, though she already had one of her own. On days when Mam didn't go to work, she took her on bike rides round the park.

All the family were keen cyclists. Even Gran had a bike, though she no longer rode it. It was very heavy and old fashioned and had cords going over the back wheel so she wouldn't get her skirts caught in it. She said she was too old for cycling now.

Recently, Ellie had seen motor bikes coming into the workshop for repairs, and the place began to smell of petrol. Mam had not been pleased when three new motor bikes were ordered and put on sale. Uncle Mick was very keen and took to riding them about the district.

'Much more exciting,' he said. 'You don't have to pedal these. Everybody will want one soon.'

Ellie heard her mother flare up at that. 'Course they won't, not everyone. Most girls will prefer a push bike.' She and Gran were cross with Mick.

Uncle Mick lived with Auntie Wilma in the rooms over the bike shop, but he used to come round and try to persuade Gran to let them have motor bikes. It got so bad, that she told him not to come any more, which made it more peaceful at home, but Mam was often furious when she came home from work. Ellie had heard her giving out over the tea table, saying she couldn't cope with Mick or cars either.

Then Mam said her brother was talking of converting the bike shop to a garage. He wanted to sell petrol and mend cars, believing that would be more profitable in the future. She and Gran were against it.

One day, Mam had been so cross when she'd come home that she could hardly get the words out to tell Gran what had happened.

'Mick wants to get rid of me. He wants to buy me out! I'm not having that.'

'Don't be hasty, think about it, Orla—'

'I keep the books, I know how much the business earns and what he's offering me is nothing like what it's worth.'

'You could just keep the books for him. He isn't very good at figures. He'd pay you for that and you could keep half of the profit you're entitled to.'

'He doesn't want me in the business. He's trying to push me out.'

Then, two days ago, Mam had come home with the news that the first car had arrived and was on show. When the place closed for the night, Gran said she'd walk down to see it. Ellie had run after her, wanting to see it too, but she didn't get a close look. Gran had glowered at it from the other side of the road, refusing to go nearer. On the way home, Gran said she was having nothing to do with it. She wouldn't go to the bike shop again, and neither must Ellie.

Ellie could see just how much upset it gave Mam and Gran to be at loggerheads with her uncle. Gran said the feud that was developing would tear the family apart.

Chapter Two

Ellie was given porridge for her breakfast. That was quite usual; but Auntie Wilma, Uncle Mick's wife, came round while she was eating and that was very unusual. Her face was screwed up with worry and her eyes were red. Her small son Ben was trying to hide behind her, clinging silently to her hand. Ellie couldn't drag her gaze from him. His blue eyes were staring silently into hers.

'Have you had breakfast?' Mam asked him, and when he shook his head, she gave him a bowl of porridge and made him climb up on the chair next to Ellie's.

Wilma started pouring out her troubles but Gran pushed a cup of tea in her hand, edged her towards the armchair and began spelling words out again.

Gran didn't approve of Auntie Wilma. Before Mick had been conscripted into the Army, he'd been engaged to a girl called Patsy Holland. The Hollands also lived in Harcourt Street, and the families had been friendly. Patsy was a nice girl, she'd been loyal, waiting for Mick to return.

But Mick had been difficult in every way, he was having rows with Orla about the business and rows with Patsy at the same time. He'd broken off his engagement, upsetting the Hollands and cooling relations between the two families.

He'd immediately taken up with Wilma, a widow older than he was, with a young son and an air of helplessness. When

Gran expressed disapproval, he'd taken Wilma to the register office and married her. He didn't tell his family or ask any of them to the wedding.

Auntie Wilma was sniffing quietly, but when she looked up her face was agonised.

'What if Mick dies? He could without regaining consciousness.'

Ellie dropped her spoon into her porridge. Mam gasped, 'If he does . . .' Her voice shook. 'Would that mean? Would that be . . . ?'

'Don't say such things,' Gran hissed. 'Not in front . . .'

'I'm worried about the business.' Wilma was scrubbing at her face with a damp handkerchief.

'I'm worried about it too,' Gran said fiercely. 'Let's hope this puts a stop to all that nonsense about turning it into a garage.'

'I mean today, with Mick in hospital . . . Will you be coming to open up, Orla?'

'Look at her,' Gran demanded. 'You can see Orla's not well. She won't be able to do much. It wouldn't be too much to ask you to run the shop for once.'

'I know nothing about bikes.' Wilma's voice was plaintive. 'I couldn't mend a puncture. I mean, I never have.'

'You can open up. If someone came in wanting a bike, you could sell them one, couldn't you? Or hire one out. Leave the repairs for the time being.'

Mam said, 'I'll probably be down later, Wilma.'

'I'm taking her down to the hospital first.' Gran was being protective. She despatched Auntie Wilma. 'It's nearly time for you to open up.' Once the door had closed behind her and her son, she added scathingly, 'Neither use nor ornament, that one.'

'She's not had an easy time, Mam. Don't be hard on her.'

George Quiltie, Wilma's first husband, had been killed on the docks, when a derrick swinging a load of cement into the hold of the *SS Alice Whiteman* had nudged him off balance and he'd fallen into the hold. Ben, his son, was eighteen months older than Ellie.

It seemed to her that, even when they'd gone, a feeling of doom hung heavily over the breakfast table. Neither Gran nor Mam said anything, apart from urging her to eat up and hurry up.

Usually, Mam walked her to school in the morning and went straight on to the bike shop. Ellie thought she intended to do the same today. She'd twisted the scarf carefully round her neck again.

'Is that to hide the bruises on your throat?' Ellie had asked. But now Mam was pallid and coughing.

'Orla, I'll take the baby to school,' Gran said. 'You look real poorly.'

'You don't look so grand yourself.'

'I've got to go to the shops anyway. Should we have offered to take Wilma's boy?'

'He goes by himself.'

'He's very quiet.'

'But he takes everything in.'

'Get your coat on, Ellie, and say goodbye to your mam.'

She did as she was told. Mam had gone to lie down on the couch and was having difficulty getting her breath, but she hugged her for longer than usual.

'I love you, Ellie,' she whispered, before kissing her goodbye. Ellie wanted to cling tighter.

Gran walked her to school, holding her hand in a tight grasp as if afraid she'd run away. Dinner time came. Ellie rarely saw her mother then, it was always Gran who met her at the school gates to take her home for something to eat. All morning, she'd been wondering if Mam was feeling better. She asked, but Gran didn't seem to hear.

Poor Gran looked really ill too and didn't want to talk. Ellie kept quiet, it was what Gran liked when she had a headache.

'Did Mam go to the hospital?' Ellie asked when she found she wasn't at home. Gran didn't say no, she wasn't herself and seemed unable to answer any of her questions, but Ellie was led to believe she had. Later that afternoon, when school finished for the day, Gran was waiting for her again.

'Are Mam's bruises better?' she asked. 'Has she come home now?'

Gran's voice was agonised. 'No, you'll not see her for a little while.'

That brought Ellie to a stop. 'Why?' This had never happened before.

Gran put her arms round her in the street and said, 'Don't you worry your pretty little head. She'll be back soon.'

'But when?' She wanted her mam here today.

Gran's hand smoothed her flyaway hair away from her forehead. 'I don't know, love.'

That was strange too. Gran always knew everything.

'Where is she, in hospital?'

'Yes . . .'

'Somebody hurt her.' She saw Gran wince at that. 'She had big bruises on her neck as well as cuts on her face and her back.'

'She fell down and hurt herself.'

'No, her knees were all right,' Ellie said. 'When I fall down, it's always my knees that get grazed.' She was sure things were being kept from her.

'Trust you to know that, you're as bright as a cart load of monkeys. She said she slipped and fell against a tandem and hurt herself. I took her to the hospital, and they're keeping her in for a bit.'

'They'll make her better, won't they? When can we go and see her?'

'Come on, let's go to the cafe now. You can have ice cream.'

Gran's closest friend was Constanzia Baldini, Franco's mother. Ellie called her Auntie Connie, though she wasn't a relation. Gran had told her how Connie's husband, Vito Baldini, had opened an ice-cream parlour in the parade of shops near where you could catch the underground train to Liverpool.

He'd set his heart on having an ice-cream parlour, but in the English winter there were few customers for that. He'd had to paint out the sign which read Ice-Cream Parlour and change it to Trattoria. He'd then planned to serve the typical Italian meals they both loved, but the locals had always called it the caff and they preferred the food they were used to. Vito had had to provide it if he wanted their custom.

He boiled large bacon joints and when cold, carved slices to serve with potato chips. It was called ham on the menu and was their most popular dish. He fried eggs and bacon to order, and served chips with almost everything. Now they had more customers, he was making salads and one additional hot meal each day. His spaghetti bolognese was growing in popularity.

'Bridie, hello. *Buon giorno.*' Vito liked to greet his customers in his native tongue. He smiled down at Ellie. 'Which ice cream today, *bambina*?'

One of Ellie's treats was coming here to choose from all the exciting flavours Uncle Vito made. She feasted her eyes first on the chocolate and then on the strawberry. She found it hard to make up her mind.

'Today, something special for you, yes?'

Ellie watched, fascinated, as he made a knickerbocker glory in the half-size glasses he kept for children.

'Strawberry, yes, vanilla and chocolate?' He always had a beaming smile for her.

'She'll love that,' Gran said.

He was layering the ice cream with syrups and fruits. Auntie Connie carried the glass to a table for her, it was brimming with cream and accompanied by wafer biscuits. Ellie climbed on a chair in front of it licking her lips. Auntie Connie pulled out a chair for herself and sat down to talk to Gran.

She and her husband were first-generation Italian immigrants and they missed the company of their fellow countrymen. Very few Italians had settled in this area, and with a name like Valentino, Gran had told her, Connie had thought at first she'd found one in her.

But Gran had been born thirty miles outside Dublin, and had kept her Irish ways and her Irish brogue. Ellie knew her grandpa had been born in Liverpool but his father had come from Naples, and he'd been proud of his Italian roots. Gran and Connie had become friends and often met up to drink tea and chat.

Connie was a lot younger than Gran, but she wore black dresses, usually covered with big white aprons. Her black hair was taken back severely into a bun, yet her face was olive skinned, unlined and smiling. She had a family of five sons. Ellie had heard her commiserate with Gran many times about their wayward children.

Ellie thought Gran's eyes were watching her warily, as though she wanted to tell Connie about the trouble at the bike shop, but wouldn't while Ellie could hear.

'The trouble with my children,' Gran said yet again, 'is their mixed heritage. Irish and Italian is an explosive mixture.'

'They're hard working,' Connie said. 'Brighter than average and quick to seize their chance in business.'

'Too quick sometimes.' Gran was spreading jam thickly on her home-baked scone.

'Orla now, you couldn't have a better daughter, the way she looked after that business while her brothers were away in the Army. A real trooper, a lovely girl, very pretty.'

'Too pretty. What have her looks brought her? Nothing but trouble.'

Ellie felt their eyes assessing her.

'You're pretty too,' Connie smiled at her. 'You've got your mother's heart-shaped face and big eyes.'

'That she has. The boys—'

'Bridie, you can be proud of your boys. Two gave their lives for their country.'

'I'm proud of them. It's Mick.'

'A handsome man. Strong looking . . .'

Ellie savoured her knickerbocker glory. Connie was right, her uncle was very strong, with broad shoulders and arms like tree trunks.

'Perhaps too strong,' Gran sighed. 'And he's very hot tempered.'

Ellie was reminded of what Auntie Wilma had said this morning. She asked, 'Did Uncle Mick die?'

Connie jerked up on her seat. 'What? D'you know I heard—'

'No, love,' Gran told her.

'But he still might?'

'We'll all die one day.' Gran looked woebegone and they listened to what was being said on the next table.

Then Connie asked brightly, 'Another cup of tea?' She got up to fetch it and Gran followed her to the counter. Ellie watched them whispering together for some time.

Gran was leaning against one of the sturdy metal stools at the counter. Everything Gran wore was old fashioned and made her seem old. She was fond of swinging black skirts that swished round her ankles, and, at home, black crocheted shawls to cover her shoulders. She had her black coat on now which showed only six inches of skirt below it. All her hats were big, this one was garlanded with grey feathers grown bare and twisted with age, so it looked like a bird's nest. It covered all her white hair which she so carefully did up in a bun.

Only Gran's grey eyes looked young. She said she had second sight and could see much more with them than other people. She could still see people who'd lived fifty years ago, and could tell lovely stories about them. Mam said it was because she was getting old and the friends and family Gran had known and loved were dead.

'But if they're dead, can she really see them?' Ellie had asked.

'She thinks she can.'

Ellie looked round the cafe; she thought it a lovely place. It was so light, with its white tables and pale tiles on the floor. It made it seem summery inside even if the rain was hurtling against the big shop windows. One of the Baldini boys had painted murals on the walls, showing a sun-drenched beach with sparkling sea and palm trees. He'd drawn flat-roofed houses too, the colour of wet sand. This must be what Italy was like.

Gran and Auntie Connie were coming back with brimming cups. 'You're right about that. Your lot always had their fists up, but mine are no better.'

'They are,' Gran said, sinking down on the chair. 'And they're all in the land of the living.'

'Three of ours have left us. We never see them.'

'They're grown men, Connie. They wanted to go back home. You can't blame them for that.'

'Milan is not home to us. I told you, we come from Cittanova, a village right down in the toe of Italy. I can't believe you don't remember me telling you that.'

'Italy's all the same to me, I've never been there. Naples is where Mario's family came from, but he never saw it.'

'I blame our Giovanni, he went to Milan and wrote glowing letters home to his brothers. I'm sure he persuaded Luigi . . . I dread seeing letters coming from Italy for our Carlo. I'm afraid . . .' Carlo was serving behind the counter now.

'You're looking for trouble before it comes. He won't want to go.'

'I'm not so sure.'

'Anyway, they've all found good jobs. If they're settling there, I can't see—'

'Giovanni helped them find jobs, but me and Vito want them here. We'd give anything to have them working in the business. It's too much for us on our own, and what's the point of building it up if there's no one to hand it on to?'

'Even if Carlo should go, there's still Franco.'

'Oh, Franco! He's more trouble than the rest of them put together.'

The shop door burst open at that moment, causing the bell to jangle fortissimo. Franco swept to the counter and leapt up on one of the stools. Like all his family he had skin that appeared permanently suntanned even in the English winter. He was slim and wiry in build. All the men were, even his father Vito. Constanzia, on the other hand, was growing heavier with the years.

'You know how wild he can be.' Disappointment with the behaviour of their sons was one of the things on which Gran and Connie never let up. 'The cheek of him sitting there like a paying customer while his pa's rushed off his feet!' Connie leapt to her feet. 'Excuse me, Bridie, I'll have to see to this.'

Gran took Ellie's hand and led her into the newspaper shop next door. As well as the evening paper, Gran bought her a colouring book and some new crayons.

'Lovely,' Ellie beamed. 'Two treats today, Gran?'

'Yes, well . . .'

After tea, she coloured in some pictures. There was a lovely one of a tiger which she crayoned in orange stripes. When bedtime came, she was thinking of Mam. Gran turned back her bed and read her a story, but Mam had always done those things.

'If Mam's in hospital, when can we go to see her?'

'I don't know, love.'

'Gran, you always know things like that. People can visit and take presents to cheer her up and make her better, can't they?'

'Not children. They don't let children in, in case they bring in some sort of infection.'

'What's that?'

'Disease, illness.'

'But I wouldn't, I'm never sick.'

'It's a rule. No children allowed in.'

In the following days, Auntie Wilma often came round to talk to Gran. She remained worried. It was some time before Ellie realised Uncle Mick was in hospital too.

Gran murmured. 'He was in the same accident as your mam.'

Ellie asked, 'Have you been down to the hospital to see them, Auntie Wilma?'

'They aren't allowed visitors,' Gran said quickly. 'Not well enough yet.'

'When will they be well enough?'

'I don't know.'

'What did happen to Uncle Mick and Mam?' Ellie demanded. 'I think they were fighting. They were always fighting, weren't they?'

'An accident,' Gran said again.

'But how did it happen? What sort of an . . . ?'

'Aren't you a nosey parker then?' Auntie Wilma asked coldly.

Ellie didn't like Auntie Wilma much. She could feel tears burning her eyes. 'I want my mam.'

Gran was trying to smile at her. 'Why don't you get out your colouring book, love? Do me another tiger.' The family were so engrossed in this other very pressing matter, that nobody was paying much attention to Ellie. She wished she was grown up so she'd know exactly what had happened.

That night when Gran was putting her to bed, she asked, 'Is Mam's new straw hat still up there?' She could see the box still on top of the wardrobe. 'The hat with pink flowers round the brim?'

'Yes.'

'She thinks a lot of that.'

'It suits her.'

Ellie looked round their bedroom. Mam's glass powder bowl with its big pink puff was still on the dressing table, her old brown coat was hanging behind the door. When Gran tucked her up and went back downstairs, Ellie got up again and pulled open the drawers in the chest. Mam's things were here: her scarves, her beads, her handkerchiefs and the blue satin nightdress Gran had given her for her birthday. Wouldn't she need that in hospital?

She opened the wardrobe, all Mam's clothes were hanging there. She flung her arms round them and buried her face in their skirts. They smelled of Mam's scent, Attar of Roses. She must be coming back. Ellie didn't think she'd leave for ever and not take any of her things with her. She threw herself back on her bed and wept.

When Franco picked up the local newspaper the following week, he found the trouble in the bike shop detailed in a big article on the front page.

He ran upstairs to his bedroom to be alone, and sat on the floor with his back wedged against the door to read it. It described the scene he and Carlo had glimpsed on that terrible afternoon. They'd both believed Mick to be dead. He'd been lying motionless, while Orla, covered with blood, had been crawling away on her hands and knees. They'd really thought she'd killed him.

Franco had had the willies ever since, he felt sick now. He'd come out in a sweat of relief when he heard Bridie say Mick was still in the land of the living. He went on to read that Michael Valentino remained unconscious in hospital while his sister was said to be very poorly.

All the details of what their quarrel was about were made clear not only to their neighbours, but to people living all over the town. Like them, the Valentinos were in business and many used the service they offered. They were well known in the district. Franco heard them being talked about at school, in the streets and the park. He guessed it would be the main topic in the caff.

Orla Valentino was popular, her customers thought her polite and efficient, but she was no better than she should be, having had a child but no husband. Her brother Mick was thought to be rude and aggressive, but he wanted to bring cars to the town; he looked to the future. Everybody took one side or the other.

In Franco's home it was spoken of as Bridie's trouble, but to him, it seemed just as much theirs. It frightened him to see how shocked his parents were. The Valentinos were their closest friends and had been for years. Franco saw the agonies of compassion his mother went through for Bridie, and in particular for little Ellie. All the horrific details must be kept from her. She was too young to understand. Ma and Bridie had spelled that out to him. Ellie must be protected.

Franco quaked. He and Carlo had done the very opposite by taking her to the bike shop on that fateful afternoon. In the bedroom they shared, they'd talked about it many times. When Franco went to the caff, they exchanged anxious whispers about it behind the kitchen door. Carlo was even more worried than he was.

'What if Ellie says something?'

'We made her promise not to.'

'But she's only a baby . . . Has she said anything to you about it since?'

'No, I don't think she understands. Either that or she's forgotten.'

'How can you be so sure?'

'Well, it isn't on her mind in the way it is on ours. She's only five, for heaven's sake.'

'Even so . . .'

'She was round at our house, sitting at the kitchen table with me yesterday, when Ma took Bridie upstairs to show her the new coat she'd bought. Ellie could have mentioned it, but she was quiet and sort of . . . Well, you know, she's sort of fretting for her mam.'

'You ought to remind her that she's promised to keep her mouth shut.'

Franco shook his head. 'I nearly did, but then I thought it better to say nothing. I mean, if she's forgotten . . .'

Carlo released a pent-up breath. 'But she'd only have to tell Bridie we took her there that afternoon, and we'd be in terrible trouble – worse trouble for keeping quiet about it.'

Over the following days, Ellie noticed people turning to look at them in the street when she was walking with Gran. She heard somebody say, 'Is that her little girl?' Other people, who at one time would say 'good morning' to Gran, now crossed the road rather than talk to them.

Gran seemed hardly to know what she was doing. 'I'm all at sixes and sevens, love.'

She forgot to wind the mantelpiece clock and Ellie was late for school. That afternoon, Gran forgot to meet her at the school gates and was shocked when Ellie came home by herself.

'I don't need to be fetched and carried all the time,' Ellie told her. 'I know the way now, I'm big enough to do it by myself.'

Meals that used always to be ready on time no longer were. Everything seemed to be too much for Gran.

Every morning, Connie sent Franco round before he went to school. He cleared out their grate, lit the fire and brought in another scuttle full of coal.

'Wait for me, I'm going to school too,' Ellie said to him when he'd finished, but he never would.

'I promised to call for my friend Denis,' he'd say, before running off. Sometimes it was Eric or Tom.

'He changes his friends as often as he changes his socks,' Gran said scornfully. 'He thinks you're too young to be bothered with.' But Ellie knew she was fond of Franco and he of her.

Ellie started running errands for Gran. She'd be sent to the shops with a bag and the money screwed up in a piece of paper on which Gran had written down what she wanted. Gran said it saved her legs.

More often than not, when Ellie came home from school, she'd find Connie in their house making an Irish stew or one of the hot pots that Gran liked. One day, she came home to find them having what Gran called a heart-to-heart talk.

A large metal strong box stood open on the table. Gran called it her treasure chest and if she was going far from home she wore the key on a silver chain round her neck. At other times, both the chain and the key were kept in the pretty china pot on her dressing table that had a rose painted on the lid.

It was a rare treat for Ellie to look through Gran's treasures. There were a lot of papers on the bottom, Gran's marriage lines and that sort of thing. Ellie was more interested in the tray with compartments that fitted over them.

She took out the gold pocket watch that had once belonged to Grandpa and wound it up. She pinned the cameo brooch to the bodice of her jumper. It was in a heavy gold setting. Gran said Grandpa had given it to her when they were married. She tried on a ring which was much too large for her finger. There were other bits and pieces, strings of beads that Gran said were not very valuable but she knew where to look if she wanted them.

'Ellie!' Gran seemed to see what she was doing for the first time. 'Who said you could play with my treasures?'

Gran's withered hands unpinned the brooch from her dress and slid everything back into the box and locked it.

'Pour her a drink of milk, Connie, would you?' Gran sank back on her armchair. Ellie took the cup and settled down between Gran's chair and the wall where she couldn't be seen. The grown-ups sometimes forgot she was there.

Connie finished chopping in the back kitchen and brought in tea for herself and Gran who sounded a bit depressed. After a while, Ellie heard her say, 'I must pull myself together, so I must, if only for the sake of the little one.'

'For your own sake,' Connie's voice came from the back kitchen, 'the little one's fine.'

'I do worry,' Gran said, 'about whether I'll be spared to see her grow up.'

'Course you will, you'll come round this. It's a terrible thing but life goes on for the rest of us.'

'But if I don't—'

'You mustn't worry about that,' Connie said briskly, clattering pans. 'Me and Vito will take care of her, you know that. We'd love to have her.'

'That's a right weight off my mind,' Gran sighed.

Another day Ellie came home from school to find Gran in tears. That really scared her, grown-ups didn't cry. 'What is it, Gran? Isn't Mam getting better?'

'I'm just being silly, a bit down,' she said, drying her eyes. 'Nothing to do with your mam,' but somehow Ellie thought it was.

More often now, after the tea things had been cleared away, Gran would pull her on the armchair beside her and put an arm round her shoulders so Ellie could nestle up against her. Then she'd tell her about growing up in Ireland fifty years ago; about her own family, the O'Malleys, who had been trying to make a living on a small-holding then, but were now scattered over America, Canada and England.

'Tell me about when Mam was a little girl,' Ellie urged, but Gran didn't seem to remember much about those days.

* * *

Connie Baldini dragged herself home from Bridie's house feeling absolutely drained. She'd gone round for a cup of tea and a chat, knowing her friend must be feeling low, but she'd never seen her like this before.

It wasn't like Bridie to sit rocking back and forth in her chair with her apron over her head. Not in the middle of the afternoon when there were things in the house that needed doing.

'I've come to cheer you up,' Connie had said in too jaunty a manner. Only realising how trite that must sound when Bridie showed her face and she saw the utter despair there.

'It's hopeless, Connie.' There'd been unshed tears in Bridie's eyes. 'I can't put this behind me. I'm weary, it's hopeless . . .'

'It's not.'

'I'm too old for this.'

'Seventy's a good age, but many . . .'

'I thought I'd be under the sods before now. My mother died at forty-nine, you know.'

'You told me. In childbirth.'

'Yes, our children bring us trouble, Connie. One way or another, they bring us our sorrows.'

'How many times have we talked about this? Our disappointment in what our children are doing, the feeling they don't love us as much as we love them, that they've turned their backs on us.'

'The worry that they're making mistakes.' Bridie sighed. 'But I've never had to worry about anything as bad as this before.'

Connie swallowed. It didn't bear thinking about. 'Don't lose heart, Bridie.'

'I have, I don't mind saying—'

'You mustn't. You've got to think of Ellie.'

31

Bridie had given her a wan smile then. 'Yes, there's Ellie. Our Orla says she's relying on me to do that.'

'You've seen Orla again?'

'I see her all the time.' Bridie's wet eyes looked into hers, and Connie caught the fey look.

'You see her in your mind's eye, you mean.'

'Orla's weeping, Connie. She's been done down. Blamed. She says it wasn't her fault.'

Ellie came home from school one afternoon and Gran stopped her taking off her red coat. 'Your Uncle Mick's come home from hospital. Come on, we'll go down to the bike shop and see how he is.'

'He's better?' Ellie felt cheered. 'When will Mam be coming out?'

'I don't know.' Gran's old face was stiff and serious.

'It can't be long now.'

'Not for a while yet, I'm afraid.'

Uncle Mick was sitting in his armchair looking just as he always had. Ellie thought he was the biggest man in town. He was huge, over six feet tall and built like a bull. Rage seemed to glitter in his dark eyes and he never spoke quietly or calmly. To Ellie, he seemed tough and aggressive and not like anyone else in her family.

'You've been lucky,' Gran told him. 'Lucky to get away with it.'

'We make our own luck,' Mick said coldly. 'You wouldn't have wanted me to die, would you? It isn't hard to guess what would have happened to our Or—'

'Hush now.' Ellie saw Gran's eyes swing round to look at her. 'We'll have none of that.'

'You think I've got off scot free, but lying in bed these last weeks has left me weak as a baby.'

'You look all right,' Ellie told him.

Wilma laughed nervously. She'd lost weight and looked scraggy.

'The doctor said I must take things easy for a while.'

'Not too easy, I hope,' Gran said sharply. 'The repair shop is filling up.' Wilma had taken on a lad for a few weeks to help out, but he could only manage the simplest of repairs.

Ellie could see Ben's blue eyes staring silently at her from a stool in the corner. She pulled at her uncle's sleeve. 'Did you see my mam in hospital?'

'No.'

'Why not? She's there too.'

Gran said, 'They have separate wards, love, the boys in one and the girls in another.'

Ellie frowned. 'If they made you better, they'll be making Mam better too, won't they? When d'you think she'll be coming out?'

She saw Auntie Wilma's lips forming silent words to him. 'What d'you mean, "Don't tell her?" ' Ellie was dancing with frustration. 'Why not? I want to know.'

Ben's stool scraped on the lino as he got up and came towards her. 'Ellie,' he said. 'Your—'

Uncle Mick sent him flying with one blow from his ham-sized fist. 'You keep your trap shut, can't you? How many times does your mother have to tell you?'

Ellie gasped. She'd never seen a child treated so roughly. Mick was feeling for her hand, looking at her as a kindly uncle would.

'I don't know, Ellie. If I could give you a date, I would.' It made her shiver. She was glad to be out in the street again and heading for home.

When the school holidays started, Gran took her away. They stayed in lodgings near the sea for a week. It was a lovely place but Ellie was still missing her mother. It was while she was there that she dreamed about her for the first time.

Ellie was coming out of afternoon school and could see Mam waiting with the other mothers at the gates. Mam had her back to her, but Ellie recognised her best blue coat and hat and the shopping basket over her arm. As she raced down the school yard, Mam turned round smiling and holding out her arms. Ellie reached her, opening her own arms to give Mam a hug, but there was nothing there. She'd vanished into thin air.

It was all the more strange because Mam used to take her to school first thing in the morning, but it was Gran who met her, Mam never had. Ellie had this dream many times, and at this point she always woke up sweating to find herself alone. Gran didn't want to talk about Mam, nobody did. Ellie remembered her as being warm and loving and couldn't believe she'd just disappear like this.

Chapter Three

One evening, Franco couldn't help but notice that Carlo was silent and curled in on himself, when he came home. He ate very little at tea time though Pa had brought gnocchi from the caff and it was one of his favourites.

Ma noticed too, and asked, 'Aren't you feeling well, Carlo?'

'I'm all right,' he muttered, but he made no move to go out to see his friends afterwards.

Then, when Ma in her bossy way said, 'Come on, Franco, you've got school tomorrow,' and pushed him up to bed at nine thirty, Carlo, for once, came upstairs with him. They shared a double bed in the back bedroom.

'What's the matter?' Franco asked, dragging his shirt over his head and throwing it on a chair.

'Mick Valentino came in today.'

'So what?'

'He went for me.'

'What d'you mean, went for you?'

'You know that fellow who comes in every morning for bacon and egg? He works nights on the docks.'

'No, how could I?'

'Well, he always sits in the window. He'd just gone and I was clearing his table when Mick came swaggering in.' Carlo let his breath out in an agonising sigh. 'Pa was in the office with the

35

rep from the coffee firm, the one he's friendly with. It was early and there was no one about.'

Franco felt under the covers on his side of the bed for his pyjamas. 'So what are you trying to tell me?'

Carlo's dark eyes were pools of fear. 'Mick's hand shot out and grabbed me by the neck of my shirt, twisting it tight.'

'What, just like that?'

'Yes, before I said anything. "You've no business to come sneaking round our bike shop," he hissed. "Wilma saw you the other day. You keep your mouth shut, you understand?" He twisted my collar with every word until I was nearly choking. "You're dead if you don't." '

' "Dead if you don't!" He was threatening you? It sounds as though Mick has something he wants to hide.' Franco shivered as he shot under the bedclothes. 'Don't forget to blow the light out.'

The bed springs were already sinking on the other side as Carlo got in beside him.

'Mick also said, "I'll be keeping an eye on you." ' Carlo's face was screwing with worry. The candle was still burning on the chest of drawers. ' "So don't try putting your oar in, now or in the future." '

Franco heard the fear in Carlo's voice and suppressed another shiver. The Valentino family's troubles were making them all nervous, they were too close.

'Tell him to take a running jump next time you see him.'

'Don't be daft, Franco.'

'Well, what exactly did you see?'

'The same as you, you idiot. We saw nothing that hasn't been in the papers; nothing that important. Just Mick flat out on the workshop floor and Orla sobbing as she struggled to her feet, all grazed and bleeding and terrified.'

Franco swallowed hard. 'I can't stop thinking about it. Whatever happened, it took place while we were there. Orla was all right, we saw her come out to the forecourt, didn't we? After that, we heard Mick raving at her. What did we hear next? Scuffling and Orla screaming and choking. That's when I think he hit her.'

'But we don't know—'

'He must have, she was all cuts and bruises. It was a bit after that when we heard the heavy crash, that could be when Mick went down.'

'You're just guessing, but so what?'

'Then it would be self defence, wouldn't it? If it was Orla who knocked him out.'

'What d'you mean, if?'

'She was already hurt, could she have found the strength?'

'Don't be daft. Somebody did.'

Franco let his breath out in an unsteady gasp. 'Wilma was there when we took a peek.'

'Wilma? She wouldn't, she's his wife. They haven't been married all that long, and they're keen on each other. She was worried stiff about Mick being in hospital. Anyway, why should she?'

'She was there,' Franco insisted.

'Of course she was there. Remember what it said in the newspaper? Wilma came down when she heard them arguing and found Mick already on the floor, unconscious, with a bleeding wound on the back of his head. She said Orla looked befuddled, she saw her stagger back and fall against a tandem, then get up and go home. She thought Mick was dead.'

'We did too, didn't we?' Franco had worried himself sick about that.

'We saw blood on his head, dripping everywhere.'

'Yes, but it was Orla who died. Mick's as right as rain and throwing his weight about.' Franco shuddered. 'I think we should go to the police and tell them. They could question him—'

'No,' Carlo hissed. 'We decided to keep our mouths shut, didn't we? It's what we want and what Mick wants. He's afraid we saw something that incriminates him, but we didn't.'

Franco shook his head. 'But why is he worried about what we saw? It must mean something did happen that he wants to keep quiet. Something happened that he's afraid we did see. I think we should tell somebody we were there. We were witnesses—'

'No, we weren't. We didn't see anything.'

'Orla's being blamed, being labelled a criminal.'

'What difference does it make now? Orla's dead,' his brother spat.

'It does to Bridie. If we don't, we'll have Mick Valentino on our backs for ever.'

'No.'

'You're a funk,' Franco said through his teeth. 'You're surely not that scared of Mick Valentino? If we went to the police, they'd question him further, find out more. I believe they could nail him for it.'

'No, Franco! There's nothing more to find out. Nothing. Besides, the less we say about that day the better. They'll want to know why we didn't say something sooner.'

Franco was scornful. 'Of course, we mustn't let Pa know his favourite son said he had the shits when he hadn't. Mustn't let Pa know about the ruse you pull to get a day off work when you want one. You know he can't let you near the food in case the customers catch it.'

His brother writhed beside him.

'Ma would be cross with her darling too. She has to work in your place, doesn't she?'

Franco wanted to cry. He knew he was letting his fear and resentment show. Carlo was the son who conformed to their parents' Italian ideas. The one who wanted to please them, to do everything the way they wanted. The one they favoured.

Carlo said coldly, 'You bunked off school too.'

'You persuaded me to. You wanted to see that round-Britain cycle race go through Liverpool.'

'I wish we hadn't. Oh God! I wish we hadn't.'

'It wasn't all that exciting.' Franco shivered again. 'Bit of a bore really.' He had another worry. 'Did Wilma see me there with you?'

'Course she did, we were together, weren't we? Mick said, "Tell your kid brother to keep his mouth shut too. Tell him I'll kill him if he squeaks. And what d'you bring Orla's baby round for?" '

Franco felt a frisson of panic. His brother was eyeing him across the sheet. 'I told him Ellie didn't see anything. He said, "You'd better be right about that. Not a peep out of any of you. Got it?" '

'He's a bully, all wind.' Franco knew it was bravado that made him say that, he was scared of Mick Valentino too.

'Look at my neck, look what he did to me. It's sore. I had to search out my chef's neck tie to hide it. Pa said how much smarter I looked with it on, and he was glad to see me wearing it.'

'I still think we should tell somebody. Pa would know what we should do. He'd want us to go to the police.'

'No!'

'You're a yellow belly—'

Carlo's punch caught him on the chin, taking him by

surprise. 'Shut up, can't you? You didn't blow the candle out.'

Franco's chin stung but he got out of bed. The lino was freezing against his feet. He took as few steps as he could and snuffed it with one breath. He leapt back on the bed, whipped the bedclothes off his brother and landed a real heavyweight in his belly. Carlo let out a cry of agony.

Franco tried to muffle it with his pillow. 'Shut it! D'you want Ma to come up?'

But she hadn't heard them. Franco settled down and pulled the blankets up round his neck. The dark that closed round him was more frightening than ever. He knew the right thing would be to speak up.

Bridie was really low and desperate for help. She kept saying she didn't know what to do. Orla was dead; she'd got the blame and been branded a criminal. Franco felt it would be off his conscience if he told Pa. It would take away the feeling that he was letting Bridie down.

Orla had always been nice to him. She'd persuaded Pa to buy him a bike for his ninth birthday and taught him to ride it.

Pa was fond of her too. During the war when nobody could get grapes, she used to cycle into the Wirral countryside to pick elderflowers and elderberries for him when they came in season. He'd had to make his wine from them in those years. And he still had a few bottles left. He spoke of the 1915 vintage as being excellent. Often, Orla's boyfriend had gone with her, the one who was killed before he could marry her.

Franco hadn't really understood at the time but he'd listened avidly when he'd heard customers in the caff discussing Orla. As he'd gown up, he'd come to understand the sense of titillation it gave older boys.

Franco knew now that the Valentinos had had their first taste of notoriety when Orla was seen to be with child but had no husband. She'd carried on working in the bike shop while heavily pregnant.

'She didn't have much choice about working,' his ma had defended her. 'Her brothers fighting on the Somme and her pa brought out of retirement to run the shop. He needed her help.'

The talk about Orla's sin and loose ways had not stopped when Ellie was born. Who the father might be became a local obsession. Elderly matrons in the neighbourhood seemed outraged.

Franco couldn't remember now where he'd heard the real facts but it seemed Orla's boyfriend had been the son of a local solicitor and, at first, Bridie had been pleased at Orla's good prospects. He'd volunteered for the Army before they'd started calling men up and been given a commission. He'd been sent to the south of England for months of training and then been killed within three weeks of reaching France.

So much for Orla's good prospects. Her love affair must have brought her heartache. She'd kept the baby though. Bridie had helped bring Ellie up. He'd heard Ellie tell people that she didn't have a father because he'd been killed in the war.

Franco decided he'd talk about being in the bike shop at that awful moment during breakfast. Once Pa knew, he'd make them do the right thing, whatever Carlo said.

As soon as Pa called them, he rushed to be dressed before Carlo. When he went down, Ma was busy scrambling eggs in the back kitchen and Pa was busy blacking his shoes.

'Here's yours.' She pushed a plate in front of Franco. 'Will you want more toast than that?'

Carlo was pulling faces at him behind Ma's back. It put him off. It was one thing to make up his mind while huddled up warm and safe in bed, and quite another to do it in the grey light of morning. Franco couldn't bring himself to go against his brother. Like him, he was scared of the trouble he'd bring on his own head. He felt just as much a weak-kneed, yellow-bellied coward as Carlo.

The tragedy had hit Franco with the force of an express train. He knew it had had the same effect on Carlo too.

If any of this did come to light, it would be Carlo who got the blame. He was sixteen, almost grown up. Franco was glad he was only twelve. A boy of his age could be more easily forgiven. He was still a child.

But he was ashamed he'd failed to do what he should. This was going to haunt him for a long time.

As Connie prepared the evening meal for her family, she told herself she was bound to feel unsettled, it was impossible not to be affected by Bridie's troubles. At lunch time, the family usually ate what the customers did not. It made sense not to waste good food, though the business was providing a reasonable profit now.

Connie was glad they were making a profit at last and that Vito had Carlo working with him. Their worst times had come when first Giovanni, then Luigi and then in his turn Bruno had decided they no longer wanted to work in Vito's trattoria but instead wanted to return to Italy.

It had always been Vito's ambition to build the business up and, when he was ready to retire, to hand it over to his sons so that they in turn could earn a good living from it. He wanted to provide for them all. Now only Carlo and Franco were left.

When her family came home for their tea, Connie felt flat. She wasn't enjoying the gnocchi she'd prepared. It was hard to get away from Bridie's dejection. She told herself she must count her blessings, she still had two sons here sharing their life. She looked up and was shocked to find Carlo's dark eyes on her. They were great pools of discomfort.

'I've been thinking . . .' He let it come out in a rush: 'Pa, I'd like to go to Milan. Giovanni says he'd put me up to start with.'

Connie's fork crashed on to her plate. 'Why? This is sudden. What's brought it on?' She'd been dreading this, she knew Vito had too. Even Franco was looking appalled.

'It's not sudden.' Carlo looked very earnest as he struggled to explain. 'It's been in my mind for some time.'

'I thought you were happy to work with me.' Vito's voice sounded strangled. 'To build up our business.'

'I am happy, Pa. But I hanker for Italy.'

Connie drew in a shuddering breath. Carlo had heard her say that. 'You've never been there.' She was indignant. 'How can you hanker for what you don't know? Your pa needs you here.'

'I know, Ma, that's why I've said nothing up to now.'

'Giovanni, Luigi, Bruno and now you.'

His father said, 'You're too young, you certainly can't go yet. You must learn more about the trade.'

'But I'd like a job with cars.'

'Cars! What do you know about cars?'

'Giovanni writes that he thinks I might get a job working in a garage in Milan.'

'Oh, Giovanni! He tempts you all away from here.'

'Don't be hasty,' Vito said slowly. 'You must think carefully about this first. It's a big step and you're very young.'

'I have thought carefully,' Carlo rushed to say. Vito held up his hand.

'At least wait until Franco is old enough to leave school and take your place. When he has learned enough to manage the job, then—'

Franco burst out, 'I don't want his job.'

Connie felt deflated and very sorry for Vito. He'd see this as the end of all his dreams. The contentment they'd both felt that their business was thriving was shattered. The rest of the meal was eaten in uncomfortable silence. She was glad to see the boys get up and go.

When they were gone, Vito seemed to sag, but he said in their native tongue which they usually used when they were alone, 'Franco is only a child. Who knows, he may change his mind in another year or so.'

'Carlo too.' But Connie was afraid it was wishful thinking. 'We won't let him go until he's twenty-one, that's young enough to leave home.'

'What if Franco should want to go too, in his turn?'

'He won't. We've brought him up differently, haven't we?'

All her other sons had been brought up to be bilingual. It had just happened, they'd heard both Italian and English spoken constantly. But when Giovanni and then Luigi and Bruno had seen themselves as Italian and had wanted to live their lives there, she and Vito had decided that the last born would hear only English. They made a great effort not to speak Italian when he could hear them. They'd discouraged the older boys from doing it.

Franco was going to be more English than the English themselves, and his lack of Italian would make it almost impossible for him to live and work in Italy.

'At least we'll always have him,' she'd said to Vito many times. 'Even if he doesn't want to work in the business.'

* * *

In bed that night with the light out, Franco pulled the blankets up round his neck and said, 'Is it because you're scared of Mick Valentino? Is that why you want to go?'

'No.' Carlo was quick to deny. 'The caff's like a treadmill. I'm fed up with it.'

'You weren't last month. Has Mick been round again trying to scare you?'

'No.'

They never went near the bike shop these days, and Franco knew his brother hated to meet Mick Valentino in the street. But he lived close, so there was no avoiding him completely. Mick had come rushing out of the railway station as Franco was passing only yesterday, a big burly man who towered over him. He'd gripped his arm with a massive fist. 'I hope your brother's had a word with you,' he'd snarled.

Franco could smell the beer fumes on his breath. He'd knocked his hand away and put out his tongue.

'You watch it,' Mick had shouted after him. It had left Franco shaken.

Carlo was a black mound beside him. Franco whispered, 'There must be something that Mick wants to keep hidden, don't you think?'

The mound stirred. 'Forget it. It's all blown over, we needn't have worried. Nobody knows we were there except Mick and Wilma and they're not going to say anything.'

But Franco couldn't forget it. It was on his conscience that they might have added something useful, but they'd been scared of Pa's wrath. He wouldn't have wanted to read their names in the papers, not for playing around in new cars and spying on Mick Valentino.

* * *

Connie Baldini knew her family was unsettled, and hoped Carlo's sudden decision to go to Milan was just a whim, brought on by a need to get away from the tragedy. Vito said his customers were talking of other things now, soon it would be forgotten.

Bridie had gone through a very bad spell but she seemed better. Her energy had come back and she was coping with her housework. She'd always had strange ideas about the afterlife and seemed obsessed with it now Orla had passed over. Vito thought it wasn't good for her.

Connie felt low herself as she washed up the breakfast crocks and looked out of the kitchen window into the rain-drenched back yard. She was afraid she'd never get used to the cold and the rain of this northern country. It brought such longing for the hot parched south she'd known in her youth; she craved to see that again.

She was twenty-two when she came to England. Vito had talked of coming for so long, they were both thinking of England as the promised land. They'd had only Giovanni then and he'd been a babe in arms. From the start she hadn't had Vito's confidence that they'd have a rosy future.

'What if,' she'd asked, 'you find you can't start your own business? What if the English don't like ice cream? What if they can't afford to spend on luxuries like that?'

'We'll have our family round us whatever happens,' Vito had said. Back home in Cittanova, the family had been the most important thing in their lives.

Although Vito had managed to start his business and they were earning a better living here than they could have done at home, the one thing they didn't have was their family round them. Giovanni, Luigi and Bruno, all brought up here and speaking English with a native accent, couldn't wait to get back to Italy. Italy was in their blood just as it was in hers and Vito's.

Connie felt she didn't really belong here, even after twenty-seven years. She couldn't forget her roots. The look of Italy was on her face, the sound of her country was still in her voice. The same with Vito, but more so. He'd never truly mastered the English language.

'I wish we could go back.' Connie felt it was the one thing she really wanted. The business had come right, but that was now keeping them here.

'One day we will,' Vito promised, but he'd been promising that for years.

'I want to see our grandchildren.' It was an ache that wouldn't go away. Giovanni had two little daughters. They looked really pretty in the photographs he'd sent, but she wanted to see them in the flesh, to hold them. And Luigi had two little sons and a third child on the way.

Family was everything to her and Vito but they didn't know their two daughters-in-law, hadn't even met them. When Connie thought of that, she felt bereft. It was better if she thought of what they did have here.

'There's Carlo,' Vito comforted. 'He's said no more about leaving us.'

Connie nodded. 'He's over that idea now. He's more settled, I think, now he has a girlfriend . . .' English, of course, but she didn't throw everything Italian back in their faces like Franco did. He was the only one who'd taken a dislike to his heritage.

Only the other day, he'd complained with angry tears in his eyes, 'I feel neither one thing nor the other. I stand out here as a foreigner, people point me out as that Eyetie, and I don't think I'd feel truly at home in Italy. Luigi says he doesn't.'

Connie knew Vito must feel that like a kick in the face. It would make him feel guilty. He and Franco had big rows; they didn't see eye to eye on anything. Franco was always ready to fight his father and it was tearing him apart.

'Coming here was meant to give us and our family a better life,' Connie mourned. 'In many ways it hasn't.'

Franco made her feel guilty too. When he'd been young, she hadn't been able to give him the love and attention that was every child's birthright.

Connie had given birth to a daughter in 1912. She'd been run down after the pregnancy and a difficult labour, but having had five sons, she and Vito had been thrilled to have the daughter they'd always wanted. They'd called her Maria Clara.

Tending to Maria Clara's needs had been a joy. Then one morning, when the baby was five weeks old, Connie had been woken by Vito's alarm clock, instead of Maria Clara's cries.

'The baby's slept through the night.' Connie had been delighted, it was the first time. She'd felt refreshed by a good night's sleep. 'I wonder if she'll wait for her feed until I've got the breakfast ready?'

Connie would never forget the blinding horror of bending over the cot and finding her baby had stopped breathing. She'd spiralled down into a black hole of deep depression after that. Robbed of any energy, she could find no pleasure in the family she had. She'd turned her back on them all.

Bridie Valentino had been like a mother to her then. She'd looked after her and her little boys and had done her best to jolly her out of it.

Connie felt she might have succeeded sooner if her father hadn't died shortly afterwards. Her heart had gone out to her mother left alone in the little house in Cittanova.

That was when Vito first promised that one day he'd take her home, but seven months later, her mother was dead too. Connie knew that for her parents, the most important thing in their lives were their children, but at their end they'd been alone.

She could hardly believe now that she'd turned away from her own sons. She'd kept breaking down in tears, been unable to do anything. Vito was very busy with the cafe during the day. It had to provide their living. Often he brought ready-cooked meals home for the family. That was as much help as he could give.

It was Bridie who came round every morning, who helped with the washing and the cleaning. The next day she'd be back to make sure the ironing was done, chatting all the time. She'd made Connie get up and dress herself neatly; made sure she ate regular meals and took her out shopping and for walks.

For months on end, Bridie had taken Franco off her hands in the afternoons so she could rest. He was a right little imp and the only one too young to go to school. Bridie had kept him quiet by telling him stories of her Irish childhood, and about the leprechauns she'd seen there, and the ghosts of her ancestors.

Franco had spent so much time round at her place that she had him believing she had second sight. There'd been no telling him it was all fairy stories. That had worried Vito a bit, but he'd thought it was inevitable, the length of time Franco had spent with her.

Things hadn't been all that easy for Bridie. She had a family of quarrelsome boys to look after too. The war years were hard for everyone, and especially hard for Bridie, with two of her sons killed in the trenches and Orla pregnant without a husband, but it was during those years that Connie gradually recovered.

She'd thought it sad that Orla's baby was unwanted, but once little Ellie was born, all that changed. Everybody wanted her. Connie had many times buried her face in Ellie's fluffy down-like hair to hide her tears, wishing her child was growing up with her. Ellie would fling her little arms round Connie's neck and hug her as if she understood.

Vito, too, had found comfort in the doll-like Ellie. For her, he'd pretend to be a horse and let her ride on his back round the living-room table. Sometimes he strode down the street with a chortling Ellie on his shoulders.

Orla had to work full time in the bike shop and Bridie had looked after Ellie then. Connie was always glad to have her for a few hours when Bridie needed to go out. Franco went round to Bridie's almost as often. He was fond of her and she said he behaved well, and always did what she asked. He'd even called her Gran at one time, picking it up from Ellie.

The two families had got on well. Orla had been a sweet girl, and Mario, Bridie's husband, had explained English legal ways to Vito and helped him start his ice-cream parlour.

Vito had admired Mario Valentino, and the way he'd built up his business. But he hadn't admired all his sons, especially not Mick. He'd always been a big rough lad, a heavy drinker and a hard fighter. Once his father died, he'd terrorised the neighbourhood. Connie was sure he bullied Bridie and Orla. You'd think a son would have more respect for his womenfolk.

She would be ever grateful to Bridie for bringing her back on an even keel; making her value Vito and her boys, and making her see that if she was depressed it affected their lives too. Bridie had made her realise she still had a lot to be grateful for.

Now that Bridie's troubles had eclipsed anything Connie had had to endure, she was wrung out with sympathy and only too willing to do what she could for her.

Connie blamed herself and her withdrawal into depression for the difficulties they were having with Franco now. She'd made him wild and rebellious and ready to fight them both and dismiss everything they thought important as useless.

The weeks were passing and building up into months. Ellie knew Uncle Mick was coming round to talk to Gran, but he only came when she was at school. She'd met him as he was leaving once or twice, and Gran never told her what they talked about.

One afternoon, as Ellie was coming up the back yard she could see Gran and Uncle Mick through the back kitchen window. He was very dark, his hair almost black and his skin swarthy. His face was screwing with rage. Gran was supporting herself against the draining board. Ellie could feel her heart beginning to hammer though it was only when she opened the back door that she heard the venom in his voice.

'I want it now. I've got every right.'

'No.' Gran's voice wavered. 'No, Mick, your father—'

She saw him give Gran's arm a vicious twist, which made her give a little screech of pain. The room seemed charged with hostility. Mick was threatening her.

Ellie felt suddenly sick with fear. Gran was too old and too frail to stand up to Uncle Mick, she had to help her. She flew at him, hammering her little fists against her uncle's beer belly.

She knew she'd knocked the wind out of him. He was swearing through clenched teeth, 'You little vixen,' as his heavy hand crashed against her head.

'Leave the child alone,' Gran screamed. Then two strong

hands gripped Ellie round the waist and she felt herself being carried towards the back door. Her head still sang, but she wanted revenge, he'd hurt Gran. This was her chance, she could reach his face now. She scratched down his cheek pressing as hard as she could.

He let out a bellow of rage and pain. She could see two long scratches oozing blood down the side of his face where her nails had dug in.

Ellie felt herself being swung down by the collar of her coat. This time his huge hand walloped against the side of her face. She kicked out at him and screamed.

'Don't you hurt the baby,' Gran shouted at him. 'Don't you dare hurt her.'

He dragged her to the back door and flung her half across the yard. The door was slammed shut and Ellie heard the key turn in the lock.

She cowered against the wash-house wall and wept, shocked and frightened. It was some minutes before she recovered enough to wonder what was going on inside. There was nobody in the back kitchen now, the house was silent.

Her face hurt and she was still shaking with sobs when she went to bang on the back door. She heard Gran's slippers shuffle towards her and the key click back.

'You poor pet.' Gran's arms went round her in a hug. She was drawn towards the old armchair by the fire, then pulled up on Gran's knee and comforted. Ellie clung to her.

'Did he hurt you, love?'

Gran had been crying too, Ellie could see tears still sparkling on her lined cheeks. 'Uncle Mick's naughty.'

It was a long time before Gran slid her down on her feet, so that she could get up to fill the kettle and make herself a cup of tea. She seemed stiff and slow. Her green strong box was on the table with the lid open. Ellie looked inside. Everything seemed to be there just as it always had been.

'What did Uncle Mick want?'

'He got what he came for,' Gran said bitterly. 'The deeds of the bike shop.'

'What does he want those for?'

'He's going to knock Grandpa's bike shop down and build a garage on the site. I've told him never to come here bothering us again. I don't think he'll dare to show his face after this.'

'Did he hurt you, Gran?'

'Not as much as he hurt you.'

Ellie didn't think that was true. She said, 'He hurt Mam, didn't he?'

Chapter Four

1922

It was the last Saturday in May and Franco was looking forward to his fourteenth birthday which fell on Monday. Soon he'd be able to leave school.

Like every other Saturday in his life, he had to get up to help in the caff. In the summer, it was the busiest day of the week. They didn't close until six in the evening.

By the time his mother had taken his breakfast plate away from him and pushed him out of the door, Carlo and his father had already opened up. There were only two customers, men coming off night work. At this time, he was expected to help prepare the meals that would be eaten later. Pa was icing his birthday cake which had been made the day before.

'Looks great,' Franco said. It really did. Pa was good at decorating cakes. Tomorrow, his parents were putting on a party for his birthday, friends and family were invited. He let his gaze linger on the luscious piece of ham waiting on the kitchen table to be baked.

Franco was put to work peeling potatoes, a job he hated. His chief job was to clear the tables of dirty dishes when the customers left and wash them up. When the cafe filled up at dinner time, it was a never-ending chore, but by then Carlo would be busy fulfilling the orders and he was often called on to help with that.

Franco didn't like doing any of it but he had to. It was what Italian families expected of their children. He'd offered to serve behind the counter or wait on the tables, wanting to be out there where he'd have a chance to talk to the girls.

'No,' Pa said. 'You aren't up to making out the bills and taking the cash yet.'

Still, though it wasn't easy to concentrate on girls while under Pa's gaze, he missed nothing. Franco wondered if Olive Makin would come in today. She was a plump blonde who'd cut off her plaits when she'd left school at Christmas. He'd seen her watching him through her lashes, and rather liked her. If she did, he'd invite her to his party tomorrow. Pa couldn't object to that.

It was a long hard slog and Franco felt shattered by six o'clock. Working here was worse than going to school. The only good thing was that Olive had agreed to come to his party.

He had to spend part of Sunday getting the tables set and helping Ma list the games they'd play, but Franco counted it well worth it. His father had played his accordion for musical chairs, and the singing and dancing. Franco thought it turned out to be a brilliant party and so did Olive, who had agreed to go to the pictures with him next week.

'Very Italian,' had been the verdict from his class mates at school the following morning. They said the only thing Italians were good at was making ice cream. They all tended to run down anything Italian. Franco felt hurt.

Now, eating his supper at the kitchen table with his family, he announced, 'I'll be glad to leave school. I'm sick of it.'

'What makes you think you'll like work any better?' Carlo scoffed, his mouth half full of mortadella.

'It's what grown-ups do, isn't it?'

His pa looked at him thoughtfully. 'When does the school close for the summer holidays?'

Franco unhooked the calendar from the wall so he could work it out. It was exciting to think he had only another month, and he'd never have to set foot in that place again.

'Right.' His father looked up. The light glinted on the gold wire frames of his spectacles. 'You'll break up on a Wednesday, you can have the rest of the week off and start with us the following Monday.

'I'll teach you the trade. Eventually when I'm ready to retire, you and Carlo can take over from me.'

Franco felt mutinous, he knew too much about this trade already.

'It'll provide you both with a good living.'

All three members of his family looked very earnest. 'Pa's very proud of this business,' Carlo murmured.

The trouble was, Pa saw the opportunity he was offering as being on a par with giving him the world. Franco wanted nothing to do with it. For one thing, he knew he'd be working under his father's eye all day and every day, at least to start with. For another, the same offer had been made to his four older brothers and three had escaped as soon as they could. Carlo said he couldn't wait to follow them.

Pa would expect him to spend every hour of every day slaving there, learning to run it on his own. He'd have to make the decisions, and Pa would tell him where he'd gone wrong if he didn't make enough profit.

'You'll have to work hard, Franco. I'll not have you dragging your feet—'

'Pa,' he groaned, 'I don't want to work in the caff. I'd hate it.'

That brought a shocked silence. His mother's disappointed gaze wouldn't leave his face.

'I keep telling you,' he insisted. 'You can't say I haven't.'

Carlo added his support. 'Pa, you told him he'd change his mind when the time came.'

'I haven't, I knew I wouldn't.' Franco felt pressurised. Pa took it too seriously. Pa thought he couldn't do anything right and was always talking about him taking responsibility and growing up. He'd be breathing down his neck all day.

'You're not a child any longer.' His father's affronted eyes met his. 'You can't sit back and do nothing. The time has come when you must realise there's more to life than having fun.'

Franco managed to wring out, 'I do.'

'So what are you going to do?'

'I'll find a job.'

'You won't find anything as good as I'm offering. You tell him, Carlo. You should count yourself lucky, not many boys get a chance like this.'

'Pa, I don't want to work in your caff. I'm not going to.' Franco rushed upstairs as soon as he'd finished eating. He was very much afraid he'd be made to. What Pa decided was law.

The following day, when Franco found himself penned down in the kitchen with Ma on one side and Pa on the other, he knew an ultimatum was coming. They had never looked more serious.

'If you're going to look for other work, you must find something with good prospects. We want you to have a career not just a job.'

'Of course, that's what I want too.' Franco felt a sneaking triumph. For the first time, he thought he might get his way.

'Ma will go down to your school and have a talk with your

headmaster. It's Mr Ratcliff, isn't it? She'll see what he suggests.'

'Pa! No need for that.'

Franco didn't want the Old Rat brought into this. He wanted to choose the job he'd do. He'd heard it wasn't easy these days, with the labour market flooded with men leaving the forces, but he'd seen jobs advertised he'd like to try.

But there was no talking Ma out of it. She came to school the next day. He was thankful he knew nothing about it until afterwards. Ma said the Old Rat had given him a good school-leaving reference and suggested he apply to the Liverpool Cotton Exchange, who were taking on trainee clerks.

Franco didn't fancy it, but Pa insisted. Ma took him for the interview and he was told right away he could start on the following Monday. It meant he'd miss the last few days at school and he wasn't sorry about that.

He went to work on the underground wearing a collar and tie and his only suit, which up until then he'd worn mainly to church. It made him feel quite grand. Not many of his classmates would find jobs like his.

The place was full of old men wearing formal suits and stiff collars, who kept telling him he was very lucky to have such a chance. Franco didn't understand what they were doing and felt out of his depth.

His job was to make the tea, run errands and see to the post. After three weeks in the job, he didn't think it was going to suit him. It was dreary, the hours seemed long and the train journey at each end of the day extended his boredom. It was too late to do anything else by the time he got home.

His late return upset the time of the evening meal. Ma said they'd eat an hour later. Carlo was very much against that, he wanted to eat his tea and go out and Pa said he was too hungry to wait. After a few days, Franco found the family had eaten and Ma was keeping his meal warm for him.

One Wednesday night, he was eating tortellini at the kitchen table when Bridie brought Ellie round.

'Be a good girl for Auntie Connie,' she was told. Bridie kissed her and said goodbye. The little girl appeared briefly at the kitchen door to stare at him with her strange amber eyes. She was wearing pink flannelette pyjamas and trailing a rug.

He said, 'You ready for bed, Ellie?'

She nodded. 'Do you want a drink of milk?' Ma asked her.

'No thank you.'

'A jam tart? No? Come to the fire then. You climb up on this armchair and we'll cover you with your rug.'

'Why is she here?' he asked Pa, who was still at the table drinking home-made wine and reading the newspaper.

'Your ma's going to look after her. Bridie's going out, a meeting or something.'

'A spiritualist meeting,' his ma told him when he asked. 'Bridie's got some funny ideas. She wants to go regularly, every week.'

Franco had heard of spiritualist meetings. They were being held in public halls and private houses all over the country.

'It's the war that's made spiritualism popular,' Pa told him. 'So many people lost their loved ones on the battlefields, it makes them believe anything, even that they can receive messages from the dead. It's no wonder it's caught on.'

'Poor Bridie.' His mother came in and started on the washing up. 'She's lost five of her six children.'

'And her husband,' Franco said. 'You can see why she wants to go.'

'She's always been interested. She used to go to spiritualist meetings with Orla.'

'How do they hear the dead speak?' Franco asked. He knew his father didn't approve, and neither did the church, which made spiritualism seem twice as exciting to him.

'They don't,' his father said. 'These so called mediums are just tricksters.'

'I'm not so sure.' Ma put her head on one side. 'There's a lot believe in it. I was reading only the other day that Sir Arthur Conan Doyle is a firm believer. He lost his eldest son on the Somme and is convinced that mediums have put him in touch with him. It's said he holds seances regularly at his home.'

Ellie was flat out by the time Franco had helped Ma dry the dishes, a chore she expected him to do. He was too tired to go out and Ellie was on the only comfortable chair not being used by his parents.

He fiddled with the crystal set Carlo had built and worried about how he could bear to work in the Cotton Exchange until he was an old man. He got up to let Bridie in when she rang the front doorbell. She seemed transformed, bursting with energy.

'A very gifted medium tonight, she put me in touch with our Eddie.'

He'd never seen Bridie's cheeks so red or her eyes so bright. He knew Eddie had been killed in 1918.

'He says he's at peace now and I mustn't grieve for him.' She seemed exultant.

Franco felt a horrible fascination. 'You heard him speak?'

'Yes, he said the little one would grow up strong and healthy.' She smiled in the direction of the sleeping Ellie. 'Of course, I most want to hear from our Orla. I asked if she was with him and he said yes, and I mustn't worry about her either. But I'm sure Orla's trying to get in touch with me. She must know I worry about her.'

Franco felt the hairs on the back of his neck begin to curl. If Orla had the power to talk to those living, she might have other powers. She might know he and Carlo had kept quiet when they should have spoken out. She might tell her mother. He wondered if she'd blame him, try to take revenge?

No, Orla wasn't the sort to take revenge, but if she was going to talk to her mother, he wanted to know exactly what she said, in case she told on him.

'Perhaps Orla will speak to you next week,' his mother said and he saw Pa purse his lips in disapproval.

For once, Bridie refused the tea his mother offered. 'I'd better get Ellie home and into bed, thanks.'

Ma nodded. 'It's a shame to wake her up. She's been asleep almost since you went. Franco will carry her back for you.'

Franco was tired but he dared not refuse. His mother had the knack of offering his services without consulting him. Many Italian parents expected to use their children like another pair of hands.

He scooped the child up. Everybody said how small and light Ellie was for her age, but she wasn't that light to carry. At the bottom of Bridie's stairs he leaned against the wall to get his breath back while she lit the candle.

Going up he thought he'd have to put her down, but he staggered into her bedroom, where Bridie turned down her bed. He rolled her in and pulled away her rug. Ellie opened her eyes and murmured something, then turned over and curled up.

'Go to sleep, love,' Bridie said, tucking her in.

Franco asked as they went downstairs, 'Will you take me with you next time you go to a spiritualist meeting?'

'No.' Bridie's face was stern.

'Why not?'

'You're not old enough.'

'I'm fifteen.'

'Don't tell such fibs, you're only just fourteen. Anyway, you've nobody on the other side to get in touch with.'

Franco couldn't tell her why he so desperately wanted to hear what Orla said. He managed to say, 'There's my sister, Maria Clara.'

'She was only a few weeks old. She couldn't speak when she died, she won't be able to speak now.'

'I'm interested, I want to see what it's like.'

'It's not a peep show, Franco. It's very serious.'

Ellie didn't like it when Gran started talking about getting a smaller bed for her, a single instead of the double.

'I like this bed,' she insisted.

Gran sighed. 'If you had a smaller bed, it would be easier to wash the sheets.'

'But when Mam comes back, we'll need the big bed.'

'Ellie, love, you have to accept that your mam isn't coming back,' Gran said gently. 'We've talked about it, haven't we?'

Ellie nodded. Gran had said she'd gone to heaven, but she talked about her as though she could still see her. She was still having dreams about her mother. Nightmares, Gran called them, but as time had gone on, they didn't disturb her so often. It took two more years before Gran said they'd have to make the best of things.

'Life's not so bad,' she told Ellie, trying to soothe away her hurts. 'We have each other and we have our friends.'

Ellie often went to play with a girl called Mary who was in her class at school and who lived in Neston Street, a short walk from her home. Sometimes Mary came to play in her house.

She came one wet Saturday, when Gran was telling Ellie about her own parents and the four sisters and three brothers she'd grown up with. Mary sat down to listen too.

Afterwards, she said Gran gave her the creeps. 'She's always talking about dead people and ghosts.'

'She's very old,' Ellie explained. 'Almost all the people she used to know are dead.'

'But she can see them.'

Ellie shook her head. 'My mam used to say she just thinks she can.'

Auntie Connie was coming round just as often, but mostly now it was for a cup of tea and a chat. Gran was managing to do much of her housework herself, she seemed her old self again.

Ellie heard Connie talking to Gran about beds. It seemed she had a friend called Norah who had a single one she wanted to swap for a double. It was a very smart bedstead and almost new.

Ellie came home from school the next day and went up to her bedroom. She knew immediately it was different though the double bed was still there. It felt strange. She let her eyes go round. The hat box was no longer on top of the wardrobe, Mam's coat no longer swung on its hook behind the door. She opened the wardrobe and her own few clothes made it seem almost empty.

That drove it home to her, Mam wasn't coming back. She went to Gran's bedroom. The half-used bottle of Attar of Roses was on her dressing table, Mam's slippers were in the wardrobe, and some of her scarves in a drawer, but most of her things were gone.

The next day, her double bed disappeared while she was at school and was replaced by a single one. It was made up with crisp sheets and a pink satin eiderdown.

'It means Mam won't be coming back, doesn't it?' Ellie could feel a tightness in her throat.

'I'm afraid she won't, love,' Gran said gently.

'Does that mean she's dead?'

Gran was smoothing the wrinkles out of her forehead and didn't answer. It was as though she couldn't talk about Mam.

Ellie was burning to know more. She had to ask, 'What made her die? She wasn't that ill, was she?'

'She was, she had an infection in her lung.'

'And she died in hospital?'

'Yes, she never came out.'

That evening, Gran and Connie took Ellie to the cinema in town. She sat between them in the dark, enthralled as she watched Mary Pickford.

'That was lovely,' she told Gran as she got ready for bed later. 'Please can we do it again?'

They did. Occasionally, others of the Baldini family came with them.

As she grew older, it seemed to Ellie that Gran seemed more grief stricken than angry with her children. She heard her saying to Connie, 'Of course, I do miss our Orla, and the child does too.' Gran's old eyes would come to rest on her.

'You still have Uncle Mick,' Ellie said.

'Oh, Mick!'

Uncle Mick had built a fine garage on the site of Grandpa's bicycle shop. It was a big building you couldn't help but see. It stood out in the way the bike shop had not. It was one of the first garages in the town, and though it was only a hundred yards or so from the Baldinis' cafe, Gran made a point of never going near it.

Mick and Wilma rarely came to the house these days. It seemed to Ellie that the family would never stop fighting.

* * *

Within a few months, Franco decided he didn't like working in the Cotton Exchange. It wasn't his sort of job at all.

'I'm learning nothing,' he complained to his pa.

'Be patient, you will,' he said from behind his newspaper.

'I'd rather be out and about, not stuck in a stuffy office all day.'

In the hour he was allowed for his lunch, Franco escaped to walk the city streets. On fine days, he found somewhere to sit to eat the sandwich he took with him, on wet days he went inside the big shops.

One morning, a van came to the door bringing a stationery order. Miss Clark, the office manager, checked the delivery while Franco and the lad who came with the van carried the reams of paper, the notebooks and boxes of pencils to the cupboards where they were stored. In the dinner hour, he saw the lad sunning himself on the Town Hall steps.

'Wish I had your job,' Franco told him. 'I'm sick of working in that office.'

'Nothing stopping you,' he told him. 'I'm going to sea. I want to see the world.'

'You're giving it up?' Franco rather fancied it.

'You bet I am. I've had enough.'

'How long have you been doing it?'

'Two years.'

'Can you drive that van?'

'Course I can.'

'But you don't. You have a driver with you.'

'He's the salesman, he lets me sometimes.'

Franco wasn't sure that was true, but when he asked about the wages, he found a van boy was paid more than he was. That made his mind up. He was going to get himself another job, and this time he wasn't going to let his pa and his teachers decide things for him.

He was pleased with himself when his plans worked out. He got the van job and gave in his notice at the Cotton Exchange. He went home knowing he'd have to tell his parents and they weren't going to like what he'd done.

Within minutes of getting home, his mother had him sitting at the living-room table and his tea out of the oven and in front of him. It was lasagne and a bit dried up. Carlo had already gone out. Pa was sitting next to him, drinking wine and reading the paper. Franco knew he had to tell them.

'Pa,' he was beginning, as the back door opened and little feet scampered into the kitchen. It was Wednesday and Ellie had come to stay with them while her gran went out. She climbed up on a chair the other side of him and eyed his plate. Good, Ma wouldn't shout so much if Ellie was taking in every word.

Franco told them as soon as Ma was back at the sink. She was furious.

'You haven't really given it a try,' she fumed. 'You've only been there three months.'

'I'll like this better, Ma. I know I will.'

'A van boy, delivering office stationery? There's no prospects in a job like that.'

'I can be a driver when I'm old enough.'

'A driver! You could have risen to head clerk in the Cotton Exchange.'

Ellie's amber eyes stared up at him. 'What's a van boy?'

'He'll just be humping packages. Loading and unloading his van.'

'I'll like it better. I have to like my job, Pa, I spend my whole life doing it.'

'Well, when you've finished your tea, perhaps you'd like to spend a little of your time helping me start some wine off.'

'I'll help you, Uncle Vito,' Ellie offered.

Franco wanted to refuse but didn't dare. He was already in his father's bad books. Even though he didn't work in the family business he was still expected to help his parents both there and in the home. Of all the jobs he was called upon to do, Franco hated most treading grapes to make wine in the wash house.

'You can buy it ready bottled in this country,' he told his pa. 'Nobody makes it here.'

'I know, but at home in Cittanova, every family made their own wine. We all had a few vines growing on our fields with a few olive trees.'

Here, Pa was friendly with the greengrocer in the same parade of shops. He let him know when there was a glut of over-ripe grapes on the wholesale market and helped him buy them cheaply.

'The lucky ones had orange trees too.'

'And everyone kept a pig and a few chickens.' Franco had heard it all before.

'A very simple life,' Vito sighed. 'We planted a few tomatoes, cucumbers and gherkins and prayed for the rain to water them.'

Pa was living in the past. He was getting older. Franco could see the grey hairs amongst his deep brown curls. Making wine was a very Italian thing to do.

'I don't know why you came if you liked it so much there,' he said.

'To make a better living for myself and my family. So you could have a better life.'

'I'd have a better life if I didn't have to help make wine.'

Pa was gentle and never raved at him however rude he was. 'It's a family tradition. One day you'll enjoy doing it.'

Franco was afraid he'd go on talking about the family for hours. Pa thought of little else. It had been his dream to come to England and start a business and now he was always moaning because his sons didn't want to work in it.

Ellie was helping them remove the stalks from the grapes and was eating quite a lot of them.

'Not too many,' his ma warned. 'They could make you sick.'

When the grapes were picked clean, Pa took off Ellie's slippers and rolled up the legs of her pyjamas and set her to jump on the grapes. She thought it was great fun and even cheered Pa up. Franco was afraid his father preferred Ellie to him. Pa liked playing with her even though Ma had to stand her in the kitchen sink to scrub at the red stains on her hands and feet. Nobody seemed to notice the red stains on her pyjamas.

Once she'd got the grapes squashed so the juice was running freely, Franco carried the great vat close to the living-room fire. The wine had to be kept warm even if the family was cold. There it bubbled and gurgled as it fermented and sometimes fizzed over so Ma complained about the mess. It gave their house a smell that nobody else's had.

Pa drank most of what he made. For him it was unthinkable to eat a dinner without wine. Carlo called it Pa's poison.

Since Pa never knew what variety of grape he'd be able to buy, and it would be a dessert variety not one meant for making wine, what he produced was unpredictable in standard and flavour. Sometimes it was a deep clear red, and Pa rolled it round his tongue with pleasure, but more often it was cloudy and sour. Either way, Franco wasn't going to touch it.

* * *

Connie Baldini was afraid it had been a mistake to let Ellie jump on the grapes. She'd washed her, but her toes were still bright pink and there was a purple streak on her face. When Bridie came to fetch her, Vito apologised, but it didn't seem to bother Bridie.

'I'm right glad that you'll have her, that I am. Every Wednesday night too,' she said.

Before she called Franco down to carry the sleeping Ellie home, Connie told her he'd left his job. 'His father's very upset and so am I.'

'Lads these days, they've no sense, that they haven't.'

'He never thinks of the future. It's what he wants now, this minute.'

When Connie was seeing them out, Bridie gripped her hand and whispered, 'A gifted medium tonight, she put me in touch with Orla. I couldn't believe it. Orla says I'm not to worry, she's watching over us.'

Connie shook her head. She should be used to Bridie talking of the dead like that, but . . .

She wanted to do her best for Bridie. Everybody went through bad patches and Bridie's was as bad as it could get. Most people came through wiser but otherwise unscathed. She was afraid Bridie's troubles were turning her mind. She was much wrapped up in her spiritualist meetings. Was it really possible to communicate with the dead?

If it was, Connie wanted to be in touch with her parents. They'd died in Italy long after she and Vito had left, and she'd never seen them again. She burned with guilt when she thought of them. She hadn't been a dutiful daughter. She shivered as she shut the door. Her life here had not turned out as she'd expected.

'They call this summer,' she said to Vito. He hadn't moved from the fire. 'I do miss the sun.'

He gave her a quick smile and turned the page of his newspaper.

One night, Franco was late getting home from work. Ma had saved a piece of cod for his tea. He was hovering behind her, starving hungry, not fond of fish but impatient to eat.

'The fish won't take a minute to fry,' she told him, 'but I have to fry the mashed potato too, to warm it up. Look, I've baked a cake for Bridie, it's on the sideboard. If you slip round with it now, your tea will be ready by the time you get back.'

Franco went, sniffing at the cake. It was some Italian speciality of Ma's. He gave Bridie's back door a rap with his knuckles and walked straight in. It was what he usually did. There was a frying pan full of sausages in onion gravy on the stove, the smell made his mouth water.

When he went into the living room, Bridie was blinking hard and pulling herself up on her chair. 'Sorry,' he said, 'did I wake you?'

'No,' she yawned behind a hand misshapen with age and rheumatism, 'I'm just tired. Our Eddie hasn't been well today, didn't go to work.'

Franco froze; Eddie was Bridie's eldest son who'd been killed in the war. She spoke of him and his tragic early death from time to time. It was so long ago, Franco hardly remembered him living here.

'I made sausage and mash for his tea,' Bridie said. 'It's his favourite, he loves the onion gravy, but he couldn't eat it. He's gone to sleep again and I can't wake him.'

'I like sausage and onion gravy.' Franco licked his lips. He liked it better than cod. He'd seen it, walked past it on his way in. He expected to be offered some. Its delicious scent hung in the air here.

'Our Orla ate it when she came home from work.'

That made him catch his breath. It sounded too real. He remembered Orla very well. Bridie could be spooky, she thought they were here with her now. That sent a thrill down his spine. He was both fascinated and repelled. His big fear was what Orla might tell her mother about him and Carlo. That row that had led to her death had altered his life too. He couldn't forget it. He tried to make a joke of it.

'I don't see them, Bridie. Eddie and Orla, where are they?'

She was staring at him then, with opaque and watery eyes. He almost forgot the cake he'd brought round. He turned back to thump it down on the living-room table. 'Ma sent you this,' he said and took to his heels.

With his fish in front of him, Franco's head was still buzzing. Mam was washing up, and Pa was still sitting at the table with a glass of wine. He told them what Bridie had said, let it all come flooding out. It had given him a shock.

'Losing five of her children is a terrible loss for her,' his father said gently. 'We all expect our children to outlive us.'

'She'd cooked for them!' Franco couldn't get over that. 'Has she got second sight or something? She was sure Eddie and Orla were there with her.'

'No,' Pa said slowly. 'She wants to see them. It eases her anguish when she does.'

'Gives me the collywobbles when she talks about them as though they're there.'

'We should be ever thankful our lads came through the war,' Ma said.

Pa refilled his glass. 'Bridie and others like her long to see their dead. It comforts them to believe they do, but in truth they see them only in their mind's eye.'

Franco wasn't sure that Pa was right. He hoped he was, because then his and Carlo's secret could not come out. But Bridie had believed her family was with her, and it had made his blood race and his heart hammer. In a way, he wanted to believe it was possible.

Chapter Five

As the months went by, Franco continued to carry the sleeping Ellie home for Bridie when she returned from her spiritualist meetings. Dread and curiosity made him ask regularly if any of her children had been in contact with her again.

She was often disappointed. Bridie told him others in the congregation had been put in contact with their loved ones, but not her. Franco understood how she felt, her appetite had been whetted and she wanted more. In a creepy sort of way, so did he.

He got up after a lie-in one Sunday morning to find Bridie drinking tea in the kitchen and chatting with his mother.

'I got it in that second-hand shop in Exmouth Street,' she was saying. 'I saw a nice copper plant pot in the window and went in to buy it, and there it was. It was meant, Connie.'

'What was?' Franco wanted to know.

'A Ouija board. I bought it instead.'

'What's that?'

'It's so I can make contact with the spirit world in my own house. My children are all round me there, it was their home. It'll be easier for them to come across.'

'For heaven's sake, Bridie,' his mother said. 'Should you be dabbling with the supernatural like that?'

'The toffs do it all the time. I read about it in the papers.'

'Don't you need a clairvoyant?' Franco took a cup from the cupboard.

'Not for this. Come round and help me try it out, Connie. Our Orla's there waiting to make contact. I feel it in my bones.' Bridie's lined face shone with conviction.

Some of the tea Franco was pouring sloshed into the saucer. 'I will,' he said. Bridie fired his interest. He was curious in a busybody sort of way. He wanted to see the ghosts she saw and how she dealt with them. If Ma's ghosts came too that would be even better.

'Aren't you scared?' his mother asked Bridie. Her own plump face showed she was.

'What is there to be scared about? My children would never harm any of us. Mario wouldn't either. You must know that. It's them I want to contact.'

She was hesitant. 'Vito wouldn't like me having anything to do with spirits.'

'He'll be going out,' Franco said. 'It's the night he checks through his stores and makes out his monthly order.'

'Well . . .' Connie didn't say she would and didn't say she wouldn't. Franco knew she was intrigued despite herself. She wanted to contact her own mother.

'Just a game, isn't it?' he said. 'Come on, Ma, say you'll go, it would please Auntie Bridie.'

Connie smiled. Bridie took that for agreement and gripped her arm in gratitude.

As soon as Pa left, Franco leapt to his feet, poked up the fire, and threw on coal from the scuttle to bank it up against their return. Then they walked up the back entry.

Bridie's living room looked different. She'd made it ready by drawing the heavy curtains. It was lit only dimly by the red glow from the fire and the candle she used to see her way upstairs when she went to bed.

'Come and sit down,' she said and Franco slid on the chair beside Ellie's.

She was wearing her pyjamas and chortling with excitement. 'We're going to play a game.'

The usual oilcloth had been taken off the table and the red chenille had been covered with a piece of black velvet. Franco brushed his palms against the soft pile and craned to see this mystical Ouija board. It was black with large gold letters round the edge. An upturned wine glass stood ready in the middle. 'What do we do, Auntie Bridie?'

'Shush.' Ma's elbow dug into his ribs. 'Be quiet, we've got to have silence.'

'Connie, will you write down the letters as they're spelled out?' Bridie pushed a pencil and paper over to his ma. Her voice sounded different.

'You must be quiet too, Ellie. Quiet for a long time. Quiet enough for us to hear voices from the spirit world. Quiet enough for the spirits to come to us.'

They all waited in dead silence for what seemed an age. Bridie's eyes were closed, she was slumped on her chair and looked as though her mind was far away. The candle flickered.

Franco closed his eyes and tried to focus on Orla Valentino. She was the dead person he knew best. If well-known important people believed it was possible to speak to the dead, it must be.

Bridie was muttering something, the sort of thing he'd heard in church, then she called out, 'Is there anyone there?'

There was another long silence. This was stirring him up.

'Are you there, Orla?'

That made him catch his breath but there was nothing but silence.

'Is there anyone to help me get in touch with Orla Valentino or Mario Valentino?'

'Or the Trapino family from Italy?' Ma added in a stage whisper.

Bridie lifted Franco's right hand and placed his forefinger on the bottom of the wine glass. He was squinting through his lashes and saw her do the same with Ellie's small finger, then she placed her own beside it.

'Come on, Connie,' she urged. Franco was all of a flutter now and thought the others were too.

'Is there anyone there?' Bridie asked again in sepulchral tones.

They were all listening. The only sound came from the fire as the red coals dropped in the grate. That left less light in the room. The atmosphere seemed charged.

Franco felt something jerk the wine glass and it began to move. He couldn't suppress a gasp, it made him feel at fever pitch. It was zigzagging across the board from one letter to the next. His mother was trying to scribble with one hand and Ellie was making soft noises like effervescent bubbles sparking in a glass of ginger pop. Then just as suddenly, the wine glass stopped.

They all sat looking at it, waiting for more. One by one they removed their fingers.

'What did it say?' Bridie could hardly get the words out.

His mother gulped. 'Quick silver.'

Franco giggled. 'What's that?'

'Shush.' Ma elbowed him again. 'Then silver for all. Showers of silver, pockets full of silver.'

'That means money,' he said. 'Money for us all.'

'It works, doesn't it?' Bridie sounded awed. 'We've got to ask questions. Let's try again.'

She blew out the candle. Now there was no light except what came from the fire. In silence, they all put their fingers back on the upturned glass. Franco closed his eyes, his heart thudding.

After a long wait, Bridie asked, 'Who is there? Who is in contact with us? Give us your name.' He heard the pent-up excitement in her voice.

This time he felt the charge go into the glass. It began to move again. Ma continued to scribble the letters it indicated. The living room felt cold despite the dying fire.

'Giovanni Trapino,' Ma gasped suddenly. 'My father!'

Franco felt his scalp crawl. Ma began speaking in Italian. He understood little, though she and Pa still spoke it together.

The wine glass continued to move, more quickly now, indicating letters. Ma seemed fraught as she scribbled them down. Then he noticed she'd taken her finger from the wine glass, doubting Thomas that she was.

Bridie was grimacing and suddenly snatched her finger away too. Franco did the same and still the glass moved round the board.

Only Ellie's finger was left. She was kneeling on her chair, her tiny body curving over the board, her flyaway hair moving when she moved, her breathing deeper and heavier than he'd ever known it.

Bridie had told him someone from the spirit world would enter a living person and he knew now it had picked on Ellie. So did Bridie. Her gaze was transfixed on her granddaughter.

At last the glass stopped. Little Ellie snatched her hand back and held it against her mouth, her cheeks were scarlet, her eyes wide and shining. They were all staring at her in silent wonder. Ma flung the pencil down. It rolled across the board. Ellie's face crumpled and she burst into tears. Ma was on her feet gathering her up in a comforting hug.

'There's nothing to be scared of, Ellie,' she murmured. 'Everything's all right, love. Perhaps you should have put her to bed, Bridie, before we started?'

'No, no,' Ellie protested.

Franco knew Bridie spent so much time thinking about the spirit world that she saw it as a normal extension of this one.

Franco felt intoxicated, he knew his mother was scared. There was something creepy about communicating with the dead.

'What did he say?' Bridie sounded all of a flutter with excitement.

His mother's voice was shaking as she said, 'Translated, something like silver in plenty for us all. Pockets full of silver. He promised modest wealth.' He'd never seen her so overawed, there were beads of sweat across the bridge of her nose.

'He says he's watching over us and will see we come to no harm. My mother and sister Philomena send their love.'

Bridie was back in the land of the living. 'Warm milk for my Ellie.' She got up to lower the saucepan on the trivet over the hot coals. 'Then off to bed with you.'

Franco sat there feeling dazed while Ellie's tears were stilled. She was just a little kid and she'd been like one possessed, nobody could tell him she hadn't been.

'You take her up, Bridie,' his mother said. 'I'll bring the milk when it's warmed.'

'Light the candle for me, Franco, and the gas while you're at it. Be careful with that mantle.'

'Was it you?' his mother demanded when they were alone.

'No, it was Ellie. You saw it. There was only her finger on the glass.' Franco's mouth was dry. 'It must have been real, Ma, mustn't it?'

'Shush,' she said. Franco knew from the way her face was working that she believed it must be.

It was only when the oilcloth was replaced on the table and they were drinking tea that they started to talk about it.

Bridie said, 'You got what you wanted, Connie, your father's been in contact.'

Ma looked pale. 'That put the fear of God into me.'

'I wanted to hear from Orla. Let's try again, just the three of us.'

'Another time,' Ma said. 'Some other time.'

'I can feel her, can't you? Orla's not far away.'

'Isn't it dangerous to interfere with the spirit world?' His mother's eyes were huge.

'Silver for us all,' Franco marvelled. Two pairs of adult eyes stared back at him. 'We'll all come into money. Could Ellie think up something like that? Could she have . . . ?'

'No,' Bridie said. 'No, she's only seven, she can't spell all that well—'

'*Mamma mia!*' his mother broke in. She looked unnerved. 'It wasn't Ellie's doing, couldn't be, it was in Italian.' She turned the paper round so they could all see the letters she'd written down.

Sweat broke out across Franco's forehead. He didn't believe his mother would play a trick on them like that, not on Bridie. Yet she was the only one here who could speak Italian – apart from those in the spirit world. He could see Bridie was thinking the same. Her mouth was open, and her upper denture had dropped.

After a long silence, she said, 'Translate it again, Connie.'

'It means something like, showers of silver. Silver in plenty for us all. That's wealth, isn't it?'

There was another thoughtful silence.

'But it doesn't make sense, not really.' Ma was impatient. 'We came to this country to find wealth and we have.'

'Not exactly wealth.' Franco was scornful.

'More wealth than if we'd stayed in Cittanova.'

Franco said, 'Wouldn't it have said gold if it meant we'd be wealthy?'

'Silver means moderate wealth, we'll be comfortably off.'

'But we are comfortably off, it's news of our loved ones we want.'

I want wealth, Franco thought. For me, if it's true, it's good news.

'It's what me and Vito talked about before we came here, all those years ago.' His mother was in deadly earnest. 'Earning enough to be able to eat properly. Making our family . . . not rich exactly, we weren't aiming that high, but making a good living so we could all be comfortable. Especially our children and our children's children.

'The Baldinis have been poverty-stricken for generations and the Trapinos have too, that's my family. Nobody had much money there, they were all trying to scratch a living from thin soil.'

'I was hoping to hear from our Orla.' Bridie wiped a tear from her cheek. 'Or at least from Eddie or Patrick – they gave their lives, Connie, and for what? The big men in parliament said we'd have a better world when the war was over, but have we?'

Franco was tingling all over. Whatever they said, it had been an eye opener for him. The dead could get in contact with this world, he didn't doubt that now. He had seen messages come from his grandfather with his own eyes.

Exciting messages too. He'd have money when he was older. Not a fortune perhaps, but enough money for comfort. He wanted to believe it. He'd have pocketfuls of silver.

* * *

Connie had been a little anxious, ever since Carlo had first told them he wanted to join his brothers in Milan. At the time, Vito had comforted her. 'There's no sense in a young lad leaving home to go all that way. We'll refuse to let him until he's at least twenty.'

'You've already told him twenty-one,' Connie reminded him.

'But Bruno went when he was only twenty.'

'At least Carlo won't expect to go any earlier. I hope he changes his mind and stays.' But she was afraid he wouldn't. With Franco refusing to work in the business, it was very important to have Carlo here.

'He's not far off his nineteenth birthday now,' Vito warned.

'But he has a girlfriend and that'll make a difference.'

She and Vito had discussed Carlo's girlfriend many times. They thought that for him, any girl would act as an anchor. She'd give him a reason to stay.

Carlo had been walking out with Myra Dewey since he was seventeen, but Connie hadn't thought the affair would last. Her other sons had soon tired of their first girlfriends.

She and Vito didn't approve of Myra, who was a year older than Carlo and wore clothes that could only be called flashy. Her blouses were cut too low at the neck and her skirts were too short.

'Short skirts are fashionable,' Carlo had objected, when Vito mentioned he'd seen her out in the street with her knees on full view, and he'd seen the neighbourhood lads looking up her hem. She wore bright red lipstick too and face powder, and she'd had her hair bobbed. She had a reputation for being 'fast'.

Myra worked as a counter assistant in the newsagent's next door to the cafe.

'Pity Fred's daughter, Rose, didn't catch his eye,' Vito mourned. 'I could get on with her, and Fred's already a friend.'

'You can't expect to choose your son's wife,' Connie retorted. 'Any girl will keep him here.'

'If she lasts,' Vito sighed. 'She's buzzing round our Carlo like a bee after honey. I can't see her keeping this up.'

But it had lasted two years. Myra's parents had come to the cafe and made themselves known. Her father was an unemployed docker and her mother looked a slut. There was also a string of younger brothers and sisters to whom Carlo was giving free ice cream. It was Franco who told Connie that Carlo was thinking of getting married.

'Getting engaged, you mean?'

'No,' Franco smirked. 'Married.'

'That's nonsense, he's too young,' she said. But Carlo broached the subject over the tea table the very next day.

Connie was shocked. 'You're only nineteen! I mean, getting married, it's a lifetime decision. You have to be sure.'

'I am,' Carlo assured her. 'Quite sure.'

'You can hardly afford to get married yet,' Vito objected. 'Not on what I'm paying you.'

Connie closed her eyes. Myra was their guarantee that Carlo wouldn't rush off to Milan. He hadn't mentioned it since Franco had refused to work in the business. He knew just how much they needed him.

'Why don't you get engaged and save up?' It was what she and Vito had done. 'I think you should wait until you're at least twenty-one.'

'We can't wait,' Carlo said slowly. 'You might as well know now, Myra's expecting.'

Connie felt her heart jerk with enough force to leave her body. 'Carlo!'

'I'm sorry, Ma.'

'You don't have to say you're sorry to me. What about Myra?'

'She's all right. She's over the first shock, she just wants to get married as soon as possible.'

'You're sure – that she really is expecting?'

'Of course we're sure.'

Vito looked as though he couldn't believe it. 'It couldn't be a false alarm?'

'No it couldn't.' Carlo sounded irritable. 'D'you think I'd have said anything before it was certain?'

Connie felt defeated. 'Then you'd better speak to Father O'Hanlon.'

'Not a church wedding, Ma. Myra doesn't go, doesn't belong . . .'

Connie took a deep breath. She'd known the Deweys weren't church folk, but they had to make the best of things. She had to keep in mind that Myra and a baby would lock Carlo to the cafe. Vito would keep his son in the business and she'd have a grandchild to look forward to.

When Connie came face to face with Myra's mother in the greengrocer's on Duke Street the following week, it seemed she wasn't all that pleased about the coming child.

'Hot-blooded Italians,' she exclaimed in defamatory tones, so that everybody in the shop turned round. Then she all but shook her fist in Connie's face.

Ellie was looking forward to Carlo's wedding. Connie and Gran couldn't stop talking about it. They made countless lists, and were in and out of each other's houses all the time. Ellie liked to sit by Gran's chair and listen.

'What do they want for a present?' Gran wanted to know.

'Well, it's traditional to pin paper money to the bride's dress, isn't it?'

'Is it?'

'Really, Bridie, you married an Italian, you should know.'

'Nobody pinned paper money on my dress. No such luck.'

'Myra's English. You can get them a pair of towels or a few cups and saucers, whatever you want. They're going to set up home, so they'll need everything.'

'I thought they were going to live with you?'

'So did I. We've got plenty of room and it would save them expense. I told Carlo that Franco could move to the little bedroom so that he and Myra could have the big back room, but he wouldn't listen to reason. "She wants a place of her own," he said, and that was that.'

'You've got a nice parlour too.'

'Yes, I said they could use that as a living room, but they've taken a couple of rooms in Beckwith Street instead. It won't be any better than I could have given them.'

'Not as good,' Gran mused.

'The house will seem so quiet without him.'

'Connie, you've still got Franco.'

'Yes, Franco.' She sighed.

Gran decided to wear her best black dress and coat. 'I'll get myself a new hat, that's all I'll need.' She said to Ellie, 'You'll have to have new, you're growing out of everything you've got. At least Mick is still paying my pension.'

One Saturday morning, they took the underground train to Liverpool and went to Blacklers, which was the biggest shop Ellie had ever been in. Gran let her choose a red dress and a brown and red hat and coat to go with it. Ellie felt very smart in her new outfit.

Towards the end of the following week, the family were going down to the cafe in the evenings to prepare the wedding feast. Ellie heard talk of hams and sausages, trifles and cakes.

Thursday, the wedding day, came at last. It was being held in the register office in the afternoon. The cafe had to open in the morning and serve lunch as usual. Ellie and Gran changed into their wedding finery early, and went down to the cafe to help Connie set it up for the party. Vito and Carlo were sent home to change.

Connie and Vito had left the register office as soon as the ceremony was over. They'd wanted to get back to the cafe to have everything ready when the newly-weds and guests arrived.

'I'd hardly feel married after that,' Connie said. 'Over in five minutes.'

'It's legal,' Vito replied. 'That's what counts.'

Looking round now, Connie felt satisfied they'd made it look festive and welcoming. They'd pushed the small tables together to make two long ones and covered them with sheets and fancy cloths. There were flowers and serviettes to make it more formal.

Vito was setting out a starter of antipasto in each place and the puddings and cakes were set out across the counter for the guests to help themselves. Vito and Franco were going to serve the main course.

Connie started to fill the sherry glasses so Franco could hand them round as soon as the party started. She enjoyed a glass of sherry and so did most ladies. They were going to serve Vito's own red grape with the meal. He had six gallons made in 1920 standing ready in their gallon containers, and he'd bought a firkin of beer for later on. A taxi was pulling up at the door. The party was about to begin.

Carlo had a broad smile fixed on his face, and his bride couldn't take her eyes off him. Everybody seemed in a party mood; it was going well. Connie was enjoying herself. She whispered to Vito that the meal was excellent.

But many of the guests were very young and Franco was lashing out the wine too readily. They were becoming rather rowdy, and soon the noise was giving Connie a headache.

They'd collapsed the tables and the guests were taking them into the back room to make space for dancing. Myra's mother carried in a table looking as though it was asking too much of her. She gazed round the kitchen sourly, taking in the pile of dirty dishes waiting to be washed up.

'Not much of a place for a wedding reception,' she said. 'I'd have thought a hotel more suitable. I believe they do lovely weddings at the Woodside.'

Connie felt a flash of anger. Her family had worked hard to achieve this. 'They do,' she agreed. 'And as the bride's mother we thought you'd be arranging it. When Myra said you weren't doing anything, we decided a little party here was better than nothing.'

Mrs Dewey looked affronted and stalked back to where she'd left her wine glass on the counter to drain the contents back. Connie watched Franco refill it.

Vito got out his accordion and started a sing-song. Myra's mother was making a show of herself, singing in a raucous voice and shrieking with laughter. All her children were there and she was encouraging them to do likewise.

Connie was afraid she'd drunk too much. When at six o'clock she started a suggestive solo dance, and Connie could see Vito was in two minds whether to stop playing, she suggested to Carlo that he take her home. When he didn't, she ordered Franco to do it straight away.

Myra's father also drank too much but he went to sleep in

the corner and gave no trouble. Vito had to wake him up and put him out of the door at one in the morning.

'It's your responsibility to see him home,' he told Carlo.

'I hope he'll be happy marrying into that family,' Vito said to Connie in a voice of doom as they were getting ready for bed.

'So do I, but Myra and a baby will peg him down. He won't go chasing off to Milan like the others.'

Less than a week after she was married, Myra was rushed into hospital and had a miscarriage.

Carlo had taken her to New Brighton for a three-day honeymoon. He said he thought Myra had done too much, she'd been determined to enjoy her break. She'd loved the fairground, especially the big dipper, and they'd gone dancing every night, staying until the dance hall closed. And when they got to bed, it was not to sleep, but Carlo didn't mention that. He thought that and all the excitement could have started off the miscarriage.

Connie was sorry there wouldn't be a baby, but she didn't think the bride and groom were.

When Ellie was ten, she came home from school one day to find Auntie Connie comforting Gran. She could see she'd been crying. There were still tears sparkling in her wrinkles.

'It's your Uncle Mick,' Connie told her.

'What's he done?'

'Had a fight with a customer,' Gran said tight lipped. 'It's all over the neighbourhood. Everybody's talking about it. It'll be in the papers again.'

'But why? What were they fighting about?' Ellie asked.

'Some say he just lost his temper and tore into a customer. The poor fellow's in a bad way with head injuries in the

Borough Hospital. You'd have thought he'd learned his lesson, wouldn't you? I wish he'd stop this fighting.'

'They were saying in the grocer's that it's a young lad he's beaten up,' Connie said. 'That he asked to have his car filled up with petrol but had no money to pay for it. That's provocation, isn't it?'

'Mario used to say customers were always right.' Gran sniffed into her handkerchief. 'That there must be no arguments with them.'

'Vito says that too,' Connie agreed. 'We're careful in the cafe. Bad for business to be otherwise.'

After tea that night, Gran put on her hat. 'Let's go down and see your Uncle Mick.'

Ellie walked down with her to the garage, but it was closed. 'It looks a grand place,' she said. It was smart and freshly painted. There were three petrol pumps, and cars were turning in before they realised they couldn't buy petrol tonight.

'Me and Grandpa used to live over the bike shop, when it first opened,' Gran sighed. 'Mick moved into those rooms when he married Wilma.'

When the garage was built in its place, Mick and Wilma had moved to a house in Livingstone Street. 'I've never been there, was never asked.' Gran sounded cross. 'I don't know the number, so we can't go.'

Ellie marvelled. 'Isn't it strange to have an uncle and not know where he lives?'

'Even stranger to have a son and not know his address,' Gran said bitterly, as they went home. 'And unless he opens, he's going to lose everything. This is no way to run a business.'

The next day when Ellie came home from school, Gran told her the garage had opened and she'd seen Mick.

'What did he say?'

'Not his fault. The man got what he deserved. He couldn't pay for the petrol and he put his fists up first. The police took Mick down to the station.'

A few days later, Ellie came home from school to find the local weekly paper on the kitchen table. There was an account of the incident.

Is this the way to treat customers? it asked. *The general public must think of their safety.*

The following week Ellie found more about it. The man was still in hospital and likely to remain there for another week or two, but he was recovering.

'He did this to Mam, didn't he?' Ellie asked. She'd never been able to put that out of her mind. But Gran just shook her head. Ellie knew she couldn't forget it either.

Many weeks later, Ellie came home from school to find Gran wasn't in. She knew where to find her and went round to Connie's. Franco opened the back door to her. Gran had a steaming cup in front of her on the kitchen table.

'Found guilty!' Connie was saying. 'That's awful.'

Ellie pulled out a chair and sat down with them. 'Uncle Mick's been found guilty?'

'Yes,' Franco said. 'Guilty of assault and battery.'

'He's been sent to prison,' Gran told her. 'Wilma's in a terrible state. It came out in court that the lad had money on him to pay. He said he was joking with your Uncle Mick but he flew at him.'

'For how long? In prison?'

'He got nine months,' Gran said bitterly. 'What a family.'

'Awful,' Connie agreed. 'Mine's not behaving either, particularly Franco.' He was making himself a bacon sandwich at the stove.

'I stay on the right side of the law, Ma.'

'Only just.'

Franco turned to wink at Ellie. She found that hard to believe.

'He's talking of going to sea.' His mother sounded exasperated.

'Cunard are advertising for restaurant staff,' he smiled. 'I quite fancy that. Going to America.'

'He's seventeen, and he's on his tenth job since leaving school.'

Ellie knew he was delivering bread from a bakery to the small shops in the neighbourhood.

'Don't you like the job you've got?'

'It's not bad.' He brought his plate to the table and sat down next to Ellie. 'But it's from a horse-drawn van. If only they'd modernise and get a motor van.'

'Is that likely?' his mother asked.

'Yes, the boss is talking of it. I'd love to be able to drive a motor.' He bit into his sandwich. 'It would be a marvellous job then.'

'I've heard all this before when you were delivering office stationery,' Connie said. 'They wouldn't let you drive, it's not what a van boy does.' She turned to Gran. 'It's the same old story, he doesn't know what he wants.'

'Can't settle.' Gran sighed.

'Franco, I do wish you'd grow up.'

Ellie giggled. 'He is grown up.' Franco towered over her. She thought him handsome.

'Seventeen,' his mother agreed. 'With less responsibility than the average seven-year-old. Can't rely on him for anything.'

Chapter Six

Connie thought Carlo and Myra had settled down well to married life. She often invited them to tea on Sundays, and Myra would put herself out to be pleasant and help her set the table like a dutiful daughter-in-law. Connie hadn't liked her to begin with, but now she was trying hard to fit into the family and she felt she'd misjudged her.

One Sunday, Myra praised the home-made scones. 'I really ought to learn to bake like this,' she said.

'I'll teach you,' Connie was quick to say.

'Actually, Pa,' Carlo put in, smiling at his wife, 'Myra and I were wondering whether you'd like her to work in the caff. With Norah leaving, you'll have to find another waitress to take her place.'

Connie could see Vito was interested. 'Why, I never thought of you . . . Would Fred mind? I mean you've been working for him for some time now.'

'Five years. I've been happy working next door but I feel like a change, and yours is a family business and I'm part of that.'

Vito said, 'Of course you are. I'd better have a word with Fred first, I don't want to upset him by taking his staff. It could be managed, I suppose.'

When they'd gone home, Connie said, 'D'you think she'll be all right?'

'Yes.' He was pleased. 'Fred says she's a good worker.'

'I never thought she'd want to join in like this. Now you'll have your family working round you. It's what you wanted, isn't it?'

'They'll be able to run the place together. Yes, it's just what I wanted.'

Within a week of Myra starting work, Vito was saying he was pleased with her. She was quick when they were busy and the customers liked her and found her friendly. Connie was in the cafe when she first heard Myra trying to say a few words in Italian. Vito was helping her to pronounce the words.

'*Buon giorno, signora. Buon giorno, signor.*'

They all laughed at her accent, but she didn't seem to mind.

'*Antipasto.*'

'*Cannelloni.*'

Myra went through the dishes several times before Vito was satisfied with her pronunciation. When Connie went home she looked out her old Italian/English dictionary and gave it to her. It pleased her that Myra was making the effort. She was the opposite of Franco's friends who always seemed to be sniping at anything Italian.

A few weeks later, Connie was setting out a midday meal for the family in the cafe kitchen and was surprised to hear Myra trying to hold a conversation in Italian with Vito.

'You're progressing fast.' Faster than Connie had when she'd learned English.

'Carlo's teaching me,' she smiled. 'He wants to go to Milan, and says I must learn to speak a bit of the language first, otherwise I'll find it hard when I get there.'

Connie felt as though she'd had the wind knocked out of her. She had to let the table take her weight. When she looked up, Vito's face was stark with shock; Carlo was putting food on plates, keeping his face turned away. This was the death knell to their hopes.

She managed to say, 'I thought he'd dropped that idea.'

'Oh no,' Myra smiled. 'He's always wanted to go, hasn't he?'

Vito barked, 'I thought you'd given up all idea of that, Carlo?'

'No, Pa.' Carlo was clearly embarrassed.

To Connie, it felt as though her whole world was collapsing. 'Your father relies on you to run the business.' She felt indignant. 'It'll be hard to replace both of you if you go now.'

Carlo said, 'We aren't going just yet. But you've always known I planned to go.'

Connie knew she and Vito had drawn their own conclusions and got it wrong. She said, 'I thought you'd want to stay here now you're married. You've made such a good start and seem settled here in the cafe. And you've set up home here.'

Myra shrugged. 'It's not much of a home, paying rent for two rooms in somebody else's house, and both of us working all the hours God sends.'

'It's not a lot of fun being a foreigner in a strange country.' Connie couldn't stop herself pointing that out. She hadn't enjoyed it.

'More fun than growing old in the back end of Birkenhead,' Myra said tartly.

To Ellie, it seemed she came home from school almost every day now, to find Gran wasn't in. She always knew where to find her and went round to Connie's. They usually had their heads together, talking about Uncle Mick.

'To have a son in prison and all the neighbours knowing . . .' Gran sounded bitter. 'It makes me ashamed. I hardly like to pass the paper shop, it's in all of the papers again.'

'Don't buy them, Gran, if it upsets you,' Ellie told her.

'She wants to know what they're saying about him,' Connie said. 'Only natural.'

Gran shook her head in despair. 'It's such a worry, with the garage and only Wilma left to run it. She says she can't cope – but she's never coped with anything.'

'She managed last time, when he was unconscious in hospital,' Connie reminded her.

'It was a bike shop then,' Gran sniffed, 'and she lived over it. Easier.'

'And she's got two young children to look after now as well. She's got her hands full all right.'

Gran sighed. 'Last week, the mechanic gave notice, this week it's the pump attendant. It's a good job that boy of hers is old enough to help.'

Ellie said, 'Ben's only twelve, Gran.'

'He's nearly thirteen and a big strong lad. He's old enough to help his mother, that he is.'

'She's keeping him off school?' Connie asked.

'Yes.'

'She'll have the school board man after her then.'

'Wilma won't cope. The place will lose money, bound to. There's no go about her. I never could fathom what Mick saw in her.' Gran clucked in distress. 'What a mess he's made of everything.'

'Knowing he's got a business to run and what she's like,' Connie said, 'you'd think he'd be careful to stay out of prison.'

'I'll have to help her,' Gran sighed. 'I'll offer to look after Mick's two little boys.'

Neither was old enough to go to school. Roy was four and full of energy, while Dougie was not quite two. She found them a handful.

'Roy's a real imp,' she complained to Connie after the first day. 'But Wilma can't have them about the garage. Somebody's got to do it.'

'Let her pay for help with the business.'

'She's trying, but says it's hard to get staff. Other garages are opening up in town now, and a good mechanic is like gold dust. She says they've had to stop doing repairs. She's turning that business away. Just selling petrol and oil now.'

'It's a man's world, isn't it? Cars and petrol.'

'Wilma says the customers aren't even coming in for that like they used to. The garage isn't making the money it should. The whole town thinks Mick is violent and dangerous, they're staying out of his way. The Valentino name is infamous since he was convicted. Wilma's talking of putting the garage up for sale. She says that's what Mick wants.'

Gran was worried sick and hadn't been well for some days. Ellie came home from school one day to find Roy screaming and kicking at the furniture, while Gran was lying on her bed cuddling the baby who was sobbing too.

'Shall I take them to the park for a while,' Ellie asked, 'while you have a little rest?'

'Would you, love?' Gran said thankfully. 'You're a good girl.' She dropped her voice. 'Better not take him near the lakes. You know what he's like.'

'Come on, Roy,' Ellie said. 'Where's your ball? We'll have a game of football in the park.'

'Can't amuse himself quietly for five minutes,' Gran fretted. 'Not like you.'

Roy was big for his age, tall as well as squarely built. He was always up to some mischief. She saw him as a smaller edition of his father.

He set off with her readily enough, walking quietly up

Ashville Road beside Dougie's pushchair. When they came to the great wrought-iron gates on each side of the road, he was pulling her to the right.

'Want to go to the lake,' he whined.

'I thought you wanted to play ball.' He had it tucked under his arm. 'This is the best side for that, there's lots of open grass.' She gripped his wrist and dragged him with her.

'Want to see the ducks,' he complained. 'There's another lake up here.'

'We haven't brought any bread for them, we'll do that tomorrow.'

The pushchair squeaked on the tarmac. Ellie was keeping a firm hold on Roy. Soon there was open grass on both sides.

'How about here?' She released her hold on Roy to turn the pushchair on to the grass. Dougie had gone to sleep. When she looked up, Roy was running away from her.

'Roy, come back.' She was afraid she'd lose him. 'Come back and we'll have a game of football.'

She tried to follow him across the playing field with the pushchair. The rough ride was waking Dougie. Roy stopped to watch some older boys kicking a ball about for a few moments, but when he saw her catching up on him, he shot off again.

'Roy, I'll tell Gran.'

Ellie was worried now. To get back home, he'd have to cross a busy road and he was only four. Even now, Gran was always reminding her to be careful on that crossing. Auntie Wilma and Gran would be furious with her if he got hurt. She could pick out his red jersey growing smaller in the distance, then he was lost in the trees.

She set off after him, but pushing Dougie's pushchair on grass was heavy going, and she couldn't go fast. When she reached the trees she couldn't see him, and the ground under the trees was even more difficult for a pushchair. She turned back to the tarmac road and was able to speed up, but the park covered almost two hundred acres, and had coppices and lakes, tennis courts and cricket pitches. There were plenty of places for Roy to hide if he wanted to. She thought he was deliberately baiting her.

She flopped down on the grass to get her breath back, thankful that Dougie was causing no trouble. What could she do?

She stared up at the sky, watching the clouds move slowly, but it had rained that morning and the grass was cold and damp. She stood up and looked round. Roy was nowhere to be seen. She set off slowly for Ashville Road. She could wait at the gates for him, but there were other gates leading out of the park. What if he went out through the main gate and didn't come this way?

Dougie woke up. She lifted him out of the pushchair and let him walk round. The shadows were lengthening and people were leaving; she was afraid to move from here now in case she missed him. She wished Roy would come, surely he'd be hungry? She was, and Dougie said he was too. She had no watch. Gran would expect them back in good time for tea at half past six and would be worried if they weren't.

She asked an old man walking a dog what the time was. 'Quarter to six,' he told her. So she'd be all right so long as Roy came soon.

Ellie had to look twice at the woebegone figure coming towards her. Yes, it was Roy, trailing his red jersey along the road. When he got close enough, she could see his shirt was dirty and had a button torn off.

She said, 'You're a naughty boy, running off like that.' He was dragging his feet and looked sullen. 'Where's your ball?'

'Some big boys took it off me.'

'Good. They wouldn't have dared if you'd stayed with me.'

'I didn't want to stay with you. I don't like you.'

'I don't like you either. Not when you do things like that. I'm going to tell your mother.'

'Ah, don't do that, Ellie. I'll get into trouble.'

'I hope you do. You deserve to.'

Ellie said nothing to Gran when they got back. She was dragging herself round the kitchen trying to get a meal on the table for them and Ellie didn't want to worry her.

'What a mess you're in, Roy,' she said. 'You've ruined your nice jersey and look at your shirt. Your mam's going to be cross with you.'

Ellie sponged his hands and face and tried to wipe some of the dirt off his clothes. Later that evening, she set out to take the boys home to Livingstone Street. Roy was subdued now, holding on to Dougie's pushchair as they went up the back entry.

The back door was open. Ellie could see Ben, tall and wiry now, filling the kettle at the kitchen sink. He came to the door when he saw her coming up the yard.

'Hello.' He smiled. He wore his pale brown hair swept straight back from his forehead, which was marred with a few pimples. His fair skin was freckled. 'Thanks for bringing them home.'

Roy tried to push past him, and he put out an arm to stop him. 'Has this little tinker behaved himself?'

'No, he's been dreadful.' She told Ben how he'd run away from her in the park and about Gran feeling ill.

'Roy, didn't Mam explain why you must behave yourself?'

'I didn't want to go to Gran's. I don't like going there and I don't like Ellie.' Roy was full of aggression, struggling to get past Ben. 'I wanted to go to the garage with Mam.'

'She has to work there.'

'She takes you, doesn't she?'

'I have to work too, it's no fun.'

'I could help.'

'Roy, if we turned our backs for five minutes, you'd be off up the road. You'd end up under a car.'

Ellie was unstrapping Dougie from his pushchair when she saw Auntie Wilma coming slowly up the back yard with a shopping bag. She looked exhausted.

'You bastard!' Roy was screaming at Ben. 'I hate you. I'll tell my dad of you.'

'Your dad's in prison,' Ben said calmly. 'I'm the man of the house now.'

Roy caught sight of his mother at that moment and ran screaming to her arms.

'What are you doing to him, Ben?' she asked sourly. 'How many times do I have to tell you to leave him alone?'

'He hit me,' Roy sobbed.

'I didn't,' Ben protested. 'Did I, Ellie? But I wish I'd thought of it, he deserves a good hiding.'

'Ellie.' Wilma turned to her. 'Look at Roy's jersey, it was clean on this morning.'

'He's torn his shirt too.'

Wilma dropped her shopping and rapidly divested him of his jersey. 'Just look at you!' She was shouting, a woman at the end of her tether. 'This shirt was almost new.'

Ellie was scared; she wasn't used to such a show of violence and rage. Wilma turned on her. 'It's too bad of you, Ellie. Why can't you look after him properly?'

'Because he won't do as he's told. Because he wouldn't stay with me and Dougie. He ran off and wouldn't come back.'

'You snitch, you liar,' Roy shouted in fury. 'Some big boys chased me. They caught me and thumped me and tore my shirt.'

Ben's bright blue eyes rolled skywards. 'Serves you right. Hope it hurt.'

Auntie Wilma raved on as she hauled him inside. 'I can't send him to his grandma's in dirty rags.'

'I want to stay with you,' Roy cried.

Wilma clucked with vexation. 'I can't have you at the garage, you know that.'

She called after Ellie. 'When d'you think I find time to wash and mend for him? I want him back clean tomorrow.'

Ellie was fuming as she went slowly home. If she were Gran, she would tell Wilma to look after her own children.

Later that night, Connie came round with some boiled ham and a cake she'd made for them. 'How's Bridie?'

'She's gone up to bed early, not feeling too well.' Ellie was heating some milk for her.

'She's trying to do too much, Ellie.'

'Yes, but she feels she has to.'

'I'd better have the boys at my place in the morning.' Connie pulled a face.

'I suppose I could stay off school.'

'No, Bridie won't want that.'

Ellie had a sinking feeling. 'We break up for the long summer holidays next week.'

'You'll get your turn at looking after them then.'

'I can't get Roy to do anything.'

'You're only eleven, love,' she told her. 'For your age, you do wonders.'

The following week, Gran was no better and wanted to see her doctor, and Ellie found herself in charge of the two boys again.

Auntie Wilma brought them round before opening up the garage.

'I've told Roy he's to do what you tell him. If he gives you any trouble I'll give him a good walloping tonight.'

It was a bright and sunny morning. 'Take them to the park,' Gran told her. 'I'd rather Roy was out of the house. You know what a mess he makes here.'

Her friend Mary Jones happened to call round to see if she could play. They always spent a lot of time together in the school holidays.

'I've got to take my cousins to the park. Do you want to come with us?' Ellie asked. She told her what Roy had done last time. 'Not that it'll be much fun with him.'

Mary was the same age but five inches taller than Ellie. 'If I look after Dougie, Roy won't be able to get away from you.'

They set off with Mary pushing Dougie's pushchair and Ellie gripping Roy's hand.

'I'd rather go to the park with you, Ellie, than stay with Mrs Baldini. I don't like her.'

'She gave you that ball.'

'It's only an old one.'

'Better than no ball at all, isn't it?'

Roy stopped to pat a stray mongrel in Ashville Road and it attached itself to them. Ellie led the way to the wide-open tracts of grass, lifted Dougie from his pushchair and prepared to kick the ball about. Mary had already started throwing sticks for the dog to fetch. He was playful, not much more than a pup, and a novelty to them. Roy was playing happily with the dog, when Ellie noticed some boys from the class above her at school coming towards them.

'There's that Valentino girl,' she heard one shout.

She recognised Tommy Watts. He said, 'Yes, that's her.'

'The Valentinos are thugs and murderers,' Eric Leyland shouted in her direction. That made Ellie shiver.

'Take no notice,' Mary said.

'Ellie Valentino, you come from a family of murderers. Your mother almost murdered your uncle,' Tommy Watts yelled. 'But he got her first.'

That took her breath away. Her mother's untimely death was never far from her thoughts, but that explanation of what had happened had not occurred to her.

Mam had almost killed Uncle Mick? 'Don't be daft,' she retorted.

Mary tossed her brown pigtails back. 'Take no notice.'

But there were five of them. Ellie felt they were surrounding her. Dougie began to whimper.

'It's true, my dad said so. You're foreigners, Eyeties. Your uncle's trying to kill off his customers now, but he won't get away with it this time.'

Ellie could hardly breathe. She knew they were referring to Uncle Mick.

'Why don't you all go back where you came from?'

'We don't want your sort here.'

The dog dropped its stick at Eric Leyland's feet and sat back wagging its tail. He threw it hard, and the scampering ball of brown fur captured the attention of the other boys.

Ellie was already strapping Dougie into his pushchair. He was wailing with distress.

'I'm going,' she said to Mary, hardly able to hold back her tears. 'They're liars too.'

'They've gone, it'll be all right now.'

'No.' Ellie gripped a kicking and wriggling Roy and set off at a furious pace. Mary followed with the pushchair. Dougie was dozing off again.

'I'm going home,' Mary announced when Harcourt Street was in sight.

'I knew it wasn't going to be much fun,' Ellie sniffed. She couldn't believe her mother would ever do such a thing. Mam had been gentle and kind and . . . But something awful had happened at the bike shop that day.

She knew Gran would not be at home. She pushed the pushchair into the Baldinis' yard, knocked on the door and went into their back kitchen. Franco was there, and she said, 'Is your mam in?'

'She's gone to the doctor's with your gran.'

Ellie burst into tears.

'Hey, come on, kid, what's the matter?' He sat down on the back door-step and pulled her down beside him.

'Some boys from school . . .'

'What have they done to you?' Franco put an arm round her shoulders while she tried to tell him. Soon, she was letting it all pour out.

'They said our family were murderers, that Uncle Mick killed my mother. That she'd tried to kill him.' She saw the shock on Franco's face.

'You poor kid, that's awful. Look, they're just trying to upset you. Don't believe what they say.'

'But it could be true.'

'Course it isn't. I know the Leylands, bullies all of them.'

'It was Tommy Watts too.'

'He doesn't know what he's talking about. Take no notice.'

The yard door scraped on the concrete as it was opened. 'Here's Ma now, she'll tell you.'

'Franco! What are you doing here?' Connie demanded.

Gran was with her. 'Tell Ellie what?' she wanted to know. 'I thought you were taking the boys to the park?'

'I did.'

Franco's arm was still round her shoulders. He hugged her closer. 'Ellie was upset. Some louts have been shouting after her, saying terrible things about her mother. I've told her it's all a pack of lies. She mustn't believe any of it. That's right, isn't it?'

Connie's kindly eyes examined Ellie's tear-stained face. 'Lads can be vicious, Ellie. You mustn't let what they say upset you.'

'Mam was kind and gentle, wasn't she, Gran? She wouldn't do . . . anything violent.'

Gran was shaking her head sadly. 'She was very gentle, love.'

Connie said, 'Let's get inside, Franco.' He was pulling Ellie to her feet too. 'Why aren't you at work?'

'I've got the sack.'

'What? Not again?'

There was a crash from inside the wash house. Gran retrieved Roy and Connie latched the door behind them. 'What for? Why've you been sacked?'

'The boss saw me doing my bareback stunt after I'd unharnessed the horse from the van.'

'Franco! Riding bareback on the cart horse?'

'It was just a bit of fun.'

'For heaven's sake, grow up, can't you? Act your age.'

Ellie asked, 'What about that job you fancied? On the passenger liners?'

'I applied for it but didn't get it. A pity.' He pulled a face. 'I'll have to look for something else.'

Connie put the kettle on, and crashed the cups and saucers as she set them out. Ellie could see she was put out. 'Come in, Bridie, and have a seat.'

Gran had Roy firmly by the hand. He was trying to swing on her skirts. She sat down and pulled him on her knee.

Connie said, 'Franco, there's a load of old toys upstairs. Can you find something for Roy to play with?'

Ellie had dried her eyes but her tears were only just under control. 'What did the doctor say, Gran?'

'I'm trying the red physic this time. He thought it would do me more good than the green.'

Franco came down with a collection of clockwork cars and wooden boats. Roy went under the table with them, and played quietly at last.

Chapter Seven

Franco had sensed his mother's reluctance to confirm what he'd told Ellie. For once, neither she nor Bridie had seemed at ease over the cup of tea. When Bridie took Ellie home, Ma poured the dregs of the teapot into her cup and collapsed on a chair.

'I told you not to talk to Ellie about her mother. Whatever made you take it on yourself?'

Franco was indignant. 'The kid was upset. I told her it wasn't true that her mother had tried to kill Mick. Isn't that what I was supposed to say?'

'Poor Bridie hasn't been able to face it for years. Not so long ago, she told me she'd tell Ellie if she asked.'

'Well, nobody told me.'

'I told you not to talk about it.'

'That was ages ago. Anyway, Ellie brought it up. I didn't have much choice.'

Ma was frowning. 'This new trouble of Mick's has raked everything up again. She was afraid Ellie might hear it from someone else.'

'Well, she has. I'm surprised it didn't happen years ago. She should have been told right away.'

'She was five, poor kid. How d'you tell her about violence like that? Her own mother dead.' He could see Ma was worried as well as cross with him.

He said slowly, 'It makes me cringe now just to think of it.' Nothing had been the same since then. Not for him and Carlo. Not for Ellie and Bridie, and certainly not for Orla.

Franco felt he knew the Valentinos well. Ma had taken him in and out of their house when he was young. It was Bridie who taught them to drink tea. They were a decent family and shouldn't have had trouble like this.

He said, 'I'm sorry, I know Bridie's got a lot to put up with, but she's had plenty of time to tell Ellie. She can do it now. I was trying to comfort her. I did what I thought was the best for the kid.'

Ma crashed her teacup down on its saucer, 'And I think I know what's best for you, Franco. You can get yourself down to the cafe right away and give a hand there.'

'Oh Ma! They won't need me, not with Myra there.'

'Go on, I mean it. Another pair of hands is always useful. If you've no job, it's the least you can do.'

Franco said nothing, but he felt he didn't deserve the sharp end of his mother's tongue. With bad grace, he went down to the cafe. It was just after midday and almost every table was filled. Pa and Carlo were busy.

'Am I glad to see you.' Carlo looked more harassed than usual as he pulled him into the kitchen. 'Make two cheese on toast and one poached egg on toast.'

Franco set about it reluctantly. As he'd walked in, he'd noticed a good-looking redhead at the corner table. She was with a girl from Morley Avenue he knew slightly, Erica something. He wanted to be out there where he'd have a chance to talk to them.

'Two minestrone with brown rolls,' Pa shouted, slapping the written orders down in front of him. 'One salad with cold sausage.'

The one good thing about the caff was that in the summer the girls came in droves for ice cream. Franco knew there was no better place to meet them and have a little chinwag. But his father would find an excuse to send him to the kitchen if he saw him talking to anyone for longer than it took to take their order. His mother thought he was the biggest flirt in the neighbourhood, and was quite likely to say that to any girl she saw him talking to.

Every place he'd worked, the blokes had talked about the fancy bits they had on the side. Franco didn't really believe them. They were middle-aged men and didn't look the sort women would fancy.

He caught sight of his reflection in the mirror positioned at the kitchen door, so they could see what was going on in the caff. When it came to getting a girl, his dark good looks helped enormously. He could see girls sizing him up in the way he sized up them.

He'd been taking Olive Makin out when he was fourteen and she'd whetted his appetite for more. Molly Dickson thought he was going steady with her now, and so did both their families. He'd met both girls here and many many more besides. He'd cheated on Molly, first with Joan Smith and then with Margery Daley, and he'd picked them up in here too.

Franco enjoyed chasing girls, but he liked to catch them too. He'd been as careful as he could be to keep this from his parents, but somehow they seemed to know. He blamed Carlo for that. He'd shown what he did by getting Myra in the family way.

Myra was looking fed up today and even Pa wasn't his usual happy self. Franco was used to hearing him laugh with the customers. He was quieter than usual today.

Franco smiled to himself. That suited him. He could do without getting the usual pep talk from Pa, about losing his job and saving himself for marriage. He wanted girls now.

Quite recently, Pa had taken him on one side and talked seriously about how important it was to control his primitive urges and how he must respect Molly. He'd said quite a lot more about his general behaviour too.

It was two hours before the rush died down, and the family gathered round the kitchen table for their own dinner. Franco was tucking into a double helping of sausage and mash when Pa got round to asking why he was here.

'Not again? I should have guessed,' he said, tight lipped. 'I suppose you've heard Carlo's news?'

'No, what?' Franco wondered if it was another baby, but Carlo's gaze was firmly fixed on his plate, and he wasn't saying anything.

Myra was sitting immediately opposite, and she gave him a radiant smile. 'We're off to Milan. Carlo's fixed it up with his brothers. Giovanni knows someone who has a trattoria where he can work and Bruno's going to put us up until we can get a place of our own.'

Franco felt as though the ground beneath his feet was being cut away.

'You've timed it right this time, Franco.' Carlo flashed him a sudden smile. 'You can take my place here.'

'He'll have a lot to learn.' Pa looked anything but pleased at the prospect. 'You've got at least five years' experience under your belt. It won't be easy with him starting from scratch.'

Franco stopped eating. This was giving him the flutters. 'Hang on, Pa. I—'

But Pa was in full flood, and didn't stop. 'A month isn't long. Don't forget, I'll have to find a replacement for Myra.'

'I know a girl who wants my job,' Myra said quickly. 'Her name's Betty.'

'How do I know I'll want her?' Franco could see Pa was getting cross.

'She's keen. I think she'll suit you.'

'Tell her to come and see me, straight away.' He was pushing his plate away before it was empty. 'At least, Franco, you're free to start now.'

'No, Pa. I'm not coming to work here. What made you think I would?'

That brought a heavy silence. They all stopped eating to stare at him.

'Grow up, Franco. It's time you saw sense. We need you here. What's the matter with you lads?'

'Pa, we've been through all this before. It's not what I want. I'll get myself another job.'

'You won't keep it if you do. You can't go on chopping and changing like this, it's getting you nowhere. You need a job with prospects. You'd have a future here.'

Franco didn't see it that way. He wanted to enjoy his life. He saw work as something he had to do to earn the money to have fun. He knew his parents would see this as rejection and he was sorry they'd be hurt yet again. He blamed Carlo for bringing this crisis on him.

Four weeks later, Franco understood they were all forgiven. Ma put on a farewell spread on the day before Carlo and Myra left, and they all went over to Lime Street Station the following evening to see them off.

Betty Leyland had been installed in Myra's job, and Danny McGuire in Carlo's. Myra knew Danny, years ago, he'd been in her class at school. He was small and slight, and seemed very keen on cooking. Pa had to admit the caff would still run without any of his sons.

By then, Franco was working in the bedding department

at the Co-op, but he wasn't sure whether he was going to like it.

The garage changed hands six months after Mick came out of prison, but Gran's health never really recovered. Over the following two years she went downhill. There were many mornings when she couldn't get out of bed. She talked with remorse of letting Mick ruin the business her husband had spent so many years building up.

'I should have put my foot down at the beginning. I wasn't firm enough. I thought he might just be right.'

Ellie tried to get her to talk about her mother but somehow Gran couldn't bring herself to do it. She sensed the horror Gran must have felt at the time and it made her more curious. She felt there was some mystery that she needed to uncover.

Gran's old eyes clouded with grief when she spoke of the sons she'd lost in the war. 'I think of them often, of what they'd be like now. They were just lads, not out of their teens.'

But about her daughter, she spoke only of the messages of comfort Orla was sending from the other side. If asked directly, she said she missed her very much. About the exact circumstances of her death, she would add nothing. As Ellie ran up and downstairs with cups of tea and hot water bottles for her, she felt a growing need to find out.

Connie popped in to see her during the day while Ellie was at school and brought them meals. From time to time, Gran would make an effort, say she felt better, and take up some of her household duties again.

Despite her worries about her grandmother, these were happy years for Ellie. She was in and out of the Baldinis' house, and she knew she could turn to Connie if she needed help.

* * *

Ellie couldn't help but see Gran was failing. She'd turned thirteen before Gran became really ill and considered herself almost grown up.

Over the last year she'd taken over more and more of the household jobs. During the last month, since Gran had taken to her bed, Ellie had looked after almost everything. For the last fortnight she hadn't gone to school. Gran needed her at home.

She sat hunched on a stool beside her grandmother's bed, her throat tight with dread. The doctor was leaving.

At the door he turned to whisper to Connie, 'She's failing fast. I'm afraid it won't be long now.'

'Can't you make her better?' Ellie choked. She was upset by what was happening and resented being treated as a child. 'I want her to get better.'

He came back to put a hand on her shoulder in a show of comfort. 'Your grandmother's very weak. Think of her. She's had a long life but recently she's suffered a lot of pain. Perhaps she'd welcome the end to it.'

'But what about me?' Ellie wailed. The hand on her shoulder patted her gently.

'Dear child, I doubt she can go on any longer.'

Ellie was frightened of what the future would bring. She cradled the wrinkled hand between her own small ones and wished she was really grown up.

Connie pushed her greying hair away from her face. 'You'll not be left on your own, love. Come on, your grandma wouldn't want you to fret.' She looked up at the doctor. 'She's brought Ellie up. The girl's distressed, bound to be.'

Connie had been in and out every day this week, bringing hot meals for Ellie and broth for Gran. She'd sent in Vito and Franco to help lift Gran out of bed for an hour, so it could be made properly. They'd laid fires and carried up buckets of coal to the bedroom. Ellie had done the rest, helping Gran wash and keeping her company.

'You must be brave. It isn't possible to help your grandmother to go on.' The doctor turned to Connie. 'She's got family, hasn't she, apart from . . . ?' He nodded towards Ellie.

'A son.'

'I think you'd better let him know.'

'Send for him?' Connie asked. Bridie had been restless last night, saying she needed to speak to Mick.

He looked grave. 'Yes, send for him, it won't be long now. I doubt she'll last the night.'

Connie put an arm round Ellie's shoulders, but nothing would comfort her. 'You stay here. I'll see to everything.'

Tears were choking Ellie as her gaze went round the room. It had changed since Gran had taken to her bed, it was a sick room now. There was a cluster of medicine bottles and pill boxes on the bed table. Tea, unwanted and cold, waited in the cup. Gran's false teeth were in a tumbler because she could no longer bear to have them in. Ellie didn't know how long she'd sat there in that silent room before Gran's cold fingers squeezed hers. She opened tired eyes.

'Ellie, I'll be up there.' Her gaze swept up to the ceiling. 'Keeping a . . . watchful eye on you. I'll see you come to no harm. Wish . . . I could stay longer, to see you grow up.'

Ellie raised the gnarled old hand to her cheek, but Gran had closed her eyes again. She sat listening to Gran struggling for breath, moaning softly, almost asleep but not quite. From time to time she grimaced, so Ellie knew she felt pain though the doctor had given her something to ease it. Gran was everything to her. She didn't know how she'd manage without her.

* * *

As Connie threw a coat round her shoulders and ran to the cafe she was blinking back her tears. She couldn't imagine life without Bridie, she needed her. That the doctor thought she was failing and wouldn't last the night brought a sense of panic. He'd told her to let Mick know.

Trust Franco not to be home when she needed him. The cafe was on the point of closing and there was no sign of Vito. Danny McGuire was washing down in the kitchen.

'Boss has gone down to the market for vegetables.'

'Oh!' Connie knew he did that on one or two evenings a week. She sagged against the door.

'Is something the matter?'

It was warm here and the tea urn hissed comfortingly, but she must do what the doctor had asked.

'It's Bridie, the doctor says she's failing fast and we should send for her son.' Danny knew Bridie, she came in often in the afternoons.

'D'you want me to go?'

'Yes, please.' She'd written down the address. 'It's New Ferry, I'm afraid.' Mick had moved to New Ferry when he'd sold the garage. It was far enough away from people who knew him.

Danny seemed quite pleased to get out of any more cleaning. 'I know New Ferry, I know this street.' Connie gave him his bus fare and told him what he must say.

'Terrible to think the old lady's dying,' he said, reaching for his coat.

When Ellie heard the front door knocker fall she ran downstairs and found Uncle Mick's bulk on the doorstep. He was towering over her.

She took a step backwards in consternation. Uncle Mick was a violent man. He terrified her. She knew what he'd done to her mother and she'd felt his fists herself on the day he'd locked her out in the yard.

'Are we in time?' he asked as he pushed past her and headed for the stairs.

'You've been very quick.' Too quick. She didn't want him frightening Gran now.

'He's asking is she still with us?' Auntie Wilma, gaunt and nervous, was with him. Ellie nodded and rushed back to her stool beside Gran's bed. They were giving her palpitations.

'Hello, Mam,' Mick was panting slightly. He was putting on a lot of weight. 'How are you?'

Gran opened her eyes and tried to smile. 'Mick.' Her voice was a faint croak.

'I'm here too, Mother,' Auntie Wilma said.

Ellie could see Gran steel herself and try to pull herself up on her pillows. 'Mick.' Her voice was stronger now. 'I'm glad you've come. I've been waiting . . . for you. You too, Wilma.'

'We're here now. We'll take care of everything.'

'Promise me you'll play fair with our Ellie.'

'Of course, Mam.'

'You remember . . . what I said when you came to see me last month? When I took that bad turn?'

'Yes.'

'Have you done it?'

'Done what?'

Gran gasped with impatience and closed her eyes for a moment to collect her strength. 'Orla owned half the business. You promised to . . . make over half the money you got for it to Ellie. It's the least you can do. Only right.'

The silence dragged on. Ellie sucked in her breath. She knew what that meant. They didn't want to give her anything.

She didn't care. The only thing she really wanted was for Gran to get better.

'It's not as easy as all that.' Uncle Mick's eyes slid uneasily from her to Gran.

'A terrible disappointment,' Wilma whispered.

Ellie could see Gran making a huge effort. 'The site . . . It was a new building . . .'

He was shaking his head. 'Didn't fetch much. It went downhill when I wasn't here to look after things. Wilma couldn't cope.' He glanced contemptuously in her direction.

'Half . . . of whatever it was . . .' Gran insisted.

'It was making a loss.'

'You stupid . . .' Gran's voice rasped. 'Always wanting to change, always fighting . . . You're a fool, Mick. If only you'd left it . . . as a bike shop.'

'No money in that.'

'But motor bikes, they would have been all right. You wouldn't have had to . . . build more.'

'Mam,' Mick asked, 'have you made a will?'

'Yes, but don't expect to get any more. What I have left is for Ellie.'

'Don't worry about Ellie. We'll look after her.' Wilma's mouth was a hard straight line.

'Better if Connie looks after her.'

'No, Mam, we'll do that.' Uncle Mick was smiling, turning from Gran to her. Ellie thought it a false smile, it didn't reach his eyes.

She saw Auntie Wilma glance coldly in her direction. 'We haven't a lot, but we'll share it with her.' To Ellie, it sounded as though she was about to take the last crust out of their mouths.

'You'll not have to pay me my pension,' Gran panted, 'and

that's been more than enough to keep us both in comfort. You'll gain a bit. Leave Ellie with Connie Baldini . . .'

'We're family. We'll take care of everything, don't you worry.'

There was another knock on the front door. 'Who can that be?' Wilma asked irritably. 'We can't be doing with callers now.' Ellie ran down to see and heard Wilma's heavy footsteps following her.

Franco was on the doorstep. 'I've brought your dinner, Ellie. It's spaghetti bolognese.' He handed over two dinner plates upended together and wrapped in a tea towel. 'Sorry to hear your gran's taken a turn for the worse. Ma said I was to ask how she was now.'

Ellie shook her head. She was fighting tears.

'No change,' Wilma snapped.

'Ma wants to know if there's anything we can do to help.'

'No. What would help at a time like this?'

Franco turned back to Ellie. 'I'll see you, kid.'

Ellie was taking her dinner upstairs. Over the last few days she'd eaten her meals beside Gran's bed.

'Come and eat that at the table,' Auntie Wilma fussed, taking the plates from her. Ellie found herself pushed into the living room and seated in front of a steaming plate of food.

'Good gracious! Call that dinner, it's nothing but worms and gravy.'

'It's Italian food,' Ellie said. 'It's nice. Gran likes it too.'

Wilma snorted with disgust. She was Merseyside born and bred. 'I can't be doing with all that foreign stuff.'

Ellie listened to her climbing the stairs and thought her strange. After all, by marrying Uncle Mick, she had become Mrs Valentino and, like Gran, that made her sound Italian. Lots of people would think she was.

Ellie struggled to eat, but tonight she just couldn't. She went back upstairs to see how Gran was. She was breathing heavily, her face greyish yellow against the white of her pillow. 'Is she asleep?'

Auntie Wilma was using her stool. 'Yes, you can see she is. Have you finished your dinner? You've been very quick.'

'I'm not hungry.'

'Go back and finish it,' she said sternly. 'Food costs money and that doesn't grow on trees. And somebody has taken the trouble to cook it and bring it for you.'

Ellie wished they hadn't come. They were coming between her and Gran. Mick was looking in the dressing-table drawers.

'You heard what your auntie said,' he thundered.

Ellie went back to the living room to try again, forcing herself to swallow despite the lump in her throat. It was nice, Connie's dinners always were, but it wouldn't go down. She was tired. Gran had woken her twice last night, calling out for a drink and more physic. She no longer knew whether it was day or night.

Ellie put her head down on the table beside the plate. It was dark outside but if she scraped her plate clean out in the yard, next door's cat would come over the wall and eat it or the birds would. Then Auntie Wilma would think she'd eaten it. Her head was swimming, and she could feel herself drifting off.

It was the sound of heavy footsteps coming downstairs that woke her. She jerked up on her chair. 'What's happened?'

'She's gone,' Wilma said briefly.

'Gone!' Ellie wailed, clutching at the neck of her jumper. 'Why didn't you fetch me?' She could feel the strength draining from her legs. 'I wanted to be with her.'

She would have run upstairs but Uncle Mick blocked the

way and swung her back. 'You didn't miss anything. She didn't speak again.'

'She wanted me with her, she told me so.'

Ellie fought him off and raced up to Gran's bed. They'd covered her face with the sheet. With thudding heart, she peeled it back. Gran looked different. She wanted to hold her hand again but that had been tucked under the bedclothes. Ellie had known this was coming, but still felt shocked and frightened. Surely Gran hadn't gone? She hadn't said a proper goodbye.

'Don't leave me, Gran,' she implored.

'She already has,' Mick said from behind her before going down to the living room again.

Ellie found Gran's hand at last and clasped it between her own. She sank back on the stool she'd occupied for so long and cried. She felt totally empty. Gran had been the centre of her world.

Ellie didn't know how long she'd been sitting there. It was very dark, she was cold and could feel herself trembling. Gran's hand was cold too and the candle was burning itself out. The last feeble flickers lit her way downstairs. Bright gas light beamed out of the living room. The door was ajar. She could hear them talking.

'Has she appointed a guardian for her?' she heard Wilma ask. 'Has she had it drawn up legally?'

'No, nothing about a guardian, nothing about appointing executors either. Trust Mam to draw up her own will, wouldn't spend the money on a solicitor.'

'I thought your family did things properly,' Wilma said spitefully.

Ellie heard a rattle of teacups. Uncle Mick said, 'Dad did. Do you reckon this is legal?'

'Probably. We could tear it up, say there wasn't one. There won't be another copy.'

'She's got savings in the bank, easier to get at them with that. Somebody has to act for a child.'

Ellie made herself push the door open and go in. She could see Gran's handwriting on the sheet of paper Auntie Wilma was holding in her hand. Alarmed, she asked, 'Is that her will?'

'No.' Uncle Mick snatched at the paper and folded it quickly, tucking it into an inside pocket of his jacket.

Ellie was sure it was. 'It's Gran's handwriting,' she accused. 'Her notepaper.'

'Yes, she's written a letter to me, asking me to look after you. We'll take you home with us.'

Ellie was taken aback. 'The Baldinis are going to look after me, Gran asked them—'

'No, we're your family.'

She burst into tears. 'You don't care about Gran, only—'

'That won't bring her back,' Mick said irritably.

It made Ellie wail with anguish. It was hard to think of anything but Gran's death.

'We've had enough to put up with tonight, without that. Spare us, for God's sake.' Mick's face was working angrily. 'You can start putting your things together. We'll take you home with us now.'

'I don't want to live with you.'

'Mam spoiled her rotten,' he added to Wilma. 'I hope we aren't going to have trouble with her.'

'It's gone midnight,' Wilma said. 'The buses won't be running. We can't go home now, unless you want to walk.'

Mick grunted. 'So it has! Better if we sleep here, then. We'd have to come back in the morning anyway to see to things.'

Wilma nodded. 'The death certificate and the undertaker.'

Ellie felt sick. She couldn't understand why they wanted to take her with them.

'You're the lucky one,' he told her. 'You can sleep in your own bed.'

Wilma's hand was on her back, propelling her upstairs to her own bedroom. Cold fingers pulled her jumper roughly over her head. 'Don't,' she sobbed. 'I can manage.'

'You'll spend all night mooning about if I leave you,' Wilma said impatiently. 'Your gran had had enough of this world. There's nothing we could do about that.'

Ellie felt her flannelette nightdress being pulled on over her vest. Within moments, her candle went and she was left weeping silently into her pillow.

As the door closed, she heard Wilma say to Uncle Mick, 'She's going to be a right ray of sunshine.'

Chapter Eight

The next morning, Uncle Mick put his head round the door of Ellie's room. 'Come on, get up. It's gone nine, we've a lot to do today. Come and show me where the food's kept. I want some breakfast.'

She pulled her bedclothes closer, feeling petrified. 'In the pantry.'

'Get up and give us a hand. No point in lying there feeling sorry for yourself.'

Ellie had a terrible sense of loss and her eyes felt sore and puffy after all the crying she'd done last night. She had to obey him. When she went downstairs five minutes later, he was lighting a fire in the living room.

He said, 'I'll have a couple of boiled eggs. There doesn't seem to be much else.'

Ellie put them in a pan to boil and began setting the table.

'Take a cup of tea up to your Auntie Wilma,' he ordered as he cracked the shell of his first egg. Ellie did as she was asked.

Wilma had made up the spare bed and had used Gran's eiderdown. She said, 'I'll be down in ten minutes. You can boil an egg for me.' She looked nervous and on edge, but she'd always tried to bully Ellie. 'Is the bread fresh? No? You can make me some thin buttered toast then.'

Ellie hardly knew what she was doing. Everything was so

different without Gran. She went down and started to make toast, deciding to have some herself. Wilma came down and complained the toast was burned.

There was a tap on the back door and Connie came in. 'How's your Gran, love?' she asked Ellie.

Ellie could feel tears prickling. Her eyes still felt funny from crying last night.

'She's gone over. In the night.'

'You poor pet.'

Ellie threw herself into Connie's arms and felt them tighten round her. She put her head down on the well-padded shoulder and wept.

'You need a quiet day. Come round to my place right away, we'll—'

'No,' Uncle Mick said fiercely. 'We're taking Ellie home with us.'

'Oh?' Ellie felt Connie straighten up in surprise. 'I understood she'd be coming to live with me.'

'We couldn't possibly trouble you.'

'She'd be no trouble. I want her. Bridie asked me if I would. She thought it best for Ellie.'

'We're family, she'll be better off with us.'

'No, Bridie was my friend, we talked about it many times. I'm sure she intended me to look after her.'

'I want to live with Connie and Vito,' Ellie choked.

'No.' Uncle Mick looked straight at her. 'My mother wrote a letter to me, asking me to look after Ellie. And she left a will—'

'I know about the will,' Connie said. 'I brought a friend round and we witnessed it for her.'

'It appoints me as Ellie's guardian. I have to insist.'

'I didn't know that.'

Ellie saw shock on Connie's face, and clung to her. 'It's not true, it can't be . . . I think he's—'

'Ellie's upset, of course. But that's the legal position as I see it. My mother appointed me as executor too.'

Connie frowned. 'I thought the will was just to leave her things to Ellie. Bridie said nothing about a legal guardian or executors or anything like that. I wouldn't have thought she'd know—'

'The will was to settle Ellie's future. My mother wouldn't leave anything as important as that to chance. I'm sure you understand?'

Ellie saw Connie's face crumple. 'That's the legal position?'

'I've said so, haven't I?'

'Can I see the will? I signed it but didn't see what was in it, but I can't believe . . . That's not what Bridie told me at the time.'

'We've packed a few things to take back with us. I'm afraid the will was one of them.'

Ellie knew they were beaten, though Connie continued to argue on her behalf. It seemed Uncle Mick wanted her to live with him. She couldn't understand why, he'd never seemed to like her much. She could feel fear growing in a hard ball in her stomach. He wasn't going to allow her to stay with the Baldinis.

'No point in trying to fight the law,' he told Connie. 'You aren't a relative and I am. You can't win.'

At last Connie, looking defeated and not far from tears, kissed Ellie and went home.

Ellie felt she'd been deserted. Gran had spoken of the time when Connie would look after her. She couldn't believe Gran would legally bind her to Uncle Mick and Auntie Wilma. Gran hadn't trusted them. Why would she write to Uncle Mick?

'I want to see the letter you said Gran wrote to you,' she said, looking him in the eye. 'I don't believe—'

'Like I told Mrs Baldini, we've packed some things to take home with us.'

Ellie stood her ground. 'The letter I saw you reading here last night.'

'We packed the documents in a suitcase where they'd be safe. We'll show them to you when we get you home. All right?' Uncle Mick pushed his cup forward for her to refill.

Ellie picked up the teapot. 'There's none left.'

'Make some more, there's a good girl. Perhaps some more toast too.'

Ellie was doing everything they asked of her. 'I can look after myself. I'll be all right here.' She wanted to prove to them she could. 'I've made breakfast for you, I can make it for myself. There's no need for me to go anywhere. I'll be at school all day and—'

Uncle Mick brought his great fist down to thump the table. 'You heard your grandmother ask me to take care of you?'

'No, what she was asking was—'

'Mother wanted me to take care of you. You'll come with us when we've done what we have to here.'

Ellie couldn't believe it. Gran had told her more than once that she'd arranged for Connie to look after her. She thought she'd heard Gran tell Mick and Wilma that. She looked at her aunt for support. For the first time she thought she saw fear in her eyes. Was everybody frightened of Uncle Mick?

'You're lucky to have relatives who can,' her aunt gulped. 'Relatives who'll put themselves out for you. Very lucky.'

Ellie didn't feel lucky. 'I don't want to put you to any trouble. I'm sure I could manage by myself. I've had to look after Gran these last few weeks as well as do the housework. I know Auntie Connie will still come in and see me right.'

'Don't be silly,' Uncle Mick burst out.

'You're too young,' Wilma told her.

'I know I could manage.'

'Don't let's have any more of this.' Mick was angry. 'It's quite impossible. Who's going to pay the rent for this house? You're coming with us.'

Ellie hesitated. 'I shall have to come back every day to go to school.'

'We can't afford bus fares like that,' Uncle Mick said, aghast. 'Not every day.'

'I'll be leaving school in a few more months.' Ellie was appalled at the thought of cutting herself off from everything and everybody she knew. 'Couldn't I . . . ?'

'There's a school you can walk to, not very far from where we live. You can go there.'

'Much better for you,' Wilma nodded. 'You'd have to get up very early to catch a bus to this part of town.'

Ellie wouldn't have minded that but she said nothing more; she knew it would do no good. She made a rush for the back door. She wasn't going to be taken away. She was going to Connie's house now. Vito and Franco wouldn't let him take her.

She got down the back yard, but couldn't get the back gate open in time. Mick's fist grabbed her by the collar and swung her round. She flinched as she glimpsed his other fist lifting to crash into her face.

'No,' Auntie Wilma cried, deflecting his arm. 'No, not here. Better if you don't. Come back inside.'

Uncle Mick slid the bolts behind them on the yard door as well as the back door, as they went in.

'Sit down, Ellie,' he said, pulling up a chair to face her. 'Now you listen to me. It's no good trying to run away, other people can't help you now. I am your closest living relative and I'm going to take care of you. There's nothing to be frightened of, you'll get a good home with us.'

Ellie shivered. 'But I want to stay with . . .' she sobbed.

'Start getting your things together,' Wilma said. 'You can bring them with you.'

'You're very ungrateful,' Mick told her. 'Wilma, you'd better go down to the doctor's to see about the death certificate. I'll take care of things here.'

When the time came to catch the bus to New Ferry, it was raining. Ellie felt weighed down with the two shopping bags and a brown paper parcel into which she'd packed some of her clothes. Gran had had two suitcases and they'd been packed tight with things Auntie Wilma wanted to bring with her. Uncle Mick carried them.

The bus came. Her uncle put her to sit on the seat in front of them. 'Two and a half to the New Ferry bus sheds,' he said, handing over coins to the conductor.

Ellie turned to whisper to Auntie Wilma, 'Gran pays full fare for me. I'm over twelve, you have to.'

'Shush.' Ellie felt some of Wilma's spittle on her cheek. 'You'd pass for ten anywhere, there's nothing of you. No point in throwing money at the wall.'

Ellie huddled back on the seat. Relatives they might be, but they were near strangers. She felt very frightened and very much alone. It seemed a long journey through streets she could barely see through the condensation on the bus windows. She hated the thought of leaving the Baldinis and their cafe, her friend Mary, and everybody she knew at school.

When Uncle Mick and Auntie Wilma had sold the garage,

they'd wanted to start afresh in a place where they weren't known, and had moved right away from the Birkenhead Park area. The house they were renting was in Bicknell Street. It had two big bay windows and was in a smoke-blackened brick terrace.

'It's not unlike your gran's house,' Wilma said. 'And it's near New Ferry Park. You'll soon feel at home here.'

The house was nothing like Gran's. It felt icy inside. Ellie shivered as she looked round the living room. The grate was full of cold ash.

'Light the fire,' Uncle Mick commanded. 'The coal shed's in the yard, you'll find what you need out there.'

Ellie looked round the untidy room and felt dazed by the speed at which her life had changed.

'Come on, jump to it.' Mick's fist thumped against her shoulder almost knocking her off balance. 'Don't expect us to wait on you while you're here.'

Feeling very low, Ellie set about it.

'You've got to get all those ashes out first,' Mick told her, 'or it'll never catch. Go easy on those sticks, you'll need some for tomorrow's fire.'

Wilma disappeared and came back a little later with Dougie. 'Isn't he growing into a big boy now?' Her pride in him was plain to see. Dougie was growing into a cheeky-looking little boy.

Ellie tried to pull herself together. 'How old are you now, Dougie?' she asked.

'Three,' he giggled.

'Three and a half,' his mother corrected. 'Our Ben's got a job now and Roy's in school. Our next-door neighbours looked after Dougie this morning.'

Ellie hated the thought of living with Uncle Mick and Roy, but she wasn't given much time to dwell on it.

'I'm hungry, get the food on the table,' Uncle Mick ordered. 'It's already late for dinner.'

The scullery sink was full of dirty dishes that Ellie had to wash before they could eat. She helped Wilma set out the cold meat and pickles. There was plenty, but she wasn't hungry.

When they'd eaten, Uncle Mick was preparing to go out.

'Where can I put my things?' she asked. 'Where am I going to sleep?' Her parcels were still on the bottom stair, where she'd left them.

Mick pursed his lips and looked as though it was the first time he'd given any thought to that. He looked at Wilma. 'Where's the best place?'

She shook her head.

'She'll have to have Ben's room,' Mick told her. 'There's nowhere else.'

'The little room up at the front,' Wilma said, her voice not much above a whisper.

Ellie took her parcels and went up to look. The bed hadn't been made and the sheets looked none too clean. Ben's clothes were tossed everywhere. She was repelled and went down again. 'Can I have clean sheets?'

Wilma looked nonplussed. 'I changed them only the other day, nothing much the matter with those.'

'They're Ben's, won't he need them?'

'Perhaps there's some in the airing cupboard.' She went to check and Ellie followed her to the hot water tank on the landing. There were no bedclothes there.

'The water doesn't get hot enough unless we have a big fire.' Wilma went down to the living room where there was a kitchen range.

'I use the oven here for airing,' she said. 'Doesn't get hot enough to cook in. Nothing works properly in this house.' She sorted through a bundle of children's underwear but there were no sheets. 'I haven't had time to wash the ones we took off. There aren't any clean ones, you'll have to use what's there for the time being.'

Ellie found a great bundle of unwashed bedclothes waiting in the wash house. They looked as though they'd been there for weeks.

Wilma said, 'I'm going to the shops to get something for tea. I'll take Dougie, the fresh air will do him good. While we're gone, you can sweep up and do a bit of dusting. Tidy the place up a bit. Be sure to take the living-room mats out to the back yard and shake them.'

'I'll do some washing first,' Ellie said defiantly.

She picked out two single sheets and some pillow cases from the pile of dirty washing, but there was no hot water and she had to boil the kettle first. She eventually pegged them out on the line in the back yard, as it was no longer raining, but she knew they'd never dry in time for her to use tonight.

She tried to clean up the living room and scullery, needing a damp cloth to remove the layers of dust that coated the furniture. Her efforts seemed to make little inroad into the mess. She was shocked to see how dirty everything was. Both Gran and Connie were fussy about cleanliness and tidiness.

She felt shattered and went upstairs to what was to be her bedroom. She straightened the bedclothes, lay down on them and wept.

Gran had said she'd be up in heaven keeping a watchful eye on her, that she'd see Ellie came to no harm. But it didn't look as though she could. Perhaps Gran had been wrong about the spirit world? Perhaps those who were dead were gone for ever.

* * *

Ellie woke to the sound of Ben's voice.

'What've you brought her here for? I'm not giving up my bedroom for her.'

Ellie trembled. She liked Ben better than her other relatives, and she didn't want to upset him by taking his bedroom. It was dark outside and the street lamps were lit. She slid off the bed and went down to join them, feeling sleep sodden and heavy.

Mick's voice was raised and threatening. He always seemed to be boiling with anger, shouting when he was ordering others about. He gave her the jitters. 'If I say you're giving it up, you are.'

They were all crowding into the narrow hall. Uncle Mick was taking off his cap and muffler, it seemed he'd just come home.

Ellie could feel the tension sparking between him and Ben. Ben's cheeks were flushed and his eyes bright with anger. 'So where am I to sleep?'

'I've made the camp bed up in the back bedroom.' Wilma's tone was placatory.

'You haven't, there's no sheets on it, just some old blankets. I'm not sleeping on that. I want a proper bed.'

'It'll only be for a night or two.'

Ben's alert and fighting eyes were watching everything around him as if ready to jump clear of trouble. 'She can sleep there then.'

'There are beds at Gran's house. We'll have them brought here.'

'And I don't want to muck in with the babies.'

'We're not babies,' Roy spat.

'I don't want your bed,' Ellie protested. 'It's filthy. I don't want to stay here.'

Mick's great fist shot out and hit her across the face, making her stagger back against Ben. She was sobbing with shock and pain.

'I'm not staying here to be belted by you. I'm going back to live with the Baldinis. It's what Gran intended, it's what I want and it's what they want.'

'You're going nowhere,' Mick growled. 'You're staying here with us.'

'But why?'

'Because I say so.' Uncle Mick's face was working with rage. 'What's the matter with you kids? You don't know when you're well off, either of you. You, Ben, will sleep on the camp bed. Like it or lump it.'

Ellie rushed back upstairs, slammed the door of Ben's room and threw herself across the bed. Her face was stinging, her body shaking with great sobs of frustration and anger.

She told herself she could find her way back to the bus shed and she knew which bus to catch. She could go back to Connie, who'd let her stay.

Ben thumped on the door and came in with his candle. 'I'm taking my things,' he told her, beginning to collect them together. 'This could be long term.' He took an armful to the back bedroom and came back.

Ellie dried her eyes. 'I'm sorry about your bed.'

'Why does he want you here?' Ben was dour.

'He said I must come so he could look after me.'

'Look after you? Ha ha. You'd better learn to look after yourself. Mick will have his reason, you can bet on that.'

'I think Gran left what she had to me, her money and her furniture. Uncle Mick wants it.'

Ben's bright blue eyes fastened on hers. 'That'll be it. If there's money on offer, he'll want it. Probably thinks it should be his – after all, she was his mother. We'll have to poke round sometime, see what we can find out.'

Ellie followed him to the back bedroom. Roy's clothes and toys were piled on the camp bed.

'I'm taking his bed,' he said. 'Give us a hand to pull it out. I want it under the light so I can read in bed.'

He positioned it in the middle of the room. Dougie's cot and the camp bed were back against the wall. 'Now Mam can't say I'm disturbing them.'

'Will Roy mind?'

'Oh, he minds. Can't you hear him screaming about it down there? Won't hurt him, he's spoiled rotten anyway.'

'I wish I didn't have to stay here.'

'So do I. I'll be out of here at the first chance.'

Ellie felt she was being used by Uncle Mick and Auntie Wilma, but though she was wary of Ben, she hoped she'd found an ally in him.

Later that night he came to look for a pullover in Ellie's room. She helped him carry the rest of his belongings to the other room and pile them round his bed.

He boasted, 'Mick doesn't hit me any more. He used to knock hell out of me.' He went on more sympathetically, 'He's got a real backhander that makes your head ring.'

'Don't I know it,' Ellie groaned. Her jaw still ached. 'You mean he'll leave you alone now he's got me to knock about?'

'No, I've figured out how to stop him in his tracks.'

'You'd better teach me. I don't want any more of this.'

'You'll be bruised by tomorrow. Bruises that show. You won't get a black eye though. He's hit too low for that.'

'So how d'you stop him then?'

'You've got to learn to dodge his fists. He's not that fast on his feet.'

Ellie was disappointed. 'Apart from that?' He was a giant of a man, towering over her. If she did dodge his first blow, she had nowhere to go if he chose to follow.

'It'd take too long to tell you. Some other time.'

'Tell me,' she cajoled. 'I want you and me to be friends.'

But Ben was already running downstairs.

Connie felt terrible. She knew she'd let Ellie down. She shouldn't have let Mick take her away. He'd frightened the whole neighbourhood here; little Ellie must be terrified.

Years ago, Bridie had taught her to make Irish stew and she'd made it regularly for her family at tea time ever since. She was thinking of how much she was missing Bridie as she stirred a fresh pan of it on the stove, when through the back kitchen window, she saw Franco whirling up the back yard.

He came slamming into the house to stand before her, his cheeks scarlet. She knew he was angry.

'Why ever did you send Danny round to tell Mick that Bridie was dying? You shouldn't have.' His face was working with anxiety. 'You know what he's like. He'll knock Ellie about, hurt her. For heaven's sake, Ma, what were you thinking of?'

Connie had been asking herself that all day. She'd been upset. What with Bridie dying and Carlo leaving, it was the end of an era, and she didn't like it.

'The doctor said I should send for her relatives . . . That she couldn't last much—'

'He didn't know how she felt about Mick. She wouldn't have wanted to see him.'

'She did, she wanted to make sure he'd make over Orla's share of the business to Ellie. She was worried that he wouldn't.'

'Was he ever likely to? You've got to think for yourself sometimes, Ma.'

Connie sucked in her breath and sank down on a chair. Vito had said much the same when he'd heard what she'd done.

'She was his mother.'

Franco was beside himself. 'I can't understand why you did it.'

'Mick's Ellie's nearest relative. He said Bridie had made him Ellie's guardian and trustee. How can we argue against that?'

'Ma, you know what a liar he is. How could you be taken in?'

'I wasn't really taken in, but—'

'If you'd done nothing, if Mick hadn't known Bridie was dying, he probably wouldn't have come near. Everything would have been as you wanted it.'

Connie knew that only too well.

'You can't let Mick take Ellie away. He'll make mincemeat of her.' She could see Franco was horrified at the thought.

That made her feel worse. 'How can I stop him now?'

'I thought you were going to look after her,' he said bitterly as he pounded across the living room and on up the stairs. 'Fine way you've got of doing that.'

Connie collapsed on the nearest chair. It would be on her conscience for ever that she'd let Ellie down. It was the last thing she'd intended. She'd sent for Mick without thinking he might change all Bridie's plans. She hadn't believed him capable of that.

Ellie found the days that followed very hard. As soon as Ben had gone to work and Roy to school, Uncle Mick said he and Wilma were going back to Gran's house.

'We've got a lot to do there. The place will have to be emptied and everything packed up.'

'I want to go with you,' Ellie said. 'I can help and I haven't brought all my things.'

'We'll take you another time,' Mick growled. 'You stay here today.'

'And take care of Dougie,' Wilma added.

It was the same the next day. 'It'll upset you to go back to that house,' Uncle Mick told her. 'Bound to.'

'It won't,' Ellie insisted. 'Please, I want to.'

'Better if you stay here.' Auntie Wilma looked as if she was trying to be sympathetic. 'You can go to the butcher's round the corner where our Ben works and get a pound of mince. Then you can have a hot meal ready for us when we come home tonight.'

Uncle Mick finally took Ellie back to Gran's house to collect the rest of her belongings, but he kept her busy packing other things, taking down curtains and rolling up rugs. She saw him and Wilma take a close look round, deciding what they wanted to keep and what should be sold.

'I think we'll take most of this furniture,' he said. 'It's a bit old fashioned but not bad stuff. We might as well take everything we can use.'

'I'd like to go and see Auntie Connie,' Ellie said when they stopped for a sandwich at lunch time.

'We haven't time to waste being sociable,' Mick snapped, but when he turned his back Ellie ran down the yard and knocked on Connie's door in the hope she'd catch her before she went down to the cafe for her dinner. It was Franco who answered.

'Ellie, how are you?' He seemed delighted to see her. 'Ma's been wondering how you're getting on, we all have. She's gone down to the caff. She'd like to see you, why don't you pop down now?'

She shook her head. 'I can't. Mick's doing his best to stop me seeing her.'

'Oh! When's the funeral? Pa was saying we should all go.'

'It's Wednesday, eleven o'clock at Flaybrick Hill Cemetery.'

'Not at St Anne's first?'

'No, just at the chapel in the cemetery. Uncle Mick says that's all that's needed.'

'Oh! Mam was talking of giving a hand with the funeral tea. Can you let her know what you want her to do?'

'Thank you, I'll ask. I've got to go, Uncle Mick's at me every minute.'

He gripped her wrist. 'Oh, Ellie! Stand up to him. Don't let him break you.'

'Where've you been?' Uncle Mick demanded when she went back, though they hadn't moved from the kitchen table.

When Ellie told them, Wilma sniffed, 'We can do without help from the likes of them. We don't want foreign stuff on our table.'

'The Baldinis have this cafe near the station. Connie could—'

'We know that,' Mick said impatiently. 'We won't be feeding the whole neighbourhood. In fact, I don't think we'll have a funeral tea at all. There won't be many at the church. Mam didn't have many friends.'

'She had a lot.' Ellie felt stricken with grief. 'Everybody liked her.'

Chapter Nine

When the morning of Bridie's funeral came, Connie felt drained. Franco's accusing eyes seemed to follow her round the house. Vito said she mustn't blame herself. She'd been upset the night her friend was dying and she hadn't been able to think straight. But she thought Vito was afraid she'd get depressed again and was trying to avoid that. She could hardly believe she'd caused Bridie's carefully thought-out plans to be so changed.

She walked up to Flaybrick Hill Cemetery between Vito and Franco. The chapel was filling up. A lot of people had known Bridie and wanted to pay their last respects. Her coffin was waiting on its bier at the front. Connie couldn't bear to look at it.

As chief mourners, Mick and Wilma came striding down the aisle in smart new black outfits and shoes that squeaked. Ellie trailed behind them wearing the outfit Bridie had bought her for Carlo's wedding, with a black ribbon stitched to the sleeve of her coat. Her face was grey and she looked downright ill. Connie's heart turned over with pity. Once the service started, she could see only the back of Ellie's head bent in misery.

The priest said a lot of complimentary things about Bridie's long life. As they filed out after the coffin Connie waited for Ellie. Her eyes were wet and red.

'This is the first funeral I've been to,' Ellie whispered. That made Connie put her arm round the small shoulders and pull her closer, searching for the words to say how sorry she was that she'd let her uncle take over like this. She couldn't find them.

Instead she said, 'Ben hasn't come?'

She shook her head. 'Mick said Ben wasn't related to Gran, and might as well go to work, that it wasn't worth him losing a day's pay.'

Connie winced. That showed how much Mick thought of his mother.

She whispered to Ellie, 'Come back and see us whenever you can. You know where to find us. We want you to.'

Ellie was blowing her nose. 'I wish I could live with you and Vito instead of Uncle Mick.'

'I'm worried about you. Have you seen your gran's will?'

She shook her head. 'I've asked to several times, but Uncle Mick always has some reason why I can't.'

The congregation followed the coffin to the grave that had been opened. Connie held back so that Mick and Wilma would go ahead with the priest, but they seemed to be making a big effort to stay close to her and Ellie.

'I am the resurrection and the life,' intoned the priest. Bridie was being put to rest in her family's grave. It felt a harrowing moment to Connie, and she could see it was heart-rending for little Ellie.

Afterwards, many stopped to kiss Ellie and whisper condolences, many shook Connie's hand.

Wilma came up then and took Ellie's arm, 'Come on, we're going to catch the bus home.'

It was only then that Connie realised there was to be no funeral tea offered to the mourners.

She said to Wilma, 'Would you and Mick like to come back to my house for a cup of tea and a piece of cake?' She was sure Bridie would be shocked at such a lack of hospitality.

'No thank you,' Wilma said coldly, as she led Ellie towards the bus stop.

Vito took her arm and turned her away. Franco was already striding out for home.

'Bridie would have expected a good send-off,' she said. 'She talked of having a wake at our cafe with you playing the accordion.'

'You mustn't worry about it, Connie.' But she felt racked with misery and worry. Why hadn't she stopped to think before she sent for Mick? She'd meant to help and look what she'd done. For once, Franco was right. She should have left Mick to stew in his own juice.

Then she could have given Bridie the funeral she would have wanted and she could have looked after Ellie in her own way.

The day after the funeral, Auntie Wilma took Ellie to see the headmistress of a nearby school. Within ten minutes of walking up the front steps she found herself sitting at the back of her new class.

They were reciting together long poems they had learned by rote. Ellie knew none of them, she'd learned different ones. She found they had been learning about Greek myths all term but she had not, and she couldn't make head or tail of the current lesson. Ellie felt at a loss – it was all so different and she knew nobody.

Back at Uncle Mick's house, she felt like Cinderella. Wilma pressed her to help about the house and look after her cousins. Roy had started school only six months earlier.

'You have to pass his school to get to your own,' Wilma told Ellie. 'You can take him with you in the mornings and bring him home at dinner time. That'll save a bit of time for me.'

Ellie dreaded having to take Roy anywhere.

'Don't let him climb those trees in the park,' Mick instructed. 'The branches are covered in soot and he'll get his clothes filthy. And he's not to go near that building site, he'll hurt himself.'

Ellie found Roy no easier to manage than he had been when she'd looked after him before.

'I don't need you to fetch me home,' he told her. 'I've been coming by myself.'

'We've got to have our dinner and get back to school. Your mam's getting it ready. She'll be cross if she has to keep it warm because we aren't there to eat it.'

Ellie also knew she'd be in trouble if she turned up without Roy. She had to insist; she took hold of his hand, but he shook her off rebelliously and trailed slowly in her wake, dragging his feet.

'You're always bossing me about,' he grumbled. 'Why did you have to come to live with us?'

'You know why. I lived with our grandmother but she died.'

'But why don't you live with your own mam and dad like everybody else? Don't they like you?'

'It's not that.' Ellie felt cold inside. She dreaded questions about her mother. Even Gran wouldn't talk about her.

'But where are they?'

'They're dead too. My dad was killed, he was a war hero.'

She knew that much, but not the where and why and how of it. Gran had always had plenty to say about other family members, but little about her father.

'I don't like you living with us,' Roy spat at her. 'I don't like you. I don't think your mam and dad liked you either, that's why they left you with Gran.'

Ellie was fighting tears again. They hadn't been far away all this month. The funeral had wrung her out but she wasn't going to let Roy see how much he could hurt her.

Later that evening, they all gathered in the living room where there was light and warmth. There was no room round the fire for her and Ben, so they sat one each end of the table, reading. Ben had taken her to the library which was just round the corner, and Auntie Wilma had signed so she could borrow books. They helped to lift her out of her drab surroundings.

Roy was playing with toy soldiers on the hearth rug. He said: 'Dad, what happened to Ellie's mam? Why can't she live with her?'

'She's up in heaven,' Auntie Wilma said. 'Like your gran.'

Ellie seized the opportunity. 'I wish you'd tell me about Mam, Uncle Mick. You were her brother and in hospital at the same time. Why did she die?'

'Her lung became infected.'

'But I don't understand about that.' Ellie was screwing up her face. 'I know she wasn't well, and had a graze on her shoulder and . . .' Mick's face was stiffening. She lost her nerve.

Ben looked up from his book. 'Poor Orla was knocked about on that day, wasn't she? Caught a few blows. Who's to say what damage was done inside.'

'Shut your mouth, you.' Mick was on his feet waving the poker at Ben. Ellie was shocked, expecting her uncle to lay into him.

Then he turned and vented his violence on the fire, poking at it in a frenzy. 'It's best forgotten.' He threw the contents of the coal scuttle into the blaze. 'No good raking up old troubles.'

Feeling she had Ben's support, Ellie tried to stand her ground. She said quietly, 'But I want to know. What happened to Mam in the bike shop that afternoon?'

'There's a lot of things I want to know too.' Uncle Mick put his angry face close to hers. 'Nothing can bring Orla back. Forget it, can't you?'

'But why won't anybody tell me? I—'

'Drop it, I say,' Uncle Mick thundered.

Wilma said slowly: 'We might as well tell her. Your mother wasn't married, Ellie, when she had you. You know what that means?'

Ellie swallowed hard. She already knew about that. She'd asked Gran one night why she had no father. Gran had sat on her bed and whispered, about how he had been an Army officer who had been posted to France in the war and been killed in the trenches before he could marry her mother.

'A tragedy for your mam,' she'd said, 'and for you. He'd have been a good father.'

Gran had sat there twisting her mouth for a while and then said, 'Some people round here made that into a scandal. They said your mam brought shame on herself, by having you when she didn't have a husband. But you were a comfort to her, she loved you.'

Ellie had accepted that long ago. Her family was different.

'Keep your mouth shut about Orla, for goodness' sake,' Uncle Mick said severely. 'Don't talk about her to the neighbours round here.'

'She brought shame on the family, let us all down,' Wilma hissed. 'And with a name like Valentino, everybody remembers.'

Ellie's mind was in turmoil for the rest of the evening. More shame than Uncle Mick, when he'd been sent to prison?

Ben's head was bent over his book. Every so often he pushed his straight hair back from his brow. She wanted to ask him about her mother, but she'd have to bide her time until they were alone.

The chance came when they were sent upstairs to bed. She followed him to his bedroom. Dougie and Roy were asleep, and the room was an untidy tip of clothes and toys.

'Thank you, Ben,' she said, 'for coming to my aid.'

'Didn't get you far.' He threw his book on his pillow, sat on his bed and started to unlace his boots.

'Do you know what happened to my mother? I really want to know.'

He shook his head. 'Can't help you there.'

'But you were living over the bike shop then. You must remember Mick being knocked out and taken to hospital.'

'Yes, graven on my mind. Mam reckons it was the start of all our troubles.'

Ellie asked eagerly, 'Did you see what happened?'

'No. When I came home from school that day, everything was normal, just as it always was. Mam was by the fire upstairs. She cut me a slice of bread and treacle and sent me out to the shops for half a pound of bacon. She'd got liver for our tea and that was to go with it. When I came back the ambulance was on the forecourt.'

'But it wouldn't have taken you five minutes from there.'

'I went to the grocer's too, for blancmange powder, and I had a halfpenny to spend on sweets. I hung about the newsagent's making up my mind. There was a lad from my class there, and we both chose lollipops. That's the truth, Ellie, I didn't see anything. Mam was hysterical when I got back, very upset. She didn't cook anything that night. We thought Mick was dead.'

'That must have upset you too.'

His glance seemed penetrating. 'I was quite pleased. I'd already had a few backhanders from him. Mam hadn't been married long then, she thought the sun shone out of him and I was getting less of her attention.' Ben lay back on his bed and sighed. 'But he wasn't dead. He came back.'

A few days later, Ellie was pleased to find a van had brought the furniture from Gran's house. The familiar pieces were like old friends. But Wilma decided the wardrobe would be better used in her own bedroom.

'Your room is too small, it wouldn't go in.'

That was true enough. Ellie did get the bed she was used to, a chair and her old dressing table. She was very glad to see her old pillows and eiderdown and have a better supply of sheets and blankets.

Ben and Roy were able to have their own beds back, and Gran's old bed was made up for Dougie. His cot was collapsed and put up in the loft.

It made Ellie feel that her future would be here. She told herself she'd have to make the best of it, that she was miserable because she was missing Gran and she'd be miserable wherever she was.

To Ellie, time seemed to pass very slowly. The weeks crawled. She felt unsettled and restless both at school and at home.

'I'd like to go and see Auntie Connie,' she said one Saturday, a month or two after the funeral.

'Go then,' Wilma said. 'You can go by yourself, can't you?'

'I need money for the bus.' Ellie had decided it was too far to walk and she wasn't sure of the way.

Auntie Wilma pulled a face. 'Money doesn't grow on trees.'

'I can go half fare.' Both Uncle Mick and Auntie Wilma seemed to think she didn't need to pay more. 'Tuppence each way.'

'I really haven't any pennies to spare. You're another mouth to feed here.'

Ellie found that hard to believe. There seemed no shortage of food on the table, there was always butter not marg, and Wilma didn't stint on meat or bought cakes. The boys had new outfits too. It almost seemed Auntie Wilma didn't want her to go and see the Baldinis.

She was thankful she didn't see much of Uncle Mick. He was usually missing at breakfast time and rocking in his chair by the fire when she came home from school in the afternoon.

'He works difficult hours,' Auntie Wilma told her. 'He has a job on the buses.'

It was Ben who told her he cleaned the buses at the New Ferry bus shed and was always complaining that his wages wouldn't stretch to keep his family. Ellie knew her gran would think that a bit of a come down after owning a share of the family business.

Within six months, Uncle Mick seemed much more optimistic about the future. One Sunday afternoon, he took Wilma and his two small sons to Brackenwood to look at some new houses that were being built.

'I believe he's thinking of buying one,' Ben told Ellie when they were left behind. He poked the fire into a blaze and pulled his stepfather's chair nearer. 'I find that almost unbelievable.'

Ellie settled herself in Auntie Wilma's chair. It wasn't often they could sit near the fire.

'I've heard him talking of emigrating to Canada,' she said, 'and taking us all.'

'And also having a slap-up holiday in Blackpool next summer.'

'And there's a firkin of beer in the wash house, and a bowl of fruit here.'

'Yep, he's come into money.' Ben's bright eyes twinkled.

'Tell me,' Ellie said, 'what's this technique you have of avoiding his clouts?'

'He's given you another?'

'Yes, he hurts.'

'Well, it's quite simple: I threatened I'd go to the police if he ever hit me again.'

'You mean you'd tell the police he's hitting you? What good would that do? He'd say we deserved it, that we have to be kept in order, disciplined and all that.'

'No, I'd tell them what he's got hidden in this house.'

Ellie pulled herself upright in the chair. 'What has he? If it works for you, it might work for me too.'

'Stolen goods.' Ben smiled. 'He does a little job every so often and brings his haul home.'

'Where is it?'

'Come on, I'll show you. It's a good time now they've all gone out.'

Ben shot up the stairs and into the front bedroom where her aunt and uncle slept. Ellie stopped in the doorway.

'Won't he be cross if we look through his belongings while he's out?'

'Cross? He'd be dancing mad. He'd bang our skulls together until they cracked.'

'D'you think we should?' Ellie was still peering in from the threshold. The bed was unmade, a rumpled mass of blankets.

'Don't be daft. You've got to look after yourself here. I'm showing you how to survive. You'd better come and see before

150

he gives you a real walloping. A single clout across the chops is just a taster of what he can really do.'

Ellie shivered.

'Up here, on top of the wardrobe, there's cigarettes.' Ben pulled a chair in front of the dressing table standing beside the wardrobe. 'Come on, take a look. You've got to get up so you can see over that ornamental bit.'

'It's Gran's wardrobe.' Ellie was indignant. It was a large Victorian mahogany piece with carved edging topping the three compartments. Once she stood on the dressing table, Ellie could see over it. There were three packages there, hidden from below. One had been opened and was spilling out packets of twenty Players Navy Cut.

'Throw me a couple down,' Ben commanded.

'Won't he know you've taken them?'

'I don't care if he does. If it's free smokes for him, it's free smokes for me.'

Ellie jumped from the dressing table. 'Where did they come from?'

'There's a tobacconist's shop at the toll bar, just round into New Ferry Road. Lots of little bowls of tobacco in the window. Dark shag and all that. You've seen it?'

'Yes.'

'Well, Mick helped do a job there. This is his share.'

'What sort of a job?'

'Burglary, you nut.'

'Oh!'

'That's why he doesn't want me going to the police. There's more. Help me move this dressing table out on to the landing and I'll show you.'

'More cigarettes?'

'More of everything.'

Ellie helped him move the ravel of Wilma's stockings, scarfs, hankies and hair brushes, and lift it out. He balanced the chair on top this time and found another to help him climb up.

'Hold this steady while I move the trap door to the loft. Oh, we need a candle first.'

When Ellie had lit the candle, he gave her a leg up. By the flickering light, she could see a litter of paper and a collection of cardboard boxes of all sizes.

'Crawl,' Ben said, when she had both feet up in the loft. 'Don't stand up. Your foot could come through the ceiling.'

She crawled to the nearest box. The contents were wrapped in newspaper. She opened one, it was a silver teapot, the whole tea set was here. In another box she found silver candlesticks. Lying under some paper were two fur coats. She was amazed.

Then a cold shiver ran down her spine. 'I think I can see . . . Yes, I'm almost sure it's Gran's strong box! She used to keep all her valuables in that.' She had to crawl closer.

Ellie's heart was in her mouth. 'It is Gran's!' She lifted the candle higher and found Ben had come up too, he was on his belly beside her.

'Can you open it?'

'The key's in the lock. She used to wear this round her neck. Oh! It's empty!' Ellie was quivering with disappointment.

'You're too late.' Ben was frowning, deep in thought. Then he shook his head. 'Come on, let's get out of here. Like I said, Mick knows I could bring a policeman here and show him these things. It makes him nervous.'

'Why doesn't he find somewhere else to hide them?'

'Maybe that isn't easy.'

'Does he sell them on or something?'

'Yes, sometimes the place empties, then another load comes.

Sometimes I hear him here in the night, but I don't come out because he brings another man with him.'

Ben chuckled. 'A few months ago, he had some nice gents' coats here. I helped myself to one and wore it to work. I thought he'd have a fit when I came home wearing it. He tore it off my back, and I got some money out of him to buy a coat. The only time I ever have.'

Ellie was shocked. 'He's a common thief.'

Ben smiled. 'Bring that candle closer. Yes, be sure to mention these stolen goods next time he starts knocking you about. It works a treat for me, it probably will for you.'

'He'll wonder how I found out.' Ellie jumped down with a thud.

'Tell him I showed you round the premises. I don't care. The more I spread his secrets round, the more nervous he gets. Ask him how much longer before he finds a buyer for those fur coats.'

'But how does he know how to go about selling on the things he steals?'

'Been in prison, hasn't he? He learned a lot in there.'

'He'll half kill you.'

'Then he'll be in big trouble, won't he? I'll drop him in it. I've got to look after myself. So have you. You try it the next time he threatens you.'

'I will, thanks.' Ellie wondered if she'd dare. Would it work for her or would she infuriate Uncle Mick even more and get twice the thrashing?

Ellie and Ben were sitting by the fire when Mick and Wilma came home. They seemed happy and pleased with their afternoon out. Over a tea of cold meat, tinned fruit and seed cake they discussed the houses they'd seen.

After listening to his mother describe a house she fancied with a marble fireplace and four bedrooms, Ben fixed his eyes on his stepfather and said with an air of assumed innocence, 'Had an unexpected windfall, have you? You're in the money?'

In the sudden stark silence, Ellie saw hate boil up in her uncle's face. Tension was sparking across the table.

'What's it got to do with you?' he snarled.

'I can't help taking an interest.' Ben's manner was deliberately insulting. 'Mam was spent up only last Thursday, could hardly wait to get her hands on my wages. We'd have gone hungry if I wasn't paid till Saturday like you.'

'Ben!' His mother seemed to be warning him. Ellie could see her uncle was enraged, a crimson tide spreading up his face.

Ben leaned back in his chair until it was balancing on two legs. 'Can't be from the usual bits and pieces you steal, I don't suppose you get anything near their value when you come to sell them on. So I have to ask, where has the money come from?'

'None of your business.'

'Definitely a windfall, I'd say. And a huge one.'

Ellie saw the veins in Mick's neck swelling with rage.

'Remember the celebrations when you prised the deeds of the bike shop out of your mother?'

'Shut your mouth,' Uncle Mick thundered.

Ellie knew he was deliberately goading his stepfather, but he turned to smile at her as though he hadn't a care in the world.

'Ellie, you were just a little kid at the time so I don't suppose you remember. Your Uncle Mick said you tried to fight him off, hammered your little fists against his chest with the ferocity of a vixen. When he brought the deeds home to show us we all

154

had a laugh about that, didn't we, Mam? As well as some good times on the money while it lasted.'

Ellie covered her face with her hands. She remembered flying at Mick very well. That was the day he'd locked her out in the yard. She hadn't understood that he was trying to bully Gran into giving him the deeds of the bike shop, but her strong box had been out on the kitchen table when he'd gone. Poor Gran had been in tears that day and hadn't been able to stop him taking them.

Ellie was petrified, unable to believe Ben could be so foolhardy as to rake all this up. He'd said Mick wouldn't dare take a swipe at him, but she held her breath, expecting it. There was fury on Mick's face, and his fists were clenching.

Suddenly he relaxed. 'You cheeky devil! There's no windfall, and if there was I'd make sure none of it came your way.'

Ellie felt sweat breaking out on her brow. Ben was right, Uncle Mick wasn't going to lay a finger on him. He was immune.

Wilma looked as uncomfortable as Ellie felt. She was torn between her husband and her son. Sometimes she supported Ben, but often, such as now, she could not.

It was plain to Ellie that Roy was on his father's side whatever wrongs he did. Dougie was too small to understand what was going on.

'If you're really going to buy a new house,' Ben was daring to go further, 'then I would benefit, we all would. We'd like that, wouldn't we, Ellie? Wouldn't mind the holiday in Blackpool either.'

'Get out, you cheeky brat.' Mick was on his feet. 'Go on, get out. You can eat in the scullery in future. I won't have you at this table.'

Roy started to giggle but stopped as his father's gaze swung to him.

Ellie understood at that moment that if Ben took her part, it was in order to get at his stepfather. He wanted to hurt him more than anything else. She wanted a friend she could trust but Ben needed an ally in the house, someone he could rely on to side with him.

Without a word he piled cake on his plate, got up slowly and stalked to the scullery. Ellie felt the angry silence close round her. She kept her eyes on her plate. When the meal was over Ben helped her wash up and then tried to return to the living room, where there was a fire.

'Your place is in the scullery,' Mick ranted. 'I don't want your ugly face near me.'

Ben retreated and Ellie heard the back door slam as he went out. Her chance to speak to him came when they were going up to bed. When they reached the landing he whirled on her.

'Why didn't you put your pennyworth in too? You should've while I'd got him down.'

'What d'you mean?'

Ben was impatient with her. 'You should have asked him if he'd taken the money your grandma meant you to have. That's what you think, isn't it?'

Ellie swallowed hard. It was. She'd been careful not to accuse her uncle of that, she was too frightened of his temper.

Ben went on. 'We found your gran's strong box, didn't we? With everything gone. What did she keep in it?'

Ellie was trying to remember. 'There was a cameo brooch, rings, beads and a gold watch that used to belong to Grandpa. That sort of thing. And important papers, like deeds to her house, insurance policies and her bank book.'

'Her will?'

'Yes, I suppose so. You never saw her will, did you?'

He shook his head. 'I heard them talking about it. I searched the house from top to bottom, but no. A day or two before, I'd seen Mick working on something in the living room, making alterations, I think. He covered it up when I went in and pretended to be reading the paper, but he had your gran's notepad beside him. I think that might have been her will. I think he must have forged another page in his own favour.'

'You're just guessing,' Ellie said suspiciously. 'You don't know.'

She saw him smile. 'Sometimes I can second guess. I need to.'

'You mean you're nosey.'

'Very. It's the only way I can keep my end up.'

'I know.'

'If my guess is right there's no proof now that your gran ever intended you to have anything. Mick is her son and he's given you a home. I heard them talking about applying for something called probate.'

'What's that?'

'I didn't know what it was either, I had to go down to the library and look it up. It means it has to be proved. It must have been, if he's got the money. So the will he put in must have appeared satisfactory. Unless you can prove it was altered or tampered with, there's nothing you can do.'

Ellie felt like crying. 'Gran said it would all be mine one day.'

'Well, you're out of luck on that,' Ben said in his matter-of-fact voice. 'He's brought all your grandma's furniture here, hasn't he? And I know he sold lots of things he didn't want, and you won't see a penny from that either. If your grandma left money, you can bet he's got his hands on that too.'

Ellie was surprised that Ben knew so much, when it hadn't come from her.

'I asked Auntie Wilma what had happened to Gran's money. She said Mick had put it in trust for me and I'd get it when I was twenty-one.'

Ben would never accuse his mother of telling lies, but his face showed what he thought of that. He said awkwardly, 'Mick probably told her to say that if you asked.'

'I asked to see Gran's will and a letter he said she'd written to him making him my legal guardian.' Both he and Wilma were always ready with reasons why it wasn't possible to show things like that to her. Either the solicitor had it, he was seeking probate or he needed to keep it for his files.

She didn't think she'd ever see any of Gran's money. Mick had taken her inheritance just as he'd taken her mother's share of the business.

'He brought me here to live with him to make it easier to take these things.'

There was contempt in Ben's voice. 'Mick is a thief and a conman and every other sort of villain. My mother should never have married him. Look what he's doing to her, turning her into a bag of nerves.'

'He was belting her last night,' Ellie said. 'I heard him, they woke me up. Why does she stay with him?'

'Search me.'

Ben went to his bedroom and switched on the light. Roy and Dougie had been put to bed an hour earlier and both were fast asleep. Ellie followed him to the door.

'I don't want to stay in this place.'

'Neither do I, but we don't have much choice, do we?'

'I could live with Auntie Connie. I'm sure she'd have me. Will you give me fourpence for bus fares so I can go and see her?'

'No.'

'Why not? You're working, I'll pay you back when I can.'

Ben lay down on his bed. 'I get paid twelve shillings a week but I'm only allowed to keep one shilling pocket money. Mick makes me pay over the rest to Mam to feed and clothe me.'

'Tuppence then, just tuppence to get there.' She could see by his face, he wasn't willing.

'It's too soon,' Ben said. 'He'd bring you straight back. He'll want your grandmother's will forgotten before he lets you go. When that's ancient history perhaps.'

Ellie knew she'd have to live here for the time being and she'd have to accept that.

'You're making yourself too useful, doing too much cleaning and cooking,' he told her.

'Your mother won't do it, she makes me.'

'Nobody can make you do what you don't want.'

Ellie was surprised. Ben usually took his mother's side.

'My mother can't manage things like she used to,' he said stiffly. 'Mick's making her like this. He's driving her dotty.'

Chapter Ten

Ellie had always looked forward to the weekends. Gran and Connie had made them enjoyable. Now when she came downstairs on a Saturday morning, Wilma had jobs lined up for her to do.

'The kitchen needs a spring clean. I want you to wash all the shelves down, including those in the food cupboard and meat safe. The larder too, and there's a lot of empty bottles and jars that could be put in the bin.'

Ellie thought Auntie Wilma lazy. She liked to lie back on her armchair and stare into the fire. But she didn't dare say so, Ben wouldn't hear a word against his mother. To him, she was as much Mick's victim as he was.

When Wilma took the younger boys shopping, Ellie started on the tasks she'd been set. Under the shelves of the larder she unearthed several boxes half filled with onion skins and soil from potatoes. Behind those were a lot of bottles and old newspapers, and also three two-pound jars that had held jam. The sticky remains were still inside. She washed them out.

When her aunt returned, Ellie helped her put the shopping away on clean shelves, and asked, 'Do you want to keep any of these jars? Gran kept them for when she made jam.'

Wilma was irritable. 'Get rid of them, I said. I don't make jam. The stove doesn't look much better.'

'I haven't done that yet.'

Ellie took the three jam jars out to the bin in the yard, but left them beside it. She knew some grocery shops paid a halfpenny on each jar if they were returned. As soon as she'd finished, she put the jars in a carrier bag and took them back to the grocer's on New Ferry Road where she thought they'd been bought. She felt a shiver of triumph when she was handed three ha'pence for them. She'd seen another similar jar on the pantry shelf, still half full of plum jam. She'd bide her time and return that one too, then she'd be able to go to see Auntie Connie.

It took another three weeks, because Auntie Wilma bought a jar of blackcurrant jam, and the plum was largely forgotten by the boys. Ellie ate as much of it as she could to use it up.

When at last she had enough money for the single bus journey, she decided to go one Sunday afternoon. Auntie Connie would lend her the return fare. She felt alight with anticipation as she set off, but by the time she was walking down Harcourt Street there was a lump the size of an egg in her throat. It was all so achingly familiar. Gran didn't seem to be far away.

There were different curtains up in her old home, and the front door had been repainted deep green. Ellie turned her face away as she passed.

She let the knocker fall on Connie's front door, and a moment later, her quick footfall was coming along the hall. Connie squealed with delight when she saw her.

'Oh, Ellie!' She threw her arms round her, hugging her on the doorstep. 'Come in. How are you?'

Vito was there beside her, patting Ellie on the back. She sobbed a little on Connie's shoulder.

'We've missed you, love. You used to be in and out of this house all the time. You and your gran.'

Such a welcome made Ellie feel she'd come home. Nothing had changed here. The scent of Sunday dinner was still heavy in the air. The remains of a large joint of beef stood on top of the stove. Connie was putting the kettle on. 'A cup of tea and a piece of my home-made cake? Yes?'

Franco came running downstairs. 'Ellie, hello. I thought I could hear your voice.'

He was smartly dressed in new grey flannels and a navy blazer, and he'd put a gloss on his dark wavy hair with Brylcreem. He pushed his feet into shoes he dragged out from under an armchair. 'How are you getting on? D'you like your new school?'

'No, I hate it. Wish I was back here.'

'Oh! What a shame!' He grimaced. 'Rotten luck, Ellie.'

'I miss you all. And Gran too.' Ellie was blinking hard to keep the tears back.

'Got to run, I'm afraid. Late already. Bye, Ellie.'

It left her shivering with disappointment.

'He's got a new girlfriend,' his father said. 'Rushing off to meet her now.'

'Her name's Pat,' Connie added, putting a cup of tea in front of Ellie. 'She works in an office. I don't know what they see in our Franco.'

'He's handsome.' He seemed to be growing more handsome as he got older. Ellie had hoped he'd be here to talk to her this afternoon.

'Don't let him hear you say that,' Connie laughed. 'He thinks he's a real swell now.'

'Done up like a dog's dinner,' his father scoffed. 'Did you see his straw boater?'

'He's changed his job again, he's on the milk now.'

'Delivering milk?'

'Yes, he has to be at work by five, but he hates getting up in the mornings.'

'He'd be able to get up, if he went to bed at a reasonable time,' his father said. 'It was past one o'clock last night when he came in.'

'Didn't I always moan to Bridie about him? We never know what he's up to. The most unpredictable of our sons.'

Connie and Vito insisted she stay and have her evening meal with them. They asked how she was getting on with her uncle and whether he'd shown her Bridie's will. Ellie told them how difficult she'd found it to get the bus fare to come and see them.

'I'm sorry things turned out like this,' Connie said, and looked so near to tears that Ellie couldn't hold her own back. 'You can come and live with us any time you want. I wish you could stay now.'

She told them what Ben had said about Mick taking her straight back.

'He thinks we could cause trouble for him,' Vito sighed.

Ellie had so much to talk about, and they made her so welcome that it was getting late when she said, 'I thought I'd go up to Flaybrick Cemetery while I'm up this end of town. If Gran's watching she'll think I've forgotten her already.'

Connie patted her arm. 'Goodness knows what she'll think of me.'

'You put flowers on Bridie's grave not so long ago,' Vito reminded her.

'Yes, I'm keeping it tidy. I go up to put flowers on little Maria Clara's grave, you see.'

When it was time for Ellie to catch the bus back, Vito slipped a half crown in her hand and told her to come again next Sunday.

'I'd like to,' she said, not wanting to leave now. 'Thank you.'

'I'll get some flowers,' Connie kissed her, 'and we'll go up to Flaybrick Cemetery together. All right?'

Connie saw Ellie out of the front door and went slowly back to the living room. Vito was raking the ash from the fire.

She was upset. 'I wish we could have Ellie here. I miss her as much as Bridie.'

'You mustn't blame yourself.'

'But I feel so guilty. Ellie's not happy there. She's not being treated right. Bridie never intended it.'

'How d'you think I feel?' Vito frowned. 'A crass coward. We've left the poor *bambina* to his tender mercies.'

'I'm frightened of him,' Connie admitted. 'Mick Valentino's a bully.'

'He's a thug, but I should have stood up to him. I was less of a man than I ought to have been.'

'You're gentle and kind,' Connie said, 'not a fighter. I'd rather have you the way you are. Why does he want Ellie? That's what I don't understand.'

'From what she says, they're using her. She's another pair of hands about the house, isn't she? But I'm afraid it's her inheritance he wanted,' Vito said.

'Bridie did have a little nest egg in the bank she meant to leave her. You remember how she kept on about Mick taking Orla's share of the business?'

'We ought to be ashamed of ourselves,' he sighed. 'We turned our backs on her, left her to cope on her own – and at a time when she was upset because of Bridie's death.'

'Mick is her closest relative, her only relative as far as we know. How can we fight him? And he said he'd banked her money for her. He may have done. We could be maligning him.'

'Connie, Ellie said Wilma refused to give her money for bus fares. They didn't want her to come here. They didn't want us to know what was going on.'

'We'll make it up to her when we can. Get her to come more often. She's growing up, she'll be leaving school soon. Perhaps Mick would let her come and live with us then.'

'Why would he? He'll be pleased she can pay for her keep.'

The following week, Ellie went to the Baldinis' house after her Sunday dinner. When Connie let her in she showed her the generous bunch of chrysanthemums she had waiting for Gran, and the posy of mixed flowers for Maria Clara's little grave.

'I'll get my coat, Ellie. The sun's come out, we might as well walk up now while it's fine.'

Flaybrick Cemetery seemed enormous and for Ellie, it brought back sad memories of Gran's bleak funeral.

'Here we are,' Connie said. 'It's the seventh grave along on this side.'

Ellie walked up the path but didn't recognise it.

'The headstone's been put back now,' Connie told her. 'I had Bridie's name added and asked them to scrape the lichens off and polish it up.'

Ellie read the five names on the black marble headstone. They had all been re-gilded, but one stood out, demanding her attention.

Orla Grace Valentino, died June 10th, 1920, beloved daughter . . .

Ellie felt paralysed, she couldn't drag her gaze away. She whispered, 'I didn't know my mother was buried here! Gran never told me. Why did I never ask?'

'She used to come up here once a week.'

'Must have been while I was at school. She never

mentioned that either. I kept on at her, asking about Mam,' Ellie breathed. 'She wouldn't talk about her. For years I went on thinking she'd come back. It was only when Gran got rid of the double bed . . .'

'Bridie wouldn't talk about her to me, either. I tried, I thought it would help, that she wouldn't fret so much if she got it off her chest. But she wouldn't or couldn't.'

'She must have said something, Auntie Connie.' Ellie shook her head. 'The night of that row in the bike shop. Mam came home in a terrible state, sort of dazed and bruised. She said she'd fallen but I think Uncle Mick hit her.'

'She told Bridie he had.'

'Did she? This is the first concrete fact . . .' Ellie shivered. She knew now how readily Mick would do that. 'Did he kill her?'

'Ellie!' Connie's face was full of compassion. 'No, your Gran took her to hospital the next day and she died there of a lung infection.'

'That's how she came to die on June the tenth? The row at the bike shop was in May.'

'Yes, May the twenty-ninth.'

Ellie groaned. 'All my life I've been haunted by it. To me, Mam just disappeared. I've always hankered to know more.'

'Bridie thought she was doing the best thing, love. You were only five.'

'But it left me with a thousand questions. What did happen that day, Auntie Connie?'

'Bridie said Orla had lashed out at Mick in return, but was confused about exactly how. She said she didn't remember picking up the starting handle, but it was assumed she'd attacked him with that. By the time the police questioned her she was too ill to say much more.'

Ellie's mind was in turmoil. 'You've told me more than anyone else,' she said, but it was all very upsetting.

There was a vase of dead flowers on the grave. Connie showed her where she could dispose of them and get fresh water. Ellie arranged the chrysanthemums they'd brought.

'Poor Gran.' The last engraving on the headstone read, *Bernadette Bridie Valentino departed this life on November 13th, 1928. Aged 79 years*. 'She'd had a hard life.'

'A widow for ten years.'

Ellie read the inscription for her grandfather: *Mario Valentino laid down his burden on the 18th January, 1918*. The first names on the stone read Patrick Luigi, aged eleven years, beloved son of Mario and Bridie Valentino, taken from this life March 3rd, 1886.

'He died of TB,' Connie murmured.

Ellie read on. 'And Orlando Niall aged 8 months, brother of the above, died December 18th, 1888.'

'Orlando died of whooping cough. The grave's full now, Ellie. No room now for any more of your family.'

On the bus home that evening, Ellie could think only of her mother. She knew a little more now about what had happened, but it had not lessened her hunger for facts. If anything she was more determined than ever to find out exactly what had happened that afternoon at the end of May.

Ellie's fourteenth birthday came at last. She'd not been able to settle at the new school, and had been counting the days until she could leave.

'Very sensible to leave straight away,' Uncle Mick agreed. 'A smart girl like you, you could get a good job. Would you like to work in a shop?'

Ellie had given a lot of thought to what she wanted. 'Yes, I'd love a job at Robbs. It's a lovely big department store and they sell beautiful clothes.'

Wilma shook her head. 'Not very practical. You'd have to get the bus into Birkenhead every morning. Fares would take a big chunk out of your wages and then there's the time it'd take. There's plenty of shops in New Ferry. I'll ask around for you.'

Auntie Wilma got her two interviews, one at Woolworths and one at the Maypole. The Maypole was one of a string of shops in the district selling dairy produce. Ellie would have preferred Woolworths, but the Maypole came up with a job offer first.

'It'll suit you to start there,' Auntie Wilma told her firmly. 'It's very handy, you can walk there in five minutes.'

Ellie left school on the Friday afternoon and started at the Maypole on the following Monday morning. She was apprehensive, not knowing quite what to expect, although she had been into the shop many times with Wilma's shopping list. The manager, Mr Duggan, gave her a white coat and cap with the Maypole badge on the front and told her to put them on. When she returned from the cloakroom, he pulled her cap down so it covered every hair on her head. Then he inspected her hands and nails for cleanliness and told her to make sure her shoes were always polished.

Then he led her into the shop. The white tiles on the walls and floor made it light and bright. There were counters round three walls, each with one or two bentwood chairs set ready for customers to use. It had an island in the centre, which was decorated with huge cheeses, whole hams and fancy pats of butter.

The manager said, 'You've a lot to learn. Always be alert to the needs of the customers and, above all, polite to them.'

Then he handed her over to Mr Owen who was in charge of the bacon counter. Her training was about to begin.

'To serve a customer,' he said, 'you've got to know the different cuts of bacon, and the difference between mild cured and smoked.'

Ellie tried to concentrate as he stabbed his finger at each white enamel tray in turn. 'Gammon, streaky, back, cut-through.' She didn't get them quite right when he asked her to repeat them.

'Cuts of boiling bacon now,' he went on. 'Corner, collar, cushion, hock. This is gammon and this shoulder.' She found that harder.

'Make sure you know them all. I'll test you again on Friday. And don't forget to learn the cheeses.'

He led her to a store room behind the shop. 'This is Alice,' he introduced. 'I'm going to hand you over to her. Alice,' he said. 'I want you to show Ellie round and explain her duties.'

'Yes, sir.' Alice wore her Maypole cap at a jaunty angle, showing a becoming amount of red hair. She yanked at Ellie's, pulling it back an inch. 'That's better. These caps make you look like a prison warder if you're not careful.' She laughed outright. Ellie was relieved. She felt more at ease with her than the men.

Alice was weighing out best New Zealand butter into pounds, half pounds and quarter pounds, from a huge bulk box of it.

'You can pat it into neat oblongs,' she told Ellie, demonstrating how it had to be done. 'Then we have to stamp the Maypole mark on it, like so, and put a piece of greaseproof paper under it, leaving the top on show. When it's bought, the paper is wrapped tight.'

It made Ellie's arms ache at first. 'You'll get used to it,' Alice laughed. She showed her how to make circular shapes to decorate the front of the counters.

That afternoon, she helped Alice unwrap whole cheeses, stick fresh labels on them and set them out in the shop.

They carried the cheeses that had been reduced by half or more, or that were crumbling or showed unsightly cuts back to the store room and Alice cut them up neatly into half-pound chunks.

'This one's Cheshire,' she beamed, stuffing a handful of cheese crumbs into her mouth. 'I like this. Write the weight and price on the label, and make sure they all have this "Cheshire" tag stuck on.'

Ellie chanted to herself, 'Stilton, Cheddar, Cheshire, Wensleydale, Derby, Leicester,' as she helped.

'We call this one Rat Trap,' Alice told her. 'It's the cheapest. Don't write anything but the price on that. If a customer asks you refer to it as "our popular-priced Cheddar".'

The shop opened at nine and closed at six in the evenings. After it closed for the day, everything had to be put away or covered and the counters and floors washed down. On Saturdays, it stayed open until nine at night, but on Thursdays it was early closing and the staff had a half day off.

Ellie was to be paid eight shillings and sixpence a week for working these hours. Auntie Wilma expected her to hand over seven shillings and sixpence and help about the house when she was at home.

Ellie liked Alice; she chatted almost non-stop. Ellie found she was less than a year older and had been working at the Maypole for nine months. 'It's all right,' she told her, 'once you get used to it.'

On her first half day, which turned out to be a very wet

afternoon, Alice suggested they go to the pictures to see Al Jolson in *The Jazz Singer*.

'It's showing at the Lyceum only a few doors along the road,' she said. 'Mustn't miss it, it's the first talking picture.'

Ellie wanted to see it, everybody did. 'I can't believe the talkies have come to New Ferry.'

'If you'd like to, we could go over to Liverpool and look round the shops next week,' Alice suggested. Ellie was glad to agree. She knew if she went home, Auntie Wilma would find some housework for her to do.

After the first week or so, she found Mr Owen on the bacon counter to be quite fatherly and Mr Duggan, the manager, kindly enough, but both were strict on cleanliness and hygiene.

Ellie found the shop hours long and the work hard, but she liked it better than school.

Ellie was pleased when Sunday mornings came round and she could have an extra hour in bed. She had to find time to clean her bedroom and wash her clothes, and Auntie Wilma always wanted her to peel the potatoes, prepare the vegetables and clear the dishes away afterwards.

Today Ben helped her. He counted Sunday dinner the best of the week and he wanted to go out as soon as he'd eaten. Ellie was finishing the washing up, when Uncle Mick put his head round the kitchen door.

'Take the boys to Sunday school, Ellie,' he said. 'Me and Wilma could do with an hour's rest.'

Ellie had heard the boys fighting in the hall. Despatching them to Sunday school was Mick's way of getting peace.

'I'll take them, but Auntie Connie's expecting me this afternoon.' It had become a regular Sunday outing for her.

'All right.' Auntie Wilma was wiping the boys' faces on

a flannel at the kitchen sink. 'Get their best coats for them, Ellie. You two, come straight home afterwards and get changed.'

On the way, Ellie held Dougie's hand and he walked quietly beside her. Roy kicked a tin can along in the gutter. Auntie Wilma had told her not to let him do that.

'You've got your best shoes on, Roy. Your mam will be cross if you scuff them.'

But Roy always wanted to kick anything he saw and he wouldn't stop. When they reached the church hall, other children were going in.

'In you go,' Ellie said.

'Bye,' Dougie called as he ran to join them.

'Don't want to,' Roy said mutinously.

'Auntie Wilma says—'

'I'm not going.' He was walking backwards, keeping out of her reach. 'I'll come with you.'

'No you won't, I'm not taking you.'

'I'll follow you.'

'You haven't got any money for the bus. Go to Sunday school, Roy.'

'I've got my collection penny.'

'You'll need more than that.'

'I'm sick of Sunday school.'

'Please go in, your mother—' Ellie stopped. Roy was running off in the opposite direction. She shrugged and turned towards the main road to catch her bus.

When she reached Connie's house, Franco was cleaning his shoes in the back yard, getting ready to go out again. She was disappointed, she wanted more of his company. He didn't seem to spend much time at home these days.

'Got yet another girlfriend,' Connie told her.

Vito snorted with disgust. 'He changes his girlfriends as often as he changes his job. They soon find out what he's like. He's more interested in having a good time than anything else. No responsibility. Not interested in doing a good job and getting promotion. No thought for the future.'

'He'll settle, sooner or later.'

'Connie, you've been saying that since he left school. I don't think he ever will.'

Ellie knew there was trouble as soon as she arrived back in Bicknell Street that night. She opened the back door and found the family crowded into the scullery. Ben was finishing a meal at the table and seemed unconcerned. Roy was snivelling over the sink in a state of undress as he washed himself. His parents were standing over him with faces like thunder.

Uncle Mick turned immediately on Ellie. 'I told you to take Roy to Sunday school.'

'I did,' she said. 'Dougie went in, but Roy refused.'

Roy was crying. 'I didn't feel like Sunday school. I wanted to go with her but she wouldn't take me.'

'He had no bus fare.'

'Look at his best coat: torn at the pocket and mud on the back – and his shoes! How did you get them like that, Roy?'

Wilma held them up. The heels were worn right down at the back and the uppers were badly scuffed. He wouldn't look at them. 'I don't know.'

'Of course you know. This isn't normal wear and tear.'

'Running—'

His father's palm slapped against his jaw. He let out a howl of pain.

'Don't play the fool. Where've you been? Where's he been, Ellie?'

She was apprehensive. 'He usually goes to play with Joey Morris and his gang.'

'Is that right?'

'Yes,' Roy muttered.

'What were you doing?'

'Nothing.'

'You can't have been doing nothing since two o'clock. You've only just come home.'

Ellie felt Uncle Mick's hand brush threateningly against her chin. 'Come on, you, what's he been doing? You were supposed to be looking after him.'

She had a sudden picture of what Mick had done to her mother and felt panic-stricken. It looked as though she was in trouble too. Her voice was little more than a whisper.

'Looks as though he's been using his shoes as brakes.'

Roy grabbed at the towel. 'Shut up, you,' he shouted.

Ellie said, 'His friend Joey has a home-made go-cart. I'd say, he's been going down a hill on that and dragging his feet to slow himself down.'

'That's it, isn't it?' His father slapped him again across his face. 'Your shoes are ruined and you've only had them two weeks.'

'We aren't made of money, you know.' His mother sounded mournful.

'You snitch,' Roy spat at Ellie. 'What are you trying to do? Make things worse for me?'

'You should have looked after him,' her uncle ranted at her. It felt as though they'd all turned against her. 'You'd no business to let him go off on his own.'

'How am I supposed to stop him?' Ellie was angry as well as terrified. 'He takes no notice of me. He goes his own sweet way, he's always off on his own. Anyway, he knows his way home.'

Wilma said, 'We've been worried stiff since Dougie came back without him . . .'

'Dougie can get home by himself.'

'He didn't know where Roy was, he thought he'd gone with you.'

'Why would I want to take him anywhere?' Ellie's voice was raised, she felt near to tears. 'Roy's nothing but trouble.'

She turned on her uncle. 'You told him to go to Sunday school, but if he won't do what you tell him, what makes you think he'll listen to me?'

Mick's angry face came close to hers. He ground out, 'Don't you dare speak to me like that.'

'It's your job to keep him in order, not mine.'

From the corner of her eye, Ellie saw him raising his arm. She knew what that meant and stepped back quickly. The blow swept past her and just clipped Roy's head. He let out a bellow of pain.

Ellie stood transfixed with horror, holding her breath. Uncle Mick was like an angry bull, pawing the ground. Menacingly, he moved closer.

Ben cleared his throat with a noisy rattle that made her glance at him. His face was telling her she must look after herself or Mick would half kill her. He was going to do that right now if she didn't speak up. She took another step back and looked him in the eye.

'I'm not going to be knocked about by you. I'll be going round to the police station if you try to clout me again.'

He snorted with rage and made a grab at her arm. 'Don't you dare touch me.' She pushed him away. 'You beat my mother up, but I'm not going to let you do that to me.'

'So now you've got two of us to keep quiet.' Ben crashed his knife and fork down on his plate and sighed with satisfaction.

Mick swore through clenched teeth. 'You bitch! You'll not get away with this.'

Ellie felt her heart miss a beat. 'I'll go round to the police station and tell them about the cigarettes on top of Gran's wardrobe.' That stopped him in his tracks.

She went on quickly. 'Ben gave me a leg up to the loft the other day. To see the silver and other stuff you've hidden up there. Stuff you've stolen.'

Ben smiled. 'I can imagine the police crawling all over this place, digging out your loot. Can't you?'

'Ben!' Wilma was wide-eyed with shock. 'You mustn't do any such thing.' For the first time, Ellie realised she was afraid of Mick too.

There was complete silence. Uncle Mick had gone limp. 'That bastard son of yours, Wilma! I'd like to wring his neck.'

Ellie stood stock still. He turned to her. 'In future, miss, when I tell you to do something, that's what you do. If you can't, you come back here and let us know.'

Ellie knew it had worked for her too. She rushed upstairs to her room, threw herself across her bed and wept into the pillow. She'd done it, she'd got the better of Uncle Mick but she'd never get used to living here with his family.

Chapter Eleven

1931

Three years had gone past and Ellie was feeling more settled. Uncle Mick had not bought himself a house, they were still living in the same rented one. He had taken his family to Blackpool for a summer holiday two years in a row, but Ellie and Ben had been left behind.

Last year, he'd bought a car, a second-hand Hispano Suiza. 'It's a real sports car,' Mick boasted. 'Not like those stodgy Fords I used to sell.'

It was parked in the road outside their house when he wasn't out driving it. Ben and Ellie were not allowed in it. Roy loved it.

Ellie had heard him boast to his school friends that his father was related to the Hollywood film star Rudolph Valentino, who had died a few years earlier of peritonitis.

'He was a first cousin,' Roy said. 'My dad inherited a small fortune from him.'

Everybody remembered Rudolph Valentino. Half the population had mourned his passing at the age of thirty-one. They believed Roy; the car was proof, wasn't it?

'Aren't you lucky?' they chorused. 'A grand car like that!'

'No,' he'd replied. 'He was sending for me to join him in Hollywood. I'd be a film star too by now.'

But Uncle Mick crashed the car one Saturday night on the way home from a public house in the town centre, putting Auntie Wilma in hospital for a month. Suddenly it seemed their years of affluence were over. He was sacked from the bus sheds and the family reduced to living on the dole, plus what he earned from selling the goods he stole.

Ellie and Ben had had their own problems. From time to time, Ben whispered that the loft had been cleared, and while there was nothing incriminating in the house, they must be careful to keep on the right side of Mick. Usually, within a week or so, more goods were stored in the loft and they had their safety net again. Then last year, the loft was cleared and remained empty.

One night, Mick ordered Ellie to make him a ham sandwich. She went to the scullery and found Ben just swallowing the last of the ham. Mick heard them talking and came in.

'You greedy brat.' His flying fist surprised Ben, catching him across the jaw. The force of it banged his head against the wall. Ben made the mistake of trying to land a punch on Mick and got a good hiding.

'I've got you kids where I want you now,' Mick gloated. 'Go to the police if you want to. They'll find nothing here.'

Scared stiff, Ellie pressed herself back against the sink, watching them. He turned on her. 'Make it cheese and pickle. And you, Ben, leave the ham alone in future. It's not for the likes of you.'

While Ellie cut the bread, Ben bathed his face in cold water. 'He's hiding his stuff somewhere else,' he muttered, 'worse luck.'

After that, Ben took some blankets to the wash house and sometimes slept out there to stay out of Mick's way. Ellie crept about the house trying not to incur his wrath, but sometimes did.

It was six months before she was woken in the night and heard more goods being put up in the loft. Ben was all smiles in the morning, and she felt mightily relieved.

It had taken her some time to find her feet at the Maypole, but after three years she was very happy there.

Both the manager and Mr Owen on the bacon counter praised her polite efficiency with customers. She'd learned to collect their purchases on the counter in front of them, and tot up the bill quickly. She was no longer the most junior member of staff. They had a new delivery boy called Ernie and a girl called Sally to help behind the counters. Ellie had been asked to show them the ropes.

She and Alice continued to go out together on Thursday afternoons. Alice always had plenty to tell her about her boyfriend Graham, who took her out every Sunday.

Ellie spent her Sundays with Connie and Vito, usually having her evening meal with them. Connie provided comfort, and her house seemed a refuge.

One of the delivery boys asked Ellie out, but she preferred Alice's company on Thursdays and the Baldinis' on Sundays. When he asked her if she already had a boyfriend she had to admit that she did not, but she thought of Franco.

She was thinking of him more and more, but was seeing less of him than she would have liked. His parents still complained about his behaviour and said he was getting worse not better. He often stayed out very late at night and woke them up when he came in.

Ellie had some sympathy for him. It seemed he could do nothing to please them. On the rare occasions when she found him at home, she would tell him how she spent her time at the Maypole, about Alice, and her life in Bicknell Street.

He listened carefully, giving her all his attention, recounting

181

anecdotes about his own job. His dark eyes had a direct and friendly gaze. Ellie thought she was falling in love with him, but she was afraid it was hopeless. Franco was seven years older than her, a man of the world now.

One hot summer Thursday, Ellie spent the morning serving in the shop feeling tantalised by the brilliant sunshine outside.

'I wish I was lying on the beach,' Alice whispered as she squeezed behind her to cut four ounces of cheddar with the wire. The manager refused to prop the shop door open even on a day like today, he said it let the flies and the dust in. The coats and caps of white drill were hot and heavy.

'What about going to New Brighton this afternoon?' Ellie whispered as Alice moved back.

'You bet, we'll have a paddle.'

'Pity we can't have a swim.'

Ellie didn't own a bathing costume but she was thinking of getting one. She bought her own clothes out of the money she was allowed to keep from her wages. She was pleased with the way they had increased over the years she'd worked.

She and Alice lived so close they usually went home in their dinner hour, but on Thursdays they brought a sandwich with them so they could go straight out. The shop sold packets of fancy biscuits to go with the cheese. Today, they bought one between them.

Ellie savoured the feeling of freedom as they crossed the road to the bus sheds where Mick used to work. She was wearing a new blue cotton dress and sandals and felt she was looking her best. It was lovely to go upstairs and ride on the front seat instead of having to work.

When they arrived, there were a lot of people strolling along New Brighton promenade on this fine day, and even swimmers in the Mersey estuary. The sun glinted on the water; sunbathers were stretched out on their towels, children were building sand castles.

'Let's have that paddle.' Alice was slipping off her sandals and running down the beach. Ellie felt truly happy, she was enjoying herself.

They sat on the sand, savouring the sights and sounds: the distant strains of Strauss waltzes from a band on the pier, dogs barking for balls to be thrown, children enjoying donkey rides. The river teemed with traffic; a passenger liner went past heading for Princes Dock. There were cargo ships of all sizes and the ferry boat came regularly to the end of the pier bringing more people. As the sun went down, a cool breeze came off the Irish Sea.

Alice dusted the sand off her feet and reached for her sandals.

'I'm hungry, let's get some chips.' They spent another half hour sitting on the prom eating them and had an ice cream each to follow.

'A gorgeous afternoon out,' Alice sighed with pleasure.

Ellie said, 'Let's not go home yet. We've hardly seen anything. I've never been to the fun fair.'

'I have. There's two here, one in the grounds of the tower and one inside that building over there.' She pointed to the other side of the prom. 'That's great on a wet day.'

'Shall we go to the tower grounds then?'

'Just to look. I want to save up for a dress like yours.'

It was fun to be in a crowd that was so obviously out to enjoy itself. They saw stands on which they could roll halfpence for prizes, others where they could throw rings on to hooks or darts at boards. For a while they stood watching men take aim in the shooting gallery, and saw a lucky winner receive a stuffed toy dog as a prize.

'We'd never win at that,' Alice said, pulling Ellie away.

'Why don't we treat ourselves to a ride on one of these roundabouts?' Ellie was keen. 'We could spare the cash for that, couldn't we?'

Alice agreed. 'Which looks the best?'

They walked round them all. Some were for children, some looked very exciting.

'The chairoplane,' Ellie decided as the hurdy-gurdy music blared out. They stood watching the double-seated chairs swing out on their chains while their occupants whooped and screamed with delight.

'Right ho.' Alice's toe was tapping to the beat. 'We'll go on this when it stops.'

At that moment, Ellie's eye was caught by a couple with their arms round each other. A second later, their chair swung up over her head. She was craning then, watching for it to come round again. Her breath came out in a shuddering gasp.

'Who's that?' Alice asked.

'Franco Baldini.'

She'd admitted to Alice that she liked him, but she'd said nothing about his girlfriends. This must be one of them. 'I told you about him.'

The couple swung behind the central pillar of the roundabout. Ellie was watching for them as they came back into view. It was Franco's dark head all right though she couldn't see his face, because he was kissing the girl who was clinging to him and screaming with delight.

The chairs were swinging lower as the ride came to an end. The girl was pretty. She was struggling to come up for air. Ellie had a glimpse of a lacy petticoat and a shapely leg.

'Come on,' Alice said, pulling her round to where a line of customers was waiting to get on the roundabout. Ellie was preparing herself to come face to face with Franco as he got off, she'd say hello and smile. But he handed over more coins to the operator and they stayed where they were for another turn.

She and Alice were only two chairs behind them, but he hadn't noticed her. All his attention was on his companion; his arm was round her shoulders, his head close to hers, his hand was going inside the low neckline of her dress.

'Wow,' Alice murmured beside her.

Ellie was touching a low ebb. She'd had a lovely afternoon until now. This was bringing home what Connie had been telling her. Franco was one for the girls.

'He is good looking,' Alice whispered. 'But you don't stand much chance there. He's besotted with the girl he's got. Do you know her?'

Ellie shook her head. Jealousy blasted through her, and she craved a chance to change places with that girl.

In bed that night, she thought hard about Franco. She knew she ought to put him right out of her mind but she couldn't. She was going to his home every Sunday, and his mother usually had plenty to say about him even if he wasn't there himself. She could stop going, of course, but the alternative was to stay at home with Ben and Auntie Wilma.

The following Sunday, she went as usual. It had been fine and warm all week but the morning felt sultry and there were heavy clouds. By early afternoon when Ellie was on the bus, there was thunder and she could see rain lashing across the park. A charity function was being held there today. The crowds were staying away and the tents and side shows looked forlorn in the wet.

She had her mackintosh but even so, she ran to the Baldinis' house when she got off. There was a big bunch of gladioli waiting on the hall table as well as the usual posy for Maria Clara's grave.

'I thought we'd go up to the cemetery,' Connie said, 'but look at the weather. We'd get soaked.'

'It could be just a heavy shower,' Vito said, turning back to his newspaper.

Connie was making a dress for herself. Ellie was helping her tack the pieces together when Franco threw open the back door and came in. He was soaked. Rain was dripping down his forehead. Ellie could see little beads of moisture on his hair; his Brylcreem didn't allow it to soak in.

Franco was in a bad mood. He'd left home at ten minutes to two to walk down to the main gates of the park to meet Sylvia Phillips. She'd seemed keen to see him again on a fourth date, though he'd felt he wasn't making much progress – she'd allowed nothing but a few kisses up to now. Franco found her attractive and saw her as a challenge.

This afternoon, there was to be a fund-raising event in the park for the local hospital. There would be side shows and competitions and brass bands playing.

'It'll be fun,' Sylvia had said, though he hadn't been all that keen to go.

It had been threatening rain when he'd set out to meet her, but it had come splashing down even before he got here. He'd waited at the main gate, trying to shelter under the arch, but so were many others and they were all being sprayed when a car went in.

He'd waited and waited, not sure whether his watch was right; it didn't keep very good time. He felt sure Sylvia was sheltering from this downpour somewhere close and she'd be along in a few minutes.

When his watch told him it was half past two, he decided

he'd waited long enough. Franco wasn't used to being stood up. He'd even bought two tickets for the show at the Argyle tonight. Perhaps he could get Doreen Withers to go with him instead?

He'd thought the rain was easing off when he set off home. He'd been wrong; the heavens had opened again and he'd been drenched. He felt very put out.

'Shake that blazer at the door, Franco,' his mother said when she saw him. 'Get the worst of the wet off before you bring it in. And change those flannels, they're wet too.'

'We thought you wouldn't be back till late,' his father said. 'What happened?'

'An absolute downpour. The do in the park got washed out.'

'I told you it was going to rain, the sky was black. You should have taken my mac when I offered it. Bet you were sorry you didn't.'

'Your mac's not fashionable,' Connie smiled. 'Too old. It would have ruined the smart effect of his blazer.'

His father's eyes surveyed him. 'The rain may have ruined it for ever.'

'I hope not.' Franco was concerned. He liked his blazer, he looked better in that than anything else. 'I buttoned it over my boater to keep that dry.'

'You've bent the brim,' Pa said unsympathetically.

Ellie set his hat on the sideboard, and piled the prayer and hymn books standing there on to the brim to flatten it. 'That should do the trick.'

'Thank you, Ellie.'

He thought about her as he went upstairs to change his trousers. He knew she was seventeen but she looked nearer twelve. Her hair was held back from her face with a black velvet Alice band. It was darker than he remembered, pale brown now rather than golden, but it had a bronze sheen on it. She was tiny. Dainty, his mother said. Ellie was not quite five feet tall and very slightly built; she looked fragile. It wasn't just her size; she looked demure in a blue dress with a Peter Pan collar. She had a childlike prettiness, but she wasn't the kind of girl that usually caught his eye. She didn't look the sort who'd be good fun. But Ellie was different, he'd watched her grow up.

Although he was seven years older, his parents still treated him like a child. Every time they were displeased with him, they'd ask, 'When are you going to grow up?' His many bosses were of like mind, but he'd come a long way since leaving school.

He'd had to accept that the jobs he'd had were on the bottom rung of the ladder, and even at home he was the lowest in the pecking order.

But girls liked him. The men he'd worked with saw getting a girl as an accolade, something to be proud of, and he had no problem doing that. Almost always he got his girl. He had power over girls and women and very much enjoyed that. It confirmed his masculinity, proved his manhood. Even his mother thought men were superior, more powerful than women.

When he went downstairs again, Ellie was making a cup of tea. She was almost as much at home in their kitchen as he was. He felt at a loose end, didn't know how he was going to fill the rest of his day. 'How's life?' he asked her.

'All right.'

'You're still working at the Maypole?'

'Yes.' She was too quiet for his taste, she volunteered little.

'Don't you hanker for a change, a more exciting job?'

'I like it there now I'm used to it.' She turned her huge amber eyes on him, as though seeking his protection.

'Better that way,' his mother said. 'Nobody but you wants to chop and change.'

'If you've nothing better to do when you've had that tea,' his father said, 'you could do a job for me.'

'What?' Franco asked suspiciously. There was always something that needed doing at the caff.

'The rain's stopped now, you could take some new crockery down for me. There's a crateful of cups here, more than we could carry all at once.'

That seemed simple enough. 'And?'

'They'll have to be washed before they're used, and the shelves need washing down.' That was more like it, they were always trying to rope him in to help.

'How about it, Ellie?' he asked. She was the sort who always waited to be asked to join in. 'Will you come too and give me a hand?'

'Yes, I'd be glad to. But what about the flowers?'

'Franco can go up to the cemetery with you. You could do that first.'

The smile that lit up her face surprised him. 'Will you?' she asked.

Poor kid, he felt sorry for her and knew all his family did.

Going up to Flaybrick on the bus was a bit of a bore. He refused to walk and felt he had to pay her fare. She'd brought a bag with a trowel and a hand fork and expected him to pull up tufts of grass and weeds from Bridie's grave. It was all sticky mud after the rain. Ellie would have stayed half the afternoon if he'd let her.

When they finally got the crockery down to the caff, he was surprised to see her put on an apron and set to at the sink. Nothing childlike about that. They'd done what was asked of them in no time, but she carried on scouring everything in sight.

'Come on,' he said. 'Leave that, we'll treat ourselves to an ice cream while we're here. We've earned it. What sort d'you fancy?'

She was not the first girl he'd brought here while the caff was closed, he had a key so he could get in whenever he wanted to. It was very handy to be able to offer ice cream as a lure and have a private place to bring his girls.

There was a room behind the kitchen, which was used partly as a store room and partly as an office. It was equipped with an old desk but had a warm rug on the floor and even a cushion that was usually used on the chair. He'd had a few sexual adventures in there, not that he'd get any of that with Ellie. She was different, his parents treated her like the daughter they'd never had.

'How are you getting on with your Uncle Mick?'

'I'm not. Can't stand cousin Roy either, he's a pain in the neck, always causing trouble.'

That made him smile. If he asked about something, she told him with transparent honesty.

'I've got a couple of tickets for a special show at the Argyle tonight. Would you like to come with me?'

Her face lit up again. Why had he thought she looked childlike? 'It's to raise funds for the General Hospital. There's a lot of big names all doing their acts free.'

'I'd love to,' she breathed.

'Right, we'd better have something more to eat than ice cream then.'

'What about getting home? Auntie Wilma will be cross if I'm late.'

'I'll come with you if there's time to catch a bus back. I'll tell them where we've been.'

'Would you do that for me?' Her big eyes gazed up into his with wholesome innocence.

'Of course.'

After he'd made scrambled eggs on toast and they'd finished off with coffee and two helpings of ice cream, Ellie helped him wash up the dishes. He always did that so as to leave no evidence.

There was still more than an hour to spare before they needed to leave for the show, and on the pretext of showing her how the store room had been rearranged, he got her in there.

He kissed her because it was what he did to all his girlfriends, and was surprised to find how warmly she responded and how attractive he found her hard thin body.

Franco acknowledged that for most girls his intentions were not honourable. His whole aim was to get them down on the rug by the desk and make love to them. But he couldn't do that to little Ellie. For one thing, it would be too easy. He could hardly count her as a conquest. For another, he'd been brought up to take care of her, protect her from the evils of the world. Not that making love was evil exactly, but he knew that if his parents found out he'd done that to Ellie, they'd kill him.

He reached for her coat. Safer for both of them to arrive early at the Argyle Theatre.

It had become a habit for Uncle Mick to walk round to the pub for a glass of beer before his Sunday dinner. One winter morning, Auntie Wilma went next door to see her neighbour, leaving Ellie to keep a watchful eye on the dinner as it cooked.

She was mooning around thinking about Franco, hoping she'd see him this afternoon. The aroma of cooking reminded her suddenly of the rice pudding Wilma had told her to take out of the stove when it was ready. She snatched open the oven door, knowing it should have been out twenty minutes ago. She was relieved to find she'd caught it in time.

From the moment last summer, when Franco had kissed her and taken her to the Argyle Theatre, she'd been living in a flurry of hope. Since then he'd taken her to New Brighton on the ferry on a cool wet autumn day, but that hadn't stopped her feeling absolutely lit up with the thrill of it.

Ellie couldn't get enough of him. She thought about him all the time. She felt much happier, more accepting of her lot, even of Uncle Mick and his family.

She wanted Franco to think of her in the way she thought of him, but instead, he seemed to be holding himself in check. He wasn't as relaxed with her as he used to be. Some Sundays, he'd already gone out when she arrived at Connie's and she didn't see him at all. Heavy with disappointment, she would have to wait another week before there was any chance of seeing him again.

Today the house was quiet, except for an occasional scurry from upstairs, where the boys were playing in their bedroom. Ben was hunched over the living-room table, absorbed in his alarm clock which he'd taken to pieces.

'I know it's old,' he murmured, 'but it's never let me down before.' It had stopped in the night, making him late for work the day before.

'Can't be too much wrong with it, probably just needs cleaning.' He'd done that in the scullery, making the smell of petrol vie with the scent of cooking. Now he was trying to put it together again.

The meal was almost ready. Ellie brought in the knives and forks.

'Your mam's going to be mad when she smells this.' Petrol had soaked into the old newspaper on which he'd laid out his clock parts.

'I'll burn it in a minute. Get rid of it,' he murmured. Ellie reached for the *News of the World*, pulled it in front of her and sat down to read for a few minutes.

There was a loud thump from upstairs but she took no notice. Suddenly Roy crashed into the room and pushed his face close to hers.

'Look what I've found.' He put a cardboard box on the table in front of her.

'What is it?' Ellie was more interested in the Sunday paper.

'You'll love these cuttings, they're all about your mother.' Roy's eyes glittered with spite.

With a thudding heart, Ellie pulled the cardboard box closer. It was half full of yellowing newspaper cuttings covered with dust.

'They're all about how she attacked my dad and nearly killed him.' Roy was gloating, she could see it on his face. 'I always knew she'd done something terrible. These prove it. Go on, read them.'

'Don't,' Ben said urgently. He was on his feet, the clock forgotten. 'Give them to me.'

'No.' Ellie picked out the top one. The strength was draining from her knees as she read the headline.

ORLA VALENTINO DIES

Orla Valentino dies while her brother recovers from his injuries. He was found with wounds on the back of his head, lying on the floor of the bike shop they owned jointly.

'If your mam hadn't died, she'd have been done for murder,' Roy spat at her.

'He murdered her, more like.'

193

'No, she hit him on the back of his head. He must have been walking away from her.'

Tears were glazing her eyes and shimmered between her and the print. She could read no more.

'Ha ha, your mother tried to murder my dad, but she failed. Instead, he got her.'

Ellie lashed out at him. The slap rang round the room a second before he began to scream.

'Ellie! Good for you,' Ben said. 'Serves you right, you little brat.'

Dougie came in clutching a toy train. 'What's happened?'

Moments later, Ellie heard the back door open as Wilma returned. 'What's all this, Ellie? What are you doing?'

'She hit me,' Roy screamed.

She was shocked to find she was becoming more like them. She'd never dared do that before, though she'd seen both his parents lay into Roy when they were angry. 'He goaded me. He said my mother tried to kill Uncle Mick.'

'So she did, it's all written here.' Roy's cheek was scarlet where she'd slapped him.

'He asked for what he got,' Ben said. He was concentrating on his clock again.

Wilma rushed to the table. 'Roy! Where did you get these?'

His belligerence going, he turned sulky. 'Under your bed.'

'Under my bed? What were you looking for?'

'Just looking,' he mumbled.

'Christmas presents,' Ben said.

'You're looking to see what we've got for you?' At that moment she caught sight of the train Dougie was hugging to him and snatched it away. 'You naughty boys! You don't deserve any presents, either of you.'

Dougie began to cry. Roy muttered, 'Don't care.'

'You will when Christmas comes. You've no business to go poking round my bedroom when I turn my back.'

She made a move to take away the box of newspaper cuttings too.

'No.' Ellie sprang to her feet and gathered it to her. 'No, I want to read them.'

'Better if you don't.' For once there was compassion on Auntie Wilma's face. 'Give them to me.'

'No.' Ellie still felt in shock, as though this wasn't really taking place. 'If this is what happened to my mother, I want to know about it. I must be the only one who doesn't.'

Wilma said slowly, 'It was all over the papers at the time.'

'I was five. I couldn't read newspapers.'

Wilma tried to explain. 'Your Uncle Mick wanted to move with the times, turn the bicycle business into a garage. Your mother wanted it to stay as it was. He went ahead and ordered some motor bikes and then a car. Orla was always arguing about it, but one day she picked up the starting handle from the car and hit Mick on the back of the head with it. She knocked him unconscious.'

'He battered her first,' Ellie said. 'She came home, I saw her.'

'Better if it's forgotten.' Ben's blue eyes stared at Ellie. 'Take no notice, it's just Roy up to his monkey tricks again, stirring up trouble.'

'Trust you, Ben,' his mother said bitterly. 'Is there nothing in this house you don't know about?'

Ben said coldly, 'I haven't found any Christmas presents for me yet.'

That made Wilma scream out, 'You're enough to drive a saint to drink. All of you. I've had enough. Ben, get that rubbish off the table before Mick comes home. You're stinking the place out.'

Ellie felt sick. She fled upstairs to her bedroom hugging the box to her chest. Slamming the door, she sank down on her bed and tipped all the cuttings out.

Her hand was shaking as she smoothed out the top one.

Disaster for local family. After five days, Michael Valentino remains unconscious in hospital. His wife, Wilma, was in tears last night. She said, 'I'm afraid they're both going to die, and the family business will be without a manager.'

She found herself skimming through them trying to get at the facts as quickly as possible. There was nothing really new. Connie had told her about all this. She was reading the same words over and over.

Dougie's head came round her door to tell her dinner was on the table. 'Mam says you're to come and eat.'

'I don't want any dinner.' Ellie felt she'd never eat again. Newspaper articles from the days when it was happening made her see the facts from a different angle, drove them home.

Years ago, some boys in the park had shouted out something about her mother being a murderer. She hadn't really believed it. Murder seemed impossibly far fetched, something that happened in films. She'd run to Franco and he'd confirmed it was all lies.

He'd told Gran and Connie when they came home, and they too had said it was all lies. But this was what they meant. Mam had hit Mick on the back of the head with a starting handle. There had been times when she'd itched to hit out at him like that. It was a miracle that Ben hadn't laid him out before now.

Ellie couldn't make up her mind what to do. After five minutes, she bundled the newspaper cuttings into a bag, took her best coat from the wardrobe, and ran out to catch the bus. She knew where to find comfort, she wanted Connie Baldini.

Chapter Twelve

The journey seemed to take an age, and Ellie felt as though she was seeing the streets through a haze. She shivered as she walked down Harcourt Street, as though there was a block of ice in her stomach. When she knocked on the Baldinis' front door she heard footsteps coming and knew immediately it was Franco. He looked surprised to see her.

'Hello, Ellie? Ma and Pa are out. Didn't they tell you they'd been invited to Rolf and Bella's for their dinner today?'

Ellie felt herself sag. 'Oh goodness, yes! Your pa's cousins in Liverpool.'

'Well, some vague relatives.'

Connie had invited her to tea and told her they'd be back about five. Yesterday Ellie had bought flowers for Gran and Maria Clara and she'd planned to go to the cemetery first. 'I forgot.' She'd left the flowers at home. Tears were burning her eyes, and she felt wretched.

'What's the matter? Come in.' He pulled her into the hall and pushed the door shut behind her. She took a step closer and put her head on his shoulder, the tears flooding out.

'What's happened, Ellie?' His arms came round her in a comforting hug.

He urged her into the kitchen. 'I'm sorry Ma's out. How can I help? I'll put the kettle on.'

'Your mother said you were invited too.'

'I was, but I came in late last night. Wasn't out of bed when they were leaving. Ma was cross with me. She was going to tell them I'd follow on.'

Ellie was pulling herself to her feet again. 'It's time you went—'

'No.' He pushed her back on the chair. 'It's already too late, they'll have started to eat. Tell me what's happened.'

'This.' She emptied the bag of old newspaper cuttings on to the table. Some fluttered to the floor. 'They're about my mother. They say she struck Uncle Mick on the back of his head and knocked him unconscious. Roy said she'd have been charged with attempted murder if she hadn't died.'

'Oh!' There was a strange look on his face.

It made her ask: 'Did you know all this?' He was tipping boiling water into the teapot. 'You did, didn't you?'

'Yes.' His dark eyes met hers straight on.

'How did you find out?' She felt anxious now. 'How . . . ?'

'I've always known.'

'What! I asked you, years ago. Some boys shouted after me in the park that my mother was a—'

'I know, I remember.'

'I ran back here, you were the only one at home then.'

'Mm, when your Uncle Mick was in prison for beating up one of his customers.'

She wanted to pummel her fists on him. 'Why didn't you tell me this? You said they were making it up, it was all lies.'

She was growing more like Mick. It took effort to resist using her fists. 'You told me to take no notice, I believed you.'

Franco caught at her wrists and pushed her back on the chair. 'Ellie, sit down and listen to me. Yes, I knew all about this at the time, we all did and kept it from you. You were only five.'

'But I asked you outright. I wasn't five then, I was . . .' She couldn't remember how old she'd been.

'Eleven or so,' he told her. 'The papers raked it up again, they called your family the fighting Valentinos. Yes, I tried to play it down, gloss over it, because I thought that's what Bridie wanted. She didn't want you to know, she was afraid it would prey on your mind.'

Ellie was calmer. 'I believed you. I really believed you.'

'You wanted to believe me, Ellie. That's what Pa said.'

Perhaps she had. 'To believe you made everything all right again.'

'Yes, that's it exactly.' She could see Franco straightening his lips. 'But there's more to it than what the newspapers said. That's not the whole story.'

'What d'you mean?'

'I'm not sure I should be telling you this. I've never told anybody . . .'

'Go on,' she said, 'you're making me curious.'

'D'you remember being in the car with me and Carlo that afternoon?'

'Yes.'

'I never mentioned it again, I thought you'd have forgotten. You were only five.'

'I remember being there with you. But when Mam was so ill, all that went out of my mind. I didn't realise . . . we must have been there at the time Uncle Mick was . . . It only occurred to me more recently . . . Franco, what did happen?'

'Wilma saw us, well you know that, but when Mick came out of hospital he threatened me and Carlo.'

'Threatened you with what?'

'To beat us up, thrash us if we opened our mouths about being there. He seems to think we saw more than we did, that we witnessed something important.'

Ellie gave rapt attention to all he was telling her. 'We heard them arguing.'

'Fighting more like. They were kicking up a racket. We told you to stay by the car, but we crept forward to take a look.'

'What did you see?'

He frowned. 'That's the silly thing, nothing that wasn't reported in the papers.'

'But what?' Ellie insisted.

'We saw your mam struggling to her feet. We saw Mick lying on the floor bleeding. We both thought he was dead, that's why we ran like hares, we wanted to get away.'

Ellie gasped. 'I didn't know . . .'

'When Mick threatened us, I was sure he must have good reason, that there must be more to it than we know.'

'You don't think my mam hit him then?'

'I don't know what to think, Ellie.'

'You should have told the police. Perhaps if you had . . .'

'I know, I wanted to and I'm very sorry I didn't. Carlo was against it. We had a big row about whether we should. You see, I'd bunked off school and Carlo had told Ma he was sick, so we could go to see some cycle race through Liverpool. We'd have had to admit to telling lies . . .'

'Yes, but . . .'

'I was a coward, Ellie.' He shrugged. 'You might as well know.'

'You were only twelve.'

'Yes, and Carlo was sixteen. I was banking on him getting the blame if it ever came out.'

Ellie shook her head. 'You are a dope, Franco.'

'It's been on my conscience for years. Your Uncle Mick terrified our Carlo. I do believe that's why he wanted to go to Milan. He wanted go where your Uncle Mick couldn't reach him.'

'Honest? Losing Carlo really upset your mam.'

'What happened that afternoon upset us all in one way or another.'

'Me included,' Ellie sighed. 'It's hard to face.'

'But easier now you're grown up.' Franco's eyes were full of sympathy.

Ellie was frowning. 'At eleven I was still thinking like a child. I couldn't take in what they were telling me. Couldn't see that anything so horrible could be true.'

She thought of those long ago days. 'Such a long time ago. You seemed grown up to me then. When Gran left me with your mother, she sometimes got you to take me to the caff for an ice cream. You used to hold my hand.'

'Orders from Ma, not to let you get run over.'

'You towered over me.'

'Still do.'

She managed a wavering smile. 'Now, I feel I've caught you up. We're both young but grown up. Equals now.'

Franco said gently, 'That's right. All this happened years ago, Ellie. The world's forgotten it. You must put it behind you.'

'I can't.'

'What I was going to say was, you mustn't let this spoil things for you now. You're doing well, holding down a job, you've got friends . . .' Ellie felt his arms tighten round her. 'Don't let this knock you down.'

Tears were prickling her eyes, and she put her head down on his shoulder to hide them.

'You've got to be strong. Come on, Ellie, I know you look as though a breath of air would bowl you over, but you are strong. Not many kids could have looked after their gran the way you did. You've got your feet on the ground, you're very strong minded. If you weren't, you wouldn't have been able to weather the kicks you've taken so far.'

Ellie sighed, then got up to rinse her face in cold water at the sink. Franco was pouring out two cups of tea. 'I'm hungry,' he said. 'Missing my Sunday dinner now.'

'So am I. I didn't stay to eat mine.'

'Let's see what there is.' He opened the larder door. 'A bit of salami, enough for a sandwich, d'you fancy that? Some broth? That's more like it.' He lit the gas under the pan. 'We'll have both.'

He was cutting bread. Feeling better, Ellie started spreading butter on the slices.

'Your gran,' he said, 'was worried about the effect it would have on you. You weren't much more than a toddler, and she was afraid it would ruin everything for you, prey on your mind for the rest of your life.

'She had your well being at heart, Ellie. We all did. It would have been awful for you when you were five.'

'Still is.'

'How could it be otherwise? But how could your gran tell you then?'

Ellie's head was spinning. She had to get the events straight in her mind. She put the newspaper cuttings in date order, so she could piece the story together. She read through them carefully. So did he.

'They reckon Uncle Mick hit Mam.' Not difficult to believe that. 'She tried to retaliate and hit him with the starting handle, knocking him unconscious.' Hadn't she learned to use her fists more since she'd lived with him?

'Except Mick seems to read something more into it.'

'That's a comfort for me to hold on to.'

'Yes, but it was Orla who died when everybody expected it would be Mick. At the time, everybody was talking about it, at home, at the caff and at school.'

'I didn't hear so much as a whisper.'

'I was ordered to keep my mouth shut. I'd have been flattened if I hadn't.'

He was right. Ellie could see that Gran couldn't have told her when she was five. Understanding that and talking it through with Franco was drawing him closer. She felt very much in love with him.

He said gently, 'We should have broken it to you as you grew older. Perhaps it would have softened the blow. But no time would have seemed quite right, would it?'

'Once Gran became ill, she hadn't the energy to think of things like this.'

'Don't let this break you, Ellie.'

On a surge of compassion, Franco reached for Ellie's hand. He wanted to look after her, help her, she was having a rotten time. Things had never been easy for her.

If her mother had died of natural causes when she was five, it would have been awful, but as it was . . . He felt churned up after re-reading all those newspaper reports about Orla. Ellie must be feeling worse.

He had a date with Sibyl Williams tonight, but he couldn't just put Ellie out on her own, not in her present state.

'We'll go down to the caff for an ice cream,' he told her. 'I just want to scribble a note first.'

She followed him into the living room, watched him take an envelope and a sheet of notepaper from the sideboard drawer. 'Am I a nuisance to you? You want to be somewhere else?'

'No, Ellie. I want to be with you.'

Dear Sibyl, he wrote. *Terribly sorry, I can't make it tonight. Domestic crisis. Can we make it Tuesday instead?*

He licked down the flap on the envelope, sealing it firmly. He could push this through Sibyl's letterbox, it wouldn't be much out of their way.

'You need taking out of yourself, and a bit more fun in your life,' he told Ellie as he helped her into her coat. Outside, in the dark street, he put an arm round her waist and pulled her close. She needed a bit of comfort too, poor kid.

'Where are we going?'

'To the caff, like I said, but I want to put this note through a friend's door.'

'You were going to take somebody else out?' He could almost feel her insecurity. It made him lie: 'I was going for a drink with a friend – a bloke.'

The lights were on upstairs in Sibyl's house. She was probably doing herself up to come out with him. He'd been going steady with her for about eight weeks, she was all right. As luck would have it, there was a street lamp right in front of her house. He hoped she wouldn't look out and see him with Ellie.

Just in case, he dropped his arm from her waist as they drew close, and was glad when they were both out of that pool of light again.

The caff felt warm inside. 'I'm not going to put the light on in here,' he said, drawing her into the shop. 'We don't want customers knocking to buy ice cream for themselves.'

His parents would be coming home soon, and they'd definitely let themselves in to see what he was up to if they saw the lights on.

He scooped up two outsize helpings of chocolate and vanilla

in the half light coming from the kitchen, picked up the box of wafers and ushered Ellie into the store room behind. He placed the two chairs side by side so they could sit up to the desk to eat. With all the other lights off and the doors shut, he felt safe enough.

When he laid his spoon down, she was close enough to put his arm round her. He pulled her closer and she put her head on his shoulder.

'Your dad makes lovely ice cream.'

He kissed her. Her big amber eyes were looking into his. She looked like a little girl, but the manner in which she clung to him and returned his kisses was all woman. He hadn't imagined Ellie could possibly be like this.

To spend an hour kissing and fondling would relax her. He always found comfort in love making. He wouldn't go all the way with Ellie, of course. He mustn't. He slid down to the rug and pulled her with him. It was a technique he practised often. He expected her to protest, but she giggled. He pulled down the green cushions and tucked one under her head.

Ellie was skinny, there was nothing of her. Her body felt rock hard against his, but there was fire in her belly and she made no attempt to resist. He was as gentle as he could be and thought she enjoyed it, even this first time.

Franco felt so relaxed that he dozed for a short while afterwards with Ellie in his arms. He woke to find her still sleeping. He looked down on her innocent childish face and felt he'd taken advantage of her, that he'd done something very wrong. Particularly so when she'd been upset. He'd never felt like this after he'd seduced any other girl. He felt sorry for Ellie. She was stirring, so he bent over and kissed her lips and her eyes flickered open.

'I'm sorry,' he said, though he hadn't meant to apologise. 'I shouldn't have done that.'

She smiled up at him. 'I love you.'

It made him hug her. 'And I love you, Ellie.' He hadn't intended that either, it just came out. He wasn't sure he really did love her, not in that way.

'So there's no need to say you're sorry, is there?'

Franco was scrambling to his feet, pulling on his pants, feeling somewhat embarrassed.

'I meant to take you out, but it's too late to go anywhere now.' But they'd had a better time here than they would have had at the pictures. Still, he shouldn't have done it.

'Do you want me to take you to see Ma? She'll be home now. You can tell her about Roy pushing those cuttings at you this morning.' She was trying to tidy her hair with her hands.

'No, it's getting late, I'd better go home.' She glanced up at him shyly. 'You've made me feel better about it. Got over the first shock. Did I make a terrible fuss?'

'You were entitled to. I'll come with you, see you home.'

He could see she was pleased that he was prepared to put himself out for her. 'I'll come in with you if you like, talk to Wilma.'

'No, no need. I'll be all right.' Her smile wavered a little, and he thought she was being brave.

It was late when Franco got home that night. He'd forgotten what the Sunday bus service was like. He'd had to wait a long time and it had been bitterly cold. He was worried stiff. He should not have made love to Ellie. He'd done it on impulse and he hadn't had any French letters and she'd been a virgin. He had his way with lots of other girls without a second thought, but she was altogether different.

He'd got into trouble years ago for taking it upon him-self to comfort Ellie when she'd come looking for his mother. He'd done that again, and if that wasn't enough, he'd pro-bably be in trouble for not turning up at Pa's cousins' for his dinner.

His parents were waiting up for him. His father pounced before he'd closed the back door.

'Where did you get to? Rolf and Bella were expecting you. They kept the dinner waiting.'

'Yes, I'm sorry . . .'

Ma looked tired and drawn. 'What's all this?'

He'd forgotten they'd left the bag of newspaper cuttings hanging on the larder door.

'Ellie brought them. She came looking for you.'

'I told her we were going out.'

'She was upset, Ma, she forgot. Those are newspaper cuttings about her mother.'

Ma grimaced. '*Mamma mia!*'

'It came as a shock to her. I wish you'd been here . . . ' He truly did, he wouldn't have made love to her then. His con-science would have been clear. 'You'd have known what to say. Poor Ellie was looking for comfort.'

'I wish I had been. I'm sorry.'

Ma was apologising to him! He'd expected a rollicking from her.

'Ellie ran out of Mick's place just before dinner. Said she couldn't face it. I had to find something for her.'

'There was broth on the stove.'

'I found it. Ellie wasn't prepared, it hit her like a bombshell, she hadn't cottoned on.'

'I think she had really.' His father sighed. 'She just couldn't face it. Didn't want to face it.'

'She told me I'd convinced her it wasn't true. You remember, years ago?'

'How was she, when you left her?'

'Better . . .' He had comforted her, but . . .

'Her gran left a letter for her,' Pa said. 'To explain about her mother . . .'

Connie sighed. 'To comfort her too. I wish we'd been here, we could have given it to her.'

He said, 'I've arranged to take her to the pictures on Wednesday. I could take it to her then.'

'She'll be coming here next Sunday. You can tell her I've got it for her.'

Since Ellie had read the newspaper cuttings, horror had paralysed her mind, the word murderer stuck in her throat. She didn't dare think about Mam dying, only days after she'd been beaten up by Uncle Mick. She must have been in pain . . .

But now, on Monday morning, she felt she'd cope if she kept her mind on Franco Baldini. She'd loved him from the sidelines for a long time. As a result of those cuttings, they'd found their way to each other and were now in a full-blown love affair. He'd been so kind, so tender and his help had come at the right moment to keep her sane.

Agonising as those revelations had been, it had all happened years ago. All the secrets of her past were out in the open, she had nothing else to fear. As Franco had said, the world had long forgotten them.

With him, it was here and now and the future. She had Franco in her life. It made a huge difference.

She told Alice at the first opportunity when she got to work. It all came spilling out, how very much in love with him she felt.

'The bloke we saw in New Brighton last summer with another girl?'

'Yes, that's him.'

'Jolly good looking. What happened to her?'

'I don't know, didn't ask. It's me he loves now.'

On Wednesday evening, Ellie rushed home, ate her tea and went out to meet him.

It was drizzling, her mac was old and shabby, and she didn't feel she was looking her best. Although she was on time, he was already waiting for her just under cover on the steps of the Lyceum picture house. He had his back to her, studying the posters advertising the programme.

'Hello, Franco.'

He turned, putting out both hands to her. 'Hello. You look different tonight.' His dark eyes beamed down at her. 'Prettier.'

She wasn't sure that was true. She had such straight hair and the fashion was for curls. Ellie had put curlers in last night, but the damp air had made most of the curl drop out.

'You look more alive, more . . . Your eyes are dancing.'

'It's meeting you.' She took his arm.

He was telling her then, that his mother had a letter for her. 'Your gran asked her to give it to you when you found out. You know, about your mother.'

'Oh!' That brought the horror flooding back to Ellie. She still pined for Gran. 'What does it say?'

'It's sealed in an envelope. We don't know.'

She could feel him urging her up the steps. He smiled. 'It's Jean Harlow, in *Platinum Blonde*. Do you fancy it?'

'This letter, why didn't you bring it for me?'

'You know what Ma's like, she feels it's important. Doesn't trust me to do anything. She said I was to ask you to come early next Sunday and have your dinner with us.'

'That would be nice.'

'She wants to give it to you herself. She feels – well, you know, sorry that she wasn't there last Sunday when you needed her.'

'This letter . . .'

He smiled. 'D'you want to go and get it now?'

Ellie breathed a sigh of relief. 'I'll be wondering for days, about Mam . . . If there's anything else . . . Would you mind? You'll miss the film.'

'No. Come on then, there's a bus in the sheds now.'

Seated on the bus, Ellie said, 'You must think I'm a nut case. You offer to treat me to the pictures and I make you go back home.'

'Ma's been keeping it for years now, I suppose she thought another few days wouldn't matter. She thought it better if you were expecting it, that you'd be prepared.'

Franco took her in through the back door. Connie was just finishing the washing up and was surprised to see them.

'Can't wait till Sunday, Ma. Ellie wants her letter now.'

'Sorry . . .'

'Oh, Ellie.' Connie's arms went round her. 'Nobody seems to get things right for you. I should have known you'd want it. It's upstairs, I'll get it. Put the kettle on, Vito, we'll have a cup of tea.'

A minute or two later, Ellie was turning the envelope over. It was addressed to Miss Eleanor Jane Valentino in Gran's spidery handwriting. She was conscious of three pairs of eyes watching her as she slit it open. She told herself they were her friends, her support.

Dearest Ellie,

I hope you'll be grown up when you're reading this, but I've no way of knowing. For a long time, I've wanted to hold you and tell you what happened to your mother, and to the family, but there was never a right time to do it. There have been so many rumours and scandals about it, I want to set it down truthfully so you understand.

Today is my 78th birthday and I'm not in the best of health. Since I may not be with you for very much longer, this seems the best way for me to do it.

I understand how painful it is for a child to lose her mother when she's very young and dependent on her. My own mother died in childbirth when I was four, but my new brother survived. I'm told that I ignored him, pretended he didn't exist.

When I was five my father married again. He not only had me and the baby to think of, but two older brothers as well.

Try as I do, I can't remember anything of my life before my stepmother arrived on the scene. It's a blank space. I know only what my father and my brothers told me. As for Jack the baby, I never managed to conquer my resentment of him.

My older brothers were rebellious, we none of us got on very well with our stepmother, though she was a good woman and I'm sure did her best. I suppose we couldn't adjust, and longed for the comfort of the old days with our real mother. It made me realise how much worse it would be for you because of how your mother died and because you had no father to look after you.

But at least you had always lived with me and that didn't have to change. I wanted to cushion you from the heartache I went through at the same age, and did my best to take your mother's place.

My children have never got on together. There has always been a chasm between Orla and Mick. That he wanted to change the bicycle shop to a garage drove an outsize wedge between them.

You were five when the terrible crisis came. Orla told me several times that Mick went berserk that afternoon and lashed out at her. That he'd put his hands round her neck and tried to strangle her.

She said she'd tried to retaliate, to get back at him, but she was confused about exactly how. She didn't remember picking up the starting handle, but it was assumed she had. She was too ill to say more when questioned.

When she was admitted to hospital, she said she'd had an accident, that she'd slipped and fallen against a tandem in the bike shop the day before, and she'd had a pain in her side ever since.

That history, and Mick being unconscious with a wound in the back of his head, made the Coroner return a verdict of accidental death on Orla.

I fear your mother didn't want to say too much about what Mick did to her. At that stage, she probably thought the whole business would all blow over and there was no point in causing more trouble for the family.

I too found it hard to talk to the police about what my children had done or not done. There were marks on Orla's neck but they chose to ignore them. Mick was thought to be the victim. It was said that the blow came from the car's starting handle and it had been delivered by a woman with only moderate strength. Sometimes a blow on the skull doesn't take much strength to harm.

Where the blame lies isn't truly clear. But Orla died and Mick recovered. She'd have been charged with inflicting grievous bodily harm if she hadn't. I loved them both. They were my children and it was tragic for us all.

I wanted us to be a happy family, but we always had our difficulties. This last trouble split me in two.

In a way, I let an early tragedy spoil my life. It gave my older brothers and me a grievance. Your mother provided her own much greater tragedy, but the last thing she would have wanted was for that to ruin your life too. Of course it altered everything for you. I don't doubt you'd have had a happier childhood with her.

I've been fearful of the consequences to you, though none of it was your fault. I don't want your loss to affect you in the way that my loss affected me.

Remember always that I want you to put this behind you and grow up with a strong mind. Your mother loved you dearly, and I always will, you've been the light of my life. We want you to be strong and happy always.

For my part, I'm not unhappy at the thought of passing over to the other side. I long to see again all the members of my family who have gone before me, especially Mario and Orla.

I've done my best to write what's in my mind, but now it's down on paper I feel I haven't said half of what I feel.

Darling Ellie, all my love,

Your Gran

Franco was brimming with emotion. He was watching Ellie in tears now as she put the letter down. His mother's eyes were wet and Pa's voice had become gruff.

'Better to have a little cry now, *bambina*.' He was patting Ellie on her back. 'Your English stiff upper lip is no good.'

Ellie offered the letter to Connie to read.

'Are you sure you want me to? It's not private?'

'Gran wouldn't mind you reading it. Any of you. You were her friends.'

'Bridie would be proud of you now.'

Franco was almost in tears himself when he read it. Bridie had always been strict with him, but she'd been fair and he'd been fond of her.

'She's trying to make you strong,' he said.

'She doesn't want me to feel sorry for myself.' Ellie was struggling for composure. He sensed she'd want to get away now she'd read her letter.

'Can we go down to the caff for an ice cream, Pa? It's too late for the pictures now.'

Franco knew how to provide his own sort of comfort once they were alone there. He ended up making love to her again, though he hadn't meant to. At least he was organised with French letters this time.

As he walked Ellie to the bus stop afterwards, she said, 'Don't bother coming all the way back to New Ferry with me. It's not far to walk when I get off.'

Franco was relieved. He thought it hardly worth going all that way for a kiss and a cuddle in the back entry, especially after what he'd just had. He was afraid he was taking too much from Ellie and giving too little in return.

He asked, 'Would you like to see that film? We could go to the Lyceum tomorrow night.'

'I'd love to see you again tomorrow, but I can't,' Ellie said. 'It's my half day off and I always go out with Alice, the girl I work with, on Thursday afternoons and we don't rush back. She's got a boyfriend but he works every afternoon like you. She says she can go out with him on other nights.'

Franco kissed her when the bus came and watched her go

inside alone. She looked vulnerable and he felt ashamed. Ellie was fair to everybody, but he was treating her as he did his other girlfriends. He decided he'd see Sibyl tomorrow, and no doubt he'd be taking her to the caff for ice cream too.

Chapter Thirteen

For Ellie, having Franco's love at this time was a lifeline. The Baldinis were her security, and she had never needed them more.

She was glad to be alone on the bus, because she wanted to think. She read through Gran's letter again feeling very moved by it. Despite the problems, Gran had given her a happy childhood. She would understand how she was feeling now.

Be strong, Gran had written. Franco had said she was already strong, but sometimes she felt as weak as the fluff on a dandelion head being blown about in the merest breeze. Put the past behind you, they'd advised, think of the future. She would, she had a life of her own now, she could make it what she wanted.

The bus turned into the terminus at New Ferry. Ellie got off and began walking to Uncle Mick's house. She was not happy about living there, but the cold terror she'd once felt for Mick was gone. Ben had shown her how to cope, she could survive. Things were easier now she was working and not totally dependent on her uncle for everything.

Mick was fond of his food and demanded not only the lion's share, but the titbits as well, but she couldn't say she'd ever gone hungry.

The younger children were petted and indulged, while she and Ben could do nothing right and were excluded from all treats. It was a house divided, and Ellie didn't like the way the family were always arguing, always shouting at the top of their voices. Sometimes Wilma screamed like an animal in pain, and these days one cross word from Mick would send her into a flood of tears. She seemed to spend a lot of time huddled on the armchair staring silently into the fire. Ben said he was afraid she was getting worse.

What Ellie really wanted was a fresh start. She wanted to leave Bicknell Street and find herself a room somewhere else. At break time at the Maypole the next day, she discussed this with Alice.

'Why not, if you aren't happy there? Course, you'd have to pay the commercial rate.'

'What's that likely to be?'

Alice reached for the newspaper Mr Owen had brought in. 'Board and lodgings, own room and packed lunch, £1 a week. Here's another for 18/6d, no mention of packed lunch though.'

'I give Auntie Wilma a pound anyway,' Ellie said. As her wages had gone up, so had her contribution to the household expenses.

'You might as well then. My mam takes ten shillings out of my pay. She says she doesn't want to skint me, she'd rather I saved a few shillings every week, and I have to buy my own clothes.'

Ellie reached for the paper. 'Where are these places?'

'Couldn't you lodge with your Italian friends?'

'They'd have me, Connie's told me. She said any time I wanted, but it would be a long way to come to work. Franco said the best thing would be to change my job, but I don't want to.'

'Oh no, don't do that. I don't want you to leave.'

'Most of these are box numbers . . .'

'Our Tom's getting married in June next year. His room will be free then. Shall I ask my mam if she'll take you as a lodger?'

'Would you?' Ellie brightened. She'd feel quite confident about moving if she could lodge with Alice's family. 'I'd like that. Tell her I'd be more than happy to pay the pound a week I pay now.'

Next morning, Alice said, 'I asked my mam about you lodging with us. She said most likely yes, if we still want it. I'll want it, of course, but it's a long time off and all Mam can think about is the wedding arrangements and getting her outfit together.'

The following Monday morning, Alice had news she couldn't wait to tell her. They were changing into their white coats.

'I'm engaged,' she laughed outright. 'Graham asked me to marry him. I'm thrilled.'

Ellie hugged her. She was feeling better, quite sure she and Franco were heading for marriage too. She'd had a lovely day with him yesterday and was meeting him again on Wednesday night. She'd told him several times how much she loved him and yesterday on that rug in the office, he'd whispered again that he loved her. She was longing for the moment when he'd get round to talking about the future.

'Of course, we'll have to wait,' Alice said regretfully. 'Graham wants us to save up for a couple of years first.'

'Two years will soon pass,' Ellie told her. 'At least you know what he wants and what you're aiming for.'

After being on her feet all day, Ellie was tired when she got home. That evening, it was almost eight o'clock by the time she'd eaten her tea and cleared up afterwards. Usually on Monday nights, she ironed the clothes she'd washed on Sunday.

The living-room grate was an old blackleaded range. In Victorian times when the house had been built, it would have been possible to cook on it, but the oven didn't get hot any more and it was used to air their washing.

She had to ask Mick to move his chair back so she could get at the oven. Ellie found it crammed tight with family clothes, and she began picking out her own things. Uncle Mick pulled out a couple of his shirts and tossed them at her.

'Now we've got an up-to-date electric iron, it won't take you many minutes,' Auntie Wilma said from her chair on the other side of the fire. She seemed brighter tonight.

Ellie bristled as she took out the electric bulb from the ceiling fixture over the scullery table and plugged in the iron.

'Last week, you forgot to iron the tablecloth, and you didn't do my green blouse properly,' Wilma complained, rattling the newspaper as she turned to another page. 'I had to put the iron on again.'

Roy was sailing his boat in the sink. He turned to watch Ellie fold an old blanket on to the table and start ironing one of her blouses. He began tossing through the pile she was about to iron.

'Where's my best shirt?' he asked. 'I want to wear it tomorrow. I'm going to a birthday party.' He let her nightdress fall on the floor. That annoyed her.

She said, as calmly as she could, 'If you want your clothes ironed, Roy, you can do them yourself when I've finished.'

'What?'

Ellie had made up her mind she wasn't going to be used as a household slave any longer. It was unreasonable to expect her to iron for the whole family.

'You're a big boy now. I loved to help Gran with the ironing when I was your age.'

222

'What's that?' Mick barked from the adjoining room.

'I was ironing until half past ten last Monday,' Ellie said.
'Wilma says it takes hardly any time with the new iron.'

'Then it wouldn't take her or Roy long either, and you all have more time here than I do.'

'You're always gadding off out,' Wilma complained.

'I'm entitled to a bit of time to myself when I come home from work. I'm not doing the family ironing in future.'

'Well I never,' Mick gasped. 'I never heard such cheek. Who do you think cooks and cleans for you?'

Now Ben had shown her how to deal with Uncle Mick, Ellie knew she'd get away with it. She told herself she had to toughen up, not worry about being shouted at.

Franco had been working as a painter and decorator for five months and was fed up with it. Mr Burns, his boss, was in business in a small way. Apart from himself, he employed his three sons, a friend of the family and also his nephew. Franco felt he was always given the worst jobs and was considered the least important worker on the team. Doing ceilings gave him neck ache, whether it was painting or papering.

Mr Burns had told him business was usually brisk in the weeks coming up to Christmas, but this year it hadn't been. Nobody would want their homes papered or painted during the holiday and they expected work to be slack afterwards. The boss told him he might have to lay him off.

On top of that, the wages were poor. Ma made him shell out ten shillings for his lodgings every week, and he liked to treat Sibyl. In fact, she expected it. She was always on the look out for presents for herself.

'That's a nice pair of gloves,' she'd say, pointing them out in a shop window, but she was good fun and well worth it.

Then he couldn't be mean with Ellie, though she expected little. She was a little straight-laced in her ways but there was adoration in her eyes when she looked at him. He liked that.

If it weren't for the free ice cream and cake he could treat them to, he didn't think he'd manage. He decided it was worth asking his boss for a rise.

'You're not much of a worker, lad,' Mr Burns said, surveying him gravely. He was a boss who was always watching. Franco could feel his eyes on his back as he worked, and he didn't like it.

He said, 'When I came to work for you, you promised to raise my pay after a few months. I can do everything you want now, you know I can. I've learned fast.'

His boss stroked his moustache. 'You don't put your back into anything, Franco. Not particular enough about your work. It's sloppy. You're too slow and you're always larking about.'

'Just another half crown,' Franco urged.

'You're not worth what I pay now. If you don't like it, you can lump it. There's plenty more who'd jump at the chance of working for me.'

Franco backed down, knowing that in the present depression, Mr Burns could be right. It was reported in the papers that there were millions out of work. He decided he'd better start looking for something else straight away. Painting and decorating was boring work, and at the same time it was back breaking. He'd like a job that was more fun, with less physical labour and which paid better.

Ellie helped to put up Christmas decorations in the shop. It was full of customers buying the special seasonal lines and they were all kept very busy, but the bosses were good humoured. Each member of staff was given a joint of ham as a gift. Ellie had already been invited to spend Christmas Day with the Baldinis, and she took hers there. She had a very nice time.

She kept Gran's letter in her handbag and took it out to read often. It was a comfort to her and it seemed to bring Gran closer. She felt she was coping, she'd get over this.

Three months into the new year, on a wet Monday morning, Ellie was taking off her hat and coat in the staff room behind the shop, when Alice came in. For once there was no colour in her face and she looked very down.

Ellie asked, 'Aren't you well?'

Alice's hand shot out and gripped her arm. 'Shush, I'll tell you later.' Her eyes went to the new girl nearby, who was buttoning up her white coat.

Ellie had no chance to speak to her alone until their ten-minute mid-morning break, which the staff took in turns. By then, she'd decided Alice was ill; she'd seen her shoot to the lavatory more than once and she seemed restless and ill at ease.

'What's the matter?' Ellie asked.

'I think . . . I was like this yesterday too. Really sick in the morning. I think I'm having a baby.'

Ellie could see her friend was panic-stricken. 'What makes you think that?'

'You little ninny.' Alice's hand gripped her arm again, her eyes wide with horror. 'Me and Graham, we do . . . you know what.'

Ellie froze, she understood. She and Franco were doing the same.

'I'm nearly four weeks late with my monthlies too . . .'

Ellie swallowed hard. She was a little late, but she was still counting it in days and living in hope. She didn't dare think of that.

'What are you going to do?'

'I haven't dared tell my mam yet. I'm terrified. We'll have to get married. We'll do it quietly in July after our Tom.'

'Well, you won't have to wait two years for it.'

'I'm excited about that,' Alice admitted. 'That's the good part. At least I'll have a husband by the time it's born.'

Ellie said nothing about her own fears. Seeing Alice in such a state had scared her stiff. Alice was right, she was a ninny not to have been worried about this before. She had mentioned it to Franco while she'd been on the rug with his arms around her.

'No, not at all likely,' he'd said with such confidence she'd believed him. 'I'm very careful, aren't I, with these French letters?'

But now the days were passing and Ellie was becoming more certain that she was in the same boat as Alice. On Sunday, she went to the Baldinis' house as usual, but she found Franco was on his way out.

'Terribly sorry, Ellie. Got to go. I'm meeting somebody who might be able to get me a job on the buses.'

She felt shocked. 'On a Sunday?'

She wanted to tell him, to have his reassurance that all would be well. She longed to hear him say he wanted to marry her, that it was what he'd always intended. They would have to do it a little sooner than they'd otherwise have done, that was all.

'His pa's a big noise in the Corporation. They run training programmes. Wouldn't it be great if I could learn to drive buses?'

Franco was always looking for new jobs. What did a new job matter, when she had this on her mind?

'Will you be back for tonight? Can we go out then?' For her, Sunday was the high point of her week. She'd been looking forward to seeing him.

'Maybe not. Next week, eh?'

His smile came easily, she couldn't get through to him. 'Wednesday night?' she suggested.

'All right. Usual time and place.'

He pecked her cheek and rushed out. She felt a pall of disappointment descend on her.

His mother shrugged. 'You know our Franco. Always looking for a new job.'

'Doesn't find it though,' Vito grunted. 'New job, and it's marvellous for six weeks, everything in the garden is lovely, then *finito*. New girlfriend, love of his life for six weeks, then *finito*.'

Ellie felt cold inside. She mustn't panic, not yet. She'd be seeing Franco on Wednesday. She'd tell him then. Vito didn't understand when he said *finito*. Franco would never do that to her. But what if . . . ? The thought made her shudder.

Connie made a fuss of her but Ellie was very worried. Even the trip to the cemetery didn't lift her spirits. She couldn't stop thinking about her own trouble. She couldn't expect help or sympathy from her aunt and uncle.

She had made up her mind to be stronger, but she hadn't expected to be tested like this so soon. This was a very adult trouble. When she was going to bed she read Gran's letter through again and slept with it under her pillow. It gave her strength.

It helped that she wasn't alone in this – Alice was in the same position and hadn't Mam been through it with her? But Mam had had Gran and Alice had her mother. Ellie told herself she had Connie. Connie would have every reason to help her.

By Monday morning, Ellie felt sick when she was getting up but better when she'd forced some porridge down and walked to the Maypole. Alice was the only other in the staff room when she was taking off her outdoor clothes. 'I've told Mam,' she whispered.

'What did she say?'

'She was cross with me for getting into trouble, shocked too, but she got over it. Specially when I said Graham wanted us to get married straight away.'

'At least you were engaged first.'

'Yes, it's just a case of bringing our plans forward. Course we won't have much money, but Mam says Graham can move in with us to start. We can even use our Tom's room as a nursery or a living room for ourselves. Sorry, Ellie, there won't be room for you to lodge with us now this has happened.'

That was the least of Ellie's worries at the moment. 'That's all right.' She wouldn't say anything to Alice until she'd told Franco. 'You feel better now it's out in the open?' She knew she would.

'You bet. Graham's had second thoughts. He thinks we should get spliced as soon as we can, not wait until July. We're going to forget the church wedding with all the trimmings, and do it in the register office without any fuss.'

'You'll have a husband. That's the important thing.'

Ellie could feel herself getting more jittery as she waited for Wednesday evening to come round. What if Franco didn't turn up? He always had until now, but Connie kept saying he wasn't reliable. If he didn't come she'd be devastated.

She had to take herself in hand. No, even if Franco didn't turn up, she wouldn't let herself get upset. She'd write to him, saying she had something important she wanted to talk about, and would he be sure to be at home on Sunday afternoon when she came.

Ellie arrived at the Lyceum Picture House five minutes

early. She knew she needn't have worried. Franco was already waiting for her. The way he looked at her told her he still loved her.

'There's a good picture on tonight.' He was enthusiastic. 'Marlene Dietrich.' He drew Ellie's arm through his and would have drawn her up the steps into the foyer.

'Do you mind if we don't go to the pictures?' Ellie stood her ground. 'I want us to talk.'

He looked at her in surprise. 'Last house will be starting soon. Can't we talk in there?'

'No.'

He looked at a loss. 'Where d'you want to go, then?'

She'd thought of the park but it was raining.

'There's a pub at the toll bar,' Franco suggested. 'How old are you now?'

'Seventeen.'

'Gosh, Ellie, you'd pass for fourteen. Better not. Is there a caff near here?'

'There is, but it closes in the evening.'

'We'll have to get the bus into town then, it'll be easier there.' Seated next to her on the bus, he asked, 'What is it you want to talk about? What's so important?'

There were other people near by, so she whispered, 'I think I'm going to have a baby.'

'What?'

She knew he'd heard, but she said it again. He was shocked. 'You can't be. I've taken precautions.'

'I've been worried about it for a few weeks. I'm pretty sure. I have the signs . . .'

'Have you been to the doctor?'

'No, of course not.'

This wasn't turning out at all as she'd hoped. He looked

shattered. She felt for his hand. 'What are we going to do about it?'

He shook his head, biting his lip in silence and staring straight ahead. Ellie waited for some response, feeling worse as the minutes crept past. The bus reached the terminus at Woodside. Everybody was getting off.

'We should have got off before now,' he said, pulling her to her feet. 'Never mind, there's the buffet in the railway station. We can get a cup of tea there.'

Ellie was terrified. She'd expected more from him than this, some decisions about the future and more concern for her. She saw an empty bench, pulled him towards it and asked again, 'What are we going to do?'

'We'll have to get married,' he said, turning to look at her for the first time. 'What do you think?'

Ellie sighed with relief and put her head down on his shoulder.

'Yes, oh yes. I do love you, Franco.'

His arm came round her. 'And I love you. We'll get married then.'

It all sounded so matter of fact, so lacking in romance and excitement, but she was going to be all right.

Franco felt guilt-stricken, and full of remorse for doing this to Ellie. She was such a child herself, it hardly seemed possible. Perhaps she was wrong. Perhaps it was all a false alarm.

'You're overdue, Ellie? Is that it?'

'Yes, over three weeks now and I felt real sickly this morning.' His heart sank. It sounded as though she could be right.

It made things doubly difficult because of who she was. Ma had always mothered Ellie. Pa would be furious with him for this too. Ellie saw marriage as her best option. His mother would tell him it was essential. There was no way he'd be able to avoid it.

He sighed. 'It doesn't look as though I'll get that job learning to drive a bus. It was all pie in the sky, but I'll have to find another job. Painting and decorating doesn't pay enough and it's killing me.'

He took her to the refreshments room and bought them each a cup of tea. 'I'm twenty-four, it's time I got married, isn't it?'

'Yes,' Ellie smiled.

With all the girls he'd had, he'd narrowly avoided marriage more than once. He valued his freedom. He wasn't sure he'd have chosen Ellie for his wife, but now he had no choice. 'We'll take a couple of rooms somewhere to start.'

'We'll be all right.'

'Got to find a better job though.'

'You will, you always do.'

Ellie was sweet really, but he was afraid he was being bamboozled into marriage. He didn't feel ready for it. He would make quite sure Ellie was having a baby before he did anything.

'Let's keep this to ourselves for a week or so,' he said. 'We won't say anything to Ma and Pa. There'll be a right rumpus when they find out. Give me time to get used to the idea first, OK?'

Ellie did as he'd asked and said nothing to Connie and Vito on the following Sundays. She had no wish to tell Wilma and Uncle Mick and though she felt sickly in the mornings she never actually vomited, so there was no reason for them to suspect she had a problem.

But she had to talk to somebody about it and on the following Thursday afternoon she told Alice.

'You too?' Alice was amazed and then gave Ellie a hug of joy. 'It's terrifying when you first realise, isn't it? Especially not being married like.'

'We're in it together.' That was a comfort to Ellie.

'We can meet afterwards and push our babies round the park in their prams.' Alice wanted to hear every detail about Franco then.

They went over to Liverpool that day and went round the big Liverpool shops, looking at prams, cots and baby clothes. They spent a few minutes in bridal wear admiring white satin gowns before moving on to formal women's wear to look at smart costumes. They tried on hats and tried to imagine themselves wearing some of the clothes.

'I won't be able to afford anything here,' Alice sighed.

'Neither will I.'

On the way back to the underground, they studied a display of engagement rings in a jeweller's shop window. 'At least we'll both have husbands in good time,' Alice consoled. 'Things could be worse.'

By the following Thursday, Alice's mood had changed, and she was exultant. 'We've arranged our wedding. It's to be on June the tenth, that's the week after next. We decided the sooner the better.'

'As soon as that?' Ellie felt envious. She'd feel so much safer if only Franco would make plans for their wedding. Saying nothing to his parents meant everything was on hold and she was finding that very hard to bear.

'It's to be a quiet wedding in the register office. For just family and one or two friends. I've asked for Thursday, Friday and Saturday off that week.'

'I feel quite excited for you.'

'It'll be on Thursday afternoon. I want you to come but you

mustn't say anything to the others here, about me getting married.'

'Why not?'

'Before you came, we had a girl working here – Joan, her name was. Well, she got married and was planning to stay on, but Mr Duggan asked her to leave. He said it was Head Office policy.'

'I don't think that's fair, not in a job like ours.' Ellie was indignant. 'I thought that rule was for professional women.'

Alice nodded. 'Mr Duggan said married women shouldn't be in a job that a man could do. Men needed work to support their families.'

'Did he take a man on?'

'No, you got her place. School leavers don't have to be paid as much as men, and Mr Owen thinks girls are better than boys. Anyway, I don't want that to happen to me. I'm going to work as long as I can, I need to, then they can stuff their job.'

'I'll keep my mouth shut,' Ellie breathed.

'We're going to have a three-night honeymoon in Prestatyn, but in the shop, I'm calling it my holiday.'

Ellie laughed. 'No more waiting. Lovely for you . . .'

'Your turn will come.'

'I'll probably do exactly what you're doing.'

'You're so thin, I can hardly believe you're in the family way. I'm not going to be able to hide this much longer.'

'The white coats we wear hide a lot. They're such heavy drill and they don't fit properly. Almost as good as maternity dresses,' Ellie giggled.

She thought her baby must be due about a month after Alice's. Ellie found her friend a great comfort. She'd helped her work out her dates and she was able to talk over her worries with her.

Chapter Fourteen

May 1932

Franco was having a hard time. He'd gone after ten jobs in the last few weeks and hadn't had one offer. He'd started by being fussy about what he would do and how much he'd be paid, but now he'd reached the stage when he'd take anything. Well, almost anything.

It was Sunday morning. Pa had his business accounts spread out on the living-room table, his mother was busy in the kitchen with the dinner. She'd got into the habit of telling Ellie to come early and have it with them. The family knew he was seeing more of her.

'Mind you treat that child right,' his father had told him.

'You'll get a piece of my mind if you don't,' his ma added. It didn't bode well for him when they found out. He'd always loved Sundays but now they weren't so easy. For the last few weeks he'd had to face Ellie's anxious eyes.

'Any luck?' she'd ask.

He'd had to say, 'No, no job yet, and you?'

She'd shake her head and whisper, 'No.' Franco had been hoping against hope that the baby was a false alarm. He'd had a false alarm with Polly Sullivan a couple of years ago, so he'd been very hopeful at first. He knew he hadn't reacted well

235

when Ellie had told him the bad news. Coming from her it was very bad news indeed. It had knocked him sideways and he'd not kept his wits about him.

He'd talked of marrying her, but he should have shown more enthusiasm. He'd been hangdog about it, reluctant even, and he knew he'd scared her. She was the last person he wanted to upset. If it was essential, he meant to do the right thing by Ellie.

When the doorbell rang, he went to let her in. Her face was paper white, except for mauve shadows under her eyes. He was shocked at her appearance. Anybody could see she was under a huge strain.

They went through the usual routine while he hung her coat on the hall stand. He knew he'd have to give up hope. There was to be no reprieve from this baby. He took her to the kitchen.

'Hello, Ellie.' Ma looked up from making the gravy, then took another look. 'Are you all right? You don't look well.'

'I'm fine.' Ellie was trying to smile and not managing it very well. It made Franco feel a real heel. She ate her dinner up, which he was glad of. She usually had a good appetite and if she'd left half of it, it would have brought more questions from Ma.

As soon as the washing up was done, he suggested he and Ellie should take a walk. It was a bright day and they'd be all right in the park.

'Remember what I told you,' Ma said to him as they were going out. It served to make him feel guiltier than ever. He'd have to try and make it up to Ellie.

He took her arm, saying, 'I think we'd better tell the family.' They'd probably go berserk when he did. He'd need Ellie alongside him; they'd be more careful what they said in her hearing. 'We can't hang on for ever hoping it's a false alarm.'

'Is that what you thought? It might be a false alarm?' Her amber eyes looked so innocent. Clearly, she'd given up hope of that weeks ago.

He knew she was eager to get on with things and get a wedding band on her finger. She seemed half afraid now that he'd take off and leave her in the lurch. He had to show her there was no danger of that. With his parents watching from the sidelines, he wouldn't dare let the poor kid down.

'No point in putting it off any longer, Ellie. The sooner we get the knot tied the better.'

That brought her first genuine smile of the day. She swung on his arm like an excited child.

'How soon? It would be such a weight off my mind.'

'My parents are going to want us to be married in church. What d'you think?'

'I don't care where, just as long as we're married.' He heard the desperation in her voice.

'Neither do I,' he said quickly.

'Alice says,' he'd heard a lot about Alice recently, 'that it can be fixed up more quickly in the register office.'

'You'd be happy with that?'

'Yes.'

'You'd not want a big day?' He'd understood girls were very keen on white weddings, with satin gowns and veils, and a slap-up reception.

'Where would we get the money for that?' she asked. 'Better if we just get on with it.'

'Come on then.' He swung her round. 'Let's go back home and make the announcement. I'll go down to the registrar's office tomorrow in my dinner hour and see if I can fix it up.' He'd push it through quickly, that would please Ellie – Ma too, when she found out. At least Carlo had paved the way for him here.

'But I've got to find a better job. That's urgent now.'

He knew it wouldn't take much for the boss to give him the sack from his painting job. It would be even harder to get another if that happened.

Franco turned his key in the front-door lock. He could feel his heart belting away as he led Ellie up the hall. Pa was dozing in the armchair, his mother reading the Sunday paper. 'You haven't had much of a walk,' she said.

'No, we came back to tell you . . .'

Pa was pulling himself up the chair and yawning.

'What?' Ma's newspaper crackled noisily.

Franco took Ellie's hand in his and smiled at her. 'We want to get married.'

'What?' Ma's jaw had dropped in surprise. 'I didn't realise . . . You two?'

Pa let out a snort of derision. '*Mamma mia*, what are you proposing to live on, lad? You're always short of money now.'

Franco saw Ellie wince at that. 'I'm looking for a better job.'

'Yes, and not finding it.'

'I will.' He knew he had to.

'Well, this is a surprise.' Ma was eyeing Ellie with concern. 'Are you sure, love? Have you thought about . . . ?'

'Very sure.' Ellie was as firm as a stone wall.

'Well, I hope you'll both be happy . . .' Ma didn't sound as though she thought they would. 'You know what Franco's like, Ellie, you've known him all your life. He isn't going to be any great shakes as a provider.'

'Give him a year or two, and he might improve,' Pa said, in

a tone that told Franco it was the last thing he expected. 'You don't have to rush into it, you're very young. You can save for a year or two.'

There was a moment's aching silence. Franco was searching desperately for the words to tell them.

'We can't wait,' Ellie said quietly, her face suddenly the colour of beetroot. 'I'm having a baby.'

Franco felt the colour drain from his face as they both eyed her abdomen. It was as flat as his own. Nothing showed with Ellie, she still looked like a schoolgirl.

'Franco!' His mother let out a cry of horror. She was on her feet, throwing her arms round Ellie. 'You poor pet, you must be worried stiff. No wonder you don't look well.'

His father looked disgusted. 'You blighter! You haven't grown up, Franco, in and out of jobs. Now this!'

'Grown up? It happened to our Carlo when he was only twenty. Must run in the family.'

That gave Pa a dig, and gave him a moment's respite. 'At least he stayed in work.'

'I'll keep the next job.'

'You'll have to. You're hardly responsible, no thought for the future.'

'You'll have to get married now,' his mother said tight lipped.

'I want to,' Franco said. 'We want to do it as soon as possible.'

'We do love each other,' Ellie said gently. He squeezed her hand.

Pa was at his most ponderous. 'Much the best thing would be to work in the business, Franco. You know well enough you won't find anything that pays better.'

Franco closed his mind to that. He wasn't ready to give up everything.

* * *

'The lad's a fool,' Connie fulminated as the door banged behind the youngsters. 'What was he thinking of? Taking such a risk with little Ellie?'

'Himself,' Vito exploded. 'Does he ever think of anybody but himself? Hot-blooded young stallion.' For them, the peace of Sunday afternoon had been shattered by the news.

'I'm ashamed of him. She's too young to saddle herself with him. What would Bridie say?'

'We both knew what he was like with the girls.'

'But Ellie?' Connie threw herself on a chair and covered her face with her hands. 'This isn't what I wanted for her. She had such a hard childhood, I want her to be happy. She deserves better than our Franco. She needs a husband who's able to look after her, give her a decent life. Someone mature and level headed.'

Vito shook his head. 'Franco won't be able to chase the girls once he's married.'

'Perhaps marriage will settle him down. He'll have to keep his job to feed his family.' Connie tried to look on the bright side. 'Ellie could be the making of him.'

'We'll see. She looks such a baby herself.'

Ellie felt better now Connie and Vito knew and the arrangements for their wedding were going ahead. She'd been disconcerted at the way they'd spoken to Franco when she'd told them there was a baby on the way. Until that moment, she hadn't asked herself if Franco would make a good husband. She was sure he would, and she loved him and wanted to be with him.

On Wednesday evening, he took her to the pictures and told her the date was fixed for June the twenty-fourth. They too would be married on the Thursday afternoon, and it would take place only two weeks after Alice's wedding.

Ellie was thrilled. Like Alice, she planned to ask for the rest of the week off. Things were going to work out as well for her as they were for her friend.

'There is one thing . . .' In the interval, Franco fished some papers from his pocket. 'Because you're under age, you'll have to get your Uncle Mick's permission to get married. It explains it all here.'

That jolted her. 'I haven't told him yet. I wasn't planning to until I'm ready to leave.' She was afraid he'd turn nasty.

'He'll sign for you, Ellie. He'll want you married now, won't he?'

Ellie was straining her eyes to read in the dim light. 'It says legal guardian. I don't know whether he is or not.'

'He told Ma he was.'

'I don't believe—'

'Just get him to sign for you, Ellie. It doesn't matter whether he is or not, it'll satisfy everybody if he signs.'

'Yes, but telling him will be awful.'

'That's how I felt about telling my family.'

Ellie tried to relax as she sat in the darkened stalls with Franco's arm round her shoulders. It was a comfort that Connie and Vito knew and she wasn't going to be left to deal with this on her own, but she wasn't looking forward to telling Uncle Mick and Auntie Wilma. 'Is there any hurry?'

'Well, we can't get married until he does.'

'I'd like to have somewhere else to live first. I'm afraid he'll turn nasty.'

Franco reached for her hand and squeezed it. 'Ma said, since we'll have so little time to find a place of our own, we can move in with them to start if we want to. She said we can use the parlour as a living room and get a double bed for my bedroom.'

Ellie was delighted. 'That's the answer. It'll get me away from Uncle Mick. I've been wanting to move out for a long time.'

'She'd take you in right away if that's what you want.'

'That's a comfort.'

Franco was frowning. 'It's all right for you to move in for a week or so, but I'm not mad about the idea of living with them when we're married. They'll be breathing down our necks the whole time. If I can't get another job though, we might have to.'

Ellie thought it the sensible thing to do in the circumstances. 'It would give us time to look round for our own place.' But she wouldn't argue with Franco if he didn't want it. It was his home and his family.

Ellie made what preparations she could. She wanted something new to wear for her wedding and bought herself a new hat in the market. It was blue felt to match her best coat, which would have to do. She went into Woolworths and found some artificial daisies to stitch round the brim and was very pleased with the result.

She hadn't much money to spend, so a pair of smart shoes and some underclothes were all she could afford. She was tempted to wear the hat for Alice's wedding first.

By the following week, Franco had more news for her. He'd found himself a new job.

'I'm made up,' he smiled triumphantly. 'Just in time, eh? I'm going to be a barman at the Mermaid pub.'

'Where's that?'

'Cunliffe Street, down in town. I could show you, we could go there for a drink.'

'Will you like working in a pub?'

'You bet. Pubs are jolly places. It'll pay better than painting and decorating and I'm fed up with that.'

'I'm so pleased.' It was lovely to see Franco excited and happy.

'So am I. The thing is, we can afford things now. We won't be so desperate for cash.'

'A honeymoon? A short one, just a few days.' She felt full of bounce. 'I'll ask for the rest of the week off, like Alice has.'

Franco was frowning. 'I've been told I can have the Thursday night off, but Friday and Saturday are busy nights at the pub. No honeymoon, I'm afraid, we won't be able to go away, not even for a few days. I'll be new in the job and can't risk—'

'Of course not.' But she felt deflated. 'The job's the important thing.'

'We could look for a couple of rooms near by. So we won't have to move in with Ma and Pa.'

'I wouldn't have minded that, but it's a long way to go to work from there, and I want to keep on for as long as I can. We'll need so many things.'

'It would be easier for you to get a bus from the town centre,' Franco agreed. 'And not so far. Come on, let's go and look round. See if we can find some rooms to rent.'

Ellie was disappointed when they didn't, and she didn't much like the Mermaid pub. Sounds of merriment could be heard before Franco opened the door. She followed him down a shabby passage. Through an open door she glimpsed the main bar, hazy with blue tobacco smoke and packed with noisy customers. She just had time to take in the row of barrels on tap on a shelf behind the mahogany counter and the spittoons and sawdust on the floor.

Franco steered her to a cramped room at the back. A bench covered with cracked maroon leatherette and showing its interior stuffing provided seating round three of the walls.

'This is where ladies come,' he whispered. There were three elderly women in one corner drinking port and lemon, and a morose couple in the other with tankards of ale. 'What would you like to drink, Ellie?'

'Lemonade please. Are all pubs like this?'

'They're all different.'

'You like this one?' She did not. 'You want to come here to work?'

'It's a job.' Franco smiled at her. 'I think I might enjoy it, there's a buzz about the place.'

Another week went by, and Ellie had her Sunday dinner with Franco's family as usual. She knew he was keen to find somewhere for them to live, and she was excited at the prospect. Franco said he'd seen several houses where there were rooms to let and he'd arranged for them both to see another this afternoon. Once the washing up was finished, they set out.

They found the address in Eldon Place, a short walk from the Mermaid pub. It was a substantial house, but looked old and in need of repair. Franco rang the doorbell. It was answered by the landlord, a burly middle-aged man wearing braces over a torn and dirty vest.

Ellie left the talking to Franco, and looked about her. All the rooms on the ground floor opened off a large hall with a handsome staircase and it seemed they would have the use of all of them. The original sitting room was large and attractive, there was a kitchen and two other rooms, all of good size. The lavatory was out in the yard.

Ellie's first impression was that she liked the rooms, but she didn't care for Mr Brunt, the landlord. He towered over her and his eyes seemed to leer at her as they followed her round.

When Franco started asking questions they found the landlord and two other tenants lived upstairs and they all used the front door and the hall. Even worse, the lavatory, yard and wash house were shared, and the only route was through their kitchen.

Ellie asked, 'There's no way we could close our rooms off?'

'No, it's rooms not a flat.' Mr Brunt was overweight with a big beer belly. 'That's what the advert said.'

'Can we have five minutes to think?' Franco led her back to the sitting room. 'What d'you reckon, Ellie?'

'It wouldn't be perfect, everybody tramping through our kitchen. The rooms are big though and this is nice, isn't it?'

Franco looked round dubiously, wrinkling his nose. 'There's an odd feeling about it, don't you think?'

'I like this room.'

'It would do, I suppose, but we wouldn't have the place to ourselves. The others I saw were worse.'

'The rent's high for what it is, but we need to get somewhere soon.'

'We need it now.'

Ellie said, 'It's this or move in with your family.'

That made up Franco's mind. 'Let's take this then. It'll do to start.'

Ellie felt such a surge of satisfaction, she laughed outright.

'We can move in straight away.' Franco laughed too.

'No, we'll need furniture.'

They walked in the park, excited now that Franco had paid two weeks' rent.

'It's ours.' Ellie could hardly believe it. They sat on a park bench and made lists of all they'd need. Franco took her back home for tea.

His mother said, 'You can take your bedroom furniture with you.'

'We'll need a double bed.'

His father looked over his glasses. 'Franco, you'll need that single one too before very much longer.'

'There's second-hand shops,' Connie reminded him. 'Much cheaper and there'd be no harm in getting your table and chairs that way.'

'It's finding the time to look,' Ellie mourned. When the Maypole was closed and she was free, so were the other shops.

'I'll look round for you,' Connie said. 'Then take you to see the best of what's on offer. Come to think of it, Seth Woodall is a good customer of ours. He has that big second-hand place, an old hall on the corner of Price Street. If I ask, he might open up for us on a Thursday.'

'That would be marvellous.' Ellie laughed. 'My friend Alice is having trouble finding the time to shop too. She's going to Liverpool with her mother this Thursday.'

'If your friend's going shopping with her mother,' Connie said, 'you can come shopping with me. I'll see you on Thursday afternoon.'

On Wednesday evening, Franco brought a message from his mother to say she'd meet her at Hamilton Square Station.

'We're going over to Liverpool? Doesn't that make it harder to have things delivered? I thought we were going to Price Street.'

The next afternoon, Connie was waiting for her by the booking office. 'Yes, we're going to Liverpool,' she smiled. 'I want you to have a new outfit for your wedding. Every bride is entitled to that.'

'I don't have the money.'

'I'm paying, it's my wedding present to you. Nothing fancy,

a costume, or a smart dress and coat. Something you'll get some wear from.'

'The baby . . . I won't be able to get into them soon.'

'A loose coat, a swing back. They're all the rage now, and you'll be able to wear the dress afterwards.'

'You're very kind, doing this for me.' She'd always found Connie generous.

'Ellie, I'm going to be your mother-in-law. It's the least I can do.'

Ellie chose, with Connie's help, a camel wool swagger coat and a dress in fawns and reds. At the last minute, Connie saw a little red hat that would set off the outfit.

'I don't know what to say.' Ellie was delighted with her new clothes. 'Thank you, I couldn't have had all these lovely things without your help. Thank you.'

'We're going home to have a meal, then I'm taking you and Franco down to Seth Woodall's place. He had a nice oak table there on Monday that I think you'll like. He said he'd open up for you and Franco at seven o'clock.'

'Great, you think of everything.'

'We'll get your rooms fixed up. Franco starts his new job next Monday, and then he'll be free in the afternoons.'

Ellie was delighted, she hadn't dared hope that things would turn out this well. She had a feeling of well-being. The Baldini family was looking after her again, just as they used to when she was a child.

Later that evening, she and Franco decided on the oak gate-legged table, four chairs and a kitchen cabinet.

'Have you any bedsteads here?' Franco asked.

'Yes, double? This way.' The bed wires were leaning against the wall. 'There's this bed head and footer in oak, or that brass one over there.'

Ellie liked the brass one, but it was a bit pitted.

'The oak,' Franco suggested. 'It's quite handsome.'

'I've got some mattresses upstairs.'

'Get a new one,' Connie advised.

Franco agreed. 'I like that armchair. No, perhaps not, there's a bad stain on the seat and it's a bit shabby.'

'I know somebody who'd recover it for you,' Seth Woodall told them. 'They'd fix the springs at the same time. It would still be cheaper than buying new.'

They chose two easy chairs. 'They don't match now,' Connie said, 'but they'll look a pair when they're recovered in the same material.'

'Red velvet would be nice.' Ellie was in seventh heaven.

Alice was in high spirits at the beginning of the following week. She laughed and giggled and talked incessantly of the little holiday she would be starting on Thursday, and the good time she was hoping to have in Prestatyn.

Mr Owen on the bacon counter laughed with her and wished he was going on holiday too.

But the manager said, 'Alice, keep your mind on what you're doing now, can't you? You've mixed the cheese labels up. Look at this, double Gloucester labelled Gorgonzola.'

Alice whispered excitedly to Ellie when they couldn't be heard by anyone else. 'We're being married at two o'clock, so you won't have time to go home and change. But don't bring your best clothes to work, I don't want anybody here to suspect.'

'What shall I do? Come like this?'

'No, you ninny. Get up early and bring your best things round to our house first. Then, when the shop closes, you can come round and change. We'll all go down on the bus to the Town Hall together.'

Ellie carried her best coat over her arm and wore her blue felt hat as she walked to Alice's house on Thursday morning. She wore her blue dress which was now only her second best, deciding she could remove her old brown coat and slip into her white drill overall without attracting attention.

Alice opened the door to her. 'I can't believe this day has come, I thought it never would.' She was flushed and running around in flannelette pyjamas.

'You've got a lovely day for it.'

'I'll hang your hat and coat here. See you at one o'clock.'

For Ellie, it seemed strange not to see Alice across the shop. All morning, she had trouble keeping her mind on what she was doing. Knowing that in two weeks she'd be getting married too sent little shivers of anticipation down her spine.

When the shop closed she hurried back to Alice's house, where her mother was dishing up bowls of soup and sandwiches to family and friends. She met Graham, the groom, for the first time and thought he seemed very much in love with Alice. He couldn't take his eyes off her.

Alice was radiant. 'I'm only just in time,' she said to Ellie up in her bedroom. It's beginning to show, but I won't care after today.'

Ellie had time to rinse her face and comb her hair. She'd made a special effort with her hair and had fashionable curls on her shoulders.

'Try my new face powder,' Alice offered, as she sprayed Ellie with her new scent. Ellie fished her own lipstick from her handbag.

Then they were off, a jolly party of fifteen going down on the bus. They arrived at the register office with ten minutes to spare and waited in a large comfortable room. Alice began to fidget while her family fussed round her.

Ellie looked round her elegant surroundings. In two weeks, when it was her turn, it would help settle her wedding-day nerves to know where she'd be coming.

They were led away and it seemed soon over. Alice was relaxed now she had a wedding ring on her finger.

The following Sunday morning, Ellie got up early to do her washing and then went to meet Franco at their rooms. He rushed up the hall when he heard her come in.

'I've just finished putting up the curtains in our bedroom, come and see.'

'You've done such a lot.' The furniture they'd bought had been delivered. 'You've made our bed up.' Ellie was thrilled.

'Ma did it. She's been bringing down bed linen and crockery and things every day.'

'It's a lovely eiderdown.' It was pink satin.

'Ma brought it.'

'She's very good to us.' Ellie smiled.

'Yes, she gave us the green curtains in the sitting room as well.'

'You've hung those too?' Ellie crossed the hall to look.

Franco pulled up just inside the door. 'Do you like this room?'

'Yes, it's the best in the whole house, lovely and big and light. What's the matter?'

'I feel . . . I don't know, there's a chill, as though something bad happened here. There's an alien presence.'

Ellie said, 'You sound like Gran.'

'You don't feel anything?'

'It's just cold.'

'I'll light the fire.'

'Franco, I'm beginning to see this place as home.'

He nodded; she knew he was as thrilled as she was. He said, 'You'll have to tell your Uncle Mick, Ellie, there's not much time left.'

Ellie was dreading that. 'Will you come with me?'

She thought Franco hesitated for a moment, but he said; 'Of course, if it will help.'

'It will.' He was someone to lean on.

'Mick terrified me at one time. I'm sure he's the reason our Carlo wanted to get away from here.'

'Terrified me too. Ben helped me get the better of him, so I'm not as scared as I used to be, but he can be difficult.'

'Right, when's the best time, then?'

'There is no best time. They'll both be there straight after tea. Uncle Mick might go down to the pub later.'

'Tonight,' he said. 'Let's do it tonight and get it over with.'

Ellie's heart was pounding as she led Franco in through the back door of the house in Bicknell Street. She was relieved to see Ben was out and she could hear the younger boys playing upstairs. Uncle Mick and Auntie Wilma were in the living room, sitting one each side the kitchen range. They looked sullen, as though they'd been bickering.

'Who's this you're bringing in?' Mick demanded rudely. Ellie's heart sank.

'Franco Baldini,' Franco said, putting out his hand. Mick ignored it.

'You remember the Baldinis?' Ellie tried to smile. 'They lived next door but one.'

'Yes, you run off to them every Sunday.' Auntie Wilma was staring at Franco. 'What d'you want?'

Mick said, 'You're from the caff, one of Vito's kids.'

'That's right.'

'So what have you come for?'

Ellie thought Franco looked very tense. She knew he'd been expecting trouble from her uncle, who was being both rude and unwelcoming.

She said as calmly as she could, 'We want to get married.'

'Married? Don't be silly, girl, you're too young. You don't want to rush into something like that.'

Ellie shivered. She heard Franco take a deep breath and say, 'It's booked to take place a week on Thursday. At the register office.'

'We'll see about that.' An angry flush ran up Mick's cheeks. 'You've no business to—'

'I know I need your permission.' Ellie was struggling to keep calm. 'I'm not twenty-one.'

'Then you'd better wait till you are. That's what I said.'

'What's all the hurry?' Ellie could see Wilma staring at her suspiciously.

She felt the heat run up her cheeks and was forced to say it. Bracing herself against the table she whispered, 'I'm having a baby.'

Uncle Mick roared out a string of obscenities. 'We might have guessed.' He was pulling a face of horror. 'Have you no shame?'

'You little slut.' Auntie Wilma was screwing her face in disgust. 'Just like your mother.'

'Hang on,' Franco came to life at last. 'There's no need to be nasty. Don't blame Ellie. If anyone is at fault, it's me.'

'What did you expect?' Wilma glared at Ellie. 'An Italian, a foreigner.'

'No more a foreigner than your husband,' Franco said. She knew he was trying to keep his temper. 'I was born and bred here.'

Ellie could hardly get her breath. She had to stop them bickering and get it settled.

'Now that you know, I take it you'd rather Franco and I were married?'

They stared back at her, but didn't answer.

'I won't be able to work for much longer. Then I wouldn't be able to pay you for my lodgings. You wouldn't want to support me and my baby?'

Mick glowered at her. 'We're not having any bastard of yours here.'

'You'll give your permission, then?'

'You bet we will,' Wilma spat.

Chapter Fifteen

Franco's mind raced with anger at the way Ellie's aunt and uncle were treating her. He'd been scared of coming. Just the thought of facing Mick Valentino in his own house had given him the jitters. He'd known Ellie was nervous about telling him; they'd both guessed he'd turn nasty.

He admired the way she'd stood up to him. She knew one blow from him could send her reeling across the room and break her bones. Yet she'd dared, and it was only her quick wits that had saved the day. She'd presented her case in such a way that those monsters saw giving permission was to their own advantage.

Franco felt he had to pull himself together and not look cowardly in front of Ellie. If she could face up to Mick Valentino, he had to.

'Well, Ellie,' he said, speaking to her and at them, 'why don't we pack your things now, so I can help you carry them?'

He turned to Wilma. 'Ellie will move out tonight. We'll come back next Sunday for the rest of her stuff.'

Wilma wasn't pleased about that. 'No need to rush, Ellie . . .'

He knew now why Wilma wanted her here. She was a lodger who didn't need looking after, one they could get to do jobs for them.

He was surprised to hear Ellie say, 'I won't be going tonight.

Can't possibly get everything packed. Couldn't carry it all at once, anyway.'

'She's got a lot of stuff,' Wilma told him.

'I'll need suitcases. Can I take those two that came from Gran's?'

'No,' Mick said. 'We use them for our holidays.'

'I'll bring them back.'

'No, I said.'

'Right, we'll take some of my things with us now,' Ellie said. 'But I'll come back tonight. Franco, come and help me pack my winter clothes, I'll not be needing them for a while.'

Franco felt himself being pulled up to her cupboard of a bedroom. 'I thought you wanted to get away from them straight away,' he whispered.

Ellie sighed. 'I half expected him to say he wasn't my legal guardian, and he wasn't going to do anything. I don't think I should leave just yet,' she said, sinking down on the bed. 'Not until he's given his permission. I don't want him to change his mind.'

'He said he'd give it. He's keen to get you out of here.'

'I know what he's like.' Ellie looked scared. 'I'd love to walk out right now and never come back, but if I do, Uncle Mick won't have to do anything to get rid of me. He won't bother doing anything, or worse, he might withhold permission just to spite me.'

Franco could see she was really concerned. 'Couldn't you threaten to tell on him? You know . . .' Ellie had told him about the stolen property she'd seen here.

'I could. I'll have to, if . . . But I don't want a fight. It'd be less of a struggle if we could get him to sign the papers first.'

Franco frowned. 'As soon as possible then?'

'Uncle Mick isn't working. He could go down to the register office tomorrow.'

He steeled himself. 'I'll go with him, make sure he does.'

'What about going to work?'

He shrugged. 'I'm giving in my notice, and I'll be leaving at the end of the week. Does it matter what the boss says?'

They went downstairs again. He watched Ellie stand in front of her uncle with her head back, looking like a fairy confronting a tiger.

'I've decided,' she said, 'to stay here until you've signed that I have your permission. Will you meet Franco outside the register office tomorrow morning?'

With bad grace, Mick agreed he would.

Ellie had packed some of her belongings in brown paper carrier bags and Franco had helped her bring them to their rooms.

'It's so peaceful here,' she said. 'I dread going back to the insults and the rows. I wish I didn't have to.'

'Stay here with me,' he urged. 'They were horrible to you.'

Ellie was tempted. 'What if he doesn't turn up tomorrow? If all goes well, it's only for one more night.'

It was time for bed when she returned to Bicknell Street. She didn't have a key, but the back door was never locked. She let herself into the scullery and found Ben making himself a cup of cocoa.

He grinned at her. 'Mam's just told me. Congratulations, Ellie, you're breaking free before me. Never thought you'd manage that.'

His stepfather called from the adjoining living room, 'You can go too, Ben, any time you like. The sooner the better. I hope your mam told you what a slut your cousin Ellie is. It'll be good riddance to bad rubbish, when we get rid of her.'

'Good night,' Ellie said as pleasantly as she could as she went through the room. The last thing she wanted was another shouting match tonight. Ben followed her upstairs with a brimming mug and perched on her dressing table.

She closed the door carefully and began telling him about needing her uncle's permission to be married. 'Not that I believe he is my legal guardian.'

'Course he isn't.' Ben was scornful. 'He said that to con you, to swindle you out of your inheritance.'

'I could do with that now, it would make a big difference.' Ellie started taking off her shoes.

'But the money's gone so you'd better forget about it.'

'Yes. I don't want to start any more rows with Mick, I just want to leave and get married.'

Ben chuckled as he got to his feet. 'At least you've learned to look after yourself, and you know which side your bread's buttered. I'll be quite sorry to see you go.'

'You'll have your bedroom back.'

'Thank goodness.' At the door, he turned to ask, 'Are you going to invite me to your wedding?'

'Yes, do come. I'd like you to. It's a week on Thursday, at three o'clock, your half day too.'

On Monday, Alice was back from her holiday, and she couldn't stop talking about it. She was so enthusiastic that Ernie, the delivery boy, who had planned to go cycling with his friend on his holiday, decided it must be to Prestatyn.

'You look so happy, I don't have to ask how you're finding married life,' Ellie whispered to Alice when they were alone.

'It's smashing, but I'm beginning to show.'

'Not in that coat.'

That evening, when Ellie was leaving the Maypole with the

rest of the staff, she found Franco waiting outside for her. He was smiling.

'Your uncle turned up, Ellie. He signed the form. Nothing can stop us going ahead now.'

'I'm so pleased! I've been wondering all day . . .'

'I knew you would be. I went in to work late and gave in my notice. I thought the boss was going to throw me out there and then, but we're in the middle of painting a church hall. So I will be working for the rest of the week.'

'I'm delighted, thrilled, made up.'

Franco asked, 'What d'you want to do now? Shall we find a cafe and get something to eat, then go to our rooms?'

Ellie said, 'While we're this close, it would be sensible to go back to Bicknell Street first. Get the rest of my things.'

'You're right.'

When Ellie let herself into the scullery, Wilma was dishing up a big pan of stew. Ben was chopping cabbage.

'Well, if it isn't our little floozy come home,' Uncle Mick jeered from the living room. 'Oh, and lover boy too.'

'There won't be enough to feed him,' Wilma said shortly.

'You won't have to feed me either,' Ellie said, though she was hungry. 'I've come to collect the rest of my things.'

She went through to the living room. Uncle Mick and the youngsters were already seated at the table waiting for their dinner.

'We're seeing the last of you? That's a relief.'

Ellie didn't answer. She felt for Franco's hand and pulled him after her.

Up in her bedroom, she said, 'I've brought some more carrier bags from the shop.' She opened her drawers and began filling the bags. 'I brought back the two we used yesterday and packed them this morning before going to work.'

Franco helped her wrap her light clothes into her heavier ones and tie them securely with string. They were both hung around with bundles and bags as they went downstairs. Ellie opened the living-room door and said, 'Right, I've got my clothes, we're going. I'd like my bedroom furniture. I'll have to arrange for it to be collected.'

The family were still eating. 'Oh no you don't.' Mick was belligerent. 'You're not taking that away.'

'The dressing table and chest were Gran's, and she and Connie found the bed for me.'

'You heard what I said, the furniture's staying here.'

'Come on.' Franco tugged at her arm. 'It's not worth having a fight over it.'

Only Ben got up to peck her cheek. 'Goodbye, Ellie, I'll miss you. All the best.'

Ellie was downcast about the furniture until they reached the house in Eldon Place, though she hadn't expected Mick to allow her to take it. Then she cheered up and twirled round the bedroom. They'd spent hours here yesterday cleaning and polishing and getting everything straight.

'Everything's so clean and tidy after Auntie Wilma's place. I'm going to love living here.'

Franco too was excited. 'I can hardly believe we've got a home of our own.' He helped her cut the strings on her bundles and she began to hang her clothes in the wardrobe.

'I'm so relieved to have left Uncle Mick's. Marvellous to think I'll never have to go back.' She felt quite hysterical, not knowing whether to laugh or cry.

Franco wandered from one room to the next. Yesterday, they'd lit a fire in the living room, and the room felt reasonably warm, but it still gave him that strange feeling in his gut. He cleared the ash from the grate and re-laid the fire, but there was no more coal here.

He was hungry and went to their kitchen to look in the larder. There was an opened packet of tea and another of sugar that he'd brought from home. He remembered the ginger biscuits he'd brought at the same time. His mother had given him a fancy tin to keep them in, and now he helped himself to two. There was nothing else.

His new home spelt freedom and privacy. Here, he and Ellie could do what they wanted. No longer would he be under the watchful gaze of his parents. He was looking forward to spending his first night here, but they had to get something to eat.

'Aren't you hungry, Ellie?'

'Starving. Do you know if there's a fish and chip shop near here?'

'I don't. Let's go home, Ma will feed us. We could ask her for something for breakfast and perhaps a bit of coal to light the fire.'

Franco couldn't help comparing the welcome they got from his family with that from Ellie's. Pa had a talent for whipping up a hot meal quickly and Ma had them sitting up to the table in no time. The problems started when he explained why Ellie was with him on a Monday night.

'You've moved in already?' Franco saw his mother's eyebrows go up. 'You didn't say you were going to. I don't think you should stay there alone, Ellie.'

'I'll be with her,' Franco said.

'I meant alone with you. Not all night. Not until you're married.'

'But I'm already . . . you know, having a baby, so what difference can it make?'

261

'Two wrongs don't make a right. It's a sin.'

Ellie smiled. 'Being with Franco doesn't seem like a sin.'

His father was on his feet. 'Franco, I agree with your mother on this. We're very shocked at the way you've behaved.'

'I'll make up a bed for you here, Ellie. You can stay with us until the wedding.'

'No,' Franco objected. 'We have a place of our own. I want to live in it.' He knew Ellie did too, but she'd found it harder to go against his parents' wishes.

'Come on, Ellie,' he said. 'Ma, we'll do without breakfast if you don't want to give us a drop of milk.'

'It's not that,' his mother said, taking a pint of milk from the larder and cutting a loaf to give them half. 'You know it's not that. Of course Ellie must have breakfast before she goes to work.'

He and Ellie had their first night in the comfort of their own bed, but for once he'd been unable to take advantage of it. He was tired. It had taken so much effort to fix this place up and get here.

Ellie was still flooding with relief that she had everything settled in time for their wedding. But Franco felt knocked sideways.

Ellie was out at the bus stop very early the next morning, she didn't want to miss the bus to work. She had no intention of telling anybody but Alice that she'd moved out of Uncle Mick's house. But as the bus drew to a halt in front of the line of passengers, she saw Mr Duggan already on board reading his newspaper.

She shot upstairs feeling unnerved, and when the bus turned into the bus sheds in New Ferry, she hung back until he got off and was crossing the road to the shop. She felt guilty.

Connie thought she was living in sin and though Ellie respected Connie's judgement, she'd gone against it. Mr Duggan would agree with Connie and anyway she'd done the most shameful thing any girl could do: she was having a baby out of wedlock. Sooner or later, Mr Duggan would find out.

Ellie knew she couldn't go on dodging him for the rest of the time she'd be working. She ran to catch him up.

'Mr Duggan,' she said as he was unlocking the shop door, 'I've changed my address. I'm no longer living in Bicknell Street.'

'Better come up to the office when you've changed,' he told her. 'I'll need your new one for my records.'

It was as easy as that. She'd made no secret of wanting to leave her uncle's house, so he probably assumed she'd done that. Ellie breathed a sigh of relief.

'You are lucky having a place of your own.' Alice was envious.

'I'm living in sin. Mr Duggan would come down on me like a ton of bricks if he knew.'

'But it's not for long. You'll soon be a respectable married woman too.'

Ellie tingled with anticipation. It was what she wanted most in all the world. To be married to Franco and to have this dread of being an unmarried mother banished for ever. She could feel excitement and relief mounting as the days came and went.

At last it was Wednesday afternoon and she had such a sense of freedom that she wouldn't be coming to work for a while.

'Your turn for a little holiday,' Mr Owen said. 'Where are you going?'

'Nowhere,' she had to say. 'I want to sort out my new home. Redecorate perhaps.' Ellie knew she'd have plenty of time for that because Franco would have to work.

* * *

When Franco started his new job at the Mermaid pub, he told everybody his name was Frank. He wanted to seem more English. Mr Secker, the licensee, was a dapper little man, with an edging of mouse-brown hair round the back of his head and a shiny dome rising through it.

'This is a good old-fashioned pub,' he told him. 'We used to make all our own beer until recently. I'll have no rowdy behaviour and no fighting in here. Anybody spoiling for a fight is to be put out. We have regulars who come in almost every night and I don't want them upset.'

'No, sir.'

'I expect punctuality and honesty from my staff. And I don't want you to bring your troubles to work with you. I aim to have a cheerful, friendly atmosphere here.'

'Sounds good to me.'

Franco thought he'd get on all right with Mr Secker. He wasn't dour like his last boss. He was handed over to a lad called Joe who was working out his notice.

'Have you worked in a pub before?'

'No, but I've been inside plenty.' He was used to adding up figures in the caff, that wasn't going to bother him. Joe was taking him along a row of five barrels on the shelf behind the bar, and drawing his attention to the labels on top which described their contents and their prices. Then along a line of bottles and the price of a tot from each. Franco found it an effort to take in all he was being told.

'Why are you leaving?' he asked.

'I'd rather not say.' The lad's voice had dropped.

'What? If I'm taking your place you ought to tell me.'

'You'll find out for yourself.'

'Come on, man. What should I look out for?'

'Well,' Joe's voice dropped another octave, 'this pub's got a bad name.'

'Ah.' Franco had already heard something of that. Several people, including his pa, had told him they'd heard it called a den of iniquity. Another called it a house of ill repute.

Joe gave him a knowing look. 'It's known locally as the Mermaid's Arms.'

'You're confusing it with the King's Arms,' he'd laughed, 'that's just round the corner.'

The King's Arms was a staid pub which took the clientele from the Queen's Hall when the show ended.

'I'm not confusing anything,' the lad said. 'Here's Gladys coming in. She's one of the barmaids.'

Gladys looked young and comely. A door banged. 'And that'll be Winnie Vickers, the other one. That's all of us now.'

The lad clearly didn't like Winnie, the atmosphere cooled, but Franco couldn't see anything to dislike about her. She had a broad smile that showed false teeth and wore a lot of magenta-coloured lipstick, which was running into the wrinkles round her mouth. He felt rather sorry for her.

'Lad's got a touch of religion,' she told him later when they were alone. 'He reckons he's holier than the rest of us. Nothing to worry about here, it's a good pub.'

Franco reckoned Winnie must be about his mother's age. She was equally stout but dressed in a very different style. Ma's dresses were high at the neck and long to the hem and were mostly black. She said black made her look slimmer, but Franco thought it was what women wore in the Italian village where she'd been raised. Ma's hair was dark brown but sprinkled with grey, and she looked a woman in late middle age. Franco thought Ma made herself look older than she was.

Winnie was doing the very opposite. He'd say her clothes were chosen to make her seem younger. The scarlet blouse was low cut and revealed cleavage that was not uninviting. She had rouged cheeks and her hair had been brightened with henna.

She was very friendly, and had dark eyes that burned into his when she spoke to him. She chatted and laughed a lot with the customers. Franco thought it a façade she put on for working behind the bar, and that really she was a very different sort of person. He told her he was getting married soon and had taken rooms in Eldon Place.

'I've got the attic rooms in a house further along Cunliffe Street,' she told him. 'Very handy for getting to work.'

Franco felt he'd done very well to find this job and that he'd enjoy it once he could find his way round.

When at last the pub closed for the night, Winnie Vickers felt exhausted, her face aching with the smile she assumed. The staff were expected to tidy up before they went home, but Gladys had already rushed off, taking a good-looking fellow back to her room, and on his first night, Frank needed to be shown everything. Winnie set about the job feeling brassed off. Frank hadn't the faintest idea of how to clean up.

It was a relief to get out of the smoky atmosphere. She could smell the river here, and the cold night air cleared her head. She had only a few yards to go down the dusty street.

Winnie climbed the stairs in the old and shabby house. The gas mantle had broken long ago and nobody had bothered to replace it, so there was no light to see the marked wallpaper and the worn linoleum, but she hauled herself up on the banister knowing every step. She counted herself lucky to have rented the attic rooms, where she could get away from the crush of humanity. This last steep flight was for her use only.

She went to her bedroom first and lit the gas, then to her living room. If she left all the doors open she could see to pour herself her usual nightcap of neat whisky. In addition, she had a cubby hole of a kitchen and another slit of a room for which she'd found little use.

The lavatory was out in the yard four floors down and she had to wash herself in the kitchen sink. She got round that by using the Ladies at the Mermaid before she left. There was a big washbowl there and she made sure there was always soap and a towel, though even there she had to run across the back yard to get to it.

The Mermaid staff and customers thought she was comfortably fixed, but she hated the grime and the shabbiness and longed to have something better. A better life than working in a back-street pub too.

Her problem, Winnie decided ruefully, was that she'd been brought up to expect something better. She'd been sent to a fee-paying day school and been taken to church twice on Sundays. Her father had been a solicitor and her grandfather a priest.

Her big mistake had been to marry Harry Vickers, an accountant, when she was nineteen. She'd wanted children but they hadn't come. He'd been a bit of a rogue, trying to make his fortune in business. When he'd been killed in the war he'd left her with big debts.

She'd couldn't return to her family: her mother had died and her father had retired and couldn't help her. She'd expected to be a wife and mother but had been forced to find work without having been trained for a career of any sort. Bar work, at least, gave her enough for food and rent.

Winnie took a sip of whisky and rolled it round her tongue. She drank too much, of course, and she'd let herself drift lower and lower through the strata of society, until she'd sunk to this.

She was always promising herself she'd make an effort to get out of here, but never did. She never had enough money to cut herself adrift from the job in the Mermaid.

Another mouthful of whisky and she could admit she was Mr Secker's backstop in the bar. She'd worked there longer than any of the others. When it came to earning a bit on the side, she knew the competition from Gladys put her in the shade, but there were still a few older customers who were prepared to pay her for the privilege. Tonight, she was quite glad to be here on her own.

On the Thursday morning, Ellie woke up to find Franco was already awake beside her. He leaned over to kiss her. 'Our wedding day,' he said.

Ellie gloried in the thought. It was lovely to have Franco here with her. He got up to make tea and brought it back to bed. A little later, he got up again to make them scrambled eggs.

He had to be at work by half ten, and would not be able to come home until the pub closed at two o'clock. Their wedding was to be at three. Ellie was too excited to settle to anything during the morning.

She got herself ready. It was a warm summer's day and she decided not to wear her coat. Her new dress and little red hat would be all she'd need. She laid out Franco's best suit. He came running in, had a quick wash and changed into his suit.

She thought how handsome he was. He looked typically Italian with skin that seemed permanently suntanned even through the English winter. She watched him comb his dark wavy hair and put on a little Brylcreem to give it a gloss. He'd grown a thin pencil moustache like Ronald Colman the film star, and he stroked a little on that too, to make it shine.

She took his arm and they walked briskly to the register office. 'This is it,' he said, straightening his tie. 'I feel quite jittery.'

Alice and Ben, and other guests, together with the Baldini family were waiting for them, and they were swept into the group.

'You look lovely,' Connie told her and started to introduce her to the guests. Vito had asked his cousin and grown-up family who owned a cafe in a suburb of Liverpool. Ellie knew the others, the newsagent and his wife from the shop next door, and Connie's friend Norah.

She'd hardly had time to say hello before they were all being ushered into a small panelled room. Ellie felt as though the ceremony for which she'd longed so much was happening to somebody else. In no time at all she felt the ring being pushed on her finger and she was a married woman.

Vito had ordered taxis to take them up to the cafe. Ellie knew Connie had deliberated at length about the best place to have the wedding breakfast. They were now too many to fit comfortably into her home and Vito and Danny had been able to prepare the feast during the morning while the cafe was open. It didn't usually close on Thursday afternoons, it was close to the park and the underground station and there was reasonable afternoon trade, but today it had closed.

The small tables had been pushed together and covered with one long starched white cloth. It was now set with glistening cutlery and bowls of pink roses. Ellie was surprised and delighted at the lengths they'd gone to.

'For a wedding, we make a slap-up feed,' Vito told her. There was a plate of antipasto to start with, followed by spaghetti bolognese then steak and chips. There were bottles of

Chianti on the table, and Ellie heard more Italian spoken than she ever had before.

People were pinning pound notes to her dress, the Italian way of giving a wedding present. Vito had made a special ice-cream cake and that was followed by coffee and strega. Then Connie brought out the wedding cake she'd made.

While Franco collapsed the tables and moved the chairs out of the way, Vito brought out his accordion and started playing dance music. Ellie found the high spirits and the camaraderie infectious. Everybody wanted to dance with her but Vito told Franco he must partner her first. Ben insisted on being next.

'This is great,' he told her. 'Franco's lot know how to enjoy themselves, not like ours. You'll be better off with them.'

'Don't I know it. I'm so glad I'm free of Uncle Mick.'

'Wish I was.' Ben looked suddenly wan.

'What's stopping you? You said once you'd like to go to sea.' They circled the floor before he answered.

'I can't leave my mother with him. It would be like abandoning her.'

Ellie remembered that occasionally she'd been woken up by shouting and sobbing in the next bedroom, and when next she saw Wilma she'd be bruised or have a black eye.

It surprised her to find Ben so protective of his mother, but she gave herself up to the fun of the moment and had a lovely time. The party went on for hours.

At eleven o'clock Franco unpinned the money from Ellie's dress and gave it to her. She thanked Connie and Vito and kissed them good night. The velvet sky was bright with stars as she walked home hanging on to Franco's arm, delighted that they'd tied the knot.

When Franco went back to work the next morning, Ellie walked to the Liverpool Savings Bank, opened an account and paid in their wedding present money. She and Franco had talked it over and decided to keep it as a nest egg. She would have much preferred to have his company over the next few days, but was quite happy pottering about their rooms, sorting things out to her satisfaction.

'Don't even think of redecorating,' Franco told her. 'The rooms aren't too bad. You take it easy, have a rest.'

Ellie did just that. She felt relief and satisfaction that she'd have someone to love her for the rest of her life and soon they'd be a real family. The future seemed golden. She was going to give their child as happy an upbringing as she could make it.

Chapter Sixteen

On Monday morning, Ellie went back to work at the Maypole feeling a different person. Her morning sickness was over and her worries were gone. She felt very happy. It was bliss living with Franco instead of Uncle Mick. She thought Franco was happy too.

Alice worked on until she was within eight weeks of the birth. By then even her drill coats couldn't hide the fact that she was pregnant. Ellie had heard the delivery boys whispering about it.

When Alice gave her notice in, she said Mr Duggan hadn't noticed.

'Did you know?' he asked Ellie the next morning, as they got off the same bus and crossed the road to the shop.

'Yes, but I didn't want to say. Alice wanted to work as long as she could. She needs the money.'

'There's a lot of people needing money,' he said severely. 'Not good for her to work in that condition. She'll make herself ill. Not good for the baby.'

'I feel fine,' Alice said when she told her. 'A bit more tired perhaps, but I can cope. You are lucky, Ellie. Nobody would guess with you.'

Ellie missed her friend when she no longer came to work. She was about to give her own notice in when she received a

273

note from Alice saying her baby had been born two weeks early.

'A baby girl,' she'd written, 'of six and a half pounds. We're both made up with her.' She'd had her baby at home. 'Come round to see her on Thursday afternoon when you leave the shop. I'll have a bowl of soup waiting for you. I'm dying to show her off.'

Ellie wrote a note to say she would and enclosed it with a card of congratulations. Alice was in bed when she got there.

'The doctor says I must stay in bed for fourteen days,' she said. 'But I feel fine.' It was Alice's mother who brought up a tray with soup and sandwiches for them both.

Ellie was thrilled to hold Alice's baby in her arms and know she'd have her own baby soon.

'She's lovely.'

Alice was looking at her baby with such love in her eyes. 'We're going to call her Audrey Alice.'

Ellie smiled. 'You're the lucky one now, to have it all behind you. What was it like? Having her?'

'Awful, I don't want to go through that again. But now, well, perhaps it was worth it.'

Christmas was almost on them again. This year, Ellie wasn't giving it her full attention, she had more important things on her mind. Connie was concerned about her and wanted her to stop work.

'Enough's enough, Ellie. If you go on any longer, I shall be afraid of you giving birth behind the counter. Give in your notice now, you deserve a rest.'

Ellie worked to within four weeks of the date her baby was expected. When she left the Maypole for the last time, she found the staff had clubbed together to buy a white wool matinée jacket for her baby, and some fancy soap and talcum powder for her. She had cards wishing her well, as well as Christmas cards.

Mr Duggan was severe with her when she went to his office to say goodbye. 'I don't know what the world's coming to. Have you girls no shame?'

Ellie didn't like that. But it gave her an enormous sense of freedom to take the bus home and know she'd be a lady of leisure for a few weeks.

On her first free morning, Connie took her down to the market. She was keen to help get the baby's layette together, and as Ellie had had little to do with babies, she was glad of her help. Connie knew how many yards of soft muslin would be needed to make napkins to protect the soft skin of the newborn, and how many yards of absorbent terry towelling would be needed to cover them. She was able to pick out the best quality and the bargains.

'You'll also need some white flannel to make binders and some flannelette for gowns.'

Ellie viewed the parcels of cloth she'd bought. 'Well, I've made a start.'

'My Christmas present from Vito this year is to be a new sewing machine, a treadle,' Connie told her. 'You can have my old one, if you'd like it. You'll find it useful for making baby clothes.'

Ellie was delighted. 'I'd love it but I've never used a sewing machine.'

'Come home with me and I'll show you how.'

Connie used one of her spare bedrooms as a sewing room. She helped Ellie cut the cloth they'd bought into squares of the right size, and showed her how to hem them on the sewing machine. Ellie started practising on scraps of material and was soon absorbed.

The newly-weds spent Christmas Day with Franco's parents as they had the year before, but Ellie enjoyed most the time she and Franco spent sitting quietly by their own fire. They decided on names for their baby: it was to be Alice for a girl and Robert for a boy. The pub was open and Franco had to work his turn, but it brought bigger wages. Ellie took great pleasure in cleaning her rooms and cooking for Franco. It seemed like playing at housekeeping.

Franco wanted only the best for his child. They went out one afternoon and he picked out a smart pram from the babyware department at Robb's, the best department store in town.

'It's lovely but very expensive,' Ellie said.

'We've still got the wedding present money.'

'We need a cot too and a hundred and one other things.' She frowned. 'I think we should leave it for the moment and see if we can get a cheaper one.'

That made her feel a spoil sport. She didn't like saying 'no' to beautiful things, but now she no longer had her own wages to rely on, Ellie was finding the money Franco handed over to her each Friday didn't go very far.

She began to keep simple accounts and after a few weeks, the result shocked them both. When they'd paid for their rent, gas and coal, there was little left over to buy food, let alone provide for the baby's needs. She was glad of Connie's thrift. All the same, Ellie spent a few contented weeks waiting for the birth of her baby.

On the last Sunday in December, the exact date she'd been told to expect the birth, she and Franco were invited to have tea at Connie's house.

'If you can,' Connie had laughed. 'If you're still in waiting.'

All day, Ellie had felt restive. She wanted the waiting time over and the baby in her arms, and felt impatient because nothing was happening. In mid afternoon she and Franco walked up to his parents' house. Tea time came and Ellie enjoyed the cold boiled ham. Franco went off to work shortly afterwards.

He kissed her. 'I'll be home about half eleven, I'll try not to wake you.'

Ellie was spending many evenings alone at home and it was a change to spend the evening with her in-laws. Connie was making more white aprons to use in the cafe on her new treadle sewing machine. Ellie was intrigued with it and asked if she might try it.

'I've been very glad of your old hand machine,' she said. 'It's come in very useful.' She'd become proficient on it.

Ellie fed one of the crisp cotton aprons under the foot and had just started sewing when she felt the first pain. When she felt the second, Connie hurried her back to the living-room fire.

She was doubling with the third when she heard Connie say, 'Vito, you'd better go round and tell the midwife.'

'I'll be all right walking home,' Ellie said. 'Tell her I'll be there.'

'We'd better start straight away.' Connie was buttoning her into her coat.

Connie had to keep a firm hold on her nerves. She mustn't show panic, it would frighten Ellie. Ellie was calm enough at the moment, but she had to stop twice in the street when a pain came, and Connie was relieved when they reached the house in Eldon Place and she could help Ellie into bed. She was even more relieved to see Vito bringing in the midwife with her bag.

She knew midwives always asked for boiled water and they wanted it cooled. She and Vito filled kettle and pans to provide it. After fifteen minutes or so the midwife came out.

'Mrs Baldini will be some time yet,' she said. 'I've another mother who's about to give birth. I'll come back later.'

'When?' Connie wanted to know.

'She's some hours off yet, love. Don't you worry. You'll stay with her?'

'Yes, of course, but what if—'

'I'm only going to Oak Street.'

'What number? In case I have to fetch you.'

'Nineteen, but there'll be no need. I'll be back in plenty of time. I've given her something for the pain, you could make her a cup of tea.'

Connie was riven with anxiety. 'You go home,' she told Vito. 'You'll have to work tomorrow come what may. You could call at the Mermaid first to see Franco. Tell him Ellie's started but he mustn't worry, the baby is still hours off being born.'

Connie was making herself sound calmer than she felt. She was worried about being left alone with Ellie. It went through her to see the girl sweating and her pains so strong. She was so tiny and frail looking.

'I'm not frail,' Ellie told her as she wiped a cooling flannel over her face.

Connie was glad to see Franco come home, but when he realised the midwife hadn't returned, he was even more anxious than she was. It had gone midnight when the midwife knocked on the front door.

'Why don't you make up a bed for the husband in the spare room?' she suggested to Connie. But when she'd done it, he refused to leave Ellie's bedside.

Connie was in and out. She had all the hot water that could possibly be needed, and had drunk so much tea she felt waterlogged. It was nearly two o'clock when the midwife first admitted she wasn't happy with Ellie's progress and uttered the word 'disproportion'.

'What's that?' Connie asked.

'Mrs Baldini is very small and the baby could be large.' She was looking at Franco. 'Where is the nearest phone box?'

She went off on her bike to ring the maternity hospital, leaving Connie more worried than ever. Franco was getting panicky. The midwife returned to say an ambulance would be coming for Ellie. It was thought better for her to go to Grange Mount Maternity Hospital.

Feeling fearful, Connie set about putting together what Ellie would need to take with her. Franco was beyond doing anything. When the ambulance arrived fifteen minutes later, Franco went with Ellie.

The first light of dawn was showing in the sky as Connie walked home. She felt utterly drained.

Ellie knew she'd had a long hard labour that had ended with two doctors attending her. They'd given her an anaesthetic and used something they'd called high forceps.

'It's a boy,' she heard them say. 'He weighs seven and a half pounds.' The baby had been placed in her arms but she'd felt so woozy she remembered nothing but a tiny red face peeping through the folds of a hospital towel.

The problem had arisen, they'd explained, because she was so small and the baby took after his father and was a healthy normal size. She knew Franco had come to the hospital with her but he'd not been allowed in the labour ward. It was afternoon when she was moved out to a bed on the ward.

Her son was now in a cradle swinging at the foot of her bed and making soft gurgling noises. Ellie felt sore and achingly tired in her limbs, but her mind was so filled with elation she couldn't keep still in her bed.

It was six in the evening and Ellie could see the other mothers in the ward changing their babies then putting them to the breast. A nurse came and lifted her baby out of his cot. He let out a howl of protest as she demonstrated to Ellie how a napkin was to be put on. .

'Time for his feed,' and before Ellie realised what she was doing the nurse had his gums clamped on her breast. She was thrilled to hold him in her arms and see him suckle. He had pale olive skin and big brown eyes just like Franco's. She wished he'd come, so she could show him his baby.

Visiting time for husbands was seven till seven thirty every evening. Like all the other mothers, as the time drew close, Ellie was watching the ward door. When the visitors were allowed to come in, it was her mother-in-law she saw heading towards her.

Connie stopped to look in the cot before placing a large bunch of daffodils on her bed and sitting down beside her.

'Oh Ellie, he's lovely. Franco's asked for an hour off tonight so he can come, but for him it's not easy. That's why they've let me pop in. Oh no, here he is already! I'll have to go, they said strictly only one visitor per patient.'

She laughed excitedly hanging over the cot. 'I'm delighted with my grandson. He's not the first, but I've never seen the others. I hope I'll see a lot of this one.'

Connie kissed Ellie goodbye. Franco bent over the cot looking enthralled, before sliding into the chair she'd vacated.

'Ellie love,' he said, and she could see tears of emotion glistening in his eyes as he reached for her hand. 'Isn't he wonderful?'

* * *

Fatherhood had crept up on Franco, taken him almost unawares. Perhaps he hadn't thought enough about Ellie, what she was going through and what it would mean. He got up to look again at his new son in the metal basket and felt such wonder.

It was hard to believe this scrap of humanity would grow into a man. A man very much like him, if Ellie was to be believed. Gently he moved the soft wrappings back so he could see more of him. Tiny and helpless, his child made him feel protective.

'Just look at his tiny ears, and his hands, so perfect.'

Ellie made him feel protective too, lying in her white bed looking absolutely spent. He promised silently that he'd always do his best for his little family. He owed her that much.

Life had been better all round since they'd been married. He hadn't expected to find it so satisfying. He'd felt at the time that he was being pushed into it, but things had been altogether more comfortable for both of them in rooms of their own. He was glad to see less of his parents and escape their complaints and niggles.

And at long last, he had a job that wasn't a tiresome bore. He'd always liked pubs. To be paid to spend time in the Mermaid pleased him, he was enjoying it. When the bell was rung to signal the end of visiting time, he was loath to leave Ellie but he had to go back.

'I've got a son,' he announced happily to customers and staff alike. 'A fine little chap of seven and a half pounds. We're going to call him Robert Francis.'

Franco had decided on the English version of his name. He wasn't having a child of his saddled with the same Italian heritage. 'He'll be Bobby for short.'

Everybody wanted to buy him a drink. Franco was happy and could see no reason to refuse, he had a lot to celebrate.

* * *

Franco woke up the next morning with a thick head and a gummy tongue and the rooms were cold in every sense without Ellie. He stayed in his lonely bed until it was time to go to work, allowing just enough time to cut a slice of bread and marmalade and make a cup of tea.

He was all right once he got to the pub, it was warm and friendly. Now he'd been working there for a while, Franco understood what Joe had been trying to tell him. It seemed to be common knowledge in the district that the Mermaid was a good place to pick up a girl for the night, from either side of the bar.

At first, he didn't think it likely that Winnie could be involved in anything like that. Perhaps she dressed to attract male attention but that was almost a uniform for a barmaid. Nobody looked less like his idea of a call girl. But more than once, he'd heard her arranging with a man to accompany her home when the pub closed.

He got on well with Winnie. She was easy going and enjoyed a laugh; what's more, she pulled her weight behind the bar. But he found it hard to believe men were willing to pay a woman as old as her for that additional service.

She wasn't good looking and didn't turn him on, she was too old. He'd never paid to satisfy what his father referred to as his primitive urges. He didn't want to. Gladys was at it too. She was in her thirties and more in demand, but she was less outgoing than Winnie.

Bill Secker sought honesty in his staff, but Franco knew he didn't have it. He saw the two women charge for drinks and ring up a lesser amount on the till than they should, so they could pocket the difference. Late in the evenings when the customers had had plenty to drink and were less likely to notice, he saw them giving short change. He said as much to Winnie.

'Can't afford to be too honest, not if we're ever to have any sort of a life, can we?'

Franco had always counted himself as honest; his parents had extolled it as a necessary virtue. He thought Winnie was right, he and Ellie wouldn't have much of a life on his wages, but he didn't like to think of himself as a thief. It took him some time to try it, but he found that helping himself to a little extra cash was an added thrill. It was that sort of pub. There was something titillating about the atmosphere which added to his enjoyment.

Ellie would be in hospital, lying-in for fourteen days, and he was really missing her. When the pub closed after the morning session, he went up to the caff where his father saved a hot meal for him.

Sunday and Thursday afternoons were all right, he could rush to the hospital and sit by Ellie's bed until four o'clock. If the evenings were busy the time went quickly and if they were slack Mr Secker would let him have an hour off to see Ellie.

His day off was on Monday, and that was harder to get through. He had to light a fire and do a bit of shopping for himself. He even rinsed through some of his shirts and hung them out on the line in the yard. He would have liked to go to the pictures that evening, but the hospital visiting time made it difficult. He spent more time at the caff and at his mother's.

For the first time in his life he felt he'd rather be at work than have a day off. Without Ellie, he felt lost at home.

Franco had other difficulties. In the last weeks of her pregnancy Ellie hadn't been exactly keen on his love making. Not that she would ever refuse him, she was not that sort, but he'd felt her reluctance and didn't like it. In the hospital she had whispered that they should wait six weeks before they made love again. He didn't know how he was going to get through all that time, but he'd do his best.

At long last the day came for Ellie to be discharged from hospital. On his way to work that morning, he called at the garage her uncle used to own, and ordered a taxi for the afternoon. All morning he could think of only one thing: Ellie and the baby were coming home.

When the pub closed he ran home, and met his mother as she was leaving.

'I've cleaned the place through and lit the fire. I brought some cake and some lasagne that will only need heating up. And I've made you a sandwich to eat now. Don't you let Ellie wait on you,' she told him. 'It'll take her time to get her strength back.'

He was already getting out the suitcase into which Ellie had packed clothes for herself and the baby. 'As if I would,' he called.

Ellie was simmering with excitement when he arrived. 'I can't wait to be home.' She had the suitcase opened in seconds. Screens were pulled round her bed for privacy and Franco was led to a seat in the hall. The nurse took the baby clothes and little Bobby was returned to him in a bundle of shawls. He was such a light weight in his arms.

It was a new life for Ellie. She was happy and felt she had everything she could possibly want. Early mornings were a time of leisurely awakenings, of feeding and playing with Bobby, all three of them cuddling together in bed.

Franco would eventually get up to make some tea and bring it back to bed. They both got dressed when the time drew close for Franco to leave for work. He cooked breakfast for them both while Ellie fed Bobby again.

When Franco had gone, she busied herself with the baby. Franco returned shortly after two o'clock for the dinner she prepared and they spent the afternoons together.

Sometimes they took the baby out for an airing, sometimes they went shopping, occasionally they stayed by their own fireside. They talked about Bobby, how much they loved him, how rewarding a baby was.

'But we don't want a big Italian family, do we?' he said. 'Two children, a son and a daughter. That's plenty.'

'Most families are bigger than that,' she'd smiled. Franco had an aversion to anything Italian. 'Right now I feel I have my hands full with just Bobby, but in a year or so I might like a little girl. Two will be fine.'

'If we have a small family, we'll be able to afford other things.' Franco's dark eyes shone as they looked into the future. 'A car, I really fancy having a car.'

That seemed an impossible dream to Ellie.

She wasn't so fond of the evenings on her own, which she found a little lonely. She cleaned and polished up her home once she'd put Bobby down for the night, and she discovered a great source of books in the public library to while away the long winter evenings.

It became routine for Connie to invite them to tea on Sundays. They wheeled Bobby up in his pram and when Franco had to go back to work, Ellie stayed on. When Bobby's bedtime came she put him to sleep in his pram and wheeled it straight to her bedroom when she got home.

Gradually she got to know the other people who rented rooms in the house in Eldon Place. She met them in the hall and from time to time they came through her kitchen when she was cooking.

Miss Minton was always very apologetic, always knocking

first if the door was closed, and pausing to pass the time of day. She was a fifty-year-old spinster who worked in an office, grey haired and grey of face; she crept softly about the house and hung large undergarments on the line in the yard to dry.

Ellie found her pleasant enough for a ten-minute chat, and she always brought in her washing if it began to rain during the day when Miss Minton was at work, but she wasn't the sort of person Ellie could make a friend of. There was a couple called Brown but Mrs Brown kept herself aloof. Miss Minton said she was a little strange in the head, but nothing to worry about.

Ellie had taken a dislike to the landlord. She didn't like the way he looked at her whenever they met. According to Miss Minton, since his wife had died two years ago, he'd become even more odd than Mrs Brown.

She was missing Alice's company. She lived a bus ride away which meant Ellie couldn't take the pram, and anyway, she had her family all round her in the evenings. Alice was looking for company in the afternoons when Ellie wanted to be with Franco. She found his working hours more of a burden than he did.

Money was still short but Franco understood. He'd got into the habit of pushing a few extra shillings into her hand from time to time.

'Where do you get this money from?' she asked.

'Tips from the pub.' He grinned at her. 'People invite me to have a drink with them, but I drink water and keep the money instead.'

March came in and the weather was wet and windy, but Ellie was beginning to think of the long light evenings to come.

'I'd like to try making myself a dress for summer,' she told Connie. She'd got her slim figure back.

'Good idea, it'll give you something to do in the evenings.'

'I've got a pattern, it was in a magazine that Miss Minton gave me.'

'Why don't we go down to the market tomorrow morning?' Connie asked. 'I might get myself a dress length too. I'll walk down to your place and pick you up.'

It was a wet morning. Ellie was glad she had the pram for Bobby. They carried it between them up the steps to the covered market, where there were several stalls selling dressmaking materials. Connie bought a length of grey and white cotton, Ellie chose a floral print in peach and white.

'Will you help me cut it out? I've never made a dress.'

'Tomorrow, yes. Vito wants me to give a hand over the lunch time.' Ellie knew she usually did, lunch time was their busy period.

Though the rain had stopped now, the roads were still wet. They were crossing Market Square on their way home when a van tooted for them to hurry out of its way. Ellie didn't see what happened next but she heard Connie's cry of pain. One minute she was walking beside her and the next she was lying on her back in the road, and the van was slithering to a halt yards from her.

'Oh! Goodness me!' Connie was trying to sit up.

'Are you all right?' Ellie retrieved her handbag and helped her to her feet. 'You're hurt?'

Ellie could see the fall had knocked the wind out of her, she was a heavy woman.

'My back.' Connie was having difficulty straightening up.

'You need something to hold on to.' Ellie guided her to the pram handle.

Connie grimaced with pain. 'What a silly thing to do.'

'You must have slipped in that horse manure.'

'Oh dear!'

'It's all up your coat. I'll sponge it for you when we get home.'

It had been Ellie's intention to go back to her rooms and Connie's to go up to the cafe, but her face was grey with pain and she was limping.

'You'd better go straight home and lie down,' Ellie told her.

'Vito's expecting me . . .'

'I could go in your place. I won't be as much use, but I'll be another pair of hands.'

'You've got Bobby to think of.'

'He's flat out now and will be all right in the store room for a couple of hours. He isn't due another feed until two.'

Back at Harcourt Street, she helped Connie upstairs to her bed. She looked very shaken and was glad to lie down.

'I've brushed the back of your coat, but it's wet and it still smells.'

'Leave it, Ellie. I'll see to it later.'

'Aspirins, they'll help. Shall I make you some tea?'

'A glass of water will do. Vito will be wondering where I am.'

'I'm going now.'

'Why don't you bring Bobby up here? He'd be better with me.' Ellie knew she loved to see him, and couldn't get enough of him. 'He'll be fine on Vito's side of the bed.'

'Bobby sleeps well between feeds. He won't trouble you much.' Ellie managed to carry him upstairs without waking him.

When she reached the cafe, it was more than busy. Vito was concerned about Connie but had no time to talk.

'What can I do to help?' Ellie asked.

'Take the orders.' He pushed a pencil and pad in her hand. 'Write down what they want and don't forget the table number.'

She reached for one of Connie's aprons, wanting to look the part. It swamped her, reaching the floor.

'You'll trip over that,' Vito took it from her. 'We've nothing to fit you. You'll do as you are.'

To Ellie, it seemed bedlam. She found it a struggle to keep on top of things. The throng of people reminded her of working in the Maypole, but there was a greater buzz of chatter here. She shot in and out of the kitchen, taking in orders and bringing out the plates of food Danny dished up.

It seemed almost a miracle when the tables emptied and they had time to speak. She filled Vito in on the details of Connie's accident. He was full of praise for the way she'd stepped in and helped.

'I'll have to go,' she said. 'Franco will be home before me, and I've nothing ready for his dinner.'

'Take something from here,' Vito said. 'What is there left, Danny?'

Ellie found herself running home with two portions of Neapolitan salad and two portions of lasagne balanced on Bobby's pram, while he wailed for his two o'clock feed. She'd quite enjoyed her busy morning.

Before Franco returned to the pub that evening, they walked up to see how his mother was.

'A little better,' she said, 'but my back still aches.'

'Would you do the same tomorrow?' Vito asked. 'Connie would be better for the rest.'

'Yes, I'd be glad to.'

'We'll pay you, of course.'

Ellie was pleased, it would ease the family budget. The following Sunday, she asked Connie how she was feeling.

'I'm fine. I could have gone back to work yesterday but I've really enjoyed staying at home. It's been lovely having Bobby here with me.'

Vito said, 'Do you fancy carrying on, Ellie? Just working for a few hours over the lunch time?'

'Yes,' Ellie said. 'But am I much use to you?'

'Ellie, you bustle round at twice Connie's pace, and you're a wizard at adding up the bills. You learn fast, you've soon got the hang of things.'

She smiled. 'I like being in the thick of things. It makes a complete change for me.'

'We're so busy these days that I've had to call on Connie more and more. I think she's finding it hard going.'

'It's six days a week with hardly a let-up,' Connie said. 'I'd love to look after Bobby instead. I could take him out shopping and to the park.'

'What about my dinner?' Franco wanted to know.

'You can both have it in the cafe. Save you rushing off to cook, Ellie.'

'That would be marvellous, but we'd be eating your profits and you're already paying me to help.'

'You'd only be offered what we haven't sold. There's always bits of this and that left over.'

'Thank you, I hardly know how—'

'You are family, after all,' Connie said.

Ellie glowed, that made her feel she belonged and that they really cared about her. 'And you're looking after Bobby for me.'

'That's my pleasure. Mostly, I'll be coming for my dinner and I'll bring him with me.'

Connie was all smiles when the arrangement was agreed. And Ellie was just as delighted. It would help the housekeeping.

Chapter Seventeen

As the evenings became lighter, Ellie was able to get out more. When it was time for Franco to go to work, she'd put Bobby in his pram and walk up to the pub with him and then walk on to the park. There was plenty going on there, always people playing on the tennis courts and sometimes a game of cricket in progress.

One evening, she sat down on a bench overlooking the duck pond, and watched some children throwing bread to the ducks. Later, two little girls came scampering towards her and climbed up on the other end of the seat. Their mother was close behind them, with an empty pushchair and a toddler just beginning to walk. She sat down, pushed her gingery hair back from her face and asked Ellie if she knew what the time was. They started to chat.

'I know your face,' Ellie said. 'I've seen you about. Do you live near Eldon Place?'

'Just round the corner from there,' she said. 'In Garnet Street, but you work in the trattoria near the Park Station, don't you? I took the kids in for ice cream on Peggy's birthday and saw you there.'

'Yes, of course . . .'

'I see you going up our street most mornings about eleven.'

'On my way to work. I remember you coming in. This is the birthday girl?'

'Yes, this is Peggy, she's six.' She put her hand on the shoulder of the larger girl. 'And this is Pat, she's four. I'm Irene Cobbold, by the way, and the baby's called Jimmy. My husband's at sea, is yours?'

'No, but he works odd hours in a pub, so I'm alone a lot.'

'I'm alone all the time,' Irene said. 'For weeks on end.'

Ellie said, 'I used to work at the Maypole, and was used to seeing a lot of people. I didn't think I'd miss them, but I do.'

Irene smiled. 'I know. I love my kids, but looking after them without Len at home, I sometimes feel cut off from the world.'

'I look forward to him coming home for months. He's deep sea, you know, and his ship only comes back to a British port every Preston Guild. We have a lovely time when he's on leave, but when he goes back I usually find I've another baby on the way.'

Ellie told her about being related to the Baldinis and how much she enjoyed working in the cafe. They walked home together. When they reached Irene's front door, she asked Ellie in to have a cup of tea.

'I'd love to.' She smiled. 'My evenings seem long and lonely.'

Together they lifted Bobby and his pram through to the kitchen. Ellie looked round with interest, the rooms were tiny compared with her own. 'I do envy you having a house of your own.'

'We could do with a bigger place. One with a hall where I could keep the pushchair.'

'Anywhere with its own front door would suit me. I want to be able to shut myself away on my own.'

Ellie could see Irene's brown eyes studying her. 'I thought you said you wanted company, that you were lonely.'

'Mm, I am.' She told her about the other tenants in the house having to walk through her hall and kitchen. 'It's Mr

Brunt, the landlord, I don't like. He sort of leers at me, tries to touch me. He gives me the creeps.'

'Have you told your husband?'

'He thinks I'm imagining it, but says find somewhere else if you want to move.'

'Have you tried?'

'Yes, but he won't want to walk five extra paces to the pub. He finds Eldon Place very handy.'

'I'll keep an eye out for you.'

Ellie thought she might have found a friend. She was happier through the summer weeks, she had a routine now. She spent Sunday evenings with Connie and Vito, and Wednesday evenings round at Irene's house. Irene said with three children to put to bed, it was impossible to come to Ellie's place late in the evenings. She warned her that it would be harder to take Bobby out in the evenings when he was older.

Ellie saw a lot of Irene. They took to each other and had a mutual need for company. On fine evenings, they often met in the park. When Irene's husband came home, Ellie expected to be ignored for the two weeks of his shore leave but Irene asked her to babysit almost every other evening. She pushed Bobby round in his pram and wheeled it up the back entry into Irene's kitchen. At the end of the evening, she wheeled the pram into her bedroom, and Bobby didn't realise he'd had his ten-o'clock feed in someone else's house.

Ellie came home after eleven one night, and after settling Bobby in her bedroom went to her kitchen to make a sandwich for Franco. She was cutting the bread when Mr Brunt came through.

'Hello, you're up late. Got a good appetite too.' His eyes were lecherous.

'It's for my husband, when he finishes work.'

'He's a lucky man. How about making one for me?'

He went on his way, leaving the back door ajar. Ellie spread margarine as quickly as she could, then put on some of the boiled bacon Franco had been given by his father. She wanted to be behind her own door before Mr Brunt returned. She didn't quite manage it. She was reaching for a plate.

'That for me then, love?' His hand brushed along her arm, making her jerk away. 'Looks delicious.' He was looking at her not the sandwich.

'You know it isn't. Let me be.'

She pushed past him and dashed to her living room, slamming the door. Too late, she realised the key was in the lock on the hall side. She leaned back against it, her heart hammering as his heavy boots crunched on the hall lino, and was sweating with relief when they passed her door and went on upstairs. She'd been afraid he was going to follow her in. She thought him repulsive.

Ellie hated the lack of privacy. There always seemed to be other people walking through her kitchen when she was cooking or cleaning. The front door slammed regularly, followed by footsteps clumping upstairs and often there were echoing voices.

If she stayed at home in the evening, Ellie liked to keep her doors closed, but once she'd put Bobby down for the night, she needed to leave them open so she could hear him if he woke.

The answer seemed to be to go to bed early, as Bobby's cot was in their bedroom, but when Franco was at work, she didn't like being undressed and in bed. There were frequent footsteps passing her door. The slithering feet belonged to Mrs Brown, Miss Minton clipped along in dainty high heels, and the heavy tread she was listening to now . . . Was it Mr Brunt? Was it her imagination or did the feet pause outside her bedroom when he saw the light shining under her door?

No, the back door hadn't slammed, it must have been Mr Brown. He was all right, barely speaking if they met. All the same, she got up and locked her door on the inside. Only then did she feel safe. But she'd have to unlock it for Franco to come in around midnight, so it was impossible to settle to sleep.

When at last Franco came, she'd been dozing off and on. 'I want to move house,' she whispered. 'I've had enough of these rooms.'

'I'm tired . . .'

'I know, so am I.'

'We'll talk about it in the morning.' He was throwing his clothes off.

'We've already talked about it lots of times. These rooms are expensive for what they are, really we can't afford them.'

Franco grunted and got into bed beside her. His feet were cold, and he put them on hers to warm them.

'Your pa says—'

'You've talked about it to him?' She felt him stiffen.

'Why not? Your mother too. They really want us to live with them. They'll rearrange the rooms to suit us.'

'You know I don't want that.'

'There'd be advantages. Built-in babysitters for a start. It would be easy for me to go out to see my friends. On your night off, we could go to the pictures.'

Franco grunted again. 'You wouldn't like it after a while. I had twenty-four years of it and I know how difficult they can be.'

'When the long winter nights come, I'd be glad of their company.'

'They'd soon get on your nerves.'

'What about a little house to ourselves then? It needn't cost much more.'

'Ellie, we can't afford this. Not really, and I don't think you'll find anywhere better. Anyway, I'm used to it now.'

Ellie decided she'd start looking seriously.

Every day, when the pub closed at two, Franco hurried up to the caff for his dinner. By the time he got up there, the number of customers coming through the doors had usually fallen off and the family were getting ready to sit round the kitchen table and eat their own meal.

Franco was a proud father, and it pleased him to see his parents making such a fuss of little Bobby. He loved spending most of his afternoons playing with him.

'I wouldn't see nearly as much of him if I had normal working hours,' he told Ellie. If he had a quibble with the new arrangements, it was that Ellie had to work to add to his earnings. It made him feel that he couldn't provide adequately for his own family. He loved his job, and thought the pub seemed a happy place.

It came as something of a surprise to hear that Gladys had given in her notice.

'Why?' he asked her.

'Got a job at a place called the Golden Lion over in Liverpool. Better pay.'

Winnie whispered some time later, 'She's been going out with one of the barmen there. Fancies him and wants to see more of him. Reckons working with him is the answer.'

Mr Secker wasn't pleased. 'I like to keep my staff. The customers like to see the same faces.'

Winnie said, 'There's a girl I know, she asked me if there

was any chance of a job here. She's got a room in the same house as me.'

'Isn't she working?'

'Yes, at the Lighterman's Arms, but at closing time the buses are difficult from there. This would be handy for her.'

Mr Secker sighed. 'Better ask her to come in and see me. On Monday if possible.'

Franco had a day off on Monday. 'Has your friend got the job?' he asked Winnie the next morning. If Secker hadn't hired her it would mean they'd have much more to do.

'Yes, she's starting the day Gladys leaves.'

'What's she like?'

'Young – well, she's twenty-nine.'

'Not that young.'

'You'll like her, everybody does. Her name's Flossie Phillips.'

Knowing she was four years older than him, Franco didn't expect to find Flossie particularly attractive, but when Winnie brought her in on her first day, he thought she was stunning.

'I'm sure we'll all get on together,' Winnie said. 'She's very friendly.'

Franco didn't doubt it. Flossie was a golden blonde, with a fulsome figure. She was curvaceous, with a narrow waist and brimming breasts, and wore a low-cut scarlet blouse that put enough cleavage on show to make his father disapprove. Franco felt the tug of physical attraction the moment her high heels came clacking behind the bar. He couldn't drag his eyes away.

Flossie kept giving him knowing glances. She spoke with a husky drawl, was jolly and always giggling. She was a huge attraction behind the bar, customers came in night after night to joke with her. She had a quick repartee and a huge smile for everyone.

Winnie had no need to teach Flossie how to short-change the customers, Franco saw her doing it, just as at times he caught Winnie at it. They were getting away with it too.

If they saw nothing wrong with cheating the customers and the licensee, Franco thought he'd be daft not to follow suit. His financial responsibilities were greater than theirs. Winnie was right, if he was to have money for smokes and an occasional drink as well as look after Ellie and the baby, he had no choice.

He'd tried it and found it easy, like taking sweets from babies. He put his qualms behind him and began doing it as regularly as the other staff.

The first time he heard a man proposition Flossie, he was shocked. She could be flirtatious, but she didn't seem that sort of a girl, she was much too nice. When time was called that night, the man was the last customer to leave and after that Franco could see him having a smoke in the porch while he waited. They were supposed to tidy up before they left. Flossie was rushing to collect a few empty glasses before she went.

When Franco left, he could see them going up the steps at 36 Cunliffe Street where she had a room. He set off for home at a rapid pace, riddled with jealousy.

It was after midnight when Franco unlocked his front door. He was always the last to come home, and had been told by the landlord to put the bolt on. He straightened up from doing it and the silence seemed absolute. There was a slight glow showing under their living-room door, otherwise the place was in darkness. He felt his way towards it. He was always hungry when he finished work, so Ellie left him a sandwich between two plates. He took a bite: cheese and pickle. Balancing the plate on his knee he sank back on an armchair still thinking about Flossie.

Ellie had turned the gas down to minimum and the room was full of shadows. It felt different tonight, colder than it should be, icy. The fire had gone out.

Franco was tired. The shadows seemed denser in one corner and something was making him peer into them. Was there something there? He saw it move. He stopped chewing and held his breath. It was a man, an old man with sad damp eyes that seemed to plead for help. There was such anguish on his face that Franco felt he could sense the turmoil in his mind. He felt the hairs on the back of his neck stand up.

'Who's there?' He jerked the words out, straining his eyes into the darkness. 'Who's there?'

There was no sound, nothing. Nothing but the shadows. Franco leapt to his feet and fled to the hall. There was no light showing under their bedroom door which meant Ellie and Bobby were asleep. He opened the door.

It was thrift that drove him back to their living room to turn out the gas, that and the thought of Ellie's displeasure if he left it burning all night. He threw off his clothes and got into bed beside her.

'Are you awake, Ellie?'

She was warm, cosy, he felt safe here. He put his cold feet on hers. It made her gasp and move away, and he snuggled into the space her body had warmed.

'I've just seen a ghost,' he told her. 'This house is haunted.'

She was only half awake. 'No.' She rolled over on her back. 'No, Franco.'

Franco was quite sure he had. Even when Bobby's cries woke him up the next morning, he was sure. He wasn't worried about ghosts of people he'd known and liked, he could trust them, but this ghost had been a soul in torment, it had scared him. He started telling Ellie all about it.

'A ghost? You imagined it, there's no such thing as ghosts.'

'Your gran believed in them.'

'Yes, but Gran was seeking comfort, trying to reach her loved ones. What are you seeking?'

'Nothing.' He went on recounting the details, trying to convince her. While they were both in the kitchen cooking their egg and bacon breakfast, Mrs Brown from upstairs came shuffling through on her way to the lavatory in the yard.

'You believe in ghosts, don't you?' Franco asked, and told her what he'd seen.

'A ghost? Here?' She was pursing her lips.

'In our living room.'

She didn't seem surprised. 'What sort of a ghost?'

'An old man. Bent, his face was screwing in agony.'

'Oh my goodness! Could it be Mr Caldwell?'

'Who's Mr Caldwell?' Franco asked, but she'd shot through the kitchen and out into the yard. 'She knows there's a ghost here,' he told Ellie. 'You can tell she knows, can't you?'

He ran upstairs and knocked on Miss Minton's door to see if she could tell him more.

'A ghost?' Her hand went to her throat.

'I saw it,' Franco insisted. 'Mrs Brown thought it might be a Mr Caldwell. Who was he?'

'He lived in your rooms.'

Franco's mouth went dry. 'What? The last tenant?'

'No, early last year. We all remember him, he was a widower and not managing well on his own. He was accused of shoplifting and was so upset he committed suicide.'

'Oh my goodness!' He felt his stomach turn over. 'In our living room?'

Mrs Brown was coming back, panting a little from climbing

the stairs. 'No, here in the stairwell. He hanged himself from the banisters and kicked the chair away.'

Franco was rubbing his hands down the sides of his trousers. They were sticky with sweat.

'Mrs Brown found him in the morning,' Miss Minton added.

'I knew it,' he breathed. 'I saw him.'

The landlord was out on the landing and overheard some of that. 'What are you trying to do?' He was belligerent towards the women. 'Scare my tenants away? Ghosts? There's no such thing here. This has always been a happy house. Keep your daft ideas to yourself.'

Franco rushed downstairs to see Ellie carrying their breakfast into their living room. They always ate there to get privacy. He followed reluctantly, telling her about Mr Caldwell.

'It still feels funny in here, as though there's a ghost. It's cold, isn't it?'

'Yes, but we haven't lit the fire. The whole house is cold.'

In the hard morning light there were no shadows. No marks on the wallpaper either, nothing to make him think of ghosts. Ellie was tucking into her breakfast.

'I don't like it here,' he said. 'You're right, perhaps we should move.'

'Franco,' she was screwing up her face in surprise, 'we agreed we'd look for a little house, that we needed a place to ourselves. Yesterday afternoon, I told you Irene had found one for us.'

Franco dipped bread into the yolk of his egg. He didn't think she had.

'It's in Garnet Street, where she lives. We could go and see it this afternoon.'

Franco knew it was an extravagance they couldn't afford, but they needed to move from here. The house was almost opposite Irene's and she was very keen for Ellie to come closer.

Ellie said she knew what to expect because the layout was the same as Irene's. They stepped through the front door straight into the living room.

'Not very big,' he said. It was half the size of their present one.

'It can be made cosy, and there's a good-size kitchen at the back. Big enough to put our table in.'

They inspected the bedrooms, two of reasonable size and one small one. They walked on down to the agent's and took a tenancy on it.

'I'll be glad to get away from the ghost,' Franco said, 'but the new place needs redecorating.'

'I'm glad to get away from Mr Brunt,' Ellie countered. 'Irene said she'd help me paint.'

The afternoons were the most convenient time for painting and papering. Franco did his best to help with the work. They were both very pleased with the new house.

'It's lovely to shut the front door and know there's only us here,' she said.

But it wasn't long before Ellie had another worry. She'd had a nagging suspicion at the back of her mind for a week or so. She tried not to think about it. After all, Bobby was only five months old and she was still feeding him herself. When she'd been in hospital for his birth, the mother in the next bed had told her that you couldn't get pregnant again all the time you were breast feeding, and the other mothers had agreed.

She was clinging to the hope that they were right. She didn't feel ready to go through pregnancy and childbirth again after so short a time. She was happy with the family she had, and didn't think they could afford another, not yet.

She put off telling Franco until six o'clock one wet June morning. Bobby woke them both crying for his feed. He was just beginning to sleep through the night. Ellie got up and changed him, then brought him into their bed as usual. He'd been slurping away happily when she'd felt such a wave of nausea, she'd had to pull Bobby off the breast and push him on the dozing Franco.

She'd retched over the kitchen sink for ages, unable to face crossing the wet yard to the lavatory in her nightdress. Bobby's screams were tearing her in two. Another baby? How would they cope?

'What's the matter?' A bleary-eyed Franco had come behind her, leaving Bobby screaming in the bedroom.

'I've been sick. Oh Lord, Franco, I think I'm pregnant again.'

'Come back to bed, you'll freeze here.'

He put an arm round her shoulders and hurried her across the hall, shivering with cold and apprehension. Ellie felt exhausted but Bobby was howling and waving his fists in anger at having his feed interrupted. She had to put him back on the breast to restore peace.

'You weren't sick last time,' Franco said.

'No, just felt sick.'

'It could be those sausages we had for tea last night, they did taste a bit funny.'

'It's not just being sick. I was almost sure before that.'

'Perhaps it's a false alarm,' he said, putting his arms round both her and the feeding baby in another hug that was meant to comfort. 'Better if we wait and see.'

Ellie felt tears start to her eyes. 'I've had one baby, I know what the signs are. I've been hoping I was wrong, but I'm not.'

'Don't upset yourself. Perhaps—'

'There's no perhaps, Franco. I'm certain.'

'I should have been more careful,' he admitted. 'French letters cost ten shillings a packet. It's hard to find that sometimes.'

'Another mouth to feed will cost more,' Ellie told him sadly.

'You said it couldn't happen yet.'

Ellie mopped at her eyes. She had, she shouldn't blame Franco. She tried to smile.

'When I was having Bobby, I thought that if only I was married I wouldn't mind how many babies I had.'

'They've still got to be fed and cared for.' Franco kissed her. 'It's come too soon, hasn't it? I'm sorry, love. Let's keep it to ourselves for a bit, eh? Until we're more used to the idea.'

Ellie tried to carry on as though it wasn't happening. It was what she'd done last time. She wanted to keep on working for Vito because she enjoyed it and because of the money.

She found pregnancy harder this time, because she had Bobby to look after. She put him on the bottle. As time went on, she found getting up in the mornings more difficult and getting through all the jobs she had to do took longer.

In the half light one morning, Franco came across the bed to her before she was really awake. He was fondling her, she knew he wanted to make love. All she wanted was to be left in peace.

He kissed her. When he moved his lips off hers she whispered, 'Bobby will wake up soon and want his feed.'

'I'll give it to him,' he said, but she pushed him off, she just couldn't be bothered, wasn't in the mood.

Franco was angry and although she said, 'All right, then,' it was too late. They'd had their first row.

When she took Bobby up to Connie's house before going on to the cafe, Connie looked at her and asked: 'Are you all right? You don't look well.'

Ellie felt the tears running down her cheeks before she could hide them. Connie's arms went round her, hugging her to her ample bosom.

She couldn't confess exactly what had caused her distress, that was too personal. 'I'm having another baby,' she said.

'I thought you were. You've got mauve shadows under your eyes, just like you had last time. That's good, isn't it?'

'I'm finding it a bit hard.' Ellie blew her nose.

'You're upset about it? I can see you are. What's wrong with having another baby? Bobby's lovely, better to have them while you're young. Your trouble, Ellie, is that you're trying to do too much. You must stop working. You've given me a lovely rest, but now it's my turn again.'

Ellie was shaking her head. She let it all come out then. How much she needed what Vito paid her; how hard she'd found it to make ends meet, and that their little nest egg of wedding money was spent. And that was without having another mouth to feed.

Franco felt guilty. Ellie had not been feeling well over the last month of her pregnancy. Bobby was a ball of energy, able to toddle round their new house, putting his fingers into everything. He kept Ellie on the go most of the day, giving her little chance to rest.

Franco wanted to make love with his usual frequency. Ellie had never shown any reluctance before, but now she did. He felt guilty if he insisted, and deprived if he didn't. To make things more difficult, the delectable Flossie was clearly interested in him. If they weren't busy, she'd follow him about the bar and her hands would reach out to touch him.

If there was nobody watching she would stroke his shoulder and laugh up into his face. Flossie exuded sexuality at every pore, he couldn't help but think of her as great fun. She was a huge temptation.

Franco knew now that, like Gladys and Winnie, she took men back to her room and took money from them. He saw many who were willing to pay up.

He'd heard her laughing with Winnie, 'I might go full time and give this job up.'

'No,' Winnie told her. 'This is where you pick the blokes up. Far better than trying to do that out on the street.'

Afterwards, he asked Winnie how long she'd known Flossie.

'Six months or so. Since she took a room in the same house.'

'Some of the customers seem to know her.'

'Flossie's well known in the district. Everybody talks about her.'

'What do they say?'

'This and that.'

'Come on, Winnie, don't hold back with me. What's the gossip?'

'Gossip is what it is. Everybody's interested in her. You know that.'

'Yes . . . I suppose you think I am too?'

Winnie laughed. 'All right, they say Flossie was married at sixteen and that she deserted her husband and two children.'

Franco straightened up, feeling shocked.

'They say she took her toddlers to her mother-in-law, telling her she was going to the hairdresser's and would be back in a couple of hours. She packed her bags instead and never returned.'

'Gossip,' he said. He didn't want to believe that of Flossie. She seemed too nice a person to desert her own toddlers.

'Safer to leave her alone, Frank.' Winnie looked serious. 'Look elsewhere if—'

'I don't pay for sex.' He was indignant that she thought he would.

She laughed. 'Not all her men have to. If Flossie fancies a man she'll do it for nothing, she enjoys it so much.'

That took Franco's breath away. He knew she fancied him and was doing her best to show it. He was tempted but determined not to succumb. He hadn't looked at another girl in all the months he'd been married to Ellie. He never would. He was going to play fair with her and keep his conscience clear.

All the same, when he got home from the pub and slid into bed beside Ellie, he was fighting his natural instincts again. It wasn't something he was used to doing.

Many nights, he suspected Ellie was only pretending to be asleep. It would take him ages to get off, and usually she was genuinely flat out before he managed it. Franco consoled himself with the thought that she would be back to normal once this second baby was born. He'd make sure there wouldn't be another for years and years.

Everything was in place for the birth. Ellie had bought another cot, and made it up with sheets and blankets. It was standing ready in their bedroom. Since they'd moved to this house, Bobby had been sleeping in another room. The midwife had arranged for Ellie to go in to Grange Mount Maternity Hospital again, and Connie had said she'd look after Bobby while she was in.

Irene Cobbold had offered to babysit Bobby if Ellie started her pains in the night and Franco had to take her to hospital. Franco was looking forward to having the second baby, but at the same time he was dreading the birth.

Bobby turned fourteen months old on the night Franco felt Ellie shaking him awake.

'Franco, I've having pains. I've started. Wake up please.'

He felt he'd only just got off to sleep. 'Oh God! What time is it?'

'Half past three.'

Franco panicked. There'd be no buses running at that time of night, and no taxis, and the nearest public phone was inside the local post office which would be closed too.

'Get dressed first.' Ellie was already dressing herself. 'Then go and wake Irene.'

'How . . . ?'

'Just hammer on the knocker and ring her bell. You'll have to wake her.'

'Her kids?'

'She says nothing wakes them.'

Irene came across the road wearing pink slippers and a coat over her nightdress. 'I'll put Bobby in his pram and take him over.'

Bobby was a big boy for his age and a tight fit when it came to sleeping in the pram. Franco tried to help but let the pram bump against the door. That woke Bobby up and he started to cry. Ellie was trying to soothe him, but doubling up in pain over his pram.

'You get off,' Irene said firmly. 'I'll see to things here.'

'Come on, Ellie.' Franco took her arm. 'I'm afraid you'll have to walk.'

'I'll be all right. Don't worry, there's plenty of time.' Reassuringly, Ellie sounded her normal self, but the next minute she was gasping as another pain came. 'Don't forget the case. I'll need my nighties and bed jacket.'

He carried the case in one hand and put his other arm round Ellie to urge her along. It seemed that every five minutes she had to stop as another pain came. Franco was scared his second child would be born in the dark street with only him to help. He felt useless, unable to cope, and he'd brought this on Ellie.

Everywhere was in darkness, and there was no traffic on the roads. He was sweating though there was a cold wind. It seemed a long long way up to Grange Mount. He was light-headed with relief when he got Ellie there safely.

He was told to ring up for news at ten the next morning so he walked home, feeling slightly sick, clutching the empty suitcase.

As soon as he arrived home, Irene came running across. 'I saw your lights go on. How's Ellie? Any news?'

He shook his head. 'She got there all right.'

'Bobby's been no trouble at all,' she reported. 'I gave him a drink of water and he went straight back to sleep. Ellie said your mother was having him. Do you want me to take him up?'

'I'd better take him. They'll want to know . . .' He glanced at the clock and couldn't believe it was nearly seven o'clock.

'Yes,' Irene said. 'My kids are up and careering round. I'll bring Bobby home then?'

Five minutes later, Franco sat down in the cold living room with Bobby asleep beside him in his pram. He dozed off, and it was nearly nine when Bobby woke him. He'd never known him sleep so late.

It was a rush then to get breakfast for them both and take Bobby up to his mother's house before he went to work. She immediately turned the pram round and insisted on going with him to the post office on Duke Street to telephone.

Franco stood in the booth waiting for the hospital operator to put him through to the midwife. He shivered as he caught his mother's eye, knowing how keen she was for news.

'Hello, Mr Baldini? Baby isn't here yet. Your wife's labour

309

is proceeding normally and she's as comfortable as we can make her. Ring again between two and three this afternoon.'

'Not yet,' he told his mother. 'I'll ring again when I come out of the pub.'

'Come to the cafe for your dinner. You should have news by then.'

Chapter Eighteen

For Franco, it was a relief to be at work, where the routine had nothing to do with his own family. He could put all his worries about Ellie on hold, he hadn't time to think of her and was glad of it.

He told Winnie and Flossie that he'd taken Ellie to hospital. They thumped him on the back and told him not to worry, his wife was in good hands. They passed on the news to their regulars who bought him drinks.

'Thanks,' he said countless times. 'I'm in need of something strong this morning. A whisky and ginger might settle my nerves.' He was copying what Flossie did with gin and orange, taking the full price but topping up his glass with ginger. He had to stay sober. Ma would half kill him if she saw him the worse for wear today.

There was quite a jolly crowd in and he began to feel better. He quite enjoyed bustling round, refilling glasses as though there was nothing else in his life.

When he walked to the cafe after the pub closed, all his family were sitting round the big table in the kitchen and demanded to know his news. He fetched the dinner Danny had put in the oven for him and sat down.

'I haven't rung yet.'

'What?' His mother was shocked, the rest chorused their

disapproval. Franco had a sinking feeling in his stomach and felt he had to have food first, but they didn't understand that. Ma pushed him out of the door before he'd finished.

He had to wait in the post office because somebody else was using the phone. Suddenly, it seemed urgent and he was twisting the paper on which he'd written the hospital number. Even when it was his turn, he had to wait for the operator to connect him and then wait again for the hospital operator to put him through to the labour ward.

'Mr Baldini?' It was the voice he'd heard this morning. 'You have a son, born a few minutes ago.' She sounded pleased. 'At half past two. He weighs six and a half pounds and both he and your wife are doing well.'

Franco slowly let out the breath he'd been holding. It was safely over.

The voice went on, 'It's visiting this afternoon, between two to four. If you come up now you can see them.'

'I will, thanks.' Franco felt light-headed, and wanted to jump for joy.

'Another son,' he marvelled as he ran back to the caff. 'Another son,' he called to his mother who was out on the step with Bobby in her arms wanting to be the first to hear. 'I'm going up to see them now.'

He caught the first bus that came. It was going to the terminus at Woodside, and he then had to run for another to get up to Grange Mount. He'd travelled miles out of his way, he could almost have walked it in the time. The wards were humming with the voices of visitors when he got there. Franco didn't know which one Ellie would be on, so he tried the one she'd been on last time. The ward sister didn't seem to know either, and told him to take a seat in the corridor.

He sat still for the first time since nine o'clock that morning, and within minutes, all his energy seeped away, leaving him aching and exhausted. He looked up to see the sister in front of him.

'Your wife's still in the labour ward. They've just finishing bathing her, she'll be coming here shortly.' He sat back and closed his eyes until he heard the trolley rattling towards him.

'Ellie?' She was lying flat, her face white and drawn, reminding Franco she'd had a harder time than he had. He got up and felt for her hand as she was pushed past.

'Just a minute, please.'

'She's my wife.'

The nurse said firmly, 'We'll make her comfortable in bed, then you can see her.'

He watched from the door as screens were pulled round to shield the process from all eyes. Another wait until he was beckoned forward and could see Ellie propped up on pillows.

He kissed her and pulled up a chair. 'How are you, Ellie?'

She yawned. 'It's another boy, he's lovely.'

'But how are you, did you have a hard time?'

'I had to have the forceps again. Not feeling my best really.'

'But it was better than last time?'

She sighed. 'They put me out both times, so I suppose much the same.'

'You'll be better tomorrow. Where's the baby?'

'Being bathed. They'll bring him here when he's done.'

'Another boy and you wanted a little girl,' he sympathised.

'Yes, but he's lovely.' She smiled and looked more like the Ellie he knew. 'I've given his name as Kenneth.'

'It's what we decided.'

'Is Bobby all right?'

'He's fine, love.'

The baby was brought in five minutes before the bell was rung at the end of visiting. Franco held him for a moment. He was red faced and wrinkled just as Bobby had been the first time he'd seen him.

He kissed Ellie, reluctant to leave her. All the other mothers had flowers, but he hadn't thought to get some for her. He went back to the caff. It was busy again, and his mother had taken Bobby home.

'Go and see Ma there,' his father told him.

Ma hung on every word he could say about the new baby and asked countless questions. He fell asleep in the chair and when he woke, she made him stay and eat a hot meal.

Franco knew he was late when he set off for work. The first customers were already in the bar when he arrived. Mr Secker, the licensee, expected him to be there half an hour beforehand to take empty casks down to the cellar and get full ones set up behind the bar. He'd had to do that himself tonight and was not in a good temper.

Winnie stood up for him. 'His wife's just had another baby boy.'

'Work doesn't stop for that,' he complained. 'All I can say, Frank, is that I hope you aren't going to have a big family. You've got to keep better time.'

While Franco was being told off, Flossie winked at him from behind the boss's back. She and Winnie were telling the customers about the new addition to his family. Many bought him a drink. 'To wet the baby's head,' they said. Franco drank more than usual. He felt he needed it; he'd had a hard day. More customers were coming in and making a beeline to be served by Flossie.

'You're looking very smart tonight,' one man told her. Something about Flossie invited personal comments. 'We haven't seen that frock before.' It was yellow, almost the colour of her hair, and cut low to show off plenty of comely bosom.

'It's new and the very latest style.' She grinned at Franco as she filled two tankards with bitter.

'She looks great in it, doesn't she?' he said to the customer.

'A bit long?' The customer was peering over the bar.

Franco whispered near her ear, 'Yes, pity we can't see more of your legs.' He wasn't keen on the longer length for skirts, which Flossie said was fashionable. She hitched her skirt up briefly, and he caught a glimpse of her stocking tops before it fell again.

'Mm, nice legs.' He smiled at the customer.

There was a lull. The small group had retreated to the other side of the room. Often they weren't busy when the doors first opened. Winnie was serving in the lounge, the boss was elsewhere. He saw Flossie look round to see if the coast was clear before her elbow dug him in the waist.

'Here, have a look at this.' She was in a flirty mood tonight. She pulled a well-worn leather bag from under the bar.

'Your handbag? Not as smart as your dress,' he teased.

'Inside, sweetheart.' Her lips, heavily emphasised with bright lipstick, blew him a kiss.

After a careful glance round, he opened it. 'What is it?'

Her beautiful blue eyes played with his. 'Take it out.'

He drew out a package wrapped in tissue paper. 'What's in it?'

Her hand pushed him back down below the level of the bar. 'Open it.'

He obeyed. Pink artificial silk bundled out into his hand. 'What's this?' His suspicions made him hesitate. He'd seen something similar in shop windows where they sold ladies' underwear.

315

'Go on,' she giggled.

He glimpsed a trimming of machine-made lace as he opened out a pair of knickers. 'Wouldn't fit me . . . Not my sort, Flossie,' he tried to joke.

She laughed aloud, showing perfect teeth. Her hand came down and jammed them back in her bag. 'Course not, they're mine, I just wanted you to know I'm keeping them here.'

He felt heat running into his cheeks.

'So I'm ready, silly.' She smiled, coming to stand closer to him than anyone else would, her breath hot and sweet in his face.

Franco was taken aback. In the past when he'd gone after girls, he'd always had to make the running. Not one of his conquests had ever offered such an open invitation.

His hot flush engulfed him. He was not sorry when a customer came close and asked for two pints of bitter so he could turn away to serve him.

Flossie had ratcheted up the temperature and had him tingling. He could hardly drag his eyes away from her. The dress swung round her sensuously as she moved, its soft fabric hugging her gently rounded hips and flat belly.

When she came to lean on the bar beside him in another idle moment, he couldn't fight the urge any longer. He slid his hand up her leg, feeling stocking tops, suspenders, a slippery satin suspender belt and just as she'd said, bare and inviting flesh.

He jerked his hand away, hardly able to breathe. She was turning him on.

It was a jolly session. One of their regulars brought in his accordion and played the popular tunes of the day. Soon he had everybody singing and there was lots of hilarity.

Flossie had a trick of pressing her body against Franco's so he felt her warmth and caught a waft of Evening in Paris. It was a delicious sensation, but he was well aware that Mr Secker could come in behind them from the other bar. So was she, she kept looking round. The risk made it all the more exciting. Every possible chance he had, he ran his hand up her skirt to stroke her soft thighs. He could hardly contain himself.

Franco loved a good time and liked to see other people enjoying themselves too. The party atmosphere lifted his mood as he leapt to refill glasses. The customers were slapping him on the back and buying him more drinks. He'd never known such generosity. He pocketed some of the money, but even so the faces and the lights were beginning to eddy round him.

At last it was closing time. Flossie took it for granted he'd go back with her to her room. The cold night air cleared his head, and he could hardly wait to get her there.

'Winnie lives upstairs,' she whispered. 'So don't make any noise. You've got a belly laugh that's unmistakable.'

He tried to run his hand up her dress again. She stopped on the dark stairs to pull him close and kiss him. It made him move her on towards her door.

'The place is a bit of a mess,' she confessed. There was silvery moonlight coming through the window. He heard the scrape of a match and stopped her lighting the gas.

'Who cares about a mess? Can't see it in this light anyway.'

He could just make out the shape of her face. She was steering him towards her bed, and all he wanted to do was to tear her clothes off.

To see her naked in the half light made him whisper, 'You're so beautiful . . .'

He'd never known a girl so passionate. Flossie was all he'd supposed, but having looked forward to it all evening, it was over in a moment.

Franco turned over in her bed and watched her get up to draw the curtains and light the gas. She was walking about naked and she really was beautiful. She hung up her new dress, picked up all their clothes from the floor and made a pot of tea. She got back in beside him to drink it.

'Don't think I haven't wanted to do this before now,' he told her.

'Lovely, stay here tonight. You've nothing to go home for.'

She put the light out and he snuggled close. She was still naked, so was he. They made love three more times before they got up to go to work the next morning. Franco felt he'd come to the end of a very long tunnel. He'd been deprived over the last months and had a lot of ground to make up.

Franco was in a turmoil for the next few days. It was the weekend so they were busy in the pub and he knew he wouldn't get to see Ellie and the new baby again before Sunday afternoon.

He had to go up to the caff for his dinner, and he had to go to see Ma and Bobby, otherwise she'd be suspicious. When she told him she'd been to tidy up their rooms he went back to pull the sheets about on the bed and lie down on it. He fell asleep for a couple of hours. When he got up, he realised she'd re-laid the fire for him in the living room. He lit it.

That night, he could hardly wait for the pub to close again. He went to spend the night with Flossie, and the following night too.

Flossie made him feel alive, free. Ever since she'd come to work at the pub, he'd fantasised about having sex with her. Now it was really happening and he could hardly believe his luck. She'd swept him into it. She could make any man's mouth water.

Flossie titillated his senses, woke him out of the rut he'd been settling into with Ellie and her flannelette nighties. With Ellie he had to face the responsibilities of earning a living and bringing up a family. There was always a clothes horse laden with nappies airing round the living-room fire. He had to fold it back before he could sit down. Bobby was always clamouring for her attention, and now there'd be two. He still loved her but it was possible to have too much of it.

Flossie made him feel more of a man. He had fun with her, he couldn't deny himself the opportunity of enjoying more of it. He wasn't in love with her, nor she with him. It was pure sex and he could handle that. He'd been well used to sexual conquests in the years before he was married.

He and Flossie were setting out for the pub one morning when Winnie came running down the stairs behind them. She clapped Franco on the back.

'You naughty boy! I thought I heard your voice last night.' She laughed. 'Flossie's room is right beneath my bedroom and I had the window open.'

Franco remembered opening Flossie's window and wished now he hadn't. He needed to keep their affair secret and was shocked that it was no longer so.

'So what?' Flossie shrugged. 'I told you I liked him.'

'But staying all night.' Winnie laughed again, and slapped Franco on the back. 'And you a married man.'

Soon afterwards, Mr Secker caught him in the cellar with his arm round Flossie. 'You're like a pair of lovebirds,' he'd said sarcastically.

It bothered Franco that his affair with Flossie had become common knowledge at the pub. It had to be kept from Ellie. Whatever happened, she must never find out. Nor must his mother.

* * *

Franco fetched Ellie home from hospital and she seemed as happy to be back with him as when she'd had Bobby. Their house lost its chilled emptiness but Ellie seemed to have less time for him. She was always busy with one child or the other.

'It'll be easier when Kenny's older and they're both on the same routine,' she said.

He knew Ellie had not been pleased to find herself pregnant again, but very soon Kenny was the apple of her eye. His mother was equally smitten with him.

At Sunday tea, they talked of Ellie going back to work in the caff in a few months' time.

'When you feel ready, Ellie,' his mother said. 'I'm looking forward to taking care of the babies.'

Ellie seemed on closer terms with his family than he was and Franco didn't like that. 'I'm not keen on Ellie going back to work at all,' he said. 'She has more than enough to do at home with two children.'

Ma put on her 'mother knows best' voice. 'Ellie needs to work. She finds it difficult to make ends meet on what you can give her.'

That cut him to the quick.

'Ellie?' She'd talked to Ma about that! They were getting together behind his back, talking about him, and letting him know he couldn't provide for his family!

Ellie smiled. 'You know I enjoy working in the cafe, Franco. It gives me a break from the babies and the cash is very handy for extras.'

When Kenny was four months old, Vito caught what he thought was a heavy cold. He stayed in the warm kitchen dishing up meals, where his cold wouldn't be noticed by customers. Connie was called on to work over the busy lunch hours, while Danny was out in the front overseeing Betty taking the orders and making out the bills. Betty was a bit of a disappointment. She had never been as quick as Myra.

Franco was enjoying an after-dinner cup of tea one afternoon when there was a tap on the front door. It was his mother, and he could see she was worried.

'Come in, Connie.' Ellie was pulling a chair up to the fire. 'There's tea in the pot, you'll have a cup?'

'I can't stay.'

Franco asked, 'What's the matter, Ma?'

'Your pa's poorly.' She could hardly get the words out. 'His cold's gone down on his chest. He's been worse these last few days, coughing and sweating at night. I made him go to the doctor. He says he's got pneumonia and sent him home to bed.'

'Goodness!' Ellie said. 'That makes it difficult for you.'

'Will you help us, Franco?'

'Of course,' he said, but he could feel his insides twisting, 'What d'you want me to do?'

Her words came out in a rush. 'See sense and come to work in the cafe now. Without Carlo, without someone else from the family, it's very hard to cope, especially when your pa isn't well.'

Franco froze. He'd guessed that was coming. His mother's face was flushed, she was very much in earnest. 'We really need you now. We'd pay you more than you earn in that pub. It's where you should be, it's your rightful place, you'd have something to work for.'

Franco closed his eyes. It was the last thing he wanted. Leave the pub? Working there was much more fun and it would mean seeing less of Flossie.

'It's what your pa and I have always wanted. As soon as you've got your hand in, you and Ellie could run the business between you.'

That didn't sound too bad, except Pa would go through the books minutely looking for trouble.

'Your pa and me, we want to go to Milan to see our other boys and their children. Then to Cittanova to see our brothers and sisters. We'd spend time there. Your pa doesn't want his life's work to go down the drain. If you took it over—'

Franco shook his head. 'Why don't you sell it? Then you could go where you like.'

He saw the pain on his mother's face and knew he'd inflicted real hurt.

'It's been on the market, Franco, for the last eighteen months, but so far no buyer. We can thank the depression for that too.'

There was dead silence. Franco took a deep breath. What was he doing? He hadn't been on good terms with them for some time and this was making matters worse.

'A cup of tea?' Ellie suggested again. He got up to get it. That started his mother talking again.

'You could come and live at our house too,' Ma offered. 'Plenty of room. Pa and I have talked it over. It's the best thing for us all.'

Franco stiffened. It was not the best thing for him. He had to fight against it.

'It'll save the rent and all the bills on your place. It'll save Ellie work too, she has more than enough to do with the children. And it's handy, just round the corner. Easier, when you have to work hard all day.'

Franco felt his hackles rise. They still expected to dictate what he did.

'No,' he said. 'No, you know it's not what I want.' They were staring at him in disbelief.

Ellie looked horrified. 'Much the best thing would be for you to work in the cafe,' she said. 'Just think of the advantages.'

She started to list them over again but he didn't want to listen. It hurt that she was openly siding with his mother. It strengthened his resolve to have his own way.

Ma lost patience with him. 'Franco, grow up, can't you? Stop behaving like an obstinate twelve-year-old.'

Even Ellie was offhand with him. 'Your pa wants it. It would make life easier all round. Why can't you just try it? Why are you being so stubborn?'

'Ma, you know . . .' It was very hard to keep refusing, especially with Pa ill, but . . . He took a deep breath and tried to smile at her.

'I'm free every afternoon, I could come and give you a hand then.'

He saw her face stiffen. 'That's not when we need help most. You know the rush is over by then.'

'I could help prepare for the next day.'

'We need someone to take your pa's place, to take charge and run it.'

Franco closed his eyes in protest. He wanted to work with Flossie.

'Not just for now, Franco, but permanently. It's time your pa retired. It's getting too much for us.'

He saw Ellie put her hand on Ma's arm. 'Connie, I could come back to work. I'd like to.'

Franco felt the pressure lift off him, but in another way, he resented what Ellie was doing. His mother snatched at it like a lifeline. 'Could you?'

'Well, wait a sec. I need to pop across the road to see if Irene will look after the babies. You won't want to do that for a week or so, not till Pa's better.'

There was relief on his mother's face now. 'If you could, that would be a great help, Ellie.'

While they waited, there was a leaden silence. His mother's dark eyes were begging him.

'Franco? You're a grown man now, I'm sure you'd settle into running the cafe, it's in your blood. Won't you try, for all our sakes?'

Franco cringed. He couldn't leave Flossie, not now. 'Danny will do it better than I can,' he muttered, pacing up and down the room. 'He's been with you a long time, he knows the ropes.'

Ellie's quick footfall came back across the street. Then the front door banged.

'I can start tomorrow,' she said, smiling at his mother. 'Irene says I can take the boys over there as early as I like, so I can come up in time to give a hand with the preparation work.'

'You're a godsend, Ellie.' Franco watched his mother get to her feet and kiss her. 'What would I do without you?'

That made Franco feel worse. In the days that followed, he stayed on after he'd had his dinner and did what he could. But as Ma had said, the rush was over by then. He could refuse his mother but it didn't stop the rush of guilt. It took many weeks before Pa was up on his feet and able to go outdoors.

Before then, Franco could see a big difference in the way the caff was run. It was Ellie who told him whether he needed to spend the afternoon there or whether he could go and collect the babies from Irene and take them to the park. Ellie was doing the ordering and fixing the menus. She'd taken charge.

He noticed a difference in his mother's attitude when she came to the caff. She was openly favouring Ellie over him. He was resentful enough to mention it to her.

'Do you wonder?' Ellie asked. 'You give them no consideration.'

His father grew stronger and slowly over several weeks began coming to the cafe, for a few hours a day, until eventually he took charge of his business again. Once he was working full time, Connie started looking after the babies. Franco got the impression she found two babies hard work, and it was decided Ellie should stop working in the afternoons so she could spend more time with her children.

Franco knew he'd let his family down and felt his self-respect ebbing away. It made him feel guilty, especially as he was seeing Flossie at work every day and she was offering such pleasure. When the pub closed, he often went home with her.

He couldn't stay in her bed for the whole night now, and it wasn't much fun crawling out after half an hour or so to come home, but he always did. When Ellie noticed he was coming home later, he told her Mr Secker was keeping the pub open an extra half hour because trade was good.

He still loved Ellie, but she seemed doll-like compared with Flossie. She was very involved with the children, and talked about them all the time. She was a good mother. All the same, he was taking great care not to get her pregnant again and she seemed pleased about that.

Franco knew his affair with Flossie was growing more important to him. More important than any he'd had before. To start with it really had been sexual attraction; sex was all he'd wanted. It had amused him to watch her drawing the men in the bar and be able to think: she likes me better than any of you. But before long he could feel his attachment strengthening. He said nothing. For a time he wouldn't even admit it to himself.

It was Flossie who brought it to a head. One night in bed, she smiled up at him as she twisted her fingers in his hair and said, 'I love you, Frank.'

It had filled him with joy that there was love on both sides. He was dazzled by Flossie.

When he thought about it the next day in broad daylight, he began to worry that his feelings were serious, perhaps too serious. He hadn't meant to get involved to this extent. They were both passionate in bed. He liked her body and missed her when he was with Ellie.

As time went on, Franco saw Flossie as a magnet. The pull of attraction he felt towards her was growing stronger. He knew he was very much in love. Working with her, he saw almost more of her than he did of Ellie and he hated her day off. He popped in to see her for a few minutes on his way to and from work. He looked forward to the days when he'd be working with her rather than Winnie, and found it hard to drag his eyes away from her to serve the customers.

She was always in his thoughts. When she was working beside him in the bar, he could smell her perfume every time she passed him. When he got home and curled up in his own bed beside the sleeping Ellie, he fantasised about taking Flossie on holiday. Imagining the things they'd do.

Another month, and his conscience began to trouble him even more. He was turning his back on Ellie. He'd stopped telling her he loved her, and worse, when he made love to her, in his mind it was Flossie he had in his arms. Ellie must never know. In his saner moments he told himself he was making a shambles of his life.

Now when he saw other men making a beeline for Flossie in the bar, he was awash with jealousy. She had her regulars, her blokes, she called them. He knew she was seeing more of one, a young commercial traveller, with yellow wavy hair and skin like alabaster. His name was Ralph Corner and Franco hated to see him come to the bar and start flirting with her. When Franco heard her blokes making arrangements with her, his palms itched, and he wanted to smash his fists in their faces.

'Not tonight,' she'd whisper to him, and Franco knew she'd have a different man in her bed. 'Got to work.'

'Give it up, Flossie,' he urged. 'I don't like you having other men.'

She'd laughed at him. 'They pay for my new hats and dresses. Besides, you have your Ellie.' Her eyes would play with his. 'What's Ellie like?'

Franco didn't want to talk about Ellie, didn't even want to think about her when he was with Flossie. He consoled himself with the thought that he was the man Flossie loved. That made him feel stronger. All the same, she was manipulating him in the way he'd manipulated his girlfriends before he was married.

For him, Flossie sparkled against a drab background. He'd thought she was interested only in the fun of the moment, but she began talking of the future, hinting she wanted to spend it with him.

One night, he and Flossie ran down the wet street to her room and threw themselves on her bed. They'd pulled the covers over themselves and lain together, but now it was time for him to get up and go home. He could hear the rain splattering against the window. He made a half-hearted move, but Flossie's arms tightened round him, preventing him from going.

'Why don't you and me go away together?' she whispered. 'We could get jobs down in London. Plenty of pubs down there. You'd like that, wouldn't you?'

It took his breath away. He pushed himself out of her arms. 'I can't do that!'

'We'd see much more of each other,' she wheedled. 'Be together all the time.'

Franco covered his face with his hands. Being with Flossie all the time would be perfect. But he couldn't!

He took a deep breath. 'I can't just walk out on my kids.' Not on Ellie either.

'Think about it.' She sounded disappointed. 'We'd both have a much better time. I want you with me.'

'I want to be with you, but . . .'

She sounded petulant. 'It's not nice, sharing you with a wife and children.'

'I don't like sharing you with other men.'

'You wouldn't have to. I'd give all that up if you took me away. We love each other, Frank. It'd be a new life for both of us.'

It thrilled Franco to think Flossie loved him, but his mind was on fire as he walked home, so that he hardly noticed the rain. He was soaked when he got there. He was cheating on Ellie and no longer knew what he wanted. He couldn't think straight.

Chapter Nineteen

Winnie Vickers was on her way to work. She locked her attic doors and ran down stairs. On the landing below, Flossie Phillips put her head out of her room.

Winnie paused. 'Are you coming?'

'Yes.' She seemed dazed, still half asleep.

At the bottom of the next flight, Winnie said, 'Come on then or we'll be late.'

'I can't rush this morning.'

'What's the matter? You didn't have a heavy night, I heard Frank leave. I thought it was quite early.'

'It was.' For once, Flossie looked washed out, her usual glow gone. Winnie waited, while she put on a spurt to catch up. 'I'm in trouble. Up the spout.'

Winnie caught at her arm. 'Flossie! What are you going to do?'

'If only Frank wasn't already married . . .'

Winnie was shocked. 'But he is. You've always known that.'

'And he won't leave his wife, I've tried that.'

'He knows?'

'Not yet.' Flossie was scurrying along now, her gaze fixed on the pavement.

Winnie could see she was upset and wanted to soothe her. 'Perhaps he'll change his mind when he does. He's keen on children.'

'Keen on that doll of a wife too.'

'She's just a kid, Flossie. Anyway, how d'you know this baby is his?'

'Good question. I want it to be his.'

'You'd better tell him then and see if he'll change his mind.'

'He's like all the other fellas. Wants only one thing. All over me till there's trouble.'

Winnie rang the bell on the back door of the pub, and Bill Secker, looking morose, as he usually did out of hours, let them in. She didn't know whether to be glad or sorry that she was too old to be caught like Flossie. The bar was still full of smoke. Winnie opened the window and propped open the door although it was a cold morning. She'd wanted children when she was young. If she'd had them her life would be very different now. She'd have someone of her own to love.

Franco took his day off on Tuesdays now. Ellie came into the bedroom and put a mug of tea beside him.

'I've washed and dressed Bobby and given him his breakfast. I've changed Kenny and fed him. There's a bottle of boiled water, that should do him till you bring him up at dinner time.'

Franco sighed. 'I wish you'd stay home with me when I have a day off.'

'You know I can't,' Ellie said. 'I've agreed to do it, and your mother would have to go in to help if I didn't.'

'It wouldn't hurt her, not one day a week,' he grumbled. 'It's not much of a rest day for me if I have to look after the boys.'

Ellie was combing her hair at the dressing table, and her eyes came up to find his reflection in the mirror. 'You said you wanted to.'

'Only that day when Ma didn't feel up to it.'

'I thought you liked having them here with you. You said you did.'

'I do, but they're wearing. I could do with a rest.'

'They need to see more of you, Franco.'

'I'm here every afternoon.'

'They go down for a sleep in the afternoon.'

Bobby came in and pulled on the eiderdown. 'Daddy, get up.'

'It'll be nice when they're old enough to enjoy a game of football.'

'Take them for a walk in the park.' Ellie was pulling on her coat. 'Don't wish your life away.'

She made him feel a heel. Franco knew he made things worse by staying in bed and leaving her to see to the boys before she went to work. He hadn't done that when Bobby was a baby. He felt bad. The bond he used to feel with Ellie seemed to have broken.

'Daddy, it's time to get up.' Bobby had the eiderdown on the floor.

He swung his feet down and reached for his clothes. He was missing Flossie already, he was even missing the chit chat at the pub. He'd try and make it up to Ellie. As soon as he was up, he washed the dishes and made the beds though he hated housework; he was doing his duty. He took the children to the park, but it was cold and he soon got fed up kicking Bobby's ball about. He took them to see the ducks.

'Bread, Daddy. Want bread.' Bobby was tugging eagerly at his trousers. 'Bread for ducks.'

'I haven't brought any.'

'Why not? Grandma always brings stale bread.'

He'd forgotten. 'We haven't got any at home.'

Kenny had kicked his covers off. Franco tucked him in again, and turned round to find Bobby paddling in the pond. He grabbed him back but his shoes and socks were soaked.

'Naughty boy,' he scolded. Ellie would be cross; his shoes were almost new. He took them off and sat Bobby on the pram. He screamed and yelled to get down.

Franco walked on, looking at his watch. He was famished. He'd had nothing but the cup of tea Ellie had brought him. Usually, he had egg and bacon before going to the pub but he couldn't be bothered making it for himself. He wanted his dinner, but he didn't want to get to the caff too early or he'd be pressed to give a hand.

At last he decided it was safe to go. He knew he'd timed it right when he found the place almost empty. Danny was dishing up a good dinner of pork chops, mash and peas in the kitchen, and Ma, who had come down to eat with them, took over the kids, sponging Bobby's hands and scolding Franco because Bobby's feet were cold. She sat him up on cushions to eat.

His pa, Danny and Ellie took it in turns to run out to the shop every time the bell pinged. Pa looked at him and said, 'It wouldn't hurt you to take your turn.'

As usual, his father was rubbing him up the wrong way but even so it was three o'clock when he stood up to leave. Kenny was asleep in the pram. Ma fastened Bobby to sit on top while Ellie put on her coat.

He felt his bad mood lifting. Ellie would be with him for the rest of the day. He was walking through the caff when he stopped, hardly able to believe his eyes. Flossie was sitting at the table in the window spooning up a knickerbocker glory. Winnie was with her and another woman he knew by sight. She too had a room at 36 Cunliffe Street. Flossie's big blue eyes looked straight into his.

'Hello, Frank.'

He recoiled, conscious of Ellie and the kids close behind. The women from the bar were eyeing them with great interest. 'Hello,' he said lamely, feeling at a loss.

'Aren't you going to introduce us?' Winnie asked.

He could hardly get the words out, he was so angry. Flossie knew how important it was that Ellie knew nothing about their affair.

'My wife, Ellie, and my boys.'

He would have gone straight out, but Ellie caught his arm. Her lips formed the word 'Who?'

'The people I work with at the pub,' he told her. 'Winnie and Flossie, and . . .'

'Edith, she's got a room in the same house as us.' She was in her mid-thirties and had a large nose and black permed hair.

'Yes, Edith.'

Ellie was smiling. 'We've seen you here before, haven't we?'

That poleaxed Franco. 'You've been before?'

'We love the ice cream,' Flossie purred. 'The best in town.'

Ma came up so he had to introduce the whole family. The ice cream he'd eaten lay like an iceberg in his stomach. Were his two worlds about to collide?

Franco had taken over the pram and was off down the street like a rabbit running for its hole.

'Wait for me,' Ellie called, running to catch up with him. 'Don't stride out like that, I can't keep up. You know my legs are shorter.'

He stopped abruptly. She thought he was going to shout at her, but he was biting his lip.

'What's the matter?' she asked.

'Nothing. I was just surprised to see the barmaids in the caff, that's all.'

More than surprised, Ellie thought, he was shocked. 'Why? They said they liked ice cream.'

'I'm used to seeing them at the pub. I suppose they seemed out of place there. Do they go often?'

'I've seen them two or three times.' Ellie could sense his discomfort. 'They call you Frank. I didn't realise they meant you at first. One of them is very good looking. You didn't say.'

Franco shrugged. 'Why should I?'

'Pretty girls draw your eye,' she dared. 'I can't help but notice.' What she'd noticed was the tension that had sparked between Franco and Flossie. The pram was gathering speed again.

'Look is all I do these days,' he told her.

'Has she been working at the pub for a long time?' His face was screwing up, and she knew he wanted her to drop this.

'Nine months or so. She came in Gladys's place.'

It bothered Ellie to see the effect Flossie had on Franco. He'd seemed anxious to find them in the caff. She felt an unaccountable rush of jealousy. 'She's beautiful.' Perhaps she was just being silly, imagining things?

Franco no longer seemed as interested in her as he used to be. Ellie had put it down to the fact that they were both busy and no longer newly-weds, but she didn't like the idea of him working at that pub now. The hours made normal family life difficult. At times he seemed to come home in the middle of the night.

Franco could see the night sky through Flossie's window. They hadn't drawn the curtains when they'd come in, they'd been in too much of a hurry to get into bed. He'd had a tiff with her in the pub about going to the caff, and they'd been at loggerheads for a couple of hours. It had been purgatory. He couldn't fight with Flossie. She'd made it up with generous apologies and it had brought greater passion to their love making.

Now, half an hour later, the full moon and brilliant stars were lighting up the room with soft silvery light. Lying here was restful after the hectic work and bright lights of the pub. Franco felt drowsy, and didn't feel like getting up and going home. He never did at this time.

'Frank.' Flossie's husky voice was sensual. He turned to look at her. Her yellow curls, spread across her pillow, were silvered by the moonlight.

'I'm in trouble,' she said. 'I'm going to have a baby.'

It was the last thing Franco was expecting. His mouth went dry, and he could feel the blood draining from his face. What had he done? 'Are you sure?'

'Quite sure. I'm three months gone.'

'Oh God!'

He could see all he'd built up with Ellie and the two babies falling down like a line of dominoes. This had never been his intention. He couldn't have two families, could barely afford to keep one. Ellie was always trying to stretch the pence.

'I wish you weren't married, Frank. It's going to be hard . . .'

'I'll help, of course I'll help. I'll do all I can.'

'You could take me away to some nice town, Brighton or Eastbourne, somewhere near the sea.'

'I can't!'

'I'd like you all to myself. We'd be a little family, nobody would ever know we weren't married.'

Franco swallowed hard. 'How do I know this baby is mine? All those other men . . .'

She put a finger across his lips. 'I always make those men wear . . . you know. You and me, well we've taken chances, haven't we?'

That was true enough. 'You said it didn't matter, it was the safe time.'

'Having your baby is quite different. I've dreamed about you and me with a baby, of being together all the time.'

'Flossie! I'm married, I already have two children. I can't leave them.'

He left her sobbing into her pillow. He felt desperate, a complete rotter, a cad. What was he going to do?

The street outside was silent, its shabbiness hidden in silvery shadows. It looked serene but Franco felt in turmoil. It was his fault and he felt responsible. It upset him to see Flossie so distressed.

But he was responsible for Ellie and the boys too. It was a huge weight on his mind. He'd never wanted responsibility of any sort and here he was torn between the two of them. What a mess he was making of everything.

Winnie could see Flossie had been crying. For once she was not her usual self in the bar. The customers were trying to chat her up and she was turning away, closed off in her own misery. It was as though a light had been turned off and the atmosphere in the bar was subdued.

It was Frank's night off and Winnie felt she was having to work harder than usual. She could hardly believe it when she heard Flossie refuse John Wilmot's request to go home with her when the pub closed. He was young and good looking, a regular of Flossie's, and she'd said she quite liked him. He worked in a solicitor's office.

Winnie saw him look in her direction, then change his mind and leave the pub as soon as his glass was empty. She knew he didn't fancy her. She didn't like that; it drained what was left of her self-esteem.

She was propositioned a little later on by an oldish man with large gaps in his yellowing teeth. She felt she couldn't stomach him and told him she already had a client for tonight, which wasn't true. She and Flossie walked home together. Winnie felt so sorry for her that she asked her up for a cup of tea.

'Frank won't say yes, and he won't say no,' Flossie admitted. 'He won't tell his wife either, he doesn't want her to know.'

'You could tell her.'

Flossie sighed. 'She's just an innocent kid – and what good would that do me?'

'Bring Frank down to earth.'

'He's not a bad sort, Winnie. I wish I'd gone to that woman in Dock Cottages for an abortion.'

'No, she nearly killed Edith that time, didn't she?'

'I know, that's what scared me off. It's too late now, anyway. I'll have to have it.'

As Winnie undressed for bed, she thought what a strange world it was. Once, she'd have loved to have a baby, but it hadn't happened, and here was Flossie dreading the birth and not wanting the child. It wasn't going to get much of a welcome or much loving care when it was born.

Franco felt he was living a nightmare. The weeks were going on. Flossie was making a big effort to hide her pregnancy from the pub customers. She bought new clothes with exactly that in mind and looked smart.

'The counter comes above the level of her waist,' Winnie said. 'It hides a lot. I've told her not to go round collecting empty glasses while the pub's full. You and I do that in future, OK?'

Franco agreed readily and rushed to do it, but he knew eventually Flossie's state would be obvious to all. The trouble was, all the pub staff and many of the customers knew he was her boyfriend. When Mr Secker found out he was furious.

'She was a good barmaid, brought the customers in, and you have to get her in the family way! So what yer going to do about it, lad?'

Franco didn't know what he could do. He was frightened. What if Ellie found out? That was a black dread. Even larger was his feeling of guilt. He loved Flossie but he loved Ellie too. He was ashamed of what he'd done to both of them. Ashamed of what he'd done to his parents too.

'I've told Flossie she'll have to go,' Bill Secker told him one night when he was the last to leave. 'Everyone can see she's got a bun in the oven now.'

Franco rushed round to her room, though he'd made no such arrangement. He didn't think she'd have a man there tonight and was afraid she'd be in tears.

Flossie had made herself a cup of tea. She shrugged. 'I knew it would happen sooner or later.'

'What will you do?'

'What can I do? I've hung on to the job for as long as possible. No hope of another with me looking like this.'

He knew she still had a few of her regular clients who went straight to her room by appointment.

She said, 'But it's difficult even with them. Some say they can feel the baby and it puts them off. Soon there'll be nothing else for it but to rely on help from my friends.' Her eyelashes fluttered. He could guess what that meant.

'I won't desert you,' he said.

He popped into her room for a few minutes several times a day. He couldn't stay away. He took her little gifts, some cigarettes, a bottle of port which she liked. He would have continued to go to her room several nights each week for sex, but she cut him down to two.

He felt she wasn't as keen on it as she used to be, but she said, 'I have to have time for my paying clients, get money where I can. I might even have to start charging you.'

'No, not that,' he pleaded. 'We love each other, don't we?' He got into the habit of putting a pound on her table when he could. 'To help with your bills,' he said. 'Not for . . .'

Millie Thorpe, the new barmaid taken on in her place, was stout and middle aged. She didn't please the customers or the boss. Flossie still came to the pub but as a customer. She kept herself looking smart and seemed to recover some of her high spirits.

She knew many of the men who drank in the bar and she was always the centre of a little group. Franco couldn't keep his eyes away from her or her men friends. He didn't like her picking up a client to take home, and in particular, he didn't like her friend Ralph Corner. He was another well-dressed young man, who followed Flossie around as though he was besotted with her.

Franco helped supply her with drinks when other customers failed to do so. So did Winnie. He watched how she did it and followed her method. She'd charge other customers the usual amount for their drinks but ring up less on the till, to cover the cost of Flossie's. Winnie was good at mental arithmetic; at the end of the night, the till was usually a penny or two over.

'Mr Secker owes her that much.' She smiled at Franco. If the boss should happen to be close by, Winnie would ring up the till with the cost of Flossie's drink and take out a few coppers to give her as change. She could always make it up later.

Franco was growing more nervous as her time drew closer. She'd booked the local midwife to deliver her at home. One morning, Franco arrived at the pub to find Winnie all smiles.

'Congratulations, you've got a daughter.' She slapped him on the back. 'She's a little angel. Born in the night with no trouble at all. Flossie says you decided her name should be Posy.'

Franco recoiled. Flossie had asked him several times, 'What are we going to call our baby?' He'd told her as nicely as he could that the name was up to her.

'Posy? I wouldn't have chosen that.'

'What did you want?'

'That's for her to choose. I don't care.'

'You do,' Winnie teased. 'She's a lovely baby.'

Franco ran along Cunliffe Street to see Flossie and the new baby before going up to the caff for his dinner. The curtains were drawn and she was lying flat on her bed. He bent over to kiss her. She moved away from him.

'Thank God that's over,' she said irritably. 'I'm shattered. Don't you want to see your daughter?'

'Where is she?'

'Here, on this side of the bed.'

Franco went to look. A drawer had been taken out of the chest and put on the floor to be used as a cradle. The baby was cocooned in flannelette, so that only her head was visible, and she seemed to be sleeping. He bent to part the covers.

She had a pretty face. He'd expected to feel the same thrill of fatherhood as he had with his sons. He felt engulfed in guilt. He should not have brought another human being into the world, not with Flossie. 'She's got a pretty face. Like you.'

'You can pick her up.'

He shivered. He didn't want to touch her.

'Go on.'

'I don't want to wake her.' He went to the other side of Flossie's bed where he couldn't see the baby. Flossie was crying. 'Did you have a hard time?'

'I've had no sleep. Winnie went to fetch the midwife when she came home from the pub and she didn't leave until after six this morning. I didn't get a wink all night. When they say labour, that's what they mean, it's hard work.'

'What time was she was born?'

'Half four. I feel as though I could sleep for a week.'

'I'll go, so you can.'

Flossie mopped at her eyes. 'I'm too keyed up to sleep. I ache all over and I'll have to feed the baby soon.'

'At least she's here with you.'

'She'll be a lot more trouble now she is.'

Ellie had been relieved but thrilled too, once her babies were born.

'Poor Flossie. It's just a matter of resting and getting your strength back now.'

'How can I rest?' she burst out. 'The midwife will be back any minute. What a life. You've no idea what having a baby means, Frank. She'll keep me on the go from morning to night if I let her. I've got another mouth to feed now and I've got to work to live. You know that.'

Franco flinched, full of remorse. He felt forced to say, 'I'll help you. I've told you that.' He fingered the coins in his pocket.

'Perhaps you will for a week or two. But for me this is a long sentence. She'll be fourteen before she can earn. I'll need help for years.'

Franco felt repelled by Flossie for the first time. She was trying to get money from him, but he ought to help support the child, that was only fair.

'Don't worry.' He put three half crowns on her bedside table. 'I'll keep it up, I promise. Seven and six a week, that's the usual amount, isn't it?' Franco knew it was, he'd gone to some trouble to find out.

'I'll be happy with that.' Flossie smiled through her tears. 'Thank you.'

Franco met Ralph Corner on the stairs as he was leaving. He broke into a run as soon as he reached the pavement. Flossie had changed, he was no longer her favourite. For the first time, he felt he was seeing her without the rose-tinted spectacles that being in love had given him.

He couldn't get the baby's beautiful face out of his mind. Her birth had had an impact like no other on him. He felt that bundle of flannelette had somehow brought him to his senses.

Flossie didn't love him. Nor was it love he'd felt for her, but lust. She'd been temptation itself. What had he been thinking of? He'd been playing about instead of seeing things as a grown man should. Ellie was worth two of Flossie.

He'd do his best for them both. But at least he hadn't run away with Flossie. He'd been tempted to do that too, but he hadn't.

As the months rolled on, Ellie was finding it hard to understand Franco. He seemed to be distancing himself further and further from his family. He said he hated the cafe; he was piqued that she worked there and enjoyed it.

They no longer went every week to have Sunday tea with his parents. Franco made excuses, saying others had invited them out. Neither would he walk up to the cafe for his dinner when the pub closed. He said it was too far and he was too tired to do that every day. Ellie took his meal home and warmed it up for him. He was less sociable these days than he used to be. He'd developed an aversion to his parents, and was on his guard against any attempt she made to draw them closer.

Ellie did her best to jolly him out of it. She tried to get him to talk about his work at the pub, asked him if he had any troubles. She knew he wasn't happy; that something was weighing on his mind. He was shutting himself away from her too, away from them all except perhaps Bobby. He still played a lot with him.

She took Franco a cup of tea in bed every morning before she left, and tried to think of different things they could do on his day off.

As a child, Ellie had seen Franco as already an adult. Then, as she'd grown older, she'd seen them as equals, but now he seemed almost childish in his stubbornness. Connie and Vito were at the centre of her life and she knew how hurt they felt by Franco's attitude.

Ellie had her routine and felt settled. She'd be content if only Franco weren't so changed.

Her evenings were not as lonely as they used to be. Connie quite often came down for a cup of tea, and Irene and her children were in and out before their bedtime. She hadn't seen much of her this week because her husband Len was home from the sea.

Irene earned a little extra cash looking after other people's children, and they kept her at home or in the park during the day. She said she was glad of adult conversation in the evenings. She didn't often visit the caff, but Ellie knew Len was bringing the whole family today for their dinner because it was a school holiday as well as being his birthday.

On rare occasions, Alice came to visit, and once or twice Connie had babysat so she could go to see her.

Ellie got up early in the mornings, leaving Franco to sleep on. As soon as she'd got her little boys up and dressed and given them their breakfast, she took them up to Connie, then went straight on to the cafe.

There, Ellie spent her mornings in the kitchen preparing meals with Danny. Vito had taught her how to cook Italian dishes and to make ice cream. He didn't come in early these days, and was leaving more of the work to her. A few customers came in for coffee and tea cakes, but they weren't busy until late morning.

Once the lunch-time rush started, she went out in front to serve the customers. She enjoyed it all, and could pull her weight in any of the different jobs. She felt part of the team as well as part of the family.

She'd soon got to know the regular customers. The women Franco worked with came quite often, and always wanted to chat to her. He'd been embarrassed to see them here but they were not. They asked Vito if he was Frank's dad, and told him his son was not at all like him.

'That would please Franco,' he said. 'He doesn't want to be like me, doesn't want to be thought Italian.'

Ellie watched Flossie through her lashes. She'd been relieved when one day, a personable man came with her and bought her lunch. They seemed very friendly; she'd seen him kiss her nose across the table. Ellie told herself she'd been imagining silly things, and was glad to find she was wrong. She'd noticed when Flossie's beautiful figure had expanded in pregnancy.

When she told Franco that Flossie was coming in several days a week with her boyfriend, he'd said, 'Didn't know she had a boyfriend. Are you sure it's Flossie? She's left the pub, couldn't work any longer.'

Chapter Twenty

May 1935

As Winnie climbed the stairs of 36 Cunliffe Street after the morning session at the Mermaid, she could hear Flossie's baby sobbing her heart out.

When she reached the landing, Edith Wilson was sitting on the top stair with her head in her hands. 'Flossie's gone out and locked her door,' she fretted. 'Isn't she awful? I can't get in to the baby.'

Edith worked at the George and Crown in the North End.

Winnie said, 'You're home early.'

'Haven't been to work this morning, I've got a migraine.'

'The landlady – she'll have a key.'

'I know, but she's gone out.'

Winnie hung over the banisters. 'Where's Flossie gone?'

'How would I know?'

After a short pause, the baby started crying more loudly, venting frustration and fear in her angry sobs.

'It's harrowing,' Edith said. 'She's been going hammer and tongs for over an hour. Probably thinks she's been abandoned. It's all right, Posy,' she called through the door. 'Mummy won't be long now.'

That quietened her for a moment. 'She hears and thinks

she's not alone after all. Flossie isn't looking after her properly.'

Winnie was beginning to sweat. Listening to the pitiful cries of such a tiny baby was going through her.

Edith said, 'I've felt ill all morning, and this is making my head pound.' Down below them the front door banged. 'Is this her?'

'I think so, yes.'

'Thank goodness!' Edith was on her feet shouting at Flossie, 'What sort of a mother are you, going out and leaving your baby locked up alone?'

Winnie saw Ralph Corner following her up the stairs. He looked very smart in a white mac and a trilby.

'What if the place burned down?'

'It hasn't,' Flossie snapped. 'Posy's perfectly all right, she just wants her feed.'

'She's due at two,' Winnie told her. 'It's now quarter to three.'

'Flossie's got to eat too,' her man friend said. 'I took her out for a hot meal.'

'Then you should have taken the baby with you,' Winnie retorted. 'Leaving her on her own – you should be ashamed of yourselves.'

'I'll go, Flossie. You've got plenty of help now. Come back tonight, shall I?'

'About six, yes.'

Edith picked Posy up from the bedside rug. 'You poor little devil! Just look at you. She's rolled out of this drawer, Flossie. It's a good job you had it on the floor.'

'I've got to make her a bottle,' Flossie said. 'There'll be no peace till she gets it.'

That was another thing neither Winnie nor Edith approved of. 'She's too young for bottles,' Winnie had told her.

'It's got to be bottles.' Flossie was adamant. 'I've got to get back to work, haven't I?'

Winnie was wrung out with pity when she looked at Posy. Her face was scarlet and her hair dark with sweat and tears. She'd worked herself up to such a frenzy that she'd freed herself from her shawls and bedding. Her shoulders were out of her nightie and her tiny body was still heaving with sobs.

Edith hugged her. She was thin and bird-like. 'You poor pet. She needs changing, a clean nappy, Flossie. Her nightie's soaking too and she'll need a clean vest.'

'I'll sponge her down,' Winnie said, 'while you find her clothes. It'll cool her, make her comfortable. Is this her towel?'

Flossie was making up a bottle for the baby with fresh milk, sugar and hot water. Winnie ran upstairs with the child. She'd washed her in her own kitchen sink several times before. Posy was quiet now but still having an occasional shudder. Her round blue eyes stared up at Winnie's face with such intensity that she kissed her. Flossie didn't deserve to have a lovely baby like this.

When she took her down again, Edith was putting a clean sheet in the drawer that served as a cradle, and going on about the dangers of her rolling out of it.

'She's getting too big for this, she needs a proper cot. She's big and strong for eight weeks.'

'Might be better if I didn't put the pillow under her,' Flossie suggested. 'She'd be lower in the drawer.'

'The pillow serves as a mattress, she wouldn't be comfortable without it.'

'She's peed on it lots of times.' Winnie was disgusted. 'It stinks. You can't use it any more. She needs a proper cot.'

'Where am I going to get the money for that?' Flossie wailed. 'I haven't worked for months. She'll have to wait.'

'You should get that fellow to buy a cot for her. I bet he's forking out for your fags and drinks. Anyway, you're starting back next week, aren't you?'

'Posy needs a pram too, so I can take her out with me.' Flossie had the bottle in the baby's mouth at last.

Winnie listened to the urgent slurping sounds as she sucked. 'I'll leave you to it.'

Edith followed her out to the landing. 'D'you fancy a cup of tea?' she asked.

'I need my dinner, I'm starving. I'll go out after, see if I can buy a cot for the poor mite. I might find something in a second-hand shop that would do her.'

'I'll come with you,' Edith said. 'Go halves if you like. Flossie isn't coping.'

'She's had babies before. Two of them. She should know what she's about.'

As Winnie went up to her attic rooms, she remembered that Flossie had walked out on her first two babies. Flossie had been in a confessional mood the night she'd told her that. She'd said she very much regretted abandoning them and was determined to keep this one.

Winnie fried herself some sausages and thought about Posy. She was the prettiest baby she'd ever seen. Good, too. Flossie had said she'd started sleeping through the night at five weeks of age. It brought a lump to Winnie's throat to find she wasn't being looked after properly.

She and Edith went out that afternoon and found just the cot for her. It was bigger than average and the side rails could be taken off to turn it into a child's bed as she grew older. The mattress was a bit stained but not too bad.

'Posy will be more comfortable in this,' Edith said.

'Safer, too. Give her room to move.'

* * *

Ellie heard the cafe door ping and saw Flossie coming in with her barmaid friends. She was coming for her dinner more often these days. If the baby was asleep, she'd be left outside in her pram and they'd keep an eye on her through the big shop window. Today, Winnie was nursing the baby on her knee. The pram was outside empty.

'Had to bring her in,' she told Ellie when she went to take their order. 'She was awake. Isn't she lovely?'

Ellie had never seen a prettier baby. She was billing and cooing happily. The door pinged again, and Irene and her family came in and occupied a nearby table.

'I'm going back to work at the Mermaid next week,' Flossie told Ellie. 'I've got to. Just been in to fix it.'

'I don't see how you can,' Winnie protested. 'Who's going to look after Posy?'

'She'll be all right in her cot.'

'She won't! You can't leave her locked in your room for hours at a time.'

'I'll feed her at ten, she always sleeps after that.'

'Not until half two, Flossie. It would be cruel.'

'She sleeps a lot.'

Ellie said, 'My friend Irene over there looks after other people's children while they go to work.'

'Does she?' Winnie jumped eagerly at the suggestion. 'Ask her, Flossie, if she'll have Posy.'

'No, I don't know her . . .'

Ellie went to the kitchen to put in their order of one lasagne and one pie and chips, and returned with meals for a table of six. When she went to take Irene's order, she had Posy on her knee and her little girls were playing with her.

She heard Irene telling Flossie she arranged for other women to child mind her regulars while her husband was on home leave, and Ellie had been in to babysit her own family several times.

For Ellie, it was a busier session than usual. Irene's family lingered over their coffee and ice cream long after Flossie and the baby had left. While Len was at the counter paying his bill and having a word with Vito, Irene whispered to Ellie that she was going to look after Posy between ten and half two when Flossie went back to work.

'The other woman wanted it,' she said.

'What about at night?'

'They said nothing about that. Perhaps she isn't going to work at night.'

'I reckon she is,' Ellie said.

Franco was feeling apprehensive. Flossie had been less friendly since he'd refused to go away with her, and she didn't seem to care whether Ellie knew about their affair or not.

His love affair with Flossie had gone sour. She was making no secret of her new boyfriend, flaunting him in the bar when she thought he was watching. He told himself she was showing her true colours; she had no loyalty, just wanted a good time with one man after another.

Franco knew he'd been like that himself when he was younger but now he wanted to cling to Ellie, to try and restore what they'd once had. He couldn't go on like this, making them both unhappy.

But he couldn't get Flossie's baby out of his mind. He had only to close his eyes to see again the pretty face wrapped tight in folds of flannelette. He felt full of remorse. He should never have risked fathering her. He'd treated Ellie very badly, his parents too. How could he make amends? If he once told Ellie, she might throw him out. He'd certainly get short shrift from his mother.

This morning, he'd joined customers and staff in welcoming Flossie back to her job at the Mermaid. Everybody said there'd be more fun in the bar from now on. Bill Secker had tried three barmaids one after the other in her place, and none of them stayed longer than a few weeks. Everybody knew Flossie drew the customers in. They were all trying to buy her drinks today.

'How's the baby?' she was being asked. 'Where is she?'

'Got somebody to take care of her.' She smiled. She'd told Franco that some days ago. It was what he'd expected and he hadn't asked who was going to do it. The less he had to do with her baby, the better.

When the pub closed after the morning session, she fell into step beside him. 'Got to pick Posy up now,' she said. Only then did he ask where she was heading.

'Garnet Street,' she said. 'That's where you live, isn't it?'

Franco's mouth fell open. 'Who's minding her?'

'Irene something . . . She's your Ellie's friend.'

He felt the blood draining from his face. 'Irene Cobbold?'

'Yes, that's it.'

'Heavens! What made you pick on her? She lives almost opposite. What if Ellie finds out?'

'Didn't you know? It was Ellie who suggested her.'

Franco found that hard to take in. Flossie was floundering. 'I didn't want anybody, but Winnie thought it was a good idea. It was her day off, and we went up to the trattoria for dinner.'

'Oh my God!' Why hadn't Ellie mentioned it? 'Does she know about you and me?'

'I don't know, do I? I haven't told her.'

Had she found out? But she hadn't said anything, or seemed in any way put out. The blood was rushing up his cheeks, he was burning hot, sweating. This was a shock. Even if Ellie didn't know, she and Flossie were moving nearer to each other. He could only see that as dangerous.

'Flossie, I don't want Posy to go there. You'll see too much of Irene.'

Her smile was glassy. He had the feeling she didn't care. 'Bit late to tell me now. I'll be careful not to say anything. There's no way she'll find out through me.'

Franco felt as though a net was closing round him. He was in a trap.

He let himself into his own house and collapsed on the armchair in the cold living room. Ellie hadn't yet come home from the caff. He wished he'd never got involved with Flossie. He should have had more sense than to bring another baby into the world. He ached with remorse.

Should he say something to Ellie? No, he mustn't drop any hints. Ellie had been with him the day he'd first seen the barmaids in the caff. Would he be better keeping his mouth shut now? He mustn't appear interested in Flossie. He couldn't make up his mind. Ellie was letting herself in before he felt ready.

'Daddy?' Bobby came rushing in to climb up on his knee. He could hear Ellie talking to Kenny as she unstrapped him from his pram.

If he said nothing, would his silence on the matter seem odd? She was going to the kitchen. He heard her light the gas and put the dinner she'd brought him into the oven to keep warm. He was a real cad, doing this to her.

'Oh!' Ellie came to the living room. 'You haven't lit the fire?'

'I've only just got in,' he lied. It made him feel worse that she'd laid it this morning before going out, and all he had to do was put a match to it. 'I'll do it now.'

On his knees on the hearth rug, he suddenly made up his mind. 'You didn't tell me Irene was going to look after Flossie's baby.'

'Didn't I? She loves babies, I'm sure she'll mother her. Posy's a lovely child, isn't she?'

He cringed, not wanting to tell a lie but he did. 'I haven't seen her yet.'

Winnie Vickers wished she didn't live so close to Flossie. She was seeing too much of what she was doing and didn't approve. Flossie wasn't looking after her baby properly. Since she and Edith had heard Posy crying behind the locked door, she hadn't trusted her. Sometimes she fed Posy on fresh milk and sometimes on condensed, whatever she had to hand. If Flossie was out of both, Posy was given a bottle of tea. It surprised Winnie that she continued to thrive.

Once Flossie was back at work, Winnie had insisted Irene take care of her during the pub's morning session, but Flossie was giving her a bottle at six and putting her down to sleep before she went back to the Mermaid for the evening session.

'I can't afford to pay a baby minder twice,' she'd said. 'And anyway, Posy sleeps through till I get back.'

Winnie was surprised to find she did. Every night when she got home, she listened as she passed Flossie's door and she'd never heard Posy crying.

'I told Irene she mustn't let her sleep during the morning,' Flossie told her. 'And I keep her awake in the afternoons. Posy's glad to sleep while I'm out at night.'

There were other things Winnie didn't like. Flossie wasn't treating Frank right. He was giving her money regularly and deserved better than he was getting. Before Flossie came back to work, she used to come to the Mermaid as a customer and chat Frank up in the bar until she could pick up a man to take back home with her. Flossie had to live, but she didn't have to make it so obvious. Winnie had seen Frank watching her and knew how he felt.

Frank still went home with her a couple of times a week, but Winnie knew the man she really welcomed to her bed was Ralph Corner.

Almost every day now, Flossie had him with her when she brought the baby home from Irene's house. She'd push her key into Winnie's hand and ask her to keep an eye on Posy because Ralph was taking her out for lunch. He was a commercial traveller in baby linen, and much of Posy's wardrobe came from him.

'Is he going to be permanent?' Winnie asked. 'A father for Posy?'

'He's already married, Winnie. Isn't that always the way for me?' Flossie looked woebegone.

'I'd be careful then. What's Frank going to think?'

'He can think what he likes.'

Winnie understood then that her affair with Frank had cooled. He understood it too and was pretty miserable behind the bar, not enjoying life as he used to. This last week, Flossie started asking her to pick Posy up and it was she who walked to Garnet Street with him.

Last night, Winnie had brought Tom Draper home with her. She'd met him in the bar and he'd been coming about once a month for many years. She liked him and wished he'd make it more often. He'd stayed what was left of the night and as he had to be at work by seven thirty, she'd got up and made him tea and toast before he left. After that she'd gone back to bed and slept late. Today was her day off and it was well after ten thirty when she'd got up again to make her breakfast. She put the two pound notes he'd left her in her handbag; she'd go out and spend them this afternoon. She was pottering about her attic in her dressing gown, when she heard footsteps running upstairs and Flossie's voice calling her. She went out on the landing.

'Winnie, be a sport and take Posy round to Irene's for me, will you?'

'Yes, what's the matter?'

'I'm late.'

'Very late, Mr Secker will be having a fit.'

'Yes, thanks a million.' Flossie pressed her key into her hand and ran back down the stairs. 'I've just fed her and there's a bottle made up.'

'You look very smart.'

Flossie was wearing her best hat and coat. Winnie leaned over the banister and could see Ralph Corner on the landing below, with a suitcase in each hand. There was something furtive about his manner. He looked up at that moment and met her gaze. He turned and rushed downstairs.

'Flossie?' Winnie was suddenly suspicious. It didn't look as though she was on her way to work. 'Where are you going?'

Flossie turned as she picked up a big bag she'd left on her landing. 'Goodbye, Winnie.'

Winnie caught a glimpse of her face, stiff with stress, then Flossie was hurtling down to the front door too. It slammed behind her.

Winnie went slowly down to the next floor. Flossie hadn't bothered to lock her door. Her room was more chaotic than usual. Drawers and cupboards had been emptied and left open, the bed unmade. Apart from Posy's things there was only tat left.

Posy was in her pram, wearing her knitted bonnet and coat, all ready to go out. She was asleep, her long lashes lying on her cheeks.

'I think your mother's just abandoned you,' Winnie told her.

Winnie sank down on Flossie's bed, feeling little darts of excitement shooting through her. She needed to think this through. She'd grown very attached to Posy. She'd always wanted a daughter and now it looked as though it might be possible. What a difference that would make to both of them. Posy was only five months old. She could grow up believing Winnie to be her mother.

But had Flossie gone for good? Winnie was afraid she might come back in a week or two, but perhaps not. Hadn't Flossie walked out on a husband and two children years ago?

She began collecting the baby clothes and equipment together. She'd take all this. She'd get Edith to help her carry Posy's cot up to her place later. Flossie had more or less cleared her room out. Winnie found a tea caddy with a little tea, some sugar and a half-used tin of condensed milk. No point in leaving those for Gertie, their landlady.

Winnie went downstairs and knocked on the landlady's door. 'Flossie seems to have gone,' she told her. 'Taken all her clothes. Did she give notice?'

'No.' Gertie released a string of oaths. 'The bitch, she owes me three weeks' rent. She's done a flit, has she?'

The landlady climbed the stairs as fast as her bulk and her bunions would allow, wanting to see for herself. Winnie followed, thrilled to know Flossie didn't intend to come back.

'Done a flit all right,' Gertie said, looking at the empty cupboards, 'no doubt about that.'

She glared angrily at the sleeping Posy. 'She's left the baby? The cheek of her! Well, I'm having nothing to do with that. She's going straight to the police station. Or the Salvation Army are nearer, perhaps they'll have her?'

Winnie said, 'I want to keep her. Bring her up as my own.'

Gertie's suspicious eyes looked into hers. 'Keep someone else's baby? You're a fool, Winnie Vickers, if you take that on.'

'I'm going to. I'll look after her.'

'See you do then. If you change your mind she'll be off to the police station. I'm not looking after her.' Winnie heard the landlady swearing again as she clumped down to her own quarters.

She sat down and pulled the pram closer so she could see the sleeping baby. She was determined to make a better life for both of them. She'd do more for the child than Flossie ever would. She'd start saving her money until she had enough to take them away from here. Then, she'd give up working as a prostitute and a barmaid, and bring Posy up properly, so she'd have nothing to be ashamed of. Posy would have a happy childhood; she'd pretend she was her mother, and a widow. Posy need never know about this place.

Winnie had always meant to get away from here. She'd dreamed of getting a respectable job and having a small house in a decent part of town, but she'd frittered away all she'd earned. It was easier to buy what comfort she could and enjoy that. She'd never saved.

But now she had Posy to think of, not just herself. For her she'd be strong. She'd find a house to rent in Formby or Southport, near the sea where she could take Posy to the beach. In her old age, she'd have Posy to look after her. By the time Posy was waking from her nap, Winnie had made her plans.

She carried her upstairs to her attic rooms, giving her little hugs of pleasure.

'This is your new home, Posy.' She took her from room to room. 'This is the kitchen, this is my bedroom and this room will be yours.' Posy gurgled with delight.

It needed cleaning out. Winnie had used it as a junk room. Everything she had no immediate use for was stored here: a basket full of clothes that needed ironing, a maiden of sheets that were airing. She'd find somewhere else for these things.

'I'm your new mother and I'll take good care of you.'

Posy was very responsive, smiling and cooing back at her. Winnie changed her nappy and put her back in her pram. She'd take her round to the pub and see what Frank said about this, and tell Bill Secker he'd need to find another barmaid.

Mr Secker lived at the pub; he had a front door that opened on to the street. Winnie knocked on that, thumping the knocker three times, but nobody answered. The landlord would be working behind the bar to cover her day off. She guessed Flossie's absence meant his wife was there too; she was always the back stop when staff didn't turn up. Winnie picked Posy up and took her into the bar.

Mr Secker didn't like that. 'Winnie, you know children aren't allowed in here,' he thundered. 'D'you want me to lose my licence?'

'I've got to speak to you.' He was ushering her towards his living room. She turned. Frank looked shocked to see her with the baby. 'And you, Frank. I've got to have a word.'

'Not now. Frank's busy serving.'

Mr Secker was in a bad mood, made worse when she told him. 'Damn Flossie! Messing me about. She only came back to work a few weeks ago. D'you know anyone to take her place?'

'I could ask Edith. She's working in a pub in the North End but it's not easy to get a bus home from there late at night. I think she's looking for a change.'

'Tell her to come straight round to see me if she wants it.' He looked at her. 'How about you coming in to give a hand tonight?'

'No, it's my day off.' Winnie didn't like the idea. 'I can't, I've got to find someone to take care of Flossie's baby. That's urgent and I've only got today. I want a word with Frank.'

'He's busy.'

'Five minutes. He's her father, he's got to do something. Please, Mr Secker.'

'Five minutes, then.'

Winnie sat down to wait. She liked Frank but she had to think of Posy now. She'd get her away to Southport sooner if she got this right.

Frank put his head nervously round the door. 'What's happened, Winnie? Why isn't Posy with Irene?'

'Didn't the boss tell you?'

'He said Flossie had gone off.'

'She's done a flit and left the baby. What are you going to do about it?'

'Me?'

'You're her father, aren't you?' Frank was the sort who had a conscience. 'Somebody will have to look after her.'

'I can't! You know I can't.'

'Well, who d'you suggest?'

That made him catch his breath. 'Won't you? I mean, I thought you liked Posy.'

'I've got to work, Frank.' Winnie could see his hand shaking. She'd got him worried now.

'I know, but Flossie worked—'

'It costs money to look after a baby. I can't afford . . . I don't see why I should.'

'I'll pay you.' He was more than eager.

'How much?'

'Seven and six a week, that's the usual maintenance for a child.'

Winnie wanted more if she could get it. 'You were paying that to Flossie and she was her mother.'

He hesitated. 'Ten shillings?'

'Then I'll need money for the baby minder. Will you pay that too?'

She saw Frank's tongue moisten his lips. He looked fraught. 'I'll give you the money, Winnie, but Irene mustn't know I have anything to do with it. You'll have to pay her. She's Ellie's friend.'

Winnie stood up and lifted Posy higher on her shoulder. 'It's a big responsibility to take on. I'll think about it,' she said.

Franco didn't know how he got through the rest of the morning. Flossie gone? He couldn't believe it. She'd turned her back on him and her baby? He'd known someone else was taking his place, but he'd not expected this.

It was an unforeseen crisis. He was worried stiff. Everybody at the pub knew Posy was his. He felt responsible but what could he do? Winnie had to be persuaded to look after her, there was nobody else.

He had Ellie and the boys to think about. He'd been deceitful, thinking only of his own needs and pleasures, and now his problems were burgeoning. How was he going to keep this from Ellie? When he thought of the money he'd promised Winnie, it brought him out in a cold sweat. He didn't know how he was going to find all that.

He went home, glad Ellie wasn't yet there. It gave him time to think, but he was no nearer a solution when he heard her key in the door and the boys scampering inside.

'It's tortellini for your dinner,' she said from the hall. Food was the last thing he wanted.

'I called in at the school on the way home. They'll take Bobby in the nursery class, when the new term starts in September. Isn't he growing up fast?

'Is something the matter?' Ellie came to the living-room door, her eyes searching his face. He felt panic-stricken. Did it show?

What he ought to do was confess his lapse with Flossie, tell her about Posy. He had to tell her everything or it would always be between them. He had to say how sorry he was and ask her forgiveness. It was the only way to get back on a better footing with Ellie. She'd be shocked, and what if she didn't forgive him?

Her amber eyes looked concerned. 'Aren't you well, Franco?'

'No.' He grasped at the straw. 'I've got a terrible belly ache. I was sick this morning at the pub.'

Looking after Posy was a labour of love for Winnie. She played with her all the time. She was growing fast, her limbs becoming rounded and dimpled. Winnie was delighted when she learned to sit up and then to crawl, and when her first word was Mamma, and she was holding her arms up to her, Winnie was filled with wonder.

Every morning, she took her to Irene's house before she went to work. There were always other children there. Irene told her they played with Posy, and she enjoyed having her dinner with them. She was a happy little girl, gurgling and babbling all the time.

Winnie knew she was turning into a bit of a money-grabber but felt that anything was justified if it was for Posy. Franco was paying up, and had told her he was relieved that she was caring for Posy.

She short-changed more customers in the bar than she'd done before. If one of them invited her to have a drink, she'd say, 'Thanks, love, I'm dying for a gin and orange.' Then she'd take only the orange and hang on to the gin money.

She brought a man home with her whenever she could. Sometimes she stole from them too, trying to take a little more from their trouser pockets than the two pounds she charged. Flossie had charged at least three pounds, more if she thought she could get it, and men had lined up to pay.

Winnie became more thrifty over her own needs, but not Posy's. She saved every penny she could for their future. She needed a safe place to hide the money, and had made a slit in Posy's mattress where she could push coins and notes into the grey flock filling. When she covered the mattress with its rubber sheet and made up Posy's cot, there was nothing showing of the treasure trove that was growing inside.

Every evening, Winnie put Posy to bed before she went to the pub at half past six. She'd told Flossie off for doing this, and she didn't like leaving her alone. Winnie asked the landlady to listen out for her and she said she heard nothing from the child.

As she grew bigger Posy became more daring and by the time she was thirteen months old she was able to climb over the cot sides. Winnie took them off, afraid she might fall while she was out working.

She now put Posy to bed wearing her walking reins over her nightdress. She'd lengthened the straps so they would fasten to her cot. If Posy woke up, she could get out of bed but not stray far. Winnie thought that was the safest thing for her, and if she was sleeping in her bed or was close to it, it kept the money safe too.

Winnie hated the life she was leading. She knew she'd drifted for too long. It had taken the baby to make her pull herself together. She was making a huge effort now and was determined to do it for Posy's sake.

Chapter Twenty-One

1936

On the Sunday nearest to Ellie's twenty-first birthday, Connie and Vito put on a party in the cafe for their friends and relatives. Ellie enjoyed her day. She wrote a note inviting Ben Quiltie but heard nothing from him. Irene came and so did Alice and her husband.

'We must see more of each other,' Alice told her. 'We're barely in touch except for Christmas and birthdays, and I miss you. I've other girlfriends now, but none close like you. Graham is my best friend these days.'

Alice had all her old bounce and zest for life. She had rosy cheeks and glowed with good health. Contentment was causing her to spread a little round her waist and hips.

'We have a house of our own now, we had to get it with two children. It's not far from Mam's place. Come and see me and have a real chinwag. We've a lot to catch up on.'

'I'd love to,' Ellie said. She needed to keep up with her friend too.

Franco wasn't joining in the fun. He was keeping his distance, hardly talking to anybody. When they were walking home afterwards, Ellie asked him again if something was the matter.

'No, it's just that they're your friends not mine,' he told her.

'Your relatives were all there, Franco.'

'I see plenty of them.'

'You hardly see your cousins from Liverpool, they were there.'

Franco seemed to have no interest in anything these days. He kept himself aloof from everybody, except the children. He played with them, taking them out to the park and teaching them ball games.

If she asked him if he loved her, he assured her he did, but she knew he had worries he didn't want to share with her. She couldn't be happy while Franco was like this.

By the next day, she was counting her blessings. She had Bobby and Kenny and they meant everything to her, she loved them very much. They had big brown eyes and dark curly hair and looked very much like Franco. She thought they'd grow up to be equally handsome.

She loved her job and was able to do it because Connie wanted to look after the boys. Connie and Vito were shoulders to lean on. Ellie was pleased with her little house in Garnet Street, and though money was very short, with what Vito paid her, they were just able to cope.

On the day she'd arranged to go and see Alice's new house, Franco was going to come up to the cafe for his dinner and would collect the boys and look after them during the afternoon.

She got off the bus in the New Ferry bus shed. Across the road she saw customers going into the Maypole, and caught a glimpse of Mr Owen behind the bacon counter. She walked past, heading for Woolworths to buy some sweets for Alice's children. Nothing seemed to have changed here, it was like stepping back into a previous life. She was enjoying being out and about with time to look round.

She paused to look in the window of the butcher's shop where Ben Quiltie used to work, and laughed when she saw Ben put a tray of mince back into the window display. He still worked here. He looked up and recognised her. The shop door was open, and they met on the step.

'Hello, Ellie.' Ben was all smiles. His straight brown hair was still swept back from his forehead, his blue eyes were still wary, but he'd grown to manhood, taller and broader. 'How are you doing?'

'Fine. Didn't you get my note inviting you to my twenty-first party?'

He shook his head. 'No, we aren't living in Bicknell Street any more. How are you getting on?'

Ellie tried to bring him up to date quickly with all that had happened since she'd moved out. Customers were trying to get in the shop, so he moved her out to the pavement.

'Ben,' his boss called from behind the counter, 'come on.'

'I want to hear about you,' Ellie said urgently. 'How are you getting on with Uncle Mick?'

'You haven't heard?'

'What?'

'Come on, lad. Stop gossiping. There's customers waiting to be served.'

'It's a long story, can't tell you now.'

'Come to the cafe for your dinner on your next half day. We'll have time to talk then. Get the bus up as soon as you close here, OK?'

'I will.'

'Ben,' his boss's voice had risen, 'I'm not paying you to chat up the girls, get yourself in here.'

'See you Thursday,' Ellie called. 'Don't forget.'

Seeing Ben brought back the bad times they'd shared. She'd

been much happier since she'd left Uncle Mick's house. She went into Woolworths and then on to Alice's house.

Ten minutes in Alice's company and it was as though they still saw each other every day. She had two little daughters. Ellie told her how much she'd wanted a girl when she was having Kenny.

Alice took her on a tour of her house. Graham, her husband, came home while Alice was setting the table for tea, a special meal because Ellie would be with them. He kissed Alice with great affection. Seeing them together brought home to Ellie that they had a much closer relationship than she had with Franco, and pointed out what she was missing. Graham was a loving husband. Ellie had expected her marriage to be like this. In the past, her own life had mirrored Alice's, but not in this respect.

Ellie was still awake when Franco came home from work at midnight. He got into bed beside her and she put her arms round him and said, 'I do love you, Franco, but we're drifting apart and I don't like it. I'm not making you happy any more. Where are we going wrong?'

For Franco that did it. It brought tears to his eyes but Ellie couldn't see with the light off. He recognised this as his chance to confess, but couldn't bring himself to do it. Telling Ellie the truth could turn her against him.

'I do love you, Ellie. I'm a rotten husband.' He mopped his tears silently on the sheet. 'I'm going to turn over a new leaf, I promise.'

She told him again she loved him and he held her close. 'I want things to be better too. We'll make it happen, Ellie.'

There had been times before when she'd seemed to invite more affection from him, but he'd felt paralysed and turned away. Other times when she'd seemed to invite confidences, but he'd felt emotionally frozen. He'd longed to get on better terms with her but he'd done such dreadful things, he didn't think she'd love him if she knew. It would break her trust in him.

For the first time he realised he must sever his connection with the Mermaid pub. He was beginning to think it might not be such a bad thing if he accepted his parents' offer of a job and a home with them. He'd been going to the caff again and having the odd meal with his parents but he could only envy Ellie's relationship with them. He couldn't get near to them.

All this was still locked inside him, as well as the frightening facts about Posy and Flossie. He couldn't bring himself to tell Ellie any of that. But he'd made a start. She still loved him, it wasn't too late to turn things round. He'd court her as he had his many girlfriends when he was young.

On Thursday, Ben Quiltie arrived at the cafe as the dinnertime rush was quietening down. Ellie had told Vito she'd asked him to come for his dinner, and he brought him straight to the kitchen. Ellie was making more gravy, and Connie and Franco were already setting out the family meal.

They talked of Ellie's children and the cafe, and other Baldini affairs. Both Ben and Franco seemed quiet. She guessed Ben didn't want to talk about Mick in front of her in-laws.

When they'd eaten, she said, 'Come home with us, Ben. I'll make a cup of tea there.'

It was only when Franco took Kenny and went to meet Bobby from school that she got Ben to open up.

'So what's this long story about Uncle Mick? What's happened to him?'

He nodded. 'It's awful. I came home from work to find Roy belting him with the poker. He had him down on the living-room floor.'

'Roy? What did you do?'

'I yanked him off and said, "Your dad isn't worth hanging for. That's what they'll do to you if you kill him." He was kicking at him too, with heavy boots on.'

'But Roy got on well with his dad.'

'His temper was up. He's just like his dad, always angry about something. He's nearly fourteen now and built like the side of a house.'

'Thirteen,' Ellie said. 'He's only thirteen. He'd never have the strength—'

'Mick had just had the plaster off his arm. Did I tell you he'd fractured it?'

'No.'

'He's been drinking too much these last few years and does nothing but sit round the house. He's not as strong as he was . . .'

'But what made Roy lift the poker to him?'

Ben shook his head again and took a deep breath. 'It seems that when Roy came home from school, Mick was arguing with Mam. Roy went to his bedroom to get out of the way, thinking it was their usual sort of tiff about next to nothing. But then he heard real ructions, Mam screaming and that. He came rushing down to find Mick thrashing her with the poker.'

Ellie was aghast. 'I never thought he'd turn against Wilma.'

'Oh yes, he's done it before. You saw her that time with the black eye, didn't you?'

'But with the poker, like that.'

'Why d'you think I stayed? Roy said he was belting the life out of Mam, he had to stop him.'

'Oh!' All this was bringing back the horror Ellie had felt when she'd lived with them. 'And now?'

'Mam's still in hospital. Mick's been charged with grievous bodily harm, having stolen goods on his premises and burglary. More charges for burglary could be brought against him. He's in prison on remand. His case comes up in a couple of months.'

Against the comforting familiarity of her own home, it sounded macabre. 'Burglary too?'

'I shopped him, Ellie.' Ben's eyes were searching into hers. 'I had to do it, the time had come. I told the police about the stolen goods in our house. They came round and went through the whole place with a fine-tooth comb. They took a lot of stuff away.'

Ellie felt sick. She was glad she wasn't living there now.

'The next day, the landlord came and told me to get out of the house. Mick hadn't paid the rent for months, and I couldn't pay him, and he didn't like the police coming round. He said it gave the place a bad name.'

'Oh my goodness! Where are you living now?'

'I took a couple of rooms in Grove Street. It's as much as I can afford but it's OK for me and the boys.'

'Heavens, Ben! How's Auntie Wilma?'

'She's getting better, slowly. This has made her see sense. Roy was trying to protect her, you see. He could get himself in real trouble that way. She's finally decided she won't have Mick back to live with us. Not ever.'

'I bet you're glad.'

'She should have done it years ago. I kept on at her, trying to persuade her.'

'But if he comes out, he'll have nowhere else to go. Won't he come looking for you? I mean you're just round the corner . . .'

'He won't find us. I'm going to sever all connections with New Ferry. I've found a small house to rent out at Eastham. We'll be in by the end of the month when Mam comes out of hospital. Roy will be leaving school this summer, so I'm hoping we'll be able to manage.'

'How long is Mick likely to stay in prison?'

Ben shrugged. 'Who's to say at this stage? It'll be measured in years not months because he's already done one stretch for assault and battery.'

Ellie said, 'He deserves all he gets.'

'When he comes out, you won't tell him where we are? He might come to the cafe.'

'Course I won't. I'll take good care to give him no clues.'

'Mam's been terrified of him for years, but she wouldn't leave him. Couldn't, she said, because she wasn't earning anything, but apart from what I earn, we've been living on what he stole. Poor Mam, she's had a terrible life with him.'

'He gave us all a terrible time,' Ellie said. 'Me and you and Gran. And I still think he killed my mam. Did you find out any more? About what happened that day at the bike shop? You promised, years ago, that you'd try.'

Ben shook his head. 'Sorry. I did ask Mam, but she's very careful what she says about it. Nothing new.'

'She was there, Ben.'

'Perhaps there's nothing more to know. Anyway, she didn't want to talk about it. I'll try again. After this, she may want to open up.'

'And you'll let me know?' Ellie was eager. 'I'm sure Auntie Wilma . . . It's been a weight on my mind for years. I swore I'd find out, but I never have.'

'Yes, if I have any news I'll come and see you at the cafe.'

Franco brought the children home and made another pot of tea. When he took it to the living room, Ellie was telling Ben about how he and Carlo had taken her to see the car at the bike shop on that tragic afternoon. They went on and on discussing it.

Franco took a gulp of tea. He'd seen it as his duty to speak up about that, but failed to do so. He'd felt less of a man ever since.

He'd never been able to put it behind him, and he didn't think Carlo had either. The Valentinos' tragedy had had a profound impact on them both.

Franco had always been glad he was only twelve at the time. A boy of that age could be forgiven and somehow he'd clung on to that. Childhood had seemed a time of warmth and security. He'd had his first glimpse of the adult world that afternoon and had been horrified by its violence. He'd been unable to deal with it. With hindsight, he felt fear had frozen him, kept him permanently at the emotional age of twelve. He'd shunned adult responsibilities ever since.

It had taken Posy's birth to bring him to his senses, and even now, he was finding it difficult to accept his part in that. He'd thought, all those years ago, that by saying nothing, he'd kept out of trouble, but it had nearly ruined his life.

'I do admire you two,' he said. 'You're both so strong. Stronger than I am.'

'Not me,' Ellie said. 'You were always telling me to be stronger, to face up to things.'

'But I couldn't do it myself.' Franco shook his head sadly.

'Ben's the strong one.' Ellie smiled at him. 'He stood between Mick and the rest of us, protecting us all. He showed me how to cope.'

When Ben left, Franco said, 'He's holding his family together, and that takes real strength. More than I'll ever have.'

'Perhaps as we get older . . .'

Franco shook his head in misery. 'I've never done what I

should. Always fought against that and gone my own way, haven't I? Everybody admires Ben but despises me.'

'I wouldn't say that.' Ellie smiled at him. 'We all love you, Franco.'

'Ma's always telling me to grow up, isn't she? It's high time I did, and got back on good terms with everybody.'

He took a deep breath and said it out loud. 'I want to leave the pub, really want to. I need to get away from it.'

He could see by her face that she was delighted. 'What will you do?' Ellie was being cautious.

'Work in the caff, if Pa will have me. I hate being at sixes and sevens with him and Ma.'

'Franco! I'm so pleased,' Ellie breathed. 'Delighted, thrilled, it's what they want too. Why don't we go up and tell them now?'

'Ellie!' Franco jumped to his feet in surprise. 'I've got to go to work. It's nearly opening time.'

'So it is, and you need something to eat. You could tell them tomorrow when you come up to the cafe for your dinner.'

'If I leave it till around closing time, I could go home with Pa and perhaps settle things.' He smiled. 'At dinner time, Danny will be there and Pa has to chase in and out after customers.'

Franco wanted to turn over a new leaf. He wanted to forget the bad things that had happened at the pub, he wanted everybody to forget them. When he was leaving for work, Ellie hugged him and said, 'This will solve so many of our problems. Make us feel closer. It's been a real afternoon for heart searching.'

'And for making up my mind about what must be done.' But Franco knew he was hoping to solve his problems without making a full confession. He needed to tell her about Flossie and Posy. He ought to, but would she still love him if he did?

Once again, he'd failed to speak up when he should have done. Ellie thought he'd changed for the better, but he hadn't. He'd kept his mouth shut again.

That same night, Winnie Vickers took a man home with her when the Mermaid closed. She showed him to her bedroom before peeping in to Posy's little room. She was fast asleep, her white-blonde curls spread out across the pillow. She was eighteen months old now and she looked a little angel.

'Not much longer, my pet,' she whispered before closing the door and tiptoeing back to the man in her room. She'd had enough of this, but she could grit her teeth and smile for just a bit longer. She always tried to show pleasure in it, faking it to give the chap his money's worth so he'd want to come again. It also speeded the man along, got it over and done with quickly.

On her next day off, Winnie meant to take the train to Southport and go round the estate agents, to see if she could rent a little house. She'd dreamed of this moment for ages, and it was now within her grasp.

She didn't want Posy to have any memory of Cunliffe Street or what went on here. It was a dump and she meant to be out of it well before Posy's second birthday.

The next morning, Winnie woke up early and looked at the sleeping face on the pillow beside her. His mouth was open showing bad teeth. He had bad breath too. She was revolted. She hardly knew him, they'd called him Tubsy in the bar, Tubsy something, she couldn't remember his surname. Not that it mattered.

He'd been drunk and she'd had to have a few drinks to hide her distaste. He hadn't seemed too bad last night, but now he needed a shave and she could see blackheads across his forehead. Thank goodness she wouldn't have to do this for much longer.

She could hear Posy waking up and rattling her bells in the next room. She began singing softly to herself. 'Ickory, ickery ock, mouse ran up the clock.'

Winnie had taught her to sing nursery rhymes and if she played records on her wind-up gramophone, Posy would lift up her feet and rock about. They called it dancing though it was far from that. Posy was great fun. Winnie lay still, listening, knowing Posy would start calling for her before long.

'Mamma?' There it was. 'Mamma?'

Winnie slid gently out of bed so as not to disturb her client, pushed her feet into her slippers and found her dressing gown. She unfastened the straps from Posy's harness and sat her on her potty. It was another source of pride to Winnie that she'd learned to use it and was advanced for her age.

She carried Posy to her cupboard-sized kitchen to warm some milk for her. She was good at drinking from a cup now. Winnie put on the kettle to make an early cup of tea for herself and her guest.

Then she fastened Posy back in her bed. Usually she'd be happy there for another hour, either sleeping or singing or rattling the beads and bells fastened to her bed head.

Winnie poured out the tea and went back to get rid of her guest. He was still asleep.

Tubsy had paid with two pound notes last night. She always made her clients pay first; getting the money out of them later could be difficult. He'd got a night's lodging out of her too, and there was no reason why she should throw that in for free. His trousers were over a chair. He'd had money in his pockets last night. She put the cups down quietly and with one last glance at the sleeping man rifled through his pockets, taking out three half crowns.

She kept a handkerchief in the pocket of her dressing gown to stop any jangling, and was sliding them in when she heard a bedspring creak. She turned round to find his dark brooding eyes watching her.

'You thieving bitch!' He jumped at her. Winnie couldn't believe such a heavily built man could move so quickly. He grabbed at her throat. She jerked herself back, but his weight crashed against her, knocking her to the floor. It winded her and twisted her back. Terror was shafting through her.

She'd meant to shout for Edith, but the only sound she made was a whimper. She was fighting to free her arms but his weight was pinning her down.

His face was inches from hers, unshaven and black with anger.

'You cheating whore.'

Winnie raised her head and bit into his fleshy chin, clamping on her jaws as hard as she could.

He let out a screech of pain and tried to pull away but she held on. Winnie wanted to scream but couldn't, because his fingers were biting into her neck. She couldn't get her breath.

Then he lifted her head and banged it back against the floor. She knew she was finished. The room was swinging round her. Everything was going black.

That morning, Franco dressed quickly and went down to the kitchen to help get the breakfast. He and Ellie had talked late into the night when he'd come home. Yesterday afternoon with Ben had sorted him out, but left him feeling drained. He was looking forward to mending the rift with his parents and getting his life back on a stable footing.

Once the house was quiet he washed up and re-laid the fire. That made him late getting to the pub. Edith was already teetering round the bar in her high heels. He was yawning.

'Missed your beauty sleep again? Been up making whoopee half the night?' she asked.

Franco thought her aggressive. She seemed to swoop at people. With her black hair and large nose she reminded him of a crow when she attacked him like this.

Mr Secker sent him down to the cellar to work on the beer. When the first customers were coming through the door, Franco asked, 'Where's Winnie this morning?'

Edith shook her head. 'I haven't seen her.'

Secker was muttering under his breath about bad time keeping, though Winnie was usually more punctual than the rest of them. It had gone eleven when he said, 'Go and see where Winnie is, Edith. Get her here before the dinner-time rush starts.'

Edith pulled on her brown hat and coat and went. There were enough customers to keep Franco busy, he hadn't time to think about anything else, but Secker was going spare. Franco looked up from serving a customer to see Edith, her hat askew, looking a wraith of her former self.

'Mr Secker, I've got to have a word.' She was tugging at his arm.

'What is it, Edith? Can't you see I'm busy?'

'In private,' she breathed. 'It's important.'

She got him moving at last. The customers were asking where Winnie was this morning and what was the matter. Franco's curiosity was aroused, but now he was the only person serving in the pub. Customers were clamouring for his attention.

It was only when a policeman in uniform pushed his way through the crowd and called, 'Is Mr Secker here?' that he began to worry about what was going on.

He directed him to Secker's private quarters, remembering then that the brewery had put in a telephone so they could contact him. But what did he want the police for? And why didn't Edith come back to give him a hand?

It was Mrs Secker who came. She thought herself a bit above serving in the bar, and only helped out in a crisis.

'What's happened?' he asked. 'Where's Winnie and Edith?'

She shook her head, looking down her nose at him as usual. 'I'll tell you later.'

It was an hour later when Edith came and touched him on the shoulder. Her face was white and drawn. 'I've come to relieve you. The police want a word.'

'What for?' Franco demanded. 'What's going on?'

Her voice was low, her face deadpan. 'Winnie's dead, murdered in her room. Strangled. I found her when I went round.'

He had to hold on to the bar to steady himself. 'Good God!'

'Go on, they're waiting for you.' She was already drawing a tankard of ale.

Franco couldn't take it in. Winnie dead? Feeling befuddled, he drifted to Mr Secker's private quarters. The policeman was sitting with his boss at the dining table, his helmet placed beside his pad, an emblem of authority.

'This is Frank, my barman,' Secker said. 'He's worked here . . . How long is it now?'

'Four years.' Franco could see his hands shaking. He put them behind his back.

'So you know the barmaids well?'

'Yes. I hear Winnie—'

The police officer interrupted. 'Give me your full name and address.'

He watched him write it down.

'Age?'

Franco's mouth was dry. His tongue felt too big for his mouth.

'Winifred Vickers was taking care of an eighteen-month-old baby . . .'

'Is she all right?'

'Yes, unharmed. It seems she was asleep in another room at the time. I understand you are the father?'

The room began to swim round Franco. This was awful. He'd never be able to keep it from Ellie after this. 'Where is . . . ? Where is the baby?'

Secker said, 'Edith's already taken her to the child minder.'

The policeman looked up from his note-taking and repeated, 'I understand you are the father.'

Franco felt his world falling apart.

Bill Secker said, 'I told him you were, that's right, isn't it? Flossie made no secret of it.'

Franco couldn't deny it, here it was common knowledge. He'd thought himself in difficulties when Flossie had gone off with Ralph Corner, but this . . .

The policeman was taking him through the whole story, his relationship with Winnie Vickers and then with Flossie Phillips. He was writing it all down. Franco could feel the blood pumping through the veins in his head. This was desperate. Things were out of control.

The policeman's gaze met his. 'I take it that as the father, you'll make other arrangements for the child's care?'

That floored him. He had to say yes, but who could he get to look after Posy now? He found himself back in the bar in front of the clamouring customers. He'd never felt so frightened before in his life. This was going to blow him apart.

Eventually, time was being called and the customers were thumping their glasses on the bar and drifting out in twos and threes. Franco set about the familiar work of clearing up, his mind anywhere but on what he was doing.

Edith and the Seckers huddled together discussing Winnie in undertones. They were as shocked and horrified as he was but her death wasn't bringing such awful consequences to them. He felt desperately sorry for Winnie, it was a horrible end, but he didn't know which way to turn. As he washed the glasses, one slid through his fingers and crashed against another, breaking both.

Mrs Secker snapped with exasperation, 'Frank, you do one job and make two more.' Slowly he began to pick up the broken pieces.

At last, he and Edith were free to go and the pub door was locked behind them.

'You'll pick Posy up?' Edith asked.

He caught at her arm. 'Will you do it? I mean will you look after her?'

She swung round on him, her black eyes sparking aggression. 'I hope you don't mean will I take Posy over and bring her up?' She must have guessed from his face that he did. 'You've got a cheek! I've got better things to do with my time. She's your baby, Frank.'

He turned away in the direction of home. For once, it didn't seem a safe place to go. Ellie would soon be there.

He hovered on the corner of Garnet Street. Irene would be expecting somebody to collect Posy, but he couldn't face it. He hurried to his own front door with his head down, unable even to look at her house.

It made him feel a coward. He flopped down on an armchair, knowing he had to light the fire. It was an effort to feel along the mantelpiece for the matches. He felt befuddled and unable to do anything.

Ellie would have to know. He couldn't think beyond that. Last night, he'd been so sure he'd be able to put Flossie and Posy behind him for ever.

Chapter Twenty-Two

Franco heard the scrape of Ellie's key in the lock.

'Hello, Franco,' she sounded cheerful, 'we're home.' Kenny came scampering into the living room to him.

'Daddy, Daddy.' He threw his little arms round Franco's knees, but for once he couldn't lift him up.

Ellie came to the door. 'I've brought bistecca for your dinner.'

He grunted, 'I suppose you mean stewed steak?' He knew he sounded grumpy.

'Yes, but it's easier to warm up if it's in gravy. It's very nice, we've all had it.'

He could hear her in the kitchen rattling pans. He had to get out there and tell her. He looked up and found she'd come back to the living-room door.

'What's the matter, Franco?'

How was he going to tell her about Flossie and the baby? He choked out, 'Something terrible happened last night . . .'

'Daddy.' Kenny had climbed up on his knee and was pulling at his pullover.

'Shut up, Kenny,' he snapped, pushing him away. Kenny began to cry.

Ellie scooped the child up and sat down with him on her knee. She was serious now. 'What's happened?'

'You know Winnie?'

'Yes, one of the barmaids, the older one.'

'She was murdered last night.'

'What? How?'

He could see by her face she was horrified, and for her it would explain why he was like this.

'I hardly know whether I'm on my head or my heels.' He covered his face with both his hands. 'Winnie took a man home with her from the pub, and he strangled her. Edith found her this morning.'

He watched Ellie's tongue moisten her lips. 'Who was he?'

'We don't know. We've seen him in the pub a few times but nobody seems to know his name or where he lives.'

Ellie's mouth still hung open. 'So he's still at large?' She was hugging Kenny to her and even the child was stunned into silence.

Franco took a deep breath. 'You remember Flossie Phillips?'

'She was the pretty one?'

'Yes, she had a baby . . .'

'I know, she brought her to the caff a few times.'

'Flossie ran off with a man sometime last year.'

'I think you told me.'

'Well, she abandoned the baby. Left it with Winnie and now there's no one to look after her.'

'Poor kid!'

He searched her face; that was sympathy, wasn't it? He went on, 'She's a lovely little girl, about eighteen months old now.'

'She's called Posy, isn't she? Irene looks after her. Where is she now?'

'With Irene.' Ellie was frowning. He dared to say, 'Wouldn't . . . wouldn't you like to have her?'

Ellie's gaze swung to meet his. 'What d'you mean, have her?'

'Bring her up with the boys.'

'No, Franco! No!'

It rattled him to have so emphatic a refusal. He tried to be persuasive. 'You said you wanted a little girl.'

'She'll have relatives somewhere, they'll want her.'

'No, she hasn't.'

'Franco, we're hard up as it is, we don't need another mouth to feed. And what about your mother? She won't want to look after her while I'm working. She wouldn't see her as another grandchild.'

'Irene's doing that. She can carry on.'

'Don't be daft, Franco. Our hands are full as it is.'

'You won't then?'

'No. No one will expect us to.'

Franco hid his face with his hands. He couldn't bring himself to tell her he was Posy's father. Not straight out, but everybody at the pub was expecting him to take responsibility for her. The police were too.

Ellie felt shaken. She could hardly believe what Franco had told her. 'It sounds more like a film than real life,' she said.

She almost let his dinner burn, but when he had it in front of him, he couldn't eat it. She could see it was really upsetting him. She made a pot of tea for them to share, but he didn't seem to want that either.

She said, 'A murderer loose here in the streets where we live? It's frightening, isn't it? Too close to home.'

Franco seemed really shut off. He was silent and chewing on his lip.

She had to ask, 'You haven't forgotten about Bobby? He's due out of school soon.' Usually Franco took Kenny up to meet him, but now he looked at her blankly, almost as though he'd never heard of Bobby.

'D'you want me to go?' She started buttoning Kenny into his coat, afraid Bobby would be out before anybody got there.

He nodded. 'You go.'

Ellie ran to the school gates, relieved to see other mothers standing about in groups. She looked from one to the other, wondering if they were talking about the murder. From their faces, they could be.

Irene came round the corner of the street towards her, pushing Posy's pram. Her face set and serious, she said, 'Have you heard? It's awful, isn't it? I can't believe . . .'

It was blustery and raining a little. The pram hood was up. Posy put her head round to see who Irene was talking to, her ash-blonde curls fluttering round her pink bonnet.

'Terrible,' Ellie agreed. 'Poor Posy, what's going to happen to her now? You look after her in the afternoons too?'

'No, I've just been up to Cunliffe Street looking for Winnie. She always comes for Posy. Before half two usually.'

The baby smiled up at Ellie, showing eight tiny teeth. 'Hello,' she said and chuckled.

'But time was going on and I thought I'd do her a favour and take Posy home. The police were there and stopped me going up to Winnie's place. Gosh, Ellie, I can't take it in.'

'You didn't know?'

'No!'

'Franco's only just told me.'

'I thought Edith was a bit odd this morning, she just wheeled Posy to my door, hammered on it and shot off without saying anything. She looked agitated but I thought that was because she was late. So late I'd thought Posy wasn't coming.'

Irene's many freckles stood out against her white skin. 'Edith's all shook up. She wouldn't let me leave Posy, she said she's having nothing to do with her.'

'Poor little mite.'

'But Winnie murdered!'

Kenny stood on tiptoe to look in the pram. Posy was playing with a stuffed rabbit that Winnie had knitted for her. He made it dance across her coverlet. She gurgled and chuckled and laughed out loud.

'I can't believe any baby could be so unlucky,' Irene said. 'Abandoned by her mother and now her guardian murdered, all before she's two years old.'

'It's as well she doesn't understand.'

'Are you going to take her, Ellie?'

Ellie felt her first qualm. Irene's eyes were studying her. 'No, why should I?'

'Edith said you were, that Franco was her father.'

Ellie couldn't get her breath. 'That's not true. No, absolutely not!'

'She said it was common knowledge at the Mermaid.'

'No!' Ellie was trembling. It couldn't be! But Franco had been in a flat spin, a state of panic. Was that why he'd asked her to have the baby? But that meant . . . She remembered Flossie's beautiful face and cringed.

Irene looked shocked now. 'Edith said he told the police he was, and that he would take responsibility for Posy.'

'No, you mustn't say such things. It's all lies.'

The children had been let out of school. Bobby had seen her and was hurtling towards her. She swept him close and kissed him.

'Hello, love. Had a good day?' It was how she usually greeted him, but this wasn't a usual day.

'Didn't you know? I mean . . .' A flush of embarrassment ran up Irene's cheeks.

Gripping a son with each hand, Ellie said, 'I've got to go.'

'Wait a minute.' Irene's girls had not yet found her. 'I don't mind looking after Posy today, or even for a few days. She's very happy in spite of everything. But I don't want her for ever.'

'You've got it wrong.' Ellie turned on her. 'Franco isn't her father.' It couldn't be true.

'Will you ask him what he wants me to do with her?'

'No.' Ellie was vehement. 'I don't believe this.'

'Ellie, I'm sorry. I thought you knew.'

Her head was spinning. Not Franco, he wouldn't. She remembered feeling a pang of jealousy when she'd caught him looking at Flossie. She didn't want to think of Flossie. She set off at the double, towing her sons.

'What's the matter, Mummy?' Bobby piped. 'Do we have to go so fast?'

Ellie felt terrible. Resentment was rising in her throat like bile. Franco had betrayed her. He'd been carrying on with Flossie behind her back. She'd felt it, she'd known they were growing apart and tried to talk to him about it. But he wouldn't, he'd kept saying everything was fine.

The house was silent when she opened the front door. The boys ran in shouting for Daddy. Franco looked up, damp-eyed, as they crashed the front door back. He was still hunched up on the armchair, hadn't moved in all the time she'd been gone.

'Go upstairs and play in your room for a bit,' she said to Bobby. It was an effort to keep her voice steady. She lifted Kenny off Franco's knee and carried him to the stairs. 'You too.'

She shut the door firmly. She was consumed with terrible anger but she had to think of the children and stay as calm as she could.

'Is it true?' she demanded in a harsh whisper. 'You're Posy's father?'

He didn't have to answer. Guilt was written all over him. 'I'm sorry, Ellie.'

'Sorry? You might have told me, instead of letting me find out from Irene.' She felt bitter about that.

'I'm sorry . . .' He looked ill.

'That doesn't make it better. You can't just say you're sorry and expect to put it behind you.'

'I know.'

'You asked me to take that baby on without telling me the truth. That was a terrible thing to do.'

'I'm sorry.'

'Don't keep saying that.' Ellie could see her whole way of life collapsing. 'Everybody knows about you and Flossie. You've admitted the baby is yours. How d'you think I feel about that?'

'What are you going to do?'

'I don't know. I can't think of anything except you've been with her . . . What did she have that I don't?' But she didn't have to ask. 'Flossie was beautiful, wasn't she?'

'Ellie . . . It was an affair which I wish had never happened, but it's all over and done with. She's been gone for over a year.'

'That doesn't make it better either.' Ellie felt bitter, even though she'd known he was one for the girls. 'How many others are there?'

'None! I've never looked at anyone else since we were married.'

'And what about the baby? It's not all over and done with for her.' Ellie couldn't believe he'd done such a thing.

'Forgive me, please,' he begged. 'I know I did wrong.' His dark eyes looked wounded.

'I can hardly take it in. I can't think . . . You've spoiled everything.' Ellie was in tears. 'I'm going up to your mother's.'

'No, stay here with me. We need to talk about this, sort it out.'

She was shaking and her anger flared up. 'How can it be sorted out? Things like this can't.' She rushed out, slamming the front door behind her, then unlocked it again.

'You've changed your mind?' Franco asked.

'No,' she spat, running upstairs. 'I'm taking the children. You'll be going to work soon.'

She buttoned their coats on again and ran them up the road like one possessed.

'Where are you taking us?' Bobby wanted to know.

'Are you cross with Daddy?' Kenny panted. 'Has he been naughty?'

Yes, she thought, he's been very naughty. She rushed them through the back yard and burst into Connie's kitchen. She was stirring a pan on the stove.

'Ellie! What's the matter?' Her gaze went to the children. 'Are they all right?'

Ellie burst into tears again. She felt bereft. 'It's Franco,' she sobbed.

'Daddy's been naughty,' Bobby said.

She felt Connie's arms go round her and pull her close against her substantial bosom. She let the tears pour out, unable to find words to tell her. She didn't know how long Connie held her, patting her back, making soothing noises.

Then she ushered the boys out to the yard and found an old tricycle and a scooter in the wash house for them to play with. 'They'll be all right for a while,' she said, steering Ellie to an armchair by the living-room fire.

Ellie found the words then to tell her what Franco had done. Her anger had gone. She was hurting now, grief-stricken and fearful.

'Ellie love, you mustn't upset yourself.' She could feel Connie's sympathy. 'You won't want to be on your own this evening. You and the boys had better stay here.'

'It's a lot of trouble for you . . .'

'Nonsense. Let's make up the bed now. You can all sleep in the double, can't you?'

Ellie tucked in sheets mechanically, slid pillowslips on pillows.

'We haven't brought our night things.'

'Best thing would be for me to fetch them,' Connie said. 'I've nothing I could lend the boys. I'll call in and see Vito. He'll have to bring something home for our tea, I haven't enough for us all. You stay here and read a story to them.'

Downstairs again, she pushed a book into Ellie's hand. 'Franco was always one for the girls,' she said sadly before calling the boys in. 'I've been half afraid of this . . .'

'What am I going to do?'

When Connie left, Kenny climbed up on Ellie's knee. Bobby pushed away the book Connie had given her. 'That's for babies.' He found his father's childhood copy of Grimms' *Fairy Tales* and wanted to choose the story. Ellie began to read 'Hansel and Gretel', though her mind was in a frenzy about very different things.

It was almost impossible to believe Winnie had been murdered. Was Franco the father of Flossie's daughter? Could she ever forgive him, ever trust him again? She was plagued with a vision of him lying naked beside Flossie, of them exchanging long, lingering kisses.

Had these things really happened or was she going mad? Was it all in her mind? Marriage had made her feel secure. She had a bond with Franco and him alone. He'd promised to forsake all other and yet . . . And if she did forgive him, how could she know he wouldn't do it again?

Franco threw himself back on the armchair. Only yesterday, he'd been planning to see his parents at this time. He'd been going to tell them he wanted to work in their caff and ask if the offer to share their home was still open.

He'd expected the rift between them to be closing by now, but if Ellie refused to come back to him, they'd want nothing to do with him. And who could blame them?

The house felt still and empty now Ellie and the boys had gone. If he lost them, this is how it would be from now on. He felt humiliated and disgraced. He'd lost his way, lost the love of his wife and his children and for what? The pleasure of the moment that Flossie had given. His life was in ruins and it was his own fault.

He should have told Ellie everything, confessed, made a clean breast of it last night, when he had the chance.

He heard the knocker rattle on the front door and ignored it. He didn't want to talk to anybody. The knocker pounded again. Reluctantly he pulled himself to his feet and went to answer it.

'Ma!' She was the last person he wanted to see but she was inside in seconds.

'What on earth do you think you're doing?' Her face was twisting with anger. 'Ellie's beside herself. She and the children will be staying up at my place. I've come for their night clothes.'

He felt numb, was staring at her unable to speak.

'Aren't you going to get them?' she demanded. With a grunt of impatience she was running upstairs to fetch them herself.

Franco followed slowly. He'd expected the lashing from her tongue.

'I'm ashamed of you, Franco. You've always been wild and chased women, but I thought you'd have the sense to give it up when you married Ellie.'

'I'm sorry—'

'It's no good saying you're sorry to me.'

'I've said it to her.'

'You're a fool, d'you know? D'you understand what you've done? You've always gone your own way and given no thought to what you're doing to others. You've no sense of responsibility. I thought you'd treat Ellie better than you did your father and me. What are you going to do about this?'

'What can I do?' Franco coiled up in anguish and wished she'd get what she'd come for and go.

'That's up to you to decide. You must put Ellie first, her and your children. I don't like what you're doing to them. But you've this baby to think of too.'

'I'm trying to think of her.' It was a cry from his heart. He didn't know Posy, hadn't seen much of her. He'd tried to put her and Flossie behind him. Forget them.

Having survived what he'd thought of as a crisis when Flossie ran off, he'd been relieved to find Winnie was happy to bring the baby up. He knew she'd do her best for the child, give her more love and attention than Flossie would have done. Franco had felt reasonably sure that, in time, they'd all be able to forget the baby's real mother.

'So where was the baby when this woman was murdered?'

'Asleep in the next room. She was unharmed – he probably didn't know she was there.'

'Don't you see it as your duty to take some responsibility for her?'

'I always have, Ma. I've paid for her keep since she was born. Seven and six a week. Well, more to Winnie.'

He'd thought paying for Posy's keep would remove the guilt he felt at fathering her, but that relief had lasted only a few days.

'Oh! And what did Ellie think about that?'

'She doesn't know.'

'Franco! She's been working to keep your boys clothed and fed, to help keep your home going, and all the time you've been carrying on with other women. You don't deserve to have Ellie.'

Franco knew it was the truth. There was nothing he could say to that. He found a brown paper carrier bag for his mother, and pushed in the children's clothes she'd collected.

'Isn't it time you were getting yourself something to eat before going back to work?'

'I don't feel like work tonight—'

'Don't be such a damn fool, of course you'll go. If you bring children into the world you've got to be prepared to support them. You can't leave everything to Ellie.'

Franco sighed. 'All this is mighty embarrassing . . .'

'Do you think your family isn't embarrassed? It's just as bad for us and we didn't bring it on ourselves. There'll be worse when it gets in the papers, I'll guarantee. You're a man, aren't you? Start acting like one for a change.'

Franco felt his mother's sharp tongue had caught him where he was raw.

'And what about your boss? How can he run his business if his staff don't feel like coming to work? You say you like the job, well you'll be needed tonight now one of his barmaids has been murdered.'

Ellie felt as though her mind was locked solid on Franco's betrayal. She couldn't move it on to anything else. She tried, but it jerked back to Flossie's body lying beside Franco's.

Vito came home and was gentle and sympathetic. 'A terrible thing to happen,' he said. 'I'm ashamed of my son.'

They ate their evening meal together and Connie helped her put the boys to bed. She'd even remembered to bring Kenny's teddy bear up for him. When Vito went back to the cafe to stock take, Connie poked the fire to a blaze, pulled up a chair for Ellie and sat down beside her.

'Franco's ruined everything,' Ellie mourned. 'He's shattered what we had, broken it, finished it. I won't let him near me again, I won't let him near the boys.'

'Ellie, you're not over the first shock yet.'

'What am I going to do?' Ellie felt another surge of anger. 'He said he loved me. I want him to go through agony like this. I want him to suffer.'

Connie said gently, 'It's better if you stay here and say these things to me. I know how hurtful it is, but if you say them to Franco, I'm afraid he'll retaliate, then you'll both have more to forgive.'

'I don't care . . .'

'You might.'

'You don't understand, Connie. I can never feel the same about him after this.'

Connie took her hand between both of her own. 'I do understand, Ellie. Vito and me, we've been through this too.'

Ellie couldn't believe it. 'But you seem so happy together, contented.'

'We haven't always been. When Franco was small, Vito had a lady friend. I was going through a bad patch at the time. I'd lost a baby girl.'

'Yes, Maria Clara.'

'I had desperately wanted a little girl, but I was left with five boys.' She poked vigorously at the fire though it didn't need it.

'I know it's wrong of me to blame my sons, and I wasn't a good mother . . .'

'I can't believe that either.' Ellie wished she could stop shaking.

'It's true enough, and probably I wasn't good company for Vito.'

'You've always seemed happy with each other.'

'No, Ellie, I railed at Vito as you've just railed against Franco. It was a woman he'd hired to help him because I wasn't in any fit state to work. My sickness was all in my head, but that made it harder to bear. It seemed like my own fault. If I'd gone on working it wouldn't have happened.

'When I found out, I was absolutely floored, just like you. I thought of going back to Italy and taking the boys. I would have done, if I'd had the money for our fares, but the cafe wasn't earning much and Vito wouldn't give me the money. He didn't want me to leave him.

'I was afraid he loved that woman and I didn't want him to go to her. I couldn't sleep, I couldn't do anything. I didn't know what I wanted, didn't know which way to turn.'

Ellie said, 'That's how I feel now.'

Connie nodded. 'I'm telling you this so you'll understand that things can get better.'

'For you perhaps.'

'For you too, if that's what you want. You must think carefully about it. Stay here with me until you're calmer and can think this through.'

When Ellie got into bed that night, she moved Bobby up, afraid her tossing and turning might wake him. She couldn't settle to sleep. Franco's betrayal was a weight on her chest.

When she was dressing the next morning, her eyes prickled for want of sleep. She had none of her usual patience with her children as she made sure their buttons were fastened and laces tied.

Connie was more than helpful. She normally looked after Kenny and today she offered to take Bobby to school. After breakfast, Ellie walked with Vito to the cafe. In a way it was a relief to busy herself with the usual routine jobs. She helped make ice cream, finding it almost soothing to keep the ice-cream maker churning.

Waiting on tables when the dinner-time rush started was harder. Everybody was talking about the murder. A copy of the local newspaper was passed round.

'It says she was a prostitute.' That caught Ellie's ear.

'No, she was a barmaid at the Mermaid.'

'That's where your fella works, isn't it, love?'

'Yes,' Ellie said, 'he knows her.'

'That pub's just a knocking shop, ain't it?'

'Here.' The newspaper was pushed forward for Ellie to read. The account was on the front page. The headline read: *Local prostitute murdered in her bed.* Ellie felt the strength drain out of her.

This morning, Miss Winifred Vickers, aged 47, was found strangled in her attic bedroom in a rooming house in Cunliffe Street, a few yards from the Mermaid Public House where she worked as a barmaid. Miss Vickers was seen to take a man home with her when the Mermaid closed last night. He has not been seen since, and is described as being between the ages of 50 and 65, of medium height and heavy build. Miss Vickers had been taking care of an eighteen-month-old baby girl who was found asleep and unharmed in the next room. The baby's father is now taking care of her.

Ellie was shocked. She could hear comments, first from this table and then from that.

'The man who did it is still at large. Just like Jack the Ripper.'

'Could be someone else's turn tonight, eh Bertha?'

'Go on, you trying to frighten me or something?'

'What is the world coming to? Why can't people live decent lives?'

When the rush was dying down, Connie brought Kenny in for his dinner as usual. Ellie was still clearing the tables in the front when Franco came.

Suddenly, he was standing over her, his face working with emotion. 'Ellie, come home . . .'

She felt she couldn't cope with him and fled to the kitchen where the others would support her. They were chattering but fell suddenly silent when they saw Franco in the doorway.

'I've come for my dinner,' he announced, looking round. Kenny slithered down from his chair to throw his arms round his legs as usual, but Ellie could see he was getting little welcome from the adults. He added less confidently, 'I hope that's all right?'

'Yes, of course,' his father said awkwardly, then went to fetch another chair and set it next to Ellie's. 'Of course, Franco.'

Conversation was unnaturally stilted. 'Any news of the murderer?' Danny enquired. 'Have they caught him yet?'

He shook his head. ''Fraid not.'

Ellie felt uncomfortable and knew the others did too. They were finishing their meal when Connie said, 'Ellie isn't coming home with you just yet. I want her and the children to stay with me for a day or two.'

Franco's face tightened. 'I want them at home with me.'

'Ellie needs peace to think about what's happened.'

He turned to look her in the face. 'Ellie?'

'Yes, I do,' she confirmed.

He sighed. 'At least talk to me. Come to the park for half an hour, please.'

That seemed so reasonable she didn't know how to refuse him.

'Be sure to bring her back to my place,' Connie said briskly as they were leaving. Ellie found herself striding out, trying to match her steps to his. He seemed eager to leave the pavements, hurried her across the main road and into the shady leafiness of Ashville Road.

'Please forgive me, Ellie,' he begged. 'I do love you. I want you and the boys to come back home. It's dreadful being there on my own.'

'I thought you were confessing everything the other day, and all the time you were keeping this back.'

They were in the park, but Ellie didn't find it any more peaceful. Her mind was in turmoil.

'What did you have to take up with her for? I thought we were happy. You went behind my back, took advantage.' Ellie shook her head in misery. 'How long were you carrying on with that woman?'

'I was a fool, Ellie. I'm sorry, I have no excuse. But Flossie's gone, you know that. It's all over, finished.'

'No.' Ellie took a deep shuddering breath. This was the part weighing heaviest. 'No, it isn't finished, there's the baby . . .'

He was biting his lip. 'I asked Irene to look after her for a few days, until . . . But I know it's asking too much. I can't expect you to bring her up.'

'No.'

'I've been making enquiries. The orphanage will take her.' He tried to take Ellie's arm, but she shook him off.

He went on, 'Most of the children there are not true

orphans, they've been rejected by their parents for one reason or another.'

Ellie felt suddenly sick. 'And that's your answer? Turn your back on Posy? You're her father, but you'll let her be brought up in an orphanage? I didn't think you were that sort of man.'

'Ellie,' he burst out angrily. 'What the hell do you want?'

'I don't know! She's your problem not mine. You must do what you think is right.'

He caught at her wrist. 'What is the right thing?'

'Who's to say?' What was right for Posy was wrong for Ellie. 'There is no answer.'

Ellie tore herself free and went running back the way they'd come.

Chapter Twenty-Three

Ellie wouldn't let herself be alone with Franco after that. He continued to come to the cafe for his dinner every day, and she could feel his soulful eyes following her about the kitchen. Before he went home alone, he'd peck at her cheek and whisper, 'Please come home.'

Connie was a tranquil presence and in a few days, Ellie began to feel calmer. When she needed to get more clothes for herself and the boys, she fetched them when she knew Franco would be at work.

She'd expected to find the place a chaotic mess, he'd never done much about the house, but instead it was neat and tidy. Their bed was made and the fire re-laid in the grate. For the first time, she felt she might return.

'Not yet,' Connie said. 'First, you must see your way forward. Have you decided what you want to do?'

'About the baby? No.'

It was a huge step to take on another child. She'd been finding things easier now Kenny was growing up. He no longer needed the pram, so it was easier to take him on the bus. In another year, he'd be going to school with Bobby. To take on Posy . . .

Yet Ellie felt sorry for her. She knew what it was to grow up without a mother, but she'd had Gran until she was thirteen. If she and Franco turned their backs on Posy, she'd have nobody.

Connie asked, 'How d'you feel about Franco now?'

Ellie covered her face with her hands and groaned. 'What can I say? I still love him. I miss him.'

Connie's arms wrapped themselves round her in a hug. 'I'm glad, that's what I hoped you'd say. Can you forgive him?'

'I don't know.'

'If you can, you can save your marriage and still have a good life together. He's truly repentant, you know.'

'Yes, he wants me to give him another chance. The boys need a father, I need a husband. It really is the best thing for us all, isn't it?'

'You're ready to try again? I'm relieved, Ellie. He's let you down badly.'

'And he has a daughter. I can't make up my mind what we should do about her. She's the real stumbling block.'

'Let him decide, love. She's his problem.'

'I don't want to take her on. We can't afford to bring another child up, but ...' Ellie was afraid she wouldn't be able to forgive herself if she cast the child off.

She started doing more, busying herself with housework and the children. One afternoon, she took Kenny to the park to kick his ball about and then went to meet Bobby when it was time for him to come out of school.

Irene was already at the school gates, leaning on the handle of Posy's pram. She smiled and waved. Ellie was embarrassed by what had passed between them the last time they'd met. She stopped, but there was no way she could avoid Irene. She was already weaving the pram through the huddle of waiting mothers.

'I'm sorry, Irene, I was nasty to you the other day – about Posy.'

'I sprung it on you, didn't I? I didn't realise you didn't know. Awful for you.'

'It was a shock.'

'I do understand.' Irene pushed her ginger fringe off her forehead. 'I hardly knew what I was doing that day either. I'd badgered Edith till she told me about Franco. I had to find out for Posy's sake. I didn't know what to do with her.'

Ellie was trying to avoid looking in the pram, but couldn't help herself. Posy's round blue eyes met hers.

'Poor little thing, I think she's missing Winnie. She's been quite tearful and it's not like her.'

Kenny offered Posy the ball. She smiled up at him and clutched it with both hands.

'It's not really clean enough for a baby,' Ellie protested.

'Isn't she pretty?' Irene said. 'And so good humoured. She likes the other children to make a fuss of her.'

Ellie couldn't drag her eyes away from the child's heart-shaped face, fair complexion and ash-blonde curls.

Irene went on, 'I've just been over to see Franco about her. I told him I don't mind looking after Posy for a few days, really she's no trouble. But Len's coming home next week, and we'll have a fortnight together. I'd like her settled somewhere else by then. You do understand?'

Ellie nodded but couldn't bring herself to say she'd take her.

The children were coming out of school, and as Irene's girls rushed towards the pram, Posy began to bounce up and down and gurgle with pleasure.

'Come and have a cup of tea with me,' Irene invited. 'I haven't seen you for days.'

Ellie muttered that she'd been staying with Connie for a little while. Bobby had found them by then, and though she hadn't intended to, she found herself falling in step with Irene. When they turned into Garnet Street, Bobby ran straight to his own house.

'We're going to Auntie Irene's,' Ellie called to him but b
then he'd rattled on the knocker. She was helping Irene to li
the pram over the doorstep when Franco opened the front do(
opposite.

'Daddy,' whooped his two sons, and he hoisted them bo
up, one with each arm, before looking across the street to Elli
He looked delighted to see them all.

'I'm going to have a cup of tea with Irene,' she calle(
feeling it was impossible to ignore him. She didn't kno
whether Irene knew about the rift between them and didn
want to get involved in a long explanation about that.

Once inside, Posy lifted dimpled baby arms to show sh
wanted to be lifted out of her pram. Irene scooped her up an
the baby arms went round her neck.

'You're lovely.' Irene kissed her, which made Posy chuckl
and press her own mouth against Irene's cheek and make kissin
noises.

'She's very responsive.' Irene smiled. 'We've all taken 1
her. I'm afraid she isn't smartly dressed – these are clothes m
kids have grown out of. Winnie used to dress her like a littl
princess. Here, you have her for a moment, I'll put the kettl
on.'

Ellie found herself holding the child while Irene rattled cup
in the kitchen. Tiny fingers were feeling her hair, the beautifu
baby face inches away from her own, the breath sweet an
milky.

Ellie felt choked with resentment that Posy was Franco
daughter but not hers. She didn't want Flossie's child. Sh
lowered her hastily to the floor. Posy could walk well, bu
dropped to her hands and knees to crawl at great speed to joi
the other children who were playing under the table.

Ellie told herself it was silly to feel resentment for the chil nd now she'd come and seen her, and held her, it was even arder to turn away.

Irene came back with the tea. 'I want her to have a home, I eally do.'

Ellie couldn't offer, really couldn't.

'Couldn't you take her for a little while, see how you get on?'

'I don't know . . .'

'It's put you in a spot, I realise that. Take her now, bring her ack tonight or tomorrow morning. Whenever you want to. I'll ook after her while you're at work.'

'Irene, we can't afford to pay for that.'

'You don't have to. We're friends, aren't we? And she's no ouble. You're back home again now, aren't you?'

'Yes,' Ellie said, thinking it was high time she was. Ten inutes later, she carried Posy across, and Irene wheeled the ram for her. She let herself in. Franco was kneeling on the oor playing some game with the boys. His face was a picture hen he looked up and found her there with Posy in her arms.

'You've come home? You've brought the baby?'

She nodded, unable to speak.

'To stay?'

Ellie swallowed the lump in her throat. 'We'll try again, ranco, shall we?'

'And the baby? You're sure about her?'

'Not exactly. She's here, let's see how we get on.'

She was having trouble keeping back her tears and saw ranco was too.

'I won't let you down again, Ellie. I promise. I'll try to be a etter husband. You're a much better person than I am. I ouldn't bear it if you left me.'

The boys amused the baby, and Ellie felt Franco's arm go und her shoulders. He made renewed promises and kissed her, but the rift was still there between them. It would take time to close that and feel the way she once had.

An hour later, Ellie said, 'We'll have to go back to your mother's now.'

Franco protested. 'You said you'd come to stay.'

'I left her preparing an evening meal for me and the boys. I need to tell her what I'm doing.'

'You always think of other people.'

'Your mother thinks of us, Franco. Why don't you come too? We'll tell her together. She'll stretch the food to do for one more. She'd like that, I know.'

As soon as Connie saw the pram being pushed into her yard, she flung open the back door and came out to put her arms round them all.

'We're getting back together,' Ellie told her. 'I'll go home tonight.'

'And you've decided to bring up the baby? Let's have a look at her. She's my granddaughter after all.' Connie had her out of the pram and was smoothing back her silvery curls. 'She's beautiful, but . . .'

The child was struggling to get down. Connie set her feet on the yard.

Ellie watched her straighten up; her mouth slightly open, her face the picture of surprise. 'You say you're her father, Franco?'

He was too embarrassed to say anything.

'You're a fool, lad.' Her voice shook. 'Just look at her, skin as white as alabaster; silvery fair hair and blue eyes. Look at your boys, is she anything like them?'

Ellie looked at Bobby and Kenny. They had lustrous dark eyes, dark brown hair and skin that seemed tinted by the Mediterranean sun. Connie was right! She'd been s overwhelmed at the thought of Posy being Franco's daughter that her mind had ceased to work.

Franco choked out, 'Her mother was a blue-eyed blonde.'

'What makes you so certain you're her father?' Connie asked. 'What guarantee d'you have? It's a fact of life, dark colouring like ours will always come through to our children.

'Look at Ellie, she's only a quarter Italian. She's fairer than us, but still quite dark.'

'She was blonde as a child.'

'My hair was an amber colour,' Ellie said. 'Amber eyes, darkish skin. Never like Posy.'

'Her mother had other men, didn't she?' Connie was looking at him pityingly. The question hung in the air between them. Ellie thought that was kinder than calling her a prostitute.

'It's your guilty conscience, son, that made you think the child was yours.'

'Flossie said she was,' he blustered.

'Well, she would, wouldn't she? Especially if you could be persuaded to pay maintenance.'

Ellie looked at Posy and drew a long unsteady breath. She was just a beautiful baby in need of a home. Connie was right, she couldn't be Franco's daughter. In a way, that made it easier to love her and care for her.

For Franco, it was a quiet morning at the pub. There were only two customers and they were talking together at the far end of the bar. Edith was damp-dusting the barrels.

'You've made your mind up then? About the baby?' Edith's dark eyes were watching him in the mirror that advertised Martell brandy.

'Yes, I've taken her home.'

'Good for you. You'll be wanting to collect her clothes then? I'd hurry up if I were you, before Gertie sells them.'

At times, Franco felt overwhelmed by the extra responsibility he'd assumed, especially when it now seemed he need not have done. 'Are they worth having?'

'Course they are. Winnie kept her lovely. Posy wanted for nothing. She has a nice cot too. The sort that turns into a child's bed.'

'I remember Winnie going on about that when she bought it. We could certainly do with it. Posy's sleeping in her pram. When our Kenny grew out of his cot, we sold it to buy him a bed.'

Edith tossed back her black hair. 'That baby's real lucky. OK, her mother abandoned her, but there's always somebody else ready and willing to take her on.'

Franco cringed. That was not how he felt about it, and he wasn't sure now whether his decision was the right one. He'd had to tussle with his conscience as well as with Ellie.

If it hadn't been for Posy, his affair with Flossie would have remained a secret. Ellie would never have found out. He wouldn't have been publicly humiliated. He wouldn't still be working here, he'd have moved on.

'Course, it was clever of Flossie to pick you as Posy's father.'

Franco felt the blood rush to his cheeks. It seemed everybody thought he was an idiot to accept her word for that. 'What d'you mean?'

Edith cackled with laughter. 'Winnie thought you were a soft touch, handing over ten bob a week to her. We thought it a bit of a joke. Well, who was to know who the father was?'

'Flossie said . . .' Franco was glad his mother wasn't listening to this. The girls had deliberately taken him for a ride.

'Flossie had no idea. She'd started going with Ralph Corne

bout the time she fell for Posy. It could have been him, it ould have been you, could have been any one of half a dozen thers, couldn't it? But you agreed it was your child.'

Franco reeled. Any man in his right mind would have isputed it. The problem was that he hadn't been in his right nind then. He'd been in love with Flossie. He hadn't realised he sort of girl she was.

He knew he'd brought this trouble on himself. His mother vas right, he was a fool. Certainly, he should never have paid naintenance money for the child. Once he'd started that there vas no way he could deny it was his.

He'd saddled himself and Ellie with bringing Posy up. He'd ery nearly ruined his marriage. Why hadn't he been able to ee that Ellie was worth two of Flossie?

Franco couldn't sleep when he got to bed that night, and his ossing and turning woke Ellie.

'I'm a bigger fool than I thought, saddling you with bringing p somebody else's baby,' he groaned. 'Ma's right, she isn't nine. Nobody can prove she is. I could deny that she's anything o do with me. They'd still have her in the orphanage, we don't ave to do it.'

Ellie was drowsy. 'Go to sleep, Franco. We've made that lecision, she's here now. We can't just say we don't want her.'

'Her mother did. Why shouldn't we do the same?'

'We aren't like that. It would be on my conscience. Besides, he's lovely.'

The next day, when the Mermaid closed after the morning ession, Franco went with Edith to 36 Cunliffe Street and found he landlady clearing out Winnie's attic.

'The baby stuff? You took your time. I've just spent the last our packing it in those cardboard boxes out on the landing. You going to give her a home then?'

409

'He's her father,' Edith said. 'Like I told you, he wants her cot too and them toys.'

'Her cot's in there. You'll have to take it to bits to get it through the door.'

It still had the bedclothes on. He could see the dent in the pillow where Posy's head had rested. Franco set about collapsing it.

Gertie stood watching with her hands on her hips. 'That's it then,' she said to Edith. 'You've already helped yourself to Winnie's things.'

Edith was cross. 'You took her best coat and some of her shoes.'

'Only because they didn't fit you.' She turned to Franco. 'Do you need a hand cart to take this stuff away?'

'Yes.'

'I'll fetch my son. He'll want a shilling for his trouble, mind you.'

It was a damp morning, there was drizzle on the window, but Franco reckoned he'd better take the stuff now while he had the chance. 'That's all right.'

It would be well worth a shilling to get her cot, which was well made and heavy.

The mattress was wrapped in a heavy rubber sheet which looked like the sort they used on adult beds in hospitals. He pulled it tighter and carried it down himself. It would serve to keep the mattress dry on the journey. Gertie's son arrived and helped to bring the cardboard boxes full of clothes. It was such a big load, they had to tie the boxes on.

He got the lad to help carry the stuff up to the little third bedroom in his house. Ellie was pleased when she saw what he'd brought. It seemed the baby would be part of his family from now on. Somehow he'd have to find the money it took to feed her.

410

* * *

That evening, Franco's trousers felt damp from his short walk to the Mermaid. Rain had lashed down all afternoon, and he could hear the wind and rain rattling against the pub windows now. Ellie had said Bobby needed a new coat and some wellingtons. He was growing out of everything.

Franco felt their only chance of survival now was to get money by short-changing the customers. With practice he'd refined his method. He always waited until the session was well advanced and they'd consumed plenty of ale. He no longer drank himself; it was safer to be cold sober. Tonight, he'd noticed two strangers drinking in the corner, and when one came up to buy another round, Franco drew two more brimming tankards and took the half crown that was offered in payment.

With the till open he took out the right change, keeping sixpence hidden between the fingers of the left hand. He used his right hand to slap the remaining coins on the bar with a flourish. He was turning to serve another customer when the man said, 'That was half a crown I gave you, mister, not two bob.'

'So it was,' he agreed readily. There was always the odd customer who noticed and the last thing Franco wanted was to argue about it. 'Have I made a mistake, given you the wrong change?'

He spread it out on the counter with his left hand dropping in the sixpence as he did so. Then he made a great play of re-counting the money knowing it would be correct. It was the customer who had to apologise for making a mistake.

Only last week, Mr Secker had taken Edith to his private room and cautioned her about short-changing customers. Franco understood only too well what she was up to, but Edith didn't use his trick of taking out the right change and keeping the coin ready to correct the amount.

If the customer wasn't happy with the change she gave, she just apologised for making a mistake and re-opened the till. If she succeeded, and mostly they both did, she took the money from the till later on, before Mr Secker emptied it to add up the takings.

Franco knew the boss could be watching him too and might even have his suspicions, but he thought of his method as fail safe.

It was Friday night. Many of their customers had received their week's pay and were indulging themselves freely. He kept one eye open for the boss. He didn't want him within hearing if he should be questioned about the change he was giving.

Another opportunity came. The customer was a regular with a particularly rude manner, whom Franco had successfully short-changed several times in the past. He paid with a two-shilling piece and Franco gave him threepence short; the threepenny Joey was the easiest coin to hide between his fingers.

He questioned his change too. Franco thought he was unlucky to have it happen twice in one night. He was about to go into his act when he realised the boss was standing behind him. He felt a rush of panic as Mr Secker turned over his left hand and forced his fingers apart revealing the small silver coin clasped between his second and third fingers. Franco realised he'd been caught in the act.

'Out the back,' Bill Secker spat between hard straight lips Franco found himself in the boss's private rooms with the door closed quietly behind him.

'I know you've been doing this for some time, Frank,' he said. 'I've seen you take money in other ways too. You think

ou're clever, don't you? Well, you aren't clever enough. Count
ourself lucky I don't call the police.'

He was rifling through his box file. 'Here's your cards. I'll
ay you up to tonight, but you'll not get a reference. Out you
o, now.'

'But I've worked here for years.' Franco was appalled. He
as trying to count up just how long.

'No point in me giving you a reference that tells the truth, is
ere? Wouldn't help you get another job.'

'Please . . .'

'I don't intend to tell lies for you. Don't come in here
gain.'

Franco was shaking as he walked home through the blustery
ain. He was shocked that he'd been dismissed on the spot;
hocked to hear himself described as a thief. He hadn't thought
f it like that. It was just one of the little ruses they all got up
, to make life a little easier.

He told himself he was tired of the job, fed up with it, that
e'd been working at the pub far too long. A change would do
im good.

He was home earlier than usual. Ellie was in bed but she
as still awake. He told her he'd been given the sack but not
hy. He didn't want her or his family to think he was a thief.
e said he and the boss had had an argument.

'A bad time to be out of work,' he mourned, remembering
at there were millions on the dole and jobs of any sort were
ard to get in this time of deep recession.

Ellie was drowsy. 'You needn't worry, your pa will want you
come and work at the cafe.'

Franco lay back and thought about it. He wasn't sure they
ould now they knew about Flossie and Posy. Ma was frosty
ith him these days. He hadn't told Pa he'd like the job in the

cafe that he'd offered him so many times. Things between them were worse than they'd ever been.

'Shall I ask him? You said it's what you want.'

'That was before ... No, Ellie, better if we let that blow over first. I'll try and get another job.'

He'd always succeeded in the past; there was no reason why he shouldn't again. Franco started looking for work in the way he used to. He decided he'd like to work with cars and went round the local garages. He soon discovered that men were applying in their hundreds for every vacancy, and there weren't many of them. He realised then his best hope of getting a job was as a barman in a different pub.

He went to see Edith who had worked in several nearby pubs, and she knew of two who might be seeking new staff. He did get to speak to both landlords, and had a story ready about being made a scapegoat for the faults of other staff, but it made no difference: his lack of a reference meant he didn't get a job.

The weeks began to pass and Franco was growing depressed. He found the dole he was entitled to was a fraction of what he'd expected because his wife was working. Even the full amount would have been barely enough to keep them.

Ellie was juggling what cash they had to cover the rent, coal and gas bills. He hadn't the price of a pint of ale in his pocket from one week's end to the next. Franco felt the whole world was against him. He hated Ellie being the sole breadwinner for his family, when everyone knew it was the man's responsibility.

He did his best to help about the house and look after Posy, but Irene and his mother were always willing to do that and thought they could do it better. It left him with time to stand about on street corners with other unemployed men. They were not cheerful company and he knew many who were going hungry. At least that wasn't happening to them because Pa was giving Ellie food from the caff. When Bobby was home from school he took the boys to collect driftwood and old plimsolls along the shore line. Anything that would burn and eke out the coal.

None of this stopped Franco feeling that at twenty-eight, his life was in ruins.

Danny had been off sick with a cough and a head cold for the last three days and Ellie had had more to do, and had worked on through the afternoons. Today, she'd been weary when the dinner-time rush was coming to an end.

Connie had arrived to have the meal with them and was setting the kitchen table. She noticed and said, 'With three children and a useless husband to look after, you're doing too much, Ellie. You'll make yourself ill. Make him see what a fool he's being.'

'I try.'

Connie had patted her shoulder. 'So do I, every time I see him.'

'That's why he's avoiding you. He's not keen to come up for his dinner any more.'

'You take what food you need,' Connie said. 'I don't want any of you to go hungry.' Vito had said much the same, but Ellie knew it wouldn't help Franco.

She was serving the few customers that remained, when she saw Ben Quiltie come in and sit down at a table she hadn't yet cleared.

'Am I too late for dinner?' he asked.

'Of course you're not.' She was piling the dirty plates together and sweeping the crumbs off the cloth. 'You're in good time to have it with the family, we're just about to eat. Come to the kitchen with me.'

He was shaking his head. 'I came to talk to you. You aske‹ me to come back if I had any news. Well, now I have.'

'Oh!' Ellie's heart seemed to bounce. 'About my mother?'

His blue eyes were brighter than ever. They'd always stare‹ into hers with unsettling intensity. 'Yes, it's what you want t‹ know. I think you'll be interested.'

Ellie felt a cold thrill run down her spine. 'I'll come an‹ have my dinner here with you. What can I get you? There' only lasagne or cottage pie left.'

'Cottage pie, then, please.'

Ellie had a word with Connie then reset the table with cutler‹ and brought two helpings of cottage pie. 'Have you move‹ house yet?' she asked as she sat down.

'Yes, we're in Eastham, got a nice little house. Very comf‹ and I've found a job in a nearby butcher's shop. Dougie ha‹ changed schools and Roy's started work at Lever's. We'v‹ severed our links with New Ferry, so if Mick ever come‹ looking for us, he won't find us.'

Ellie's stomach was churning. 'When does his case com‹ up?'

'End of next month.'

'And Auntie Wilma, how is she now?'

'Home from hospital, but her back's still painful and she's ‹ bag of nerves. She's not able to do much.'

Ellie shook her head. Wilma never had done much. 'An‹ she's told you something? About what happened that afternoo‹ at the bike shop?'

'Yes. When I started probing, it all came flooding out. Man‹ said it was the first time she'd ever let a word of it pass her lip‹ – except to Mick, of course. I think she had to talk about it t‹ get it off her mind.'

Ellie stopped eating. 'And? Come on, tell me.'

'You know your mother was arguing with Mick and why. Well, it seems the row got out of hand. He became violent and tried to choke her.'

'Ben, I've always known that, she had bruises on her neck.'

'Yes, well, Mam told me last night that she heard a commotion in the bike shop and went down to see what was happening.'

Ben lowered his voice though they had the cafe almost to themselves. 'She said Orla was on the floor and Mick had her by the throat. He was like a wild thing, throttling her and screaming at her. Orla was past helping herself, she was already losing consciousness. Mam said she panicked. She thought he was going to kill her.'

Ellie gasped. 'She lied to the police? Then it must have been Wilma . . . ?'

'Yes, she picked up the starting handle. She said Mick didn't know his own strength and could be brutal, and she had to stop him. She meant to hit him on his shoulder but he moved and the blow struck him on the back of his head.

'She was terrified when the police started questioning her. She said Mick was unconscious when she came downstairs – to protect herself, you understand. She'd knocked him out; she thought she'd killed him.'

'She summoned an ambulance?'

'Yes. She also said your mother was on her feet but she seemed shocked and dizzy, and that she saw her fall against a tandem that was upended on its handlebars. She knocked it over, then within moments, she pulled herself to her feet and went home.'

Ellie had stopped eating. 'That changes everything, doesn't it?'

'Mam had to say that. After all, she'd told the police she'd found Mick lying unconscious on the workshop floor with a wound on the back of his head. Somebody had to have struck him.'

'Oh my God! She blamed my mother.'

'Yes. Orla had gone by the time the ambulance arrived and Mick remained unconscious for six days. His wounds were thought to have been inflicted by a woman. Not very much force was used, but on the head it doesn't always take much.'

'They suspected the wrong woman.' Ellie was angry. 'I know Gran went through hell at that time. Orla was being blamed for something she didn't do, that would be why.'

'Yes. It's been on Mam's conscience, Ellie, if that's any comfort. It's turned her into a nervous wreck.'

'It was a terrible thing to do.'

Ben nodded. 'She was shocked, I'm sure. Hardly knew what she was doing.'

'Protecting herself.' Ellie couldn't help feeling bitter about that. 'Poor Gran. I wish she could have known the truth. She wanted to hear Orla's side of the story. She spent years trying to contact her in the next world.'

'What?' Ben was surprised.

'I mean at spiritualist meetings and through seances. She believed in all that sort of thing.' Ellie shook her head. 'You'd have thought the police would have investigated more thoroughly.'

Ben leaned over and took a bottle of sauce off a nearby table. 'It seems Orla corroborated Mam's story. When she was admitted to hospital the next day, she said her injuries were caused by a fall. She didn't accuse Mick of assaulting her.'

'Why not?'

'Possibly she didn't remember exactly what had taken place. Mick was her brother and he was unconscious at the time.'

'But there must have been fingerprints on the starting handle.'

'Yes, everybody's were, including Mam's. She said it was lying close to Mick when she came downstairs, that she picked it up to move it when she knelt to look at him. It was considered normal for Orla and Mick to have handled it.'

Ellie shuddered.

Ben went on, 'As Mick had a wound on the back of his head, it was assumed Orla had struck him as he turned away and her fall was an accident that happened afterwards. Therefore, at her inquest, the coroner returned a verdict of accidental death. She fractured a rib in her fall, by the way, and it pierced her lung. It became infected and . . .' Ben stopped. 'It must be awful for you, listening to all this.'

Ellie's teeth were on edge. She grimaced. 'I've always wondered about it, wanted to know. Go on, Ben, so Wilma . . .'

'Mam thought Mick was going to die and Orla would be charged with his murder, everybody did. But it went the other way. Mick recovered and your mam died. It was difficult to decide who was the victim and who the aggressor. No charges were ever brought.'

'But it was Wilma who hit Mick!'

'She'd planned never to tell him, but she was so scared by what had happened that she couldn't keep it back. He told her to keep her mouth shut and not to change her story.'

Ellie said coldly, 'If the police knew Wilma had done it, she could have been charged with grievous bodily harm. It might even be assumed she'd attacked my mother too, and that would be murder or manslaughter.'

'As it turned out, if the police had known the true facts, Mick could have been charged with Orla's murder. They know now.'

'Auntie Wilma's told them?'

'Yes, she felt she had to. She couldn't live with it on her

conscience any longer. You wouldn't know her, Ellie, she's so changed.'

'Will she be charged with perjury or something?'

'I don't know. She wasn't under oath when she lied, but she certainly perverted the course of justice. We'll have to wait and see. I hope after all this time, they'll let things be.'

'To think,' Ellie said, 'I was a few yards away when all this was happening, playing with Franco and Carlo in that car on the forecourt. I saw Auntie Wilma come out and shout at them.' She sighed. 'At least Mick's got his just deserts this time, and Auntie Wilma . . .'

'She's been paying for the lies she told ever since.' Ben shook his head. 'We've all been paying for those lies, haven't we?'

Ellie pushed her plate away. She couldn't finish her dinner, though Ben had a clean plate.

'Pudding?' she asked. 'There's jam tart or ice cream. Or both since it's you.'

'No thanks, I've had enough.'

'Tea then? We'll have one here. Danny's off sick, so I can't go home yet.'

'I can't stay too long, Ellie. I've arranged to go out this evening. I've got a girlfriend now, and we're going to the pictures.'

Ellie smiled. 'I'm pleased for you. Very pleased. You need some fun in your life. What's her name?'

'Emily. Yes, life's going to be better from now on.'

Chapter Twenty-Four

Ellie felt overwhelmed by what Ben had told her. Vito was at his desk in the office, so she went in and talked it over with him.

'After all this time . . . To find it was Wilma . . .' He tried to comfort her. 'Don't let it open up old wounds, Ellie love, it was such a long time ago.'

'But Wilma—'

'Try not to dwell on what she did. It won't do any good now.'

She ran up to tell Connie, and talked it all through again. She knew it touched Connie on a raw spot.

'It was horrible to hear people saying such awful things about your mam. Poor Bridie, if she'd known Orla was totally innocent, it would have been a great comfort to her. When I think of her searching beyond the grave, when she could have heard the true story so near to home. She might have got it out of Wilma if she'd tried.'

Although Ellie was late, she walked slowly home, her mind whirling. It wasn't going to open old wounds as Vito feared, rather it soothed them. And she was able to put the part Wilma had played into perspective, but she'd always be grateful to Ben for making things clear to her. He was the one with real strength and courage.

As soon as she got in, she told Franco, letting it all come out. He held her close in a comforting hug.

She said, 'Poor Mam, she had a horrible end, but at least I understand what happened to her now. I feel as though her name has been cleared, the slate has been wiped clean. At last I can close the door on what happened that afternoon.'

'So it was Wilma!' Franco smiled. 'I always felt it must be. And at last she's admitted it was her who knocked Mick out . . .'

'Franco, she went to my mam's aid. Mick might have killed her outright, if she hadn't. I don't blame Wilma . . .'

'You can blame her for not speaking up sooner,' Franco said sharply.

'Yes, she could have set all our minds at rest,' she agreed. 'And if you and Carlo had spoken up about what you saw, she might have had to. More questions would have been asked, wouldn't they?'

She could see from Franco's face that he found that hurtful.

'Don't get upset,' she said. 'Don't go back into your shell.' She'd expected him to be less touchy, back to his normal self, by now.

'No.' He was biting his lip. 'I have to face up to what I've done. I've made mistakes.'

'Yes,' she said gently. 'If you can put all that behind you we'll be all right.'

Before his affair with Flossie came to light he'd said he wanted to work in the cafe and was ready to move in with his parents. Now, though he'd lost his job and it was urgent that he did, he'd changed his mind again.

Ellie knew he had to resolve this. They were getting deeper into debt with each week that passed; he had to have work. She couldn't hold back her tears.

'Look, Ellie,' he sounded a bit short, 'you've got to turn your back on what happened to your mother now. Not let it bother you. D'you think you can?'

She mopped at her eyes, trying not to sound impatient. 'Yes, I'm already doing that. For me it's over.'

She was weeping for Franco not her mother, though it was hearing about her end that had made her emotional. She took a deep shuddering breath. 'Franco, you also have problems you need to put behind you. Big problems. Please say you'll try.'

Ellie's request took Franco by surprise. 'Yes,' he said, almost without thinking. He knew Ellie was right, he wasn't putting anything behind him.

Her lips brushed his lightly. 'We're both going to put the past behind us.'

'Yes,' he had to agree.

'And think of the future.' Her amber eyes were searching his face. 'Do what's best for us. I've come back to you and I brought Posy to live with us. It's what you said you wanted.'

Franco said, 'I mustn't forget that.'

'I didn't mean . . .'

'I know, Ellie, you've bent over backwards for me.'

She'd told him she'd forgiven him for what he'd done with Flossie and had never mentioned her name since.

'Now you no longer believe you're Posy's father, it's easier to take to her, isn't it? Everybody else thinks she's lovely.'

'She's a beautiful baby, but . . .' She reminded him of Flossie.

'You know what you should do, Franco.'

He'd always known what he should do, but never done it. This was what he usually turned his back on.

'Then why don't you tell your pa you want the job in the cafe?' she urged.

Franco ran his hands through his hair. 'It looks as though I only want it because I can't get anything else.'

'Well, don't you?'

'It would look like I'm begging for a favour while I'm down. I should have gone to work there when Pa was ill. They needed me then. I want to be on good terms with them, make amends . . .'

'Then tell them. They'll want you, I know.'

Franco sucked his lip. 'Pa hasn't mentioned it again? About me going to work there?'

'No. You've turned it down so many times, Franco, they've given up hope.'

'They won't want me, not after the way I treated you. They're on your side.'

'They will. Let me tell them you've changed your mind.'

He shook his head. 'Let me think about it. The customers know what I did, they know about Flossie and Posy.'

Even if his family didn't think he was her father, people in the neighbourhood still believed he was. He felt ashamed.

When Ellie left for work the next morning, taking the children with her, Franco felt at his lowest ebb. He'd sunk to join the dregs of society.

His family thought him the worst sort of a fool to believe Posy was his. He couldn't believe now that he'd accepted what Flossie had told him. Why hadn't it occurred to him that she might not know herself? Or that she might deliberately lie? Ralph Corner had yellow hair and fair skin, why hadn't he thought of that?

Ellie was back with him but her trust in him had gone. The bond between them was weaker. His affair with Flossie was like a high wall between them. He wanted to knock it down but didn't know how. Perhaps in time, if he worked at it, but he was losing hope. He didn't seem to get anything right.

He couldn't get a job. He couldn't do anything. He was adrift.

Ellie knew Franco was trying to do more to help with the housework. Today, he'd said he'd buy two pennyworth of bones from the butcher and get some old and damaged vegetables from the back of the market to make soup. He was also hoping to get some bruised apples to make an apple pie. He knew how to cook, he'd learned at the cafe.

When she got home, Ellie found a bright fire in the living room. It felt cosy. Posy was in her playpen in the corner. She picked her up and kissed her. She could hear the boys playing upstairs in their bedroom. The creak of bedsprings told her they were jumping on their beds, one of their favourite pastimes.

'Stop that, Bobby,' she called upstairs. 'You'll ruin your mattress. How many times do I have to tell you?' She heard two thuds on the ceiling as they jumped off, followed by lots of giggles. Franco came from the kitchen, looking miserable.

'Why don't you stop them, Franco? We'll have to get Bobby a new bed if this goes on.'

'Don't start moaning the minute you get in,' he said.

That wasn't like Franco. It brought Ellie up sharply. 'Is everything all right?'

'How can it be all right?'

'I just meant . . .'

'Sorry, not a good day.' He put his arms round her then and gave her a hug. 'I had to pay threepence for bones and there were no old vegetables being thrown out at the market.'

'There's others after them too,' she said. 'You need to get there earlier.'

'Don't start complaining.'

The bedsprings were creaking again in Posy's room. The boys were giggling in there now.

She ignored it and said quietly, 'I'm not complaining. I'm not trying to find fault with what you do. Why are you angry?'

'I'm not angry . . . Just fed up. Well, Ma put her oar in today when I collected Posy.'

'She means well.'

'She nags all the time. I wish you wouldn't talk about me behind my back. It makes me feel small.'

Ellie's patience snapped. She wanted to shake him. 'You're touchy and bad tempered. You aren't happy,' she told him fiercely. 'I don't know why you're being so stubborn. You're too proud to tell your mother and father that you want the job you've turned down so many times.'

Franco slumped on to a chair by the fire, suddenly pale and silent.

Ellie went to the kitchen feeling she'd said too much. Bickering like this set them at each other's throats for days, doubling their troubles. The soup was simmering on the stove. She started to dish it up into bowls. She was hungry and the boys always were.

'What does pride and loss of face matter?' she said as she took them to the living-room table. 'We can't afford to live here like this, Franco. We're getting deeper into debt. You must ask your pa for a job.' She called the children to come down for their tea.

Franco flashed her a frosty look. She remembered that Posy had gone upstairs to the boys. She could climb up safely enough but didn't look too secure when she was coming down. Ellie went to make sure she didn't fall.

She lifted the baby into her high chair, broke some bread into her soup bowl and pushed it towards her. Posy could feed herself, but she made no move to lift her spoon. Each of her tiny fists was clenched round something.

'What have you got here, Posy?'

Posy was fascinated with Bobby's marbles and Ellie was afraid she'd swallow one. She'd told Bobby to keep them out of her reach, but marbles were what she expected to find. She prised back the little fingers to see two half crowns. Posy giggled and slowly opened her other hand to show another two half crowns.

Ellie stared in disbelief. 'Where did you get those?'

The child laughed up at her. 'Ickory, ickory, ock. Mouse ran up the clock.'

'No, no, where did you get this money?'

'Money?' Franco came to see. 'Real money?'

Bobby craned forward to look. 'It's magic.'

The meal was forgotten as the boys crowded round, astonished and thrilled. Finding herself the centre of attention, Posy carried on singing. The whole family was laughing with her.

Ellie couldn't help but see Franco was completely awestruck. 'It's from the life beyond. Somebody there is helping us. Helping Posy pay for her keep.'

Ellie knew he believed in the supernatural, but was surprised all the same. 'Why should it be?'

'She won't find money lying around this house, so where else could it come from?'

'Did some well-wisher put it into her pram while you had her out? Your mother?'

'No, it's Winnie helping us.' His eyes had that far-away look in them, as though they could see into the world beyond.

'You're always thinking the dead can reach us.'

His face was full of wonder. 'A pocketful of silver! This was predicted years ago. At that seance your gran held. You were there, you remember?'

'Vaguely.' Ellie remembered being frightened. She turned the coins over in her hand. 'It's real enough. Not spirit money.'

Franco put one between his teeth and bit it. 'Yes, there's ten shillings here. It's a gift from the other side.'

'Posy's a little angel,' Bobby sang out. 'We can buy what we want now.'

'Posy can make money,' Kenny chortled.

'If only she can keep doing it, we'll never be poor again.' Franco beamed at her.

'Like the goose that lays golden eggs but much nicer,' Bobby said.

They all made much of Posy, hugging and kissing her.

Ellie was surprised at the effect the money was having on Franco. His mood had changed completely. From being depressed and morose, he was exultant.

'We went to Posy's aid and now she's helping us. We can get more coal tomorrow. We'll be all right if she can keep doing this.'

'Franco!' He seemed to be at Bobby's level when it came to fairy tales. They were egging each other on, demanding that Posy tell them where exactly she'd found the money.

The soup had gone cold on their plates. Ellie poured it back in the pan and took it to the kitchen to reheat. When she brought it back, the four half crowns were lined up along the table and they couldn't stop talking about them. At bedtime, the children were still excited and far from sleep.

Ellie was tired and wanted peace to think about it. She hurried the boys into their pyjamas and gave Franco a book from which to read a bedtime story. She washed Posy's hands

428

and face, put on the napkin she still wore at night and took her upstairs to her bed.

This morning, when she'd got Posy up, she'd found her napkin had leaked and her bottom sheet was wet. Ellie had pulled it free and left it soaking in the kitchen sink. Franco had washed it and put it out on the line, but he'd done nothing about making up her bed again. The boys had been jumping on it, enjoying the rebound of the springs. The big mackintosh sheet had almost slid off.

Ellie sighed with impatience. Franco had promised to do the housework but was only half doing it. Then she felt she was being unfair. He was doing his best.

Posy was drowsy now. To free her own hands, she tucked her up in their own bed. She took a clean cot sheet and went back to Posy's room, ripped off the protective rubber and turned the mattress over.

As she did so, she heard something drop out and roll across the lino. She went down on her hands and knees to slide it out from under the chest of drawers. A two-shilling piece sparkled in her hand. She straightened up, surprise and pleasure mingling with disbelief. Where had the money come from?

She turned to Posy's bed and examined the mattress carefully. There was a slit in the side where somebody had cut it open, and dark grey flock was spilling out. She knew now where Posy had found the money.

The hole was large enough for Ellie to put her hand in. She felt round for coins but brought out a roll of bank notes held together with a rubber band. Her fingers shook as she counted them. She had to do it twice to be sure. Twenty pounds!

She went back to the mattress and put in her hand again. Another roll of used bank notes, and another. Ellie was tingling all over. She wanted to dance. What a lovely surprise! She could hear Franco saying goodnight to the boys in the next room. She took a deep breath to steady herself and went to kiss her sons goodnight.

Franco had been reading 'Jack and the Beanstalk' for the umpteenth time, and found, for once, the boys were not interested.

'How d'you think Posy makes the money, Daddy?' Kenny wanted to know.

Like them, he couldn't get over the way Ellie had opened Posy's little fist and found silver coins grasped in it.

It was bringing back memories of his childhood, things he hadn't thought about for years. Bridie's seance. The prediction from the spirit world that the four of them would be showered with silver, that they'd have, if not exactly wealth, then enough money to live on in comfort.

It was all coming back to him. Quick silver were the words Ma had used. Well, Posy was quick silver itself, and she'd given them silver. All those years ago, Bridie and Ma had agreed it meant they'd be given pennies from heaven.

Could it be that those predictions which had excited him so much were coming true? The money had come at a time when they really needed it.

Ellie came in, her face radiating the excitement they all felt. 'Time to settle down now,' she told the boys, tucking them in. Franco felt himself being pulled out. She put out the light and closed the door carefully, then dragged him into Posy's little room. She didn't have to say anything. He saw the money spread out on the chest of drawers and let out a whoop of surprise and delight.

'What's the matter, Daddy?' Bobby called. Ellie had her forefinger held against her lips.

'Nothing.'

'I heard you. Have you found something else that's nice?'

'No. Go to sleep.'

There was silence. 'We can't tell the boys about this,' Ellie whispered, 'not yet anyway. We'll never get them to sleep, if we do.'

Franco went to turn over the money and started counting.

'Twenty pounds,' Ellie said. 'And there's more.'

Franco couldn't wait to scoop out all there was in the mattress. There was more, much more. A few coins, three old guineas, but mostly used bank notes. The pile on the chest grew. They removed most of the mattress filling too. It was all over the floor before they were satisfied they'd taken out all the money.

Ellie looked tired. 'We'll have to stuff all this flock back in and sew the hole up.'

'This is tedious.' He was trying to spread it to the corners of the mattress. 'It looks lumpy.'

'Posy will never notice. It'll flatten down with use.'

While Ellie sewed up the hole, he took one of Posy's pillow cases from the drawer and scooped the money into it. 'I'll take it to our room to count. We'll put it out of sight then.'

Posy was fast asleep on their bed and didn't wake up when he put the light on. He found the notes were already counted out into lots of twenty pounds.

'Come and help me make her cot up,' Ellie hissed from the door.

He did. 'Sorry, I meant to do it this morning. I forgot.' Ellie carried Posy through and put her into her own bed without waking her.

Back in their own room, she was smiling. 'Nothing paranormal about this, it's a treasure trove we've found.'

Franco wasn't convinced. 'It was predicted we'd be given enough to be comfortable for life. Posy is paying for her keep.'

'Don't be a nut, Franco. Forget the ghosts and the spirit world, stay in this one. Somebody hid this money in the mattress. Would it be her mother? Would she save this for Posy?'

'Flossie couldn't save a penny. She wasn't the type. Anyway, she wasn't that concerned about Posy.'

'Winnie was concerned about her,' Ellie said. 'This might be hers. Could she save?'

'I wouldn't have thought this much.' Franco felt bemused. 'But now I come to think of it, Winnie had big ideas about taking Posy away. I thought it sounded an impossible dream. She said she'd give up bar work and all the rest . . . Find a nice house for them somewhere like West Kirby or Southport.'

'Not a dream,' Ellie said. 'She was saving to do it, making progress too.'

'D'you know, I got the impression . . . that she wouldn't be working at the Mermaid for much longer.'

'Poor Winnie. It wasn't her fault she didn't manage it.'

'Fancy hiding it in Posy's mattress. Why not the bank?'

'Did she leave a bank book?'

'I don't know. If she did, somebody else took it.'

'Then the mattress was a safer place.'

It was getting late. They went to bed still talking about the money and the barmaids who'd worked at the Mermaid.

'This will be the making of us,' Franco chortled. 'We can pay off all our debts. We won't have to worry about anything for ages.'

'No, Franco!' Ellie was aghast. 'It's Posy's money not ours.'

'But we can use it to look after her, give her a better life. That's only fair.'

'No!' Ellie protested. 'No. What did Mick do with the money Gran left for me? Exactly that, and you railed against him and we both thought he'd done me down.'

'But Winnie didn't leave a will.'

'If she had, she wouldn't have left the money to us. We'll put this in the bank for Posy. She can have it when she's twenty-one. That's what Winnie would want.'

'But we'll have to feed and clothe her. How can we do that?'

'Well, perhaps spend a little of it on clothes and shoes for her but that's all.'

'But what can we do about our own debts?'

'What Winnie did. Stand on our own feet. Work our way out of this mess.'

Franco was shocked at the difference between Ellie's standards of integrity and his own. Shocked that he'd thought real money could have come from the spirit world. Even he could see now it was ridiculous to think there was a psychic explanation.

If Winnie could get a grip on her life and do that, surely he could stand on his own feet too?

Finding Posy's treasure trove had made almost as big an impact on him as seeing Mick lying on the bike shop floor had all those years ago.

The next morning, Franco woke to a feeling of well-being. He'd ask his father for the job in the caff. The solution was in his own hands, it always had been. Ellie was brimming with happiness.

'Can we see Posy's half crowns again?' Bobby asked. 'They haven't disappeared in the night?'

Franco spun them along the breakfast table, and the boys laughed with excitement. It seemed a good omen. While Ellie got ready for work, he put Posy in her pram. They dropped Bobby off at school on the way to the caff.

When they arrived, his father was tinkering with the tea urn, and seemed surprised to see him. There were two customers in on separate tables, each tucking into egg and bacon.

'We'd like a word, Pa,' Franco said. 'In private, please.' Ellie was taking Posy from her pram.

'Come to the office then.'

He led the way. As they went through the kitchen, Danny was scraping fairy-cake mix into paper cases. Kenny wanted to lick the bowl and stayed with him. It was a while since Franco had been in the little back office. He couldn't help but think of his youthful excesses as he stood on the mat.

'Well?' His father perched against his desk and looked at him over his spectacles.

Now he'd come to the point Franco was nervous. He blurted out, 'If you're still willing to give me a job here, Pa, I'd be very grateful.'

He half expected him to say, 'Now you're on the dole and can't get anything else?' But his father's face lit up as never before. 'You'll come and work here?' It was as though he couldn't believe his ears. 'You're sure?'

'Yes, if you'll have me. I really need the job.'

Pa's arms came round him in a hug. 'Franco, we need you too. Start today, right now, before you change your mind.'

'Thanks, Pa.' He was struggling with tears of gratitude. He hadn't expected to be welcomed like this.

Vito was enthusiastic. 'When you've got your hand in, I want you and Ellie to run this place between you. But you know that, I've spelled it out to you often enough. Your mother thinks it's time I retired.'

Franco was shaking hands on it when Kenny came in with

cake mix round his mouth. He said, 'I'd better take the children up to Ma's before I start.'

'Yes, tell her the good news. She'll be made up, I promise you. You'd better go with him, Ellie, to make sure he comes straight back.'

'I told you he'd want you.' Ellie was fizzing with pleasure. He put his arm round her waist as they walked up. She reminded him to wipe the pram wheels before he helped lift it into the back kitchen.

'Ma?' he called. She came running downstairs, looking surprised to see them all.

'Good news, Connie.' Ellie smiled. 'Very good news. Franco's starting work today at the cafe.'

She threw her arms round him and shrieked with pleasure. Posy began to shriek too.

'At last!' Connie laughed. 'I'm so glad you've changed your mind.'

He tried to explain then how he'd come to refuse their offers for so long.

'I think I lost my way when I was twelve, the day Orla and Mick had their fight in the bike shop.'

They sat down at the kitchen table while he told his mother what he and Carlo had done that day.

'Mick frightened the life out of both of us. I was glad I wasn't grown up. I knew if there was trouble about us keeping quiet, Carlo would take the brunt of the blame.'

He'd wanted to remain a child, it seemed safer. But adults had power over their children and as he'd grown older he hadn't been prepared to accept that.

He wanted no more secrets. 'I rejected all discipline.'

Ma said, 'You had no self-discipline either, that was the problem.'

'I sought pleasure and thought only of myself. I believed that was the way to a happy life.'

'And what did it do for you, Franco?'

It had put him at odds with Ellie and his family, left him without a job or any self-respect. He'd touched bottom and even then had expected the supernatural to bail him out. He'd been creating his own problems and walking away from them.

Franco sighed. 'I should have seen you had my welfare in mind. I wasn't man enough to accept what you were offering.'

Ellie said slowly, 'Sometimes the mind plays tricks, Franco. It makes you see things in the wrong light, believe things that aren't true.'

Connie had a wry smile. 'I wasn't far wrong then when I kept telling you to grow up?'

'You were right,' Ellie told her.

'I've come of age now.'

'We're all pleased to hear that. Very pleased.'

His mother was smiling. 'Your pa promised me a long holiday in Italy once the future of the cafe was settled. I'm going to make sure we take it. It'll be the trip of a lifetime for us.'

She could hardly sit still. 'Will you move in here too? There's plenty of space. We've always had a large family round us. With just Vito and me, we rattle round. Say you will.'

Franco looked at Ellie. She was nodding her agreement, all smiles.

'Yes, Ma, we'll be glad to come,' he said.

For Ellie, it was a busy day at the cafe, but to have Franco there working beside her made all the difference. She could relax and look to the future with confidence.

When the cafe closed they had to rush to the nearby shops.

They bought special treats for their tea, and then collected the children from Connie and took them for a walk in the park.

At home, with the evening meal cleared away, they played with the little ones. Ellie was finding Posy a delight. She was more advanced than her boys had been at eighteen months and didn't demand a lot of attention. She could walk and climb stairs and feed herself.

Bobby was prompting her to recite her favourite nursery rhyme.

'Ickory, ickory, ock, mouse ran up the clock.'

Posy knew it all the way through, and when she finished she jumped up and down and laughed. They all clapped her performance, which made her more excited. She was a happy child.

Franco said, 'Winnie must have played with her and taught her these things.'

'Everybody takes to her,' Ellie said, smiling. 'Bobby and Kenny are delighted with her.' They were teaching her 'Baa Baa Black Sheep'. She copied everything they did. 'Connie's very attached to her now. You will be too, if you let yourself.'

Franco smiled. 'Like the rest of you, I'm dazzled by Posy. I can't get over the wonderful surprise she gave us. She's brought me to my senses.'

'Posy's binding us together,' Ellie said. 'Life's different now she's with us. I know she's another mouth to feed but she's worth it. She's great fun.'

Franco looked at the clock. 'We ought to start packing, decide what we want to take and what we'll sell off.'

'Not tonight,' she yawned.

When they'd put the children to bed they went downstairs together to make their bedtime cocoa, but found they'd let the fire go out. Ellie yawned again.

'An early night, after all that excitement,' he suggested. 'We can have our cocoa in bed.'

'It's been a lovely evening.' Ellie snuggled down happily under the blankets. Franco put his arms round her and held her tight.

'What an idiot I've been, Ellie. I'm sorry. I thought I could escape my past when Winnie was so ready to look after Posy. I believed I could leave the pub, wipe the slate clean and still keep the worst things hidden from you and Ma. I was ready to do it, but it would've been wrong.'

Ellie whispered, 'You were like two different people. At the Mermaid, you were Frank. Working there changed you.'

There he'd been ready to cheat customers out of their change, lie, and go behind Ellie's back. That was no way to live.

'It wasn't the pub that changed me. It was the afternoon Carlo and I took you to the bike shop.'

Ellie went on. 'But here, and at the cafe, you're Franco, a much more caring person.'

'I'll try to be in future,' he promised. He'd been brought up to be honest and fair with everybody, but it had taken Ellie to show him what he should do with Posy's money. His standard of honesty had shocked her. He wanted her approval and the approval of his parents, and knew he'd never find happiness unless he accepted their ways.

'I'm going to be Franco from now on. After what I did, I hardly deserve to be forgiven by you and Ma.'

'I love you,' Ellie said. 'So does she. Love isn't conditional.'

'I'm so happy,' Franco murmured. 'I feel as though our marriage is on an even keel again. I'm going to try to keep it this way, I'm going to try very hard.'

Ellie listened to Franco's steady breathing and knew he'd fallen asleep almost while he was talking. She knew now Franco wasn't perfect, he wasn't going to find it easy to change, but she felt events had made him grow up at last.

She was sure they could make their marriage work if they both tried hard enough. It was what they wanted now. They had both realised that the only way to happiness was to rebuild their trust in each other.